THROWN
by a
CURVE

Titles by Jaci Burton

Wild Rider Series
RIDING WILD
RIDING TEMPTATION
RIDING ON INSTINCT
RIDING THE NIGHT

WILD, WICKED, & WANTON
BOUND, BRANDED, & BRAZEN

Play-by-Play Novels
THE PERFECT PLAY
CHANGING THE GAME
TAKING A SHOT
PLAYING TO WIN
THROWN BY A CURVE

Anthologies

UNLACED
(with Jasmine Haynes, Joey W. Hill, and Denise Rossetti)

EXCLUSIVE
(with Eden Bradley and Lisa Renee Jones)

LACED WITH DESIRE
(with Jasmine Haynes, Joey W. Hill, and Denise Rossetti)

NAUTI AND WILD
(with Lora Leigh)

Specials

"The Ties That Bind" from UNLACED

THROWN
by a
CURVE

JACI BURTON

BERKLEY SENSATION, NEW YORK

THE BERKLEY PUBLISHING GROUP
Published by the Penguin Group
Penguin Group (USA) Inc.
375 Hudson Street, New York, New York 10014, USA

USA / Canada / UK / Ireland / Australia / New Zealand / India / South Africa / China

Penguin Books Ltd., Registered Offices: 80 Strand, London WC2R 0RL, England

THROWN BY A CURVE

This book is an original publication of The Berkley Publishing Group.

Berkley Sensation Books are published by The Berkley Publishing Group,
BERKLEY SENSATION® is a registered trademark of Penguin Group (USA) Inc.
The "B" design is a trademark of Penguin Group (USA) Inc.

ISBN: 978-1-62490-076-1

PRINTED IN THE UNITED STATES OF AMERICA

Cover photo by Claudio Marinesco.
Cover design by Rita Frangie.
Interior text design by Kristin del Rosario.

This book is dedicated to the amazing people at Summit Physical Therapy, especially Bret, my therapist, who worked so diligently on my shoulder for so many months so I could continue to do my job. I think you're all miracle workers and I appreciate everything you do. And thanks for all the sometimes painful, but useful, hands-on learning.

ACKNOWLEDGMENTS

To my editor, Kate Seaver, and my agent, Kimberly Whalen, for their unwavering dedication to making a book rock hard. Y'all are my saviors. Thank you, thank you, thank you.

ONE

GARRETT SCOTT SAT IN THE ST. LOUIS RIVERS THERAPY room facing an entire team of sports medicine specialists, all wearing looks of doom on their faces.

From the team doctor to the therapists who'd been working on his shoulder for the past six months, their faces said it all—he wasn't ready to pitch yet.

He was tired of it. Tired of being molded and manipulated and poked and prodded like some kind of experiment. His shoulder wasn't getting any better, and he still couldn't throw a pitch. He was done. His career was over, and no amount of fake hopeful expressions would make him believe any differently.

"Let's go over to the pulleys," Max said. "If we increase the weight . . ."

"No. It's not going to help. I don't have my full range of motion, and no pulleys, no weighted balls, no water therapy, and no amount of stretching is going to get it back."

"You don't know that, Garrett," Max said. As head of the sports medicine team, when Max had a plan, everyone listened. "We haven't finished your therapy, and the season hasn't started yet. There's plenty of time."

Phil, the team doctor, nodded. "Max is right. You haven't given it enough time."

Garrett glared at them both. "I said no. This has been going nowhere, and we all know it."

Everyone started talking at once, but it was all white noise to him. They were blowing smoke up his ass about how he was going to pitch come April.

He'd heard it before, all the pats on the back and the encouragement that didn't mean anything if you couldn't get a ball across the plate. They were just words. Empty promises.

The only one who didn't say anything was the woman hovering in the background. Dark hair pulled back into a ponytail, she wore the same team-color polo shirt and khaki pants as the men, and held a digital notebook. And she was giving him a look. A pissed-off one.

"You haven't said anything," he said, focusing his gaze on her. "What do you think?"

She blinked and held her notebook close to her chest. "Me?"

"Yeah."

"I'm not in charge of your recovery. There are people here with much more experience than me."

"You've watched my therapy, haven't you?"

"Yes."

"Then what do you think?"

They all turned to her, watching and waiting. She finally shrugged. "I think your team is right. You'll pitch."

She moved forward, and he got a good look at her. Despite the ugly uniforms they all wore, she was pretty, one of the two women on the sports therapy team. He'd thought them interchangeable and hadn't paid much attention, because they were both brunettes, just blurs passing by while he was doing therapy with Max and some of the other senior members of the team. Now that she was closer, he really noticed this one. She had stunning blue eyes and a pretty mouth; he was definitely paying attention now that she'd spoken.

"My arm is stiff."

"Because you're babying it, because you won't give it your all. Your therapists know what they're doing, but you fight them."

As soon as she said it, her eyes widened. Max crossed his arms, and Garrett could tell he was pissed.

Garrett wasn't. His lips quirked. "Go on."

"Look, I didn't mean to insult you."

"Yeah, you did. You've sat back quietly for all these months, and you obviously have something on your mind. Spill it."

She looked up at Max, who shook his head.

"Don't look at him," Garrett said. "Tell me what I'm doing wrong."

She sat next to him on the bench and laid her notebook down, her gaze lifting to his.

"Fine. You're argumentative, confrontational, and a general pain in the ass to deal with. Honestly, no one wants to work with you because you fight your recovery. Half of healing is mental, and your head is the biggest obstacle to getting you back on the mound."

Huh. He glanced up at the others, who did their best to look away. "I see."

But when he turned back to—he had no idea what her name was. "What's your name?"

"Alicia."

"Okay, Alicia. You think you can make me a pitcher again?"

She gave him a confident smirk. "I know I can, if you pull your head out of your ass and work with me."

He liked her confidence. He liked her. She sure as hell was better looking than the rest of the sports medicine group he'd worked with all these months. And she smelled good.

"Alicia," Max warned. "Why don't you head up to the office, and I'll finish up here with Garrett?"

Alicia nodded, then stood and left the room.

Garrett laughed, the first time he'd laughed in a long damn time. "It's okay, Max. I like her. She's honest."

As soon as the door closed, he turned to Max.

"I want her in charge of my therapy."

"Absolutely not," Phil said, interjecting himself into the conversation. "As your doctor, I'm advising against it. Max is the head of sports medicine for the team. He's the best. Alicia doesn't have the experience he has."

"I don't give a shit if she's the water girl. She's confident. She's a sports medicine specialist, certified to do therapy like the rest of you, isn't she?"

"Well, yes," Max said.

"Then I want to work with her."

"You have a multimillion-dollar arm, Garrett," Max said. "I'm not entrusting it to her."

Garrett stood and stretched, then looked at Manny Magee, the St. Louis Rivers coach, who'd been sitting in the corner of the room, silently taking it all in. "These guys have all been working on me for months, and I haven't seen the results needed to throw a single goddamn pitch. I want Alicia to give it a try."

Manny stood and ambled over. He was tough and always honest, so Garrett knew Manny would give it to him straight. "That's because she's right. Physically, you're healing fine from the injury. A lot of your problem is you're resisting the treatment."

Maybe Manny was right, but Garrett doubted it. What he needed was a new therapist. If Alicia and her smart mouth could get the job done, then maybe his career wasn't over.

He looked at Manny—at all of them.

"I need a change. What we're doing isn't working. And maybe someone new can help with that."

"I don't give a damn if a circus clown does your therapy, as long as you're on the mound opening day," Manny said. "Just be ready for the season. We need your arm."

SHIT. SHIT. SHIT. ALICIA MASSAGED THE GIANT HEAD-ache that had taken refuge between her eyes and counted down the minutes until her boss entered the office and fired her.

She'd always had a smart mouth, always spoke first and thought later. But to insult the entire St. Louis Rivers sports medicine team in one sentence had been a serious, colossal fuckup. She'd had some major success as a therapist and had been getting great feedback from her boss in the time she'd been here. This was the job of her dreams, and to make matters worse, her cousin played for this team. Gavin was going to kill her.

The frustrating part was, she knew she was right. Garrett Scott was a seriously amazing pitcher. His injury had been bad, but there was no reason to think he wouldn't come back and be a great pitcher again, providing he cooperated with his rehabilitation. The problem was, he was the worst patient she'd ever seen in terms of cooperation. He resisted therapy, he argued with the treatment plan, and she knew damn well he wasn't doing his at-home exercises. He was one of those athletes who thought of himself as some kind of superhero. Get injured, do rehab, and be fine in a few weeks.

Unfortunately, serious injuries didn't work that way, no matter how young or virile you were. You had to work at your own recovery. The team had done a good job on their part. Garrett just hadn't done any of his part. He blew off his therapists with jokes and promises to do better the next time. And they all liked him, so they placated him.

Ugh.

He wasn't responding to traditional treatment. Which meant he needed a new plan, something she'd been working on during her off days. She'd wanted to present it to Max and Phil, but her methods were a little beyond the norm, and she knew they'd never go for it, especially not for Garrett.

Now, it didn't matter since she wasn't going to be treating any of the Rivers players any longer.

Idiot. She should have just kept her mouth shut and told Garrett that he should listen to whatever Max told him. This was going to be her penance for having a mind of her own. And a big mouth.

She lifted her head as Phil and Max came through the door, along with the Rivers coach, Manny Magee.

Great. They brought the coach with them. She was definitely fired. Manny had a reputation for being fiery and loud. She might even get yelled at before they canned her ass.

She sat up straight and lifted her chin, determined to take it like the professional she was.

Correction. If she was a professional, she probably wouldn't have told the Rivers star pitcher to pull his head out of his ass.

"Alicia," Phil said. "What you said to Garrett downstairs . . ."

"Yes, sir. I know. I was out of line. I'm sorry."

"Actually," Manny said, "it was exactly what he needed to hear."

She frowned and shifted her gaze to the coach. "Excuse me?"

"Garrett has been the perfect specimen of a pitcher for five seasons," Manny said. "We plucked him out of college ball, he spent six months in AAA before we brought him up, and he's been in our starting rotation ever since, with one of the lowest ERAs of any pitcher in the league. He's won the Cy Young Award twice, pitched a near perfect game last year, and held the strikeout record the past two seasons. He's the golden boy."

She'd reviewed his file. She knew his record. But hearing it from Manny gave her an understanding. "He's never failed."

Manny nodded. "At anything. He doesn't know how. So this injury threw him for a loop, ya know? The kid is one of the nicest people I've ever worked with, so don't take his black moods to heart. He'll get that kindness back once he finds his footing."

She looked from Manny to Phil to Max. "Wait. I'm not fired?"

Max didn't smile at her. She could tell he was still angry about what went down in the treatment room. "No, Alicia. You're not fired. Instead, we're putting you in charge of Garrett Scott's rehab."

Again—oh, shit. That's what she got for opening her mouth.

Phil and Max went over her new assignment.

"I want to try some unconventional treatment methods with him," she said to Max.

Max balked, but she figured if she didn't suggest it now, she might as well hand Garrett right back to him.

"Look. He's resisting. And yes, a lot of it is in his head. But some of his problem is boredom. His treatment is rote. He's used to the plan you've run him through, and so is his body. Let me try this. If it doesn't work, we'll alter the plan."

Max looked to Phil, who shrugged. "I agree it's not a standard plan, but alternative therapies do have a high success rate with some athletes. It could work."

Max shrugged then turned to Alicia. "Give it a try. I want weekly reports."

Excited, she nodded. "Yes, sir."

When Garrett came in a few minutes after they left, she stood, suddenly nervous. She'd always been a fan. The Rivers were, after all, her hometown team. And Garrett was nothing short of the most gorgeous man she'd ever laid eyes on. Six feet four inches of dark-haired, dark-eyed intensity, with a leanly honed body that was a work of art.

She'd spent her adult life studying body mechanics. She loved sports and sports players, and Garrett was one of the best. She'd watched him in the workout room, day in and day out, sweating through his therapy. From day one of his injury, when he could barely move his shoulder, she'd ached for him, wished she could be in there helping him.

And now he was all hers. Talk about a huge responsibility.

"They told you?"

She swallowed. "Yes. My question is . . . why me?"

He shrugged. "Because you stood up to me. I need to work with someone who isn't going to take shit from me. The rest of them tell me what they think I want to hear. They pacify me. I don't think you'll do that."

She needed to relax. Think of him as a patient, not a hot man standing only inches away.

"No, I definitely won't do that. I'm not going to take shit from you. But I am going to help you. You have to believe that. And believe in yourself. That's the first step."

He studied her then nodded. "Sure. I cleared your schedule, so you're only going to work with me."

She arched a brow. "You know, I can work with more than one player."

"Probably. But I need you concentrating on my recovery."

A little ego there. Understandable. She'd deal with it. "Okay."

"Then let's get started."

"We will. On Monday. I'll need a few days to develop your

treatment plan. Since today's Friday, the weekend will give me the time I need."

"Fine." He whipped out his phone. "What's your number?"

She gave it to him.

"Okay, good. I'll call you on Sunday, and we can get stuff set up. Does that work for you?"

"Sure." He gave her his number, and she pulled her phone out of her pocket to add it in.

He punched the info into his phone then lifted his gaze to hers. "What's your last name?"

"Riley."

His lips lifted. "Any relation to Gavin?"

"Actually, he's my cousin."

He looked up. "No shit. Is that how you got this job?"

He wasn't the first person to ask that question, and it always annoyed her. "No. I got this job because I'm good at sports medicine. I'm so good at sports medicine that you'll be pitching come April, Garrett. Which has nothing to do with my cousin and everything to do with me."

He laughed. "Man, have you got some attitude. I like you, Alicia."

She wasn't sure how she felt about him. Jury was still out. She headed to the door. "You won't like me when I start kicking your ass, Garrett."

TWO

ALICIA PULLED UP TO THE CURB AT HER AUNT AND uncle's house. She was obviously the last to arrive, because the driveway was full. She hoped they hadn't started dinner without her. She was starving. She'd worked all weekend, buried in Garrett's file, going over everything about his injury. She'd spent Friday night and Saturday reviewing his notes and writing her treatment plan, so she'd be free on Sunday to enjoy family time.

Plus, she hadn't seen her cousin Mick's wife, Tara, since the hospital, and Alicia was dying to get her hands on the new baby.

As she walked in the door, the baby's cries tugged at her heart. She headed into the living room and found Tara, her mother, and her aunt huddled over a small blue wrapped bundle.

"Okay, you can all get out of my way," she said as she slipped out of her coat and tossed her bag on a nearby chair. "I need to hold little Sam."

Tara turned and sent a tired but giddy smile her way. "Take a number. You might have to fight Sam's grandma and aunt Cara for him."

"They get to see him more than I do." She squirted some antibacterial gel onto her hands, rubbed it in, then held out her arms. "Come on, Aunt Kathleen. I know for a fact you've been camped on Mick and Tara's doorstep since he was born three weeks ago."

Kathleen sighed. "You bet your cute little butt I have. It's been a long time since we've had a baby in the family. And little Sam here is the brightest thing to come around since I started getting new daughters-in-law." She gave a little wink to Tara, who took a seat on the sofa.

Kathleen handed Sam over to Alicia. She took him and pulled him against her chest. He was awake, and his big blue eyes regarded her with a curious stare. His cheeks were full and pink. He had dark hair like Mick, but she saw a lot of Tara in him, too.

Alicia walked over to the sofa and sat next to Tara, who looked about ready to pass out.

"He's gorgeous," she said, sliding her fingers across his soft, chubby cheek.

Tara leaned forward and smiled. "I think so. He looks like Mick."

Alicia shifted her glance from the baby to Tara. "And you. His chin and his mouth are definitely yours."

"You think so? I only see Mick when I look at him."

"Oh, I definitely see you. And Nathan."

Tara sighed. "Nathan says that, too. He tries to act like he doesn't care since he's almost a man himself now. But he's over the moon about having a baby brother. And when he sees Mick fussing over the baby, it's like Mick's giving him permission to do the same."

"Well, you know how it is with guys."

"I do. I still have a hard time wrapping my head around the fact that I'm the mother of a newborn and also a son who'll be eighteen this year. That's quite a spread."

Alicia laid her hand on Tara's. "And isn't it wonderful that you get a second chance to do it all over again?"

Tara regarded her. "When you put it like that . . . you're right. I'm so lucky." Her eyes filled with tears. "Oh, shit. Here come the hormones again."

Kathleen laughed. "Expect those for a while, honey. I've told you they come and go."

Tara grabbed a tissue from the box Alicia's aunt held out for her. "I know. It's been so long that I forgot what it was like. Poor Mick. As if my pregnancy wasn't bad enough, now he has to deal with this postpartum nonsense."

Alicia cuddled Sam's warmth against her chest. "Oh, but look at the result. How could he complain?"

"No complaints here," Mick said as he walked in and slid onto the sofa next to Tara. He pressed a kiss to Tara's lips and pulled her against his side. "You can cry all you want, or yell at me anytime those hormones act up." Mick gazed over at Alicia and gave her a giant grin as he looked with pride at his son. "Because look what you gave me."

"Look what we made together," Tara said, lifting a loving gaze to Mick.

"Okay, it's getting all nauseating in here. The room is so filled with love and baby hormones I might have to take a step outside just to get a cold slap of frigid air."

Alicia laughed. Leave it to Gavin's wife, Elizabeth, to break the weepy mood. "Hey, Liz."

"Hey, yourself. I see you're holding my new nephew. And time's up."

Alicia stood. "You want your turn?"

Elizabeth took the baby from her. "Honey, this baby will likely never have a minute's peace when he's over here for family gatherings."

"Isn't that the truth?" Alicia's mom said, throwing her arm around Kathleen. "I suppose we should go check on dinner."

"Might as well," Kathleen said with a sigh. "I obviously won't get another turn with Sam for a while."

"You'll get your turn plenty, Mom," Mick said. "Tara loves that you come over to help. And she needs it. She's out of practice with this new-mom thing, as you can tell."

Alicia glanced over to see Tara's head resting on Mick's shoulder. She was sound asleep.

"Oh, poor thing," Kathleen said. "Was she up late again last night?"

"Yeah. Sam eats every three hours, and since she's breastfeeding, she's up, too. I get to do the diaper changes, though."

"Now, who would have thought diapers and poop would be something you'd be excited about?" Gavin asked as he crowded into the room. He peeked over his wife's shoulder. "You're a natural at that, babe. Maybe we should have our own kid soon."

"That would require you to stay in one place long enough for me to jump your bones so you could get me pregnant."

"I'm not hearing this," Kathleen said. "Come on, Cara. Let's go work on dinner."

"Making babies, are you?" Alicia asked.

Liz shrugged. "We're practicing making babies."

Gavin wrapped his arms around Liz. "That's the fun part."

"I don't want to hear this," Mick said from his spot on the sofa.

"Too bad. You're stuck there with your passed-out wife," Gavin said. "Is this what happens when they give birth? They sleep all the time?"

"The wife or the baby?" Alicia asked, nudging Gavin in the ribs.

"Both," Mick said with a wide grin.

Alicia rolled her eyes. "I'm going in the kitchen to help Mom and Aunt Kathleen. Where's Jenna?"

"She called," Liz said. "Said she and Ty will be a few minutes late."

Alicia nodded and went down the hall, meeting her mom and her aunt in the kitchen.

"Where are Dad and Uncle Jimmy?"

"Tinkering on something in the garage with Nathan," her aunt said, giving Alicia a knowing look.

"Oh." In other words, avoiding the women. Not that she could blame them. It got a little crowded in here when the entire family showed up. "Cole and Savannah doing okay?"

"They're fine," her mother said. "Still taking an extended vacation after the end of football season. I think last time I heard from him they were in . . . What was it I said to you, Kathleen?"

"St. Lucia? St. Thomas? I can't remember which it was."

Her mother waved a knife in the air and shrugged. "I don't recall. They're taking a few weeks, hitting a couple of islands to just be alone together. That's all I know."

"Sounds fun," Alicia said. The two of them deserved it. It had been a tough season but a great one. Her brother's team had made it all the way to the championship before they lost. Cole had been pissed, but he'd really clicked with the team. She was glad. Meeting Savannah had changed his life in ways none of them could have ever imagined. She'd not only changed his professional attitude, the two of them had also fallen in love in the process. Alicia was happy for both of them.

"How's work, Alicia?" her mom asked, handing her a knife and a couple of tomatoes so she could help make the salad. The one thing about family dinners was they assumed if you stepped into the kitchen, you were there to help. No one even blinked when handed a task. She washed her hands and dug in.

"Oh, work? It's . . . interesting."

Her mother paused as she opened the oven door. "Does that mean you're enjoying it?"

"Of course. I love it. It's everything I wanted and more."

"I'm so glad to hear that."

She didn't want to talk about this new assignment with her mother or with her aunt. But when she finished the salad and headed down the hall, Liz was coming up. Alicia grabbed her by the arm.

"I need to talk to you."

"Okay. Sure."

"Let's go upstairs."

"Tara's up there. She just went up to feed Sam."

"Good. She can listen in."

Jenna peeked her head in around the living room wall. She was slipping her coat off. Her cheeks were red, and she was rubbing her hands. "Oooh, gossip? Can I come? I need something hot and juicy to warm me up. It's freezing out there."

Alicia hugged her. "Of course you can come."

"Great." She turned to Ty, who was right behind her. "You're on your own. Find the men."

Ty nodded and wandered down the hall. "First I'll find the beer."

Jenna rolled her eyes and followed them up the stairs.

Liz knocked softly on the door to Aunt Kathleen's bedroom. "Tara, we're invading you."

"Hey, guys, come on in. Just feeding Sam."

Liz pushed the door open, and they all piled in. Tara was in Aunt Kathleen's rocking chair, Sam to her breast.

Alicia sighed. Tara looked so serene as she rocked the baby in her arms.

"You sure we're not bothering you?"

"Not at all. I'd love the company. Otherwise, I might fall asleep again."

Alicia laughed. "Okay."

"So, what's going on?" Liz asked.

"I've been assigned to Garrett Scott's rehab."

Liz arched a brow. "Garrett Scott, huh? That's interesting."

Jenna rolled onto her side on the bed. "He's a hottie. Shoulder injury, right?"

"Yes. He's been rehabbing for several months with no progress."

"So, what's the problem?" Tara asked.

"He was working with one of the senior members of the team. Actually, several senior members. Until I opened my big mouth, and said he had his head up his ass and wasn't cooperating with his treatment plan."

Liz snorted. "That sounds like something you'd say."

"I know, right? I just couldn't keep my mouth shut. Then again, it wasn't entirely my fault. He did ask my opinion."

"So you felt free to give it to him," Liz said with a smirk.

Alicia sighed. "I did. And before I could blink Garrett said he wanted me assigned to him. Just me. I thought I was going to get fired, and instead, I'm in charge of his recovery."

Jenna sat up and crossed her legs over each other. "Wow. That's big. Are you feeling intimidated?"

This was why she needed her girls. They knew exactly how she felt. "More than intimidated. I'm scared to death."

"You can handle this, Alicia," Tara said as she lifted Sam over her shoulder and rubbed his back. "You know what you're doing."

"Tara's right." Liz squeezed her hand. "We've talked about this. You went into this field because it's all you ever wanted to do. You love sports and medicine. This is your shot to do something monumental. Rehabbing Garrett and being successful at it could be a huge step in your career."

She looked at all of them. "What if I screw this up? Garrett is their number one pitcher."

"You won't screw it up," Tara said, smiling when Sam let out a tiny burp. "You know what you're doing. This is what you've trained for."

"Tara's right," Jenna said. "You're going to get Garrett's shoulder in shape and get him back on the pitcher's mound."

Liz nodded. "Have some faith in yourself. And go kick his ass."

THREE

MONDAY DAWNED OVERCAST, SPITTING SNOWFLAKES and promising a big-ass storm later in the day.

These were the kinds of days that caused Garrett's shoulder to ache like a son of a bitch. So when he arrived at the team practice facility early, he was happy to see Alicia already there.

She had her digital notebook in hand, her hair pulled back in its customary ponytail, and she was wearing that hideous uniform everyone from the sports medicine team wore. No makeup, very plain, except she wasn't plain. How had he not noticed her before? Caught up in his own misery, probably, because Alicia was pretty. There was something about her that made him see through the ugly uniform and lack of makeup.

Maybe it was the promise she'd made to help him pitch again. But it was more than that, because he also liked the sparkle in her eyes—it reminded him of the sky in the summer. And her mouth— he really liked her mouth, especially when she smiled. He wanted to see her smile more. He'd bet she was gorgeous when she smiled. It didn't hurt that she was pretty, and not all made-up and dressed like she wanted to be taken out to lunch or shopping like the women he usually hung out with.

She came to meet him when he pushed through the door.

"Good morning. Are you ready for this?" she asked.

"I'm stiff, I'm sore, and my shoulder hates this weather."

She nodded. "Don't worry. We'll put some heat on it to warm you up first, then we'll get to work."

He followed her to one of the private rooms.

"Take off your jacket and get comfortable on the table. I'll go get a heating pad. If you brought some music with you, you can get that started."

He had brought his MP3 player, and it was obvious Alicia wasn't going to have a conversation with him. Usually, he and the guys would shoot the shit for about an hour then do some therapy. This was going to be different.

He tucked in his earbuds and turned on some music. Alicia came back and put hot pads on his shoulder, then turned down the lights and left the room without a word.

Fine. Whatever. He didn't need her to be his best friend. The heat felt good, so he settled in, closed his eyes, and immersed himself in the music.

The ten minutes passed too fast. He could have gone to sleep, but she pulled the pads off, leaving him chilled. He grabbed his jacket, but she stopped him.

"You won't need that right now. Come with me."

She took him into the workout room and sat him down on the arm bike.

"This will get you warmed up. I'll be back shortly."

She set the time for five minutes and walked away.

Again.

Wasn't this fun? At least the TV was on, set to sports news. He pedaled away and caught up on sports, but he also watched Alicia out of the corner of his eye. She went into the office, chatted with Phil and Max. They looked over whatever she had in her electronic notebook. There was a lot of nodding going on. Talking about him, no doubt.

When his bell rang, she was right there next to him.

"Ready?" she asked as he climbed off the bike.

"I've been ready."

"Good. Come over here."

She led him to the doorway.

"Reach your arms to the top of the beam," she said.

He turned to her. "What?"

"Lift your arms up, straight overhead. Touch the overhead."

He did. His left arm went up just fine, but he winced when he straightened the right. And he wasn't straightening it as easily as the left arm.

"It's just a stretch, nothing too strenuous. Keep it up there and try to straighten your right arm, keeping your arm as close to your ear as you can."

She stood behind him, silently watching.

"See anything?"

"Yes. Now, drop your arms, shake them out for a few seconds, and do it again."

He gave her a look over his shoulder. "This doesn't seem to accomplish anything."

"That's why you're the pitcher and I'm the therapist. Do it again, and hold for a count of ten each time."

He shrugged but reached for the top of the doorway again.

She had him do it five more times. By the last time, it felt like his form was much better. She came up behind him and grasped his shoulders, pushing against the muscles and tendons.

"Right side feels tight," he said.

"Of course it feels tight. You don't move enough. You don't stretch enough. The more you keep your arm immobile, the more scar tissue forms. That's half your problem."

He turned to face her. "And the other half is?"

She tapped the side of her head. "You thinking that your career is over. And because of it, you don't do your home exercises like you should. And because you don't do your home exercises like you should, your shoulder isn't healing. Self-fulfilling prophecy and all that."

Garrett didn't like how easily Alicia had him pegged. Then again, wasn't that the reason he'd chosen her in the first place? She'd seen right through him, had told him what he needed. And what he needed was someone to push him.

He needed to get back on the mound. He was twenty-nine years old and still had a lot of years left to pitch. He wasn't going to let this injury derail his career. Being out of commission this long had fucked with his head, and he didn't know how to change that.

The one thing he'd always had was control—over his pitches, over his career, and over his life. The past year he'd lost all of it, and he wanted it back. All the team doctors and athletic directors and therapists hadn't helped him get it back.

The therapists he had befriended had done nothing but enable him, allowing him to make excuses and not get the strength in his arm back.

Was that what he wanted?

Maybe Alicia was the key. She seemed confident in her ability to help him, so he had to trust in her. He was running out of options.

He looked down at her, wondering how much he could challenge her. "You're kind of short."

She snorted. "Oh, but I'm mighty. Just you wait and see."

He liked that she didn't insult easy. "You must have brothers."

"One. And cousins. You don't scare me."

"Wasn't trying to."

"Let's go for a walk," she suggested.

"Aren't you going to work out my shoulder?"

"In good time."

"You know it's winter out there."

She cocked her head to the side. "Yes, I do. Afraid of a little weather?"

"No." He hated cold weather. If he'd wanted to be in cold weather, he'd have played football.

"Good. Put your coat on."

"Is this part of my therapy?"

She grabbed her coat. "No. I love freezing my ass off and thought you might want to join me."

"You're kind of a smart-ass," he said as he slid into his heavy winter jacket then his beanie.

"Yeah, I've never heard that one before." She slipped her hat over her head. "Everything I do with you is part of your therapy. Let's go."

They walked outside the facility, and Garrett slunk farther into his jacket. The darkness of the morning hadn't given way to any sunshine, and the wind had picked up even more, so it felt colder. They walked up the stairs and down the street.

Alicia was practically bouncing as she lifted her face to the sky. She turned to him. "It's supposed to snow today."

"Yeah, like a foot of it or something."

"I know. It's exciting."

He caught the grin on her face, and just as he had imagined, it transformed her from pretty to beautiful. Her cheeks rounded, and her lips curved into something so sexy it stole his breath. He tried not to notice, but it was hard not to. "You like snow."

"I love it. I love all weather, actually. There's nothing like a big snowstorm while you're cuddled inside the house in your pajamas with a steaming cup of hot chocolate and a great romance novel."

And now he'd have to get that mental picture out of his head. He wondered what her hair would look like out of that ponytail, waves of dark curls spilling over her shoulders. Though the fantasy would be better if she was reclining on the sofa naked.

He decided this whole therapy thing would go a lot better if he didn't find her sexy. Bathrobe, fuzzy slippers, her face slathered in some kind of green facial cream, and maybe her hair in curlers.

"Reach up and grab that thin limb on the tree," she said as they walked.

He stopped and pulled his head out of the fantasy. "Huh?"

"That limb on the tree ahead. Keep walking, but just grab the limb as we walk by."

"And do what with it?"

"Here. I'll show you the first time." She strolled ahead of him then slowed down as she stepped under a tree with low-hanging limbs. She reached up with her right arm and grabbed one of the thinner limbs, held on as she walked past.

Ah. He got it. "You want me to stretch the back of my shoulder by grabbing on to tree limbs."

"Yes, but don't jerk it. Do it gently. Slow your pace as we walk under the trees. Just pause, hang on to the limb, and really feel the stretch."

"Got it." And he did the next time, and the next; she'd chosen a heavily tree-lined street.

"This is a lot less boring than the pulleys."

"Even if you are freezing your ass off?" she asked with a wry smile.

"Even if."

"It's always nice to get out of the facility. I like being outdoors, breathing in fresh air. Plus, you needed a change in your therapy. And you need to get out of your head. It's very doom and gloom in there."

"So you think me yanking on tree limbs is going to fool my body—and my mental state—into thinking this really isn't therapy?"

She laughed. "No. I know you're not stupid. You'll still know this is therapy. It's just using different mechanics."

By the time they'd walked a mile, he could definitely feel it in his shoulder. Plus, she made him do it leaning to the side and from the front. They walked into the facility, and he wasn't cold anymore. He peeled off his hat and his jacket, and went to the break room for a bottle of water.

Alicia met him at the door. "Ready for some serious work now?"

He paused mid-drink. "I thought we were done."

"That was just a warm-up. Now that your muscles and tendons are toasty, we're really going to dig in."

"Yeah, I don't think so. I'm a little sore."

She marched over to him and pushed on his back. "Being a wuss isn't allowed. Head over to the pulleys."

"I thought jerking on the tree limbs was in lieu of the pulleys."

She adjusted the weights for him. "You would think that, wouldn't you? But no. Three sets of ten."

He looked down at the weights, which were set heavier than they'd been before. Then he looked up at Alicia. "This isn't going to wreck my shoulder?"

"Nope. Start lifting. I'll be here watching your progress."

He went through the routine, waiting for some sharp, knifelike pain to signal that he was right, that the weights were too heavy.

The pain didn't come. It hurt, but therapy always did.

Though, it was a lot less painful so far because he had Alicia to push him around. Maybe this could work.

* * *

ADMITTEDLY, ALICIA WAS NERVOUS. NOT JUST A LITTLE nervous, but a whole bundle of jammed-up tension that had settled right between her shoulder blades as she worked through this first session with Garrett.

There was a mountain of pressure on her to do this right, and a lot riding on this—Garrett's career. If she didn't get his shoulder working again, and not just working minimally, but fully enough that he could pitch and pitch well, then she'd likely be out of a job. Sports medicine specialists were hired—especially by a baseball team—because they were the best. Throughout her time in school and at the orthopedic clinic she'd worked for prior to being hired by the Rivers, she'd prided herself on being damn good at sports medicine. She'd studied anatomy and physiology before she'd ever stepped foot in a college classroom, had worked on her brother's and cousins' aches and pains, and had watched athletes' mechanics and studied their injuries.

This is what she'd spent her life training for. Now was her chance to prove herself.

She put Garrett on the leg press to give his shoulder a break and also to balance his workout. She took a moment to ogle his muscles as he lay back and pushed a sizeable amount of weight. Since he'd warmed up, he'd shed his sweats and was down to his shorts, his thighs flexing as he pushed up on the press.

If she wasn't an employee of the team, she'd be all over him like she was sure many women were. But fantasizing about the hot pitcher wasn't going to happen, no matter how amazing his body was or how sexy his eyes were when he glanced up at her.

He was her patient, and he was going to remain firmly rooted in that spot.

He sat up after locking the weights into place.

"So, how experienced are you at this, Alicia?"

"I have plenty of therapeutic experience."

He dropped his chin then lifted his eyes. "Right. Tons, I'll bet." This wasn't the first time she'd been questioned by one of the athletes about her background. "I have a master's degree in sports medicine. I both interned and worked for some of the best orthopedic surgeons out there before I was hired by the Rivers. I've been working in this field for seven years. But if you have any doubts about working with me, you can feel free to—"

He held up his hands. "Touchy subject, obviously."

"Hey, you're the one who wanted me. If you've changed your mind, just let me know, and I'll turn you over to Max again."

"I haven't."

"Good." She picked up her notebook and sat on one of the benches. She was irritated but more at herself than at Garrett. She was being overly sensitive, and she knew it, and it wasn't his fault. Well, indirectly it was, because he'd placed her in this position by singling her out and putting her in charge of his recovery.

"Why me?"

He frowned. "Huh?"

"Why did you choose me? You had to know I don't have half the experience of some other members of the team."

"I told you why. Because you didn't take any of my shit and you told me exactly how you'd handle me."

"I see."

"So . . ." He looked down at his shoulder then back at her. "Handle me."

She really wished she hadn't picked up the sexual innuendo in what he said. Which was probably all in her mind and not at all in his words. She wished he was ugly or unpleasant to deal with.

Even when he was whiny and complaining, there was still an underlying charm about him. He might be a pain in some areas of his recovery that made him cranky, but that she could handle. He was also friendly, and oh, dear God, was he gorgeous and sexy, and he had a body she wanted to get her hands on in much more than a therapeutic way.

But this was her golden opportunity, so she was going to have to separate her . . . urges from her job.

"So . . . are we done here?" he asked.

"Nice try. Our time together isn't up yet."

"My shoulder feels like a limp noodle."

"And you're not the therapist, so suck it up and sit there until I tell you you're done."

She walked away to get the stretch bands and the ball, mainly to create distance. The less she chatted with him, the less she'd think about him on a personal level. When she brought him the bands, he gave her a dubious look.

"We should be beyond this."

"And you like to cut corners. That's why your therapy isn't progressing. Let's do this."

He blew out a loud, frustrated sigh but did the routine she laid out. She turned some relaxing music on.

"I'd prefer something harder."

She tried not to wince. For some reason, everything he said conjured up sex in her head. She'd like something harder, too, but it wasn't music she was thinking about. And she needed to stop acting like a lust-filled teenager for the love of God.

"This is relaxing. I want your muscles liquid, not tensed up."

"You could always give me a massage after."

"You want a massage therapist, I'll bring one in. That's not what the team is paying me to do."

"Oh, so you will bring in a masseuse for me?"

She stood beside him, watching and making notes while he pulled at the bands. "If I think one is warranted."

"Yeah? And how will you know?"

"After I finish you off, I'll see how your muscles feel."

"How come you won't do the massage yourself? My other trainers did."

"Good for them."

"But you don't want to climb on me and massage me. It's too personal for you."

Now *that* was innuendo. Plain and clear. She slanted him a glare. "Well, now I know what kind of massages you get."

"Huh?"

"Climb on?"

He laughed. "Okay, I was exaggerating. But I know you all give massages. Except you, obviously."

She met his gaze and couldn't tell if he was teasing her, challenging her, or plain trying to annoy her. She chalked his attitude up to sore muscles and decided to give him a break. "I didn't say that."

"I know you all are trained in massage because one of the guys told me."

"Yes, we are. But that's not our primary focus as therapists. I tend to frown on doing it because I don't want my patients to look on me as a glorified masseuse."

"You mean because you're a woman."

"No, because I worked my ass off to become a therapist. And not a massage therapist."

"Again . . . touchy."

"I'm not touchy. And you're finished here. Let's move on."

She put him through a routine of circuit training with various upper body machines, with the objective of strengthening his shoulder.

"You gave me heavier weights when we started," he said as he dragged the pulley forward.

"I know."

He frowned as she had him do another set with only twenty pounds of weight. When he bent to adjust the pin to a heavier weight, she stopped him.

"These are too light. I'm not getting any benefit."

She tilted her head to look at him. "Last time I looked, you weren't in charge. Do another set with this weight."

He gave her a look through his narrowed gaze that led her to believe they were about to argue the point, but then he straightened and did the set.

"Your form is good, so let's up the weight."

"Finally."

She bit back a retort. He was frustrated, and she knew that. She had a plan. She increased the weight in ten-pound increments after each set until she saw him struggle.

Impressive. And encouraging. His shoulder could bear a lot of weight, at least on the pulley.

"Now, let's pull from the side. This will be harder."

"I know."

Once again, she started with lighter weights and gradually increased. He couldn't handle as much weight, but she monitored him for signs of pain. When she saw the wince, she ended the session and marked it in her notes.

"I could do more. Now that we're into it, I can see the benefit. It's not hurting as much, and my shoulder can handle it."

"That's enough for our first go-round."

"I need to push myself," he said as he followed her to the next circuit. "You said so yourself."

She turned to face him. "And if you reinjure the shoulder, you'll be back pulling ten pounds again, and you'll miss the season. Is that what you want?"

"No."

"All right, then." She took him through the rest of the circuit, arguing with him the whole way about how much weight he could handle. She remained firm, refusing to allow him to press or lift any more weight than what was in her therapy plan, much to his irritation.

"We're done," she finally said after an hour.

"That's it?"

"A little while ago you wanted to be done."

He paused. "Well, that was earlier. I've got a second wind, and I can go longer."

"We're finished. Now, I'll stretch you. Go lie down."

"That's not enough. We need to do more."

"It's enough for now. I'll give you a good stretch, and you'll be begging me to leave you alone for the rest of the day."

"We'll see."

Alicia gave him a sly smile.

Garrett dragged his fingers through his hair and laid on his back on the padded table.

Logically, Garrett knew how therapy worked. It was a slow, methodical process, and nothing changed dramatically the first day. But goddamn it, he expected miracles.

He'd need a miracle in order to start pitching again. He was investing a lot in his decision to go with Alicia as his therapist. He hadn't been blinded by her beauty or great body. He'd depended entirely on gut instinct and the way she'd talked to him.

Now, as she loomed over him, he sucked in a breath and hoped for the best.

"You ready for this?" she asked.

He shrugged. "Sure."

She lifted his arm over his head, doing the basic stretches he was used to. Nothing hurt, but it always felt good to get stretched out after a therapy session. He closed his eyes and imagined himself on the mound, throwing a curveball to a batter, followed by the umpire signaling a strike.

Yeah, that's where he needed to put his focus, and if he had to ride Alicia hard to get her to push him, that's where he'd—

"Jesus Christ!" His eyes shot open when she bent his arm back, then to the side. Hot, stinging pain made his eyes water. "That fucking hurts."

"Take deep breaths," she said, her voice soothing, as she did the same damn thing with his arm.

He wasn't a wimp, and he had a pretty high pain tolerance, but that shit was painful as hell. "What are you doing?"

"Breaking up scar tissue. Pushing you to your limits. That's what you want, isn't it?"

"Yeah. But I thought—"

"Shhh," she said, taking his arm back in a pitcher's rotation position. "Just breathe and try to relax through this."

"How long are you going to stretch me?"

"About thirty minutes."

He could be dead in thirty minutes if she kept this up. He gritted his teeth and sucked it up like a man, trying not to moan when she kneeled beside him and, he was certain, pulled his shoulder right out of its socket.

Okay, maybe he exaggerated, but it sure felt like she was twisting his shoulder into unnatural positions. And he didn't like it.

The room was getting hot, the pain more intense. Having something to bite down on wouldn't hurt, either, because Alicia was relentless. And she wouldn't stop. He needed just a one-fucking-minute break, so he could take a goddamn breath, but she went on and on and on until he was panting like he was about to give birth.

"Tell me about the best game you ever pitched," she asked as she worked on his arm.

Momentarily distracted from the pain, he lifted his gaze to hers. "What?"

"What was your best game?"

He thought about it for a second. "Against Chicago. Tied in the ninth. I had pitched the whole game. Grueling back and forth. Coach wanted to pull me several times, thought I was getting tired, but he relented and let me stay in." He winced when she drew his arm back for a long stretch.

"Just take deep breaths," she said, her voice soft and comforting. "You're tied in the ninth. Home game?"

He breathed in and out, and she released the tension on his arm. "Yeah. So I face the first batter, who swung at a curve and hit a grounder to first. Second batter popped up to center. The third one was tougher, throwing off fouls on my fastballs, but I figured I could get him because his timing was off. Either that or he was gonna wallop a big one off me. But I dug in and nailed one right past him. He struck out swinging."

She stopped and looked down at him. "Hard to have that kind of juice on your ball that late in the game."

He smiled up at her. "Yeah. Our guys scored a run in the next inning, and we won the game."

"Good game, then."

"Yup."

She held out her hand. "And good session. We're done here."

Relieved as hell, he sat up. "Thanks."

She leaned him against the wall then put an ice pack on his shoulder.

"Ten minutes with the ice pack, then you're all done."

She'd distracted him during the toughest part of the stretch by making him talk to her.

He watched her while she typed into her notebook, part of him hating her for the wicked-hard stretch, the other part of him just not able to figure her out yet.

She looked up and met his gaze. "You're giving me strange looks. Was it too hard for you?"

"It was fine." His shoulder was still throbbing.

"Your jaw is clenched. You should try to relax." She took the ice pack away and sat across from him. "It's only going to get harder from here on out. Think you can handle it?"

For a split second, he pondered going back to the other trainers. He was used to their brand of therapy. This had been . . . different. It had been hard. But there was something about Alicia that clicked for him. And he'd asked for this, so he was going to take it. "You're sure this is going to work."

"Positive."

"Then I can take whatever you dish out."

"Good. If you're sore later, I'll rub you down."

Later? He was sore now. "I thought you didn't give massages."

She gave him a look over her shoulder as she left the room. "I'll make an exception for you since you look like you're about to cry. But I warned you that working with me wasn't going to be a vacation, didn't I? I'm not going to go easy on you, Garrett. If you don't want to work with me, say so now, and we'll make adjustments."

She waited, the challenge in her eyes really damn clear. He liked that about her, and no way in hell was he going to cave.

"If you can dish it out, I can take it. Let's do this."

FOUR

IT HAD BEEN A WEEK AND A HALF. TEN HORRIBLE DAYS of therapy that Alicia thought might kill her.

Physically, Garrett was doing all right. He was taking a toll on her emotional state, though, because his constant griping was a pain in her butt.

She either worked him too hard or not hard enough. Nothing she did was right. No wonder the team coddled him. They obviously did whatever he asked to shut him the hell up. He might be pretty on the outside, but she had thoughts of running for the duct tape to slap over his mouth whenever he showed up for therapy.

Even worse, everyone else had left at the beginning of the week for spring training in Florida, which left her alone with Garrett. The first few days she'd had the other therapists to talk to when things had gotten rough. And they'd commiserated, because they'd all worked with him.

Now she was alone, though both Phil and Max had told her

she could call them if an emergency came up related to Garrett's condition or if she had a question. Annamarie, one of the other therapists and a good friend, said to call her if she just needed to vent.

She'd likely have to call Annamarie just to whine at her. Probably every day.

Like today, because Garrett was an hour late. She used the time to update her notes and work on her upcoming treatment plan for him, but when another half hour ticked off, she dialed his cell.

He answered with a sleepy, "Yeah."

"You were supposed to be here over an hour ago."

"Who is this?"

Alicia sucked in a hard breath. "Your therapist."

"Oh." He paused, and she heard a yawn. "Sorry, Alicia. I must have overslept."

"No kidding. How about you get your ass in here?"

Another yawn. She tapped her foot.

"How about we just skip today? My arm's kind of sore anyway."

"I don't think so. Grab some coffee and get dressed."

She could have sworn she heard a snore.

"Garrett. Are you there?"

"Huh? Oh, yeah. I'll be there tomorrow. Promise, k?"

Then she heard a click. "Hello? Garrett? Garrett?"

She stared at her phone.

"That son of a bitch." He'd hung up on her.

Unbelievable. That play might have worked on someone else, especially when the facility had other injured players to focus on. Did he think she was going to enjoy the day off and go shopping or maybe read a book? Hell no.

He'd asked for her, and like it or not, he was going to get her. She pulled up his address from his file, grabbed her coat and car keys, and stormed out the door.

* * *

THERE WAS A RELENTLESS POUNDING IN GARRETT'S head. He'd had a few beers last night, but he didn't recall any whiskey or tequila, so he shouldn't have a hangover.

He pulled the pillow over his head, but then he heard the bell ringing. He searched under the pillow on the other side of the bed and grabbed his phone, cracking his eyelids open to peer at the display.

No, wasn't the phone.

There was that pounding again.

What. The. Fuck?

It took him a few seconds to figure out it was the door. And the doorbell. Simultaneously. He dropped his head to the pillow again. Whoever it was would go away when he didn't answer.

Except they didn't. The banging and ringing continued.

Shit. He rolled out of bed and slid into his sweatpants, went to the door, and peered through the peephole.

"Really?" He unlocked the door and pulled it open. Alicia stood there with a sweet smile on her face.

"Morning, sunshine. Ready for therapy?"

"Uh, no. I *was* sleeping."

She pushed through the door. "Not anymore. So you might as well get dressed."

He couldn't believe she'd come to his house. He wanted to shut the door in her face. But since she was here . . .

"I need coffee." He walked past her, and since he heard her footsteps behind him as he made his way to the kitchen, he assumed she'd come in.

At least she was quiet. While the coffee was brewing, he grabbed two cups, got out the cream and sugar, and turned to face her.

Her gaze drifted down to where his sweats were slung around

his hips. He realized then that he was barely dressed, just the sweats that he'd grabbed so he could see who was at the door.

And she had noticed. And he noticed that she was looking.

He cracked a smile at that. Crossed his arms as she made a visual inspection of his abs and chest. When her gaze reached his face, she blushed.

Nice.

But she stayed silent. "Might as well take your coat off."

"That's not necessary. I can wait while you get dressed."

"I need to take a shower."

He saw her make a quick scan of his exposed skin again. If she didn't stop that ogling, she was going to give him a hard-on. She looked cute all bundled up in her coat and hat and gloves, her cheeks rosy from blushing.

"Shed the outerwear and have a cup."

She tugged off her cap and shrugged out of her coat. "Fine."

He laughed as her hair flew in all directions from static cling, which made her glare at him. "What?"

He walked over to her and smoothed her hair down. "You look like you stuck your finger in a light socket."

Her eyes widened, and she slapped his hands away, grabbed a ponytail holder from her wrist, and gathered her hair up in it. "And you aren't making me any happier this morning."

He walked to the coffeemaker and poured two cups. "Maybe you're the one who needs to go back to bed. You're cranky."

"You're right. I am cranky because you're making light of what I consider serious business, which is your recovery and your career."

"Your cup is on the counter. Cream and sugar are there if you want it."

He leaned against the counter and took a drink. Then another, waiting for the surge of caffeine to give him the jolt he'd need to deal with Alicia this morning.

Fortunately, she wandered over, picked up the cup, and grabbed some sugar to add to it, then leaned beside him to silently
drink.

Silence. He liked that word. He'd gotten through his first cup
and was on his second before she spoke again.

"You think this is fun for me?"

He looked down at her, feeling a lot more charitable now that
he was fully awake. "Probably not. But you could have just let one
day slide."

She sat her cup on the counter and turned to face him. "One
day can make all the difference in your recovery. I've studied your
chart. It's not just one day, Garrett. You've let a lot of days slide
since your injury. And the team let you. That's not going to happen
with me. If I have to camp out on your doorstep and drag your lazy
ass out of bed every day, then I will. If I have to move in with you
and kick you out of bed to get you to cooperate, then that's what's
going to happen. But one way or the other, you're going to get the
therapy you need to get your arm in shape come game day."

Now that he was sufficiently awake, he was geared up for battle.
He turned to her. "I don't need a goddamn babysitter."

"Then stop behaving like a child and act like an adult. One who
takes his responsibilities seriously."

He arched a brow and crossed his arms. "So I sleep in one
morning, and I've suddenly failed?"

"You cancelled your therapy sessions thirty-four times before I
took over."

He cocked a brow. "You counted?"

"Yes. And while you think missing one session doesn't make a
difference, blowing off thirty-four sessions does. That's why you're
not improving. That's why you're not on the mound throwing
pitches yet. Have you even had a ball in your hand since you've
been injured?"

He changed his mind. He didn't like Alicia after all, and frankly, he hated her ball-busting attitude.

"Answer me. Have you?"

"No."

"Then stop blowing me off and start taking this therapy seriously. Maybe then we'll get somewhere."

Tired of listening to her, he pushed off the counter. "I'm going to take a shower."

She trailed after him.

He turned to her in the middle of the hallway. "You going to follow me into the shower?"

That finally got through to her. She stopped. "I'll wait here."

He looked her up and down. Just the thought of her stripping down to continue their argument in the shower was enough to make his dick twitch to life. He needed to get away from her before he did something really stupid, like suggest they use their energy on something more productive, like sex.

And then she'd really be pissed off at him.

He pivoted and headed into the bedroom, stripped off his sweats and turned the shower on, blowing out a frustrated breath as he stepped under the steamy water.

He'd always hated being told what to do. Being in this business, it was all about the rules, including where you fit in the rotation.

Hell, at the rate he was going, he'd be lucky to be in the rotation at all. If he didn't rehab well, he could end up losing his job as a starter, a job he'd worked his ass off to get and to hold on to. Instead, he could wind up as a middle-inning reliever, tossing a few pitches every couple of games when needed. If he pitched at all.

Or he could end up spending this season rehabbing his arm in the minors.

He shoved his face under the spray and thought about what that might be like.

The one thing he knew about the majors was that once you went backward, you very rarely got a shot at coming back up.

He pulled his head away from the water and scrubbed his hand over his face, turned off the shower, and grabbed a towel. After the steam cleared in the bathroom, he took a look in the mirror.

Maybe Alicia was right. God, he hated to admit that, but maybe it was time to take this therapy thing more seriously.

Or at least think about taking it more seriously. He still wasn't convinced any of this was doing any good. But maybe he should give it more time—give her more time—to make it all work.

He threw on clean clothes, combed his hair, and came out of his room. Alicia was staring out the back door into his backyard.

She turned when she heard him come out.

"Okay, let's get this therapy thing going."

She walked over to grab her coat. "About damn time."

He smiled as he pulled his jacket off the back of the chair. Yeah, he still liked her sass.

He followed her to the treatment facility and got out of his car.

"Wait," she said as he headed to the door.

"What?"

"You didn't eat."

"No. Didn't have time."

"You need to fuel up first."

He leaned against his car. "What? And ruin your carefully crafted time line?"

"Funny. Come on."

They walked across the street to Denny's. Alicia ordered a cup of coffee and some juice while Garrett ordered the full breakfast.

"Nothing to eat for you?" he asked.

"I already ate breakfast. I was on time and waiting for you at the facility two hours ago."

"Okay, I get it. I was an asshole," he said as he downed a glass of juice.

She didn't answer, so obviously, she agreed with him. Then she went quiet. She'd brought her notebook, so he contented himself with playing a game on his phone.

"You get that this is all for your benefit, right?"

He waited to answer her while the waitress delivered his food. "Part of me does. The other part of me just wanted to sleep in this morning."

"That other part of you needed a wake-up call."

He dug into his eggs. "Yeah, well, that part of me doesn't like you very much." He swallowed. "Sorry."

"I don't need you to like me, Garrett. I just need you to follow the plan."

"And just what is the plan for today? More of the same?"

She smiled. "No. I have something fun in mind for today's therapy."

Fun, huh? Nothing about therapy was fun.

After he finished eating, they headed back to the facility. Alicia stopped at her car. "Get in."

"We're not going to train in there?"

"Not today."

He climbed into her car and put on his seat belt. "So, where are we going?"

She pulled out of the parking lot, keeping her gaze straight ahead. "Not far."

He had a chance to watch her as she drove. Carefully. With both hands on the wheel, and never once taking her attention off the road.

He also noticed she didn't have her uniform on today, something he hadn't paid much attention to when she'd shown up at his house.

"No team uniform today?"

"Nope." She pulled off the highway and pulled into what at first looked like a gym.

Then he realized it wasn't a gym at all.

"Seriously?" he asked as she parked. "A rock climbing facility?"

She finally turned to him. "It'll be great therapy. Plus, tons of fun."

Nothing that had "therapy" in it was ever fun. But he got out and slid into step next to her.

"Ever rock climbed before?" she asked as they headed inside.

He didn't know what he expected, but tons of walls with different-sized colorful rocks wasn't it. "Uh, no. You?"

She grabbed a clipboard from the front desk. "As a matter of fact, I have. It's a tremendous form of exercise for your entire body, especially for your shoulders."

"Hey, Alicia."

Garrett looked over as a muscular guy came to the desk. Alicia smiled at him.

"Hi, Dave."

"I have everything set up for you and Garrett. Hi, I'm Dave."

"Nice to meet you, Dave." Garrett shook his hand.

"I'm a big fan of the Rivers. I understand you're doing some shoulder therapy. I hope it gets you back on the mound soon."

"Me, too."

He was handed a clipboard and a form that basically said if he fell to his death, it wasn't their fault, along with some other information about safety. He filled it out and signed it.

"Right this way," Dave said.

Garrett walked behind as Alicia and Dave stayed close together talking. Or rather—Dave talked. Alicia tilted her head back and laughed. And Garrett felt like a third wheel, though he had no idea why. It wasn't like Dave and Alicia were on some kind of date.

As far as he knew, anyway. He didn't know anything about her personal life. Dave could be her boyfriend, and he was helping her with Garrett's therapy.

Lucky guy if that was the case. Out of those loose-fitting team uniforms, she had one hell of a body. Tight workout pants and a tank top hugged her body in a way the team uniforms never had.

She was slender but not skinny. The woman had muscle tone like she worked out and curves in all the right places.

"Okay, Garrett, let's get you in a harness," Dave said, and proceeded to hook him up. Alicia seemed to know what she was doing as she climbed into the gear herself then headed over to him.

"You're climbing with me?" Garrett asked.

Alicia grinned. "Of course. I'll be right next to you the entire time. I need to watch your form and make sure you don't injure your shoulder."

She led him to one of the walls and leaned against it, raising her arms. "We'll stretch out first."

After they stretched, she put her foot on one of the rocks. "Just follow along next to me. We'll go easy at first."

He tilted his head back and stared up at the top of the wall, his shoulder aching at the thought of how much work it was going to take to get there.

Alicia laid her hand on his shoulder. "We'll only go as far as you think you can handle—and as far as I think you can take—no farther, okay?"

He studied the top, then slipped on his gloves and grabbed the rope. "Don't sweat it. I can handle this."

The first ten feet or so were pretty easy, a stretch that felt pretty good to his shoulder. And he had to admit this was much more fun than doing repetitive exercises at the training facility. By the time they were halfway up the wall, though, he was drenched in sweat, and his shoulder felt like it was about to pop right out of the socket.

Alicia, on the other hand, sailed up the wall like a spider on the run. She made it look easy and wasn't even winded. Right now she was above him, dangling by holding on to a rock one-handed as she looked down at him.

"How's it going?" she asked.

He gritted his teeth. "Great."

"Any pain?"

He swiped at his brow with the back of his arm. "I'm fine."

She climbed down until she was level with him. "Garrett. If you're in pain, I need to know. We're not doing this for fun, you know."

"Really? I thought we *were* doing this for fun."

She cocked her head to the side. "Seriously. How do you feel?"

"My shoulder hurts."

She frowned. "Hurts really bad, hurts a little, or something in between?"

"It's tolerable. Not that bad."

She reached over and put her hand on the back of his shoulder, gave it a squeeze. "Muscles aren't too tight. Are you sure you want to go on?"

"Yeah."

"Okay. Let me know if it gets to be too much."

"Let's just keep moving."

Her lips curved. "I think you like the challenge."

"Do you want to hang here and talk, or do you want to get to the top of this wall?"

"Let's get climbing."

He had to admit, watching her butt was a good distraction, and since she was above him, he had a pretty-damn-good view of her fine ass and her legs as she swung from one rock to the other. She had a tank top on that showcased the muscles of her back.

He'd like to get her naked and see what her body really looked like.

Maybe he could talk her out of wearing those ugly uniforms. She was a lot more pleasant to look at in this outfit.

"Still doing all right?" she asked.

"Great." They'd made it three-quarters of the way. Even Alicia was sweating now, and Garrett's shoulder no longer had any feeling in it. He wasn't sure when he reached for a rock if he'd be able to hold on. But he'd be damned if he'd quit. If Alicia could make it, so could he.

She waited while he grabbed the nearest rock and pulled himself up. He'd never tell her he used his legs to hoist himself up.

"You're looking a little shaky. Is your shoulder hurting?"

"Hell, yes, it's hurting. But we're close to the top. I can make it."

She crossed over several rocks above him and ended up on his left side. He mustered up whatever he had deep within him to keep pace with her. And when Alicia's foot slipped on a rock, despite the harness and the ropes the handlers held them steady with, he reached out with his left arm to grab her around the waist.

"Crap," she said, holding herself close to the wall.

He pulled her tightly against him. "You okay?"

"Here I was thinking I was such a monkey. I do this all the time, and I've never once slipped."

She was still shaking. He kept his arm around her, despite the strain on his other shoulder. He could handle this. "Just take deep breaths. We're in no hurry to go anywhere."

She lifted her gaze to his, and he was struck by the clear blue of her eyes. Eyes that held more than a little bit of fear at the moment.

"I'm the one who's supposed to be taking care of you," she said.

"I didn't slip," he said, his lips curving.

"Smart-ass. Thanks for grabbing me."

"You weren't in any danger since you're harnessed up and they have you in check on the ground."

"True. But it's still pretty scary to lose your footing this far up. I'm grateful you reached out for me, even though you shouldn't have. It could have hurt your shoulder."

He arched a brow. "No way was I going to let you fall—or dangle or whatever it was that could have happened to you."

She stared at him, and then, as if she realized he was holding her, she gently shifted away.

"I'm all right now, but if it's okay with you, can we descend?"

"Sure. My shoulder's pretty much done for, anyway."

Going down was a hell of a lot easier than going up had been, though they still had to take their time. Garrett kept his focus on Alicia the whole time, making sure she took each step slow and steady. She did, not scrambling around on the rocks the way she had on the way up.

"Are you all right?" Dave asked when they reached bottom and unhooked.

She gave Dave a bright smile. "I'm fine. My foot slipped. I'm so glad Garrett was there to grab me."

"You were perfectly safe up there with your harness and us down here anchoring you with the rope, you know," Dave said.

Garrett read the defensiveness in Dave's tone. He crossed his arms and tried not to smirk about it. Though Dave was right and Alicia had been safe, Garrett liked knowing he'd been the one up there to catch her. For months now he'd felt useless, his bum shoulder making him feel inadequate. He might not have caught her with his injured shoulder today, but he'd held on to the rock with his sore arm, and grabbed her with his good one.

To Garrett, that spelled victory.

"Logically, I know I was fine up there," Alicia said. "And there's no way I could have fallen since I was hooked up to a harness. But there's nothing like having someone there to grab on to. Garrett was a hero for me today." She turned to him and laid her hand on his arm. "Thank you again."

"No problem." He walked away with a big smile on his face, leaving Alicia to wrap everything up with Dave. Once she'd finished, she grabbed her bag, and they walked out.

"So what's next?"

"We need to go back to the facility so I can assess your shoulder and ice it down."

"Okay."

They headed back, and when they arrived, she laid him down on one of the therapy tables.

"I want to do a light stretch and check your range of motion."

"No other exercises today?"

She shook her head. "The rock climbing was enough torture on your arm, don't you think?"

He definitely thought so, but he wasn't sure what her plan was.

After she worked on his arm a bit, he had to admit, the ice pack felt good on his throbbing shoulder. Alicia sat on the bench next to him, focused on her notebook.

"That was fun today."

She lifted her head and smiled. "I'm glad you enjoyed it. Your arm got a fabulous stretch. It really helped your range of motion."

"So . . . could we do it again sometime?"

Her brows rose. "Sure."

He didn't know what her other plans were for therapy, but anything other than this day-to-day bullshit he'd been enduring for months sounded like a good idea to him.

FIVE

AFTER GARRETT LEFT FOR THE DAY, ALICIA STAYED behind to clean up the room and review today's session. A session that wouldn't have happened at all if she hadn't gone chasing after Garrett.

Which hadn't turned out too badly after all. He might be a pain in the butt about getting to therapy, but once they got going, he was all in.

She had to admit she'd had fun today. Even though she'd monitored Garrett and his progress, rock climbing was one of her favorite things to do. And it was good therapy for his shoulder, so why not combine something he seemed to enjoy with something therapeutic?

Maybe this wasn't going to be as tough as she thought.

And maybe aliens were real.

She knew better. Today had gone pretty smoothly, despite the unpromising start. That didn't mean it was going to be all sunshine and roses. She'd read Garrett's file, knew his rehab was one of the more difficult ones. She was going to have to watch him very closely, every day, if she was going to succeed in getting him back on the mound by April.

No pressure or anything.

Needing a break from that nerve-wracking thought, she decided to catch up with Annamarie via a phone chat. She was happy to talk and said they were all having a great time in Florida.

Color her jealous. They were enjoying themselves in a sunny warm climate while Alicia was alone here and freezing with one difficult client that she'd had to hunt down this morning like the elusive Bigfoot.

Her cell rang. She looked at the display, pleased to see it was Phil.

"Hello, Alicia. I just called to get a report on Garrett."

She filled him in on Garrett's progress.

"So he's still dragging his heels," Phil said.

"Somewhat, but despite the rough morning, we had a good treatment day. His recovery is going well. The cold weather isn't helping him any, though. He's stiff, and I know it affects him. I'd really like to work him out somewhere warmer, where I could do some outdoor activities with him."

"You have a point. Let's bring him down to Florida. I agree you can make better headway with him here."

"When should we come?"

"As soon as possible. I'd like you and Garrett to get together and plan this out. I want you close to him, Alicia. His therapy is important. So, figure out a plan, and the team will handle it from there."

"Okay. I'll let him know. Thanks."

She hung up then dialed Garrett's number. This time he picked up the phone.

"What? You want round two today?"

She couldn't help but smile. "You're off the hook the rest of the day."

"Lucky me. So, what's up?"

"I talked to Phil, and he suggested we head down to Florida to continue your rehab in a warmer climate."

"Sounds great to me. When do we go?"

"As soon as possible. Would you like to discuss that now? We need to make travel arrangements, figure out when we're going to leave, where we're going to stay, and discuss your therapy plan for when we get there."

He paused a minute. "Yeah, we can do all that. Look, I'm going to have pizza tonight. Why don't you come on over, and we'll plan it out in person rather than over the phone?"

His place for dinner? That sounded so . . . personal. Then again, her entire existence was centered around Garrett right now, so why not? It would give her a chance to check on him and see how he was faring after the rock climbing today.

"Okay. Sure. What time?"

"Six is good for me."

"I'll be there."

She hung up, then chewed her lower lip, remembering what it was like to walk in on him that morning, that first shock of awareness at seeing him with his sweats barely hanging on his hips and the rest of him gloriously bare.

She'd had to struggle to engage her brain and focus on why she was there.

But oh, that image of him remained burned in the back of her head.

Garrett Scott was so damn sexy, and he had an amazing body she'd love to get her hands on. Though she did put her hands on him, didn't she? Too bad she only got to feel up his shoulder.

By the time she'd finished up work for the day, she decided she'd better get lascivious thoughts of other parts of Garrett's body out of her head. The only part of him she would allow herself to think about was his shoulder. The rest of him was off-limits.

Before she headed to Garrett's, she went home to take a shower and change clothes, deciding on her favorite pair of dark skinny jeans, her black boots, and a sweater. Though she wasn't sure why she didn't just go directly to his house. What difference did it make what she wore or what she smelled like? This was just pizza and planning the trip to Florida. Disgusted with herself for being such a girl, she also curled her hair and put on makeup and earrings.

Garrett answered the door, and she was pleased to see him fully covered since her imagination had already gone wild once today. He wore a pair of cargos and a long-sleeved shirt that clung to his torso, outlining all those muscled contours she wanted to run her hands over.

Off-limits, remember, Alicia?

Right. Shoulder only. She wouldn't even look at his body, except his awesome ass as he walked away.

She sighed.

"Hey. You look . . . different," he said as she slid out of her coat and handed it to him.

"I don't wear that uniform all the time, you know."

"Yeah, so I noticed when we were rock climbing today. You should get out of that uniform more often."

She cocked her head to the side. He'd noticed?

He hung her coat in the closet right inside the door. "Take a seat in the living room. You want a beer or something?"

"No, thank you. I'm driving."

"Right. Okay. I'll order the pizza. I like pepperoni. How about you?"

"Uh, I'm a vegetarian. So, cheese for me."

He gave her a look. "No, shit. Okay, cheese pizza it is."

"You can put meat on your side, or on the whole thing. I can just pick it off, you know."

"I like cheese pizza. Would you like a soda? I have iced tea, too. Or I could make coffee."

She grabbed a spot on the sofa. "Iced tea would be great. But don't go to any trouble. I can get it for myself."

His lips curved as he walked by. "I'm pretty sure I can fix you a glass of tea, Alicia. You want sugar?"

"No. Plain is fine with me. Thanks."

She'd barely paid attention to his place when she'd stormed in this morning, because she'd been so focused on him and getting him to therapy. Now that she was more relaxed, she looked around.

Wow. It was nice here. Roomy living room with a sectional, big screen television, lots of video games, surround sound. The room was artfully decorated in shades of taupe and brown that lent a masculine feel to the room. The hardwood floors only added to the hominess of the place, and there were area rugs spread around in a way that looked haphazard, but she knew was deliberate.

Someone had decorated. Unless Garrett had that kind of flair.

"Did you decorate the place yourself?"

"Huh?" he asked as he came in with their drinks then looked around as she motioned to the living area. "Oh. Hell, no. If it were up to me, there'd be like a folding table in here, and I'd be sitting on the floor. Some chick at the furniture store recommended a decorator, who took care of everything."

"She did a good job. I guess I'm just surprised that you live in a nicely furnished house, you being a single guy and all. Most of the guys I know live in apartments or a condo."

He laughed as he flopped onto the sofa next to her. "I like big spaces. I did my time in apartments. Too cramped for me."

"Well, you're a big guy. I could see why that wouldn't work for you."

"How about you?"

"An apartment. I'm not a big guy, so it suits my purposes."

He gave her a long once-over, the kind that a man gave a woman he was definitely noticing. It made the room seem awfully warm. "No, you're definitely not big . . . or a guy."

She laughed. "No, I'm not. But I have lived with a big guy. And sharing a tiny bathroom with my brother growing up wasn't fun. The apartment I live in now is like a castle by comparison."

"College was like that for me. I shared a bathroom with three other guys. Not anything I ever want to do again."

"I did that in college, too, though I shared a bathroom with about fifteen women."

He made a face. "All those hair products."

She laughed. "Hey, we managed. And how did you score a suite?"

"Athletic dorm. It wasn't too bad."

"No kidding. You got lucky. You went to college in Oklahoma, right?"

"Yeah." He leaned back on the sofa with his drink. "In fact, there's a get-together with some of the guys from my dorm coming up. Haven't seen some of them in a while."

"Are you going?"

He shrugged. "I haven't thought much about it. Been focusing on the shoulder thing, you know."

"You should go. It would be good for you to reconnect with your friends from college."

"Maybe." He took a long swallow of his drink, and she studied him, the way his body moved. Some of that was the nature of her job. She watched every athlete's body, always looking for signs of injury, watching their body mechanics to see if she could correct anything they did that might point out a weakness. But with Garrett she found she simply enjoyed watching him . . . and his body.

She shook that thought away. "I sense hesitation. How long has it been since you've seen your friends?"

"I don't know. Like I said. It's been awhile."

"Oh, you should definitely go. I love hanging out with my college friends."

He snorted. "You're a girl."

"What does that have to do with it?"

"Girls like all that rehashing of the past. Guys . . . not so much. We move forward."

"That's such crap. Guys have shown up at our college get-togethers, and they have just as good a time as the women do. So, what's holding you back?"

He didn't answer. Then it hit her. "It's your injury, isn't it? You want to go back to your friends as a big success. And right now you feel like a failure."

He narrowed his gaze at her. "That's not it. I told you, I forgot about it until just now, because I've been focusing on rehab."

She didn't believe him. "You've been a success. You *are* one. Look at your career."

"That's in the past."

"Oh, please. Look at your accomplishments at such a young age. You're a Cy Young Award winner. Come on. Don't you want to celebrate that with your friends?"

"In sports you're only as good as your current season."

She wanted to smack him in the shoulder—the uninjured one, anyway. "That sounds like a line fed by media. You watch too many sportscasts. How many athletes do you know of who never even make it to the majors, who never get their shots to play the big games? You have, and you've played so well. Don't let this injury define you when it's nothing more than a bump in the road."

Garrett stared at Alicia. She gave a good speech, but he wasn't sure if he believed her. He wanted to, but she just didn't know how it was in sports. One day you were on top of the world—the next you were out the door. You were only as good as the last pitch you threw, and he hadn't thrown one since August of last year. Not only did his team measure his success that way, so would the media. And the fans.

And his friends.

Okay, his friends wouldn't judge him on his success or lack of it. That's why they were still his friends. But he judged himself, and that was enough. He just didn't want to have to . . . explain.

"When's your get-together?"

"I don't know. Sometime this month. It's not a big deal."

She blew out a breath. "So, when is it?"

"Geez, I don't know. The date's in an email Gray—one of my roommates—sent me."

Alicia rolled her eyes. "Oh, my God, Garrett. Do you have it handy where you could look it up?"

"It's on my phone."

"Go get it. Find out when it is."

"Why are you so interested?"

She gave him a smile. "Just consider it therapy. Will you go get it?"

She was pretty when she smiled. Really pretty. Like not making him think of her as his Attila the Hun therapist kind of pretty. He got up and went down the hall, came back with his phone, which he'd scanned for Gray's email while he'd made his way back to the sofa. "It's this weekend, actually. Too late now. We have to head to Florida."

He handed her his phone so she could read the email. She looked at it then lifted her head to look at him. "It's not too late at all. It would only delay the trip to Florida by a couple of days. You should definitely go. Are all your friends baseball players?"

"No. We had guys from every sport holed up together in the athletic dorm."

"That's so interesting. How many of them have gone on to play professional sports?"

He smiled. He hadn't thought about the guys in a long time, hadn't seen them in a while. It would be good to catch up. "From my core group—all of them."

She arched a brow. "Really? That's amazing. And now my curiosity is high. I want to know who these guys are."

He thought about it for a minute. Ridiculous idea. He wasn't even going. But if he was . . . "You could come with me."

She looked as surprised by his comment as he was when the thought popped into his head.

"What?"

But now that he'd said it, it made sense. "Sure. Come with me. I'll introduce you."

"Oh, I don't think so. I mean you should totally go. You'll have a good time. And you really should reconnect with your friends."

"This was your idea."

"I know. It was my idea for *you* to go."

He liked that she looked so uncomfortable, with her deer-in-the-headlights, wide-eyed expression. Since she made him so damned uncomfortable all the time, it was nice to turn the tables on her.

"Hey, you're supposed to be with me all the time anyway. You wouldn't let me blow off one day of therapy. You'd let me be away for a three-day weekend to go to this reunion?"

She opened her mouth, then shut it.

Perfect. He had her now.

"Okay, you might have a point there."

He never made an argument without one.

"Uh, where would we be going exactly?"

"Not that far. Central Oklahoma. Just a short drive down the highway. And we could work out at the lodge facility. There's state-of-the-art equipment there."

She cocked her head to the side, mulling it over. "Okay."

The doorbell rang, and Garrett went to grab the pizza from the delivery boy. They ate while planning logistics for both the weekend coming up and for the subsequent trip to Florida.

"I'll need to order certain equipment for your workouts. And I'd really like to have access to a pool."

"There's one at the beach house I stay at. We could use that one."

She arched a brow. "Really? You have a beach house?"

He grinned. "I rent it from a couple I know. I don't like hotels. It's bad enough I have to deal with them throughout the season. At least during preseason I have the beach house."

"All right. I can work with that."

"Actually, you could stay there, too. There's a guesthouse."

She pondered the idea. She'd figured she'd stay at the same hotel as the team, but this would make more sense, especially if there was a guesthouse. "Okay, that works. We can commute together to the team facility."

"Yeah, we can do that. But there's also a gym room that has a lot of exercise equipment."

"Really?" She got out her notepad. "Tell me what's in there. I'll be sure to order in whatever else we need."

He gave her a list, and she made some notes.

"This will work out great. I'll need to call Max and get things ironed out for the delay. He was expecting us to make plans to head down there right away."

"Make the call."

"Now?"

"I don't see why not. If Max or Phil has a problem with me taking that trip to Oklahoma, they'll let you know. And then I'll talk them out of it."

She rolled her eyes. "Do you always get your way?"

"Not always, but it's nice when I do."

She grabbed her cell and dialed Phil's number. As team doctor, he'd have the final say. As Garrett suspected, Phil was fine with the delay and was happy Alicia was going with Garrett to continue his therapy.

She hung up and laid her phone down. "We're all set."

"Good." He leaned back in the dining-room chair.

"What's going to happen when you don't get what you want?"

"You think everything goes my way all the time?"

"Seems that way."

He shook his head. "Honey, if I got everything I wanted, I'd be in Florida throwing pitches right now."

She laid her hand over his. "I'll get you there, Garrett. I promise."

He looked down at her hand, so small over his. Hard to believe those hands could wreak so much pain on his shoulder. He lifted his gaze to hers. "I'll keep trying to believe that."

She stared into his eyes. "You have to believe in me and trust me. I'll do whatever it takes to get you back on that mound."

For some reason the low tone of her voice, the slight rasp in it coupled with the intimacy of her hand on his made his balls quiver. He wanted to make some quip about doing whatever it took, but hell, he wasn't a teenager anymore and sexual innuendo would be stupid. He was already attracted to her, and now he'd invited her to spend the weekend with him.

He pulled his hand away and started to clean away the remnants of their dinner.

"You bought. Why don't you let me take care of cleaning up this mess?"

She gathered up their plates and the pizza box before he could object. And then she did the dishes, so he leaned against the stove and watched her.

"I can do all that, you know."

She threw him a look over her shoulder then smiled. "So can I. There were only a couple of plates and salad bowls."

When she finished, she dried her hands on the towel and leaned her hands against the sink. "I guess that's it."

"Thanks for doing the dishes."

"Thanks for the pizza."

She tilted her head back, and he wanted to kiss her. His dick quivered at the thought of pushing her against the counter and feeling her body pressed against his. He was hot with the sudden rush of desire, and he had no idea what to do with it.

Her gaze hit his, and he knew then that she realized what he was thinking. She licked her lips, which only made his dick get harder.

She took a shaky breath. "Well, I should probably go. I have a lot to do to get ready for both these trips."

She was obviously a lot smarter than he was, or at least more clearheaded.

He took a step back. "Okay. Sure."

He'd never seen anyone flee the scene so fast. She grabbed her coat. "I'll talk to you tomorrow, then. Thanks again for the pizza."

She was out the door like someone with superpowers, tossing him a wave over her head as she dashed to her car.

He lingered at the door after she pulled out of the driveway, needing the cold blast of air to cool him down.

Dumb move, Garrett. The last thing he needed was to get involved with Alicia. Or even think about her in any way other than as his therapist.

And now he was going to spend the weekend with her.

Great.

S I X

THIS WAS WHAT ALICIA GOT FOR OPENING HER MOUTH and butting in.

If she hadn't pushed Garrett about reconnecting with his friends, she could have had a weekend off. Instead, she was working this weekend. And not only was she working, she was heading to a strange city with someone she really didn't know that well, to meet a bunch of other people she didn't know at all.

Sounded like fun. Then again, she'd always thrived on adventure, so she decided she was going to look on this as a new undertaking. Besides, she was supposed to be working every day on Garrett's arm until he was able to take the mound, so he'd been right when he said she would have to start following him around wherever he went.

No pressure there or anything. And to add to that, the other night in his kitchen he had looked at her in a way she was sure had crossed the line from professional into something dangerously personal. She could have sworn that he'd wanted to kiss her. And since she had looked at him the same way, had felt a sudden physical chemistry with him that had nothing to do with the business of therapy, she'd hightailed it out of there before she'd done something really stupid, like let him kiss her.

That would have been disastrous.

But it also likely would have been very, very good. She couldn't help looking at his mouth. Garrett had an amazing, full bottom lip that just begged to be kissed. She wanted to tug at it with her teeth then rub her cheek against the stubble of beard that always seemed to pepper his lower jaw.

She wondered how that slight beard would feel rubbing against her thighs.

Heating at the thought, she spared a glance at him as he drove them down the turnpike. They'd been on the road for eight hours, she was tired, her butt was numb, and Garrett had been strangely quiet the entire time.

Her fantasizing about his mouth—and that jaw of his—wasn't helping matters any.

"How's the shoulder doing?" she asked, deciding to put her thoughts to more businesslike use.

He glanced her way. "It's fine, thanks."

"Do you need me to drive?"

He snorted. "No. I think I've got this."

"You don't have to get all manly on me. I'm perfectly capable of sharing the driving duties."

"And I'd be white knuckling it the whole time. I prefer to drive."

She arched a brow. "You've been in the car with me. I'm a very good driver."

"You drive like an old lady."

She gasped. "I do not."

He laughed. "Yes, you do. All careful, driving the speed limit, both hands on the wheel."

He was making fun of her. But he sure looked hot behind the wheel with his dark shades and his big body occupying the driver's seat of his SUV. She was so used to her very ancient compact car, this was like being in some luxury tank with leather seats, a great sound system, and a navigation system. And since the scenery along the way was nice and Garrett was content to do the driving, she leaned back in the seat and enjoyed the view.

Since they'd gotten up early and she hadn't slept much the night before, she was sleepy and drifted off. When she woke, Garrett was pulling into a gas station. She stretched and climbed out of the car to use the restroom and grab something to drink. He followed her inside, got a drink for himself along with a few snacks.

She peered into the bag he handed her after he paid for their stuff. "Chips and a candy bar?"

"Road food," he said as they climbed back into the car.

"Not nutritious."

He tore open the bag of chips. "It'll do until we get into town and grab something more substantial." He laid the bag in the center console. "And I'll share."

The chips did smell good, though she wasn't a big chip eater. But she was hungry, so she dug in and ate a few. She never could resist the lure of salty chips, and after eating a handful, she licked the salt off the tips of each of her fingers.

She caught him looking at her, realized he was watching her lick her fingers. And not in a disgusted Why-don't-you-use-a-napkin? kind of way, but more of a You-could-be-sucking-my-cock-instead kind of way. Which got her thinking about his cock. Her belly tightened, her nipples tingled, and it suddenly got very warm in the car.

She grabbed a napkin and wiped her hand, then looked out the window to distract herself, but her thoughts drifted. She closed her eyes, and mental images of her fingers and Garrett's mouth got all jumbled together in her head.

She'd rather be licking his fingers, which got her thinking about his mouth again. That was the problem with long road trips. Too much time for the imagination to run wild, and she had a very vivid imagination. There would be plenty of time on the road for him to take her hand and ask her why she was licking her own fingers when he could do that for her. She could lean across the seat and slide her finger across his bottom lip, let his tongue snake out until he sucked one of her fingers in his mouth. He'd tell her that her fingers tasted good, and she'd tell him she wanted his cock in her mouth. Her breathing quickened, and her nipples hardened.

She let out a soft groan.

"Something wrong?"

Her eyes shot open, and she jerked to face him. "What?"

"You . . . moaned or something. Are you having some kind of pain?"

"Oh. No." She rubbed her temple. "Just a little headache."

He frowned. "You should take some Tylenol."

"Yes. I'll do that."

Good God, she was an imbecile. No more sex daydreams for her.

Focus, Alicia.

HEADACHE, HIS ASS. ALICIA HAD BEEN THINKING about sex. He knew when a woman was in pain and when a woman was turned on, and she was definitely turned on. Her eyes were closed, and she'd practically been writhing in her seat.

Which had made him want to groan. And his dick was hard

from watching her. He didn't know what she'd been thinking about, but between watching her lick her fingers and then scoot around in her seat, he was about to come in his pants.

Fuck. This whole trip was a bad idea. She was driving him crazy, and they hadn't even gotten to the lodge yet. He was never going to survive the weekend.

He should have never agreed to take this trip, let alone bring Alicia with him. First, he was going to have to explain to the guys why he wasn't in Florida for spring training, and then he was going to have to explain who Alicia was.

He never brought women to meet the guys. Of course, once they knew about the injury, he supposed explaining Alicia would be moot anyway. He'd just tell them she was his therapist, and that would take care of that. At least he wasn't bringing a girlfriend with him. The guys were all single and still pretty wild and crazy. They'd hate the idea of a woman—or some wife or girlfriend—coming along to these weekends.

He raked his fingers through his hair, already imagining the nightmare to come.

He pulled into the front of the lodge. It had been a long time since he'd been here. Nothing had changed. It still had that country club feel to it with its manicured lawns and perfectly sculpted bushes. He always thought the main building resembled a castle, with its dark stone face and turrets. The first time he'd come, he'd expected to have to cross a moat to get to the main building.

"This is really amazing," Alicia said, unbuckling her seat belt to go inside with him.

"Yeah, it is." He'd been here plenty of times before with Gray, whose dad had a club membership.

It was cool inside, and Alicia tucked the edges of her coat around her. This early in the season there weren't going to be too many golfers on the grounds, except for the diehards who played year-round. If there wasn't snow on the ground, they'd be getting in their eighteen holes, no matter what.

He saw a few of them walking past, seemingly oblivious to the forty-degree temperatures outside. Some even wore short-sleeved shirts.

Garrett was a warm-weather guy himself and couldn't wait for the more mellow temperatures of Florida.

He went to the front desk and got them checked in, requesting adjoining rooms.

"Thanks for that," she said after he handed off her room key to her. "That'll make it easier for me to come in and take care of you if you need me."

He shuddered out an exhale as his mind swam with visuals of just how he'd like her to take care of him, but he brushed those thoughts aside as he saw Gray heading his way.

Showtime.

ALICIA STOPPED IN HER TRACKS AS ONE SEXY PACKAGE of a man pulled Garrett up in a bear hug. She thought Garrett's looks could stop traffic, but this guy? Wow. He was magazine ready, looked like he could own this lodge, with his patrician looks, perfect face, and striking whiskey brown eyes. He was as tall as Garrett, with the same lean but muscular look. His worn jeans hugged his lean frame and his long-sleeved Henley shirt clung to every sculpted muscle of his chest and arms.

"I didn't think you were coming," the guy said. "Shouldn't you be in Florida?"

Garrett shrugged. "Shoulder injury. Still working on rehab."

"Oh, right. I heard about that. I'm sorry, man. That sucks." The man's gaze shifted to Alicia, and he offered up a smile that made Alicia's toes curl. "And who's this?"

"Sorry. Alicia Riley, this is Gray Preston."

He shook her hand. "Nice to meet you, Alicia."

"Same here, Gray."

"Alicia is my physical therapist."

Gray's smile turned to something a little sexier. "Is that what we're calling it these days?"

Alicia laughed. "No, I'm really his therapist. I work for the team."

Gray arched a brow and shifted his gaze to Garrett. "So, the team pays for it? Quite a perk."

"You're an asshole, Gray," Garrett said.

"That's what my father tells me."

"Your father's a prick."

Gray slapped him on the back. "And that's why you've always been one of my good friends. Go on and get settled in. Trevor's already in the bar, likely the center of attention."

Garrett laughed. "Of course he is. What about Drew?"

"Haven't seen him yet."

"Okay. We'll see you soon." He led Alicia to the elevator and, once inside, pushed the button for the second floor.

"Gray is interesting."

He nodded. "Yeah. His father is Senator Mitchell Preston."

She turned to him as they got out of the elevator and walked down the hall. "I've heard about the senator. Very staunch and no-nonsense. Gray doesn't seem at all like him."

"He isn't. Wait till you get to know him." Garrett stopped at a room. "This one's yours."

"Oh. Okay. I'll get unpacked and changed. Meet you outside in fifteen minutes?"

"Sure."

She went into the room and put her bag on the bed, hung everything up and went into the bathroom to unpack her toiletries.

She fixed her makeup and brushed out her hair, then went into the closet to ponder what to wear.

They were meeting in the bar, so she decided on a pair of jeans, a long-sleeved shirt, and her boots, figuring understated would be a good choice.

When she came out of her room, Garrett wasn't there, so she knocked on his door. He opened it.

"Sorry. Grabbed a quick shower."

His hair was still damp, the ends curling. She inhaled his fresh, piney scent, which made her want to inch closer and bury her face in his neck. Instead, she took a step back.

"That's okay. Are you ready or should I just go wait in my room?"

"No, I'm ready."

He closed the door and stood there, scanning her.

She frowned and looked down at her clothes. "What's wrong? Am I not dressed right?"

"Uh, no. You look very nice."

Relieved, she relaxed. "Thanks. I wasn't sure what was going on the rest of the day, so I figured I'd go casual."

"You're fine. Let's go."

He was acting strange. Maybe it was the long drive. He might be uncomfortable. "We should get in a workout today, make sure we at least stretch out your shoulder."

"Okay. We'll do that later."

"We're burning daylight already."

"I'll make sure to whine and complain about how much I hurt so that you don't forget."

She laughed. "You can do that, but trust me, I won't forget. That's the whole reason I'm here, remember?"

"Right. Though Gray thought you were hired for another reason."

She laughed. "Yes. Which I thought was wildly funny. Imagine someone like me, an escort."

He gave her a long look. "You could pull it off."

"Not in yoga pants with my hair in a ponytail."

He stopped as they walked off the elevator on the first floor. "You don't give yourself enough credit, Alicia."

She gaped as him. "I'm not sure whether to be flattered or insulted."

"Be flattered." He placed his hand on the small of her back and directed her down the darkly paneled hallway, away from the main entrance. The bar was tucked just inside some doors that led outside to what she imagined was the golf course.

The bar was painted a rich burgundy and cream, separated by wainscoting along the wall. The place looked just as expensive as everything else she'd seen of the lodge, with wood tables and booths spread around, some pool tables, and televisions mounted above the bar and throughout the room showing various sports. It was kind of like Riley's, her aunt and uncle's bar, only way more upscale. There was a thick oak bar served by two bartenders wearing long-sleeved shirts and vests. Their shirts even had pleats. Fancy.

Definitely not the kind of bar she usually frequented. There weren't even any peanuts on the floor. In fact, she was pretty sure she could eat off this floor.

Gray was seated in one of the booths in the corner, along with several other guys. As her eyes adjusted to the dark, she wondered if she was being punked. They all stood up, and it was like walking into a cover shoot for a magazine. Several hot men smiled at her as she and Garrett approached.

Maybe she should have dressed up more. Dashed on some perfume or something. Because, damn.

"The ever-elusive Garrett Scott finally shows up," one of them said, sticking out a hand.

"Surprised to see you here, Trevor," Garrett said. "Figured you'd be stripped down to your underwear doing another photo shoot for a magazine or a billboard somewhere."

Now Alicia knew why that guy looked familiar. Trevor Shay's oh-so-hot body was plastered up . . . everywhere. On billboards, across magazines, on the sides of buses, and in commercials. He had been one hot commodity for the past few years, because he'd been playing football and baseball, and was very good at both of them. He was also a known ladies' man.

Trevor grinned. "Yeah, well. I took the weekend off to drink beer with you assholes." Finally noticing Alicia, he said, "Oh. Sorry. Didn't mean to cuss."

"It's all right. I'm Alicia Riley."

"Trevor Shay. Nice to meet you. So, you're Garrett's . . . girl-friend?"

"Therapist," she corrected.

Trevor lifted a brow. "Therapist? Got Mommy issues, Scott?"

"Ha ha. She's my *physical* therapist. She works for the Rivers."

"Oh, yeah. You fucked up your shoulder because you can't throw for shit."

Garrett shook his head. "I'm not even going to dignify that comment with a return insult about how some of us can't make up our minds about what sports to play when we grow up."

Trevor grinned. "Yeah, and maybe some of us are so damn good we get to play both."

Garrett rolled his eyes. "You keep thinking that, buddy. Where's Drew?"

"He can't make it," Trevor said. "He's got a game tonight. Said to tell everyone to kiss his ass and not talk about him while he's not here to defend himself."

"So, that means we're going to talk about him, right?" Garrett asked.

"You know it," Gray said, lifting a glass in toast.

Garrett introduced her to a couple of other guys. Alicia was glad she was good at remembering names and faces.

"Make room, dickheads, so we can sit."

They did, and Alicia slid over in the booth. Garrett leaned over. "I'm sorry, but these guys are all assholes. There's going to be cursing and name-calling."

"Yes. Feel free to join in, especially if you have dirt on Garrett," Gray said.

Alicia laughed. "Oh, no. I plan to just listen. And make mental notes. Maybe write a tell-all book in the future."

"I like her," Gray said to Garrett. "She's a smart-ass like us."

Alicia just smiled, and when one of the waiters came over—impeccably dressed like the bartenders—she ordered a drink. A soda.

"Oh, come on, Alicia. You're here to relax and have fun," Trevor said. "Fun means hard liquor."

"Hard for me to be clearheaded and take those mental notes if I'm fuzzy with alcohol. Soda it is for me."

"Buzzkill," Trevor said. "You being the only woman in the bunch, how are we all going to get you drunk and take advantage of you?"

"You aren't," Garrett said, and then ordered a beer.

"I thought you said she worked for the team?"

"She does. Which means hands off, Trevor. I mean it."

Alicia kind of liked the firmness of his statement, even though she was fully aware Trevor was just kidding and Garrett was only protecting an employee of the Rivers. Not someone who belonged to him.

"Maybe it's not just a work thing." Trevor picked up his beer and slanted a look toward Gray and the other guys.

"Maybe it isn't," Gray said, tipping his beer toward Trevor. "But if it is, that means Alicia is available. So, are you seeing someone?"

How was she supposed to answer that? "Um . . . no, I'm not."

Garrett turned to her. "You should run now while you still have a chance. A weekend with these jokers and who knows how you'll end up."

"She'll be in love with me by the end of the weekend," Trevor said, waggling his brows. "I'm irresistible, you know."

"Hey. I'm the one with all the money. And the charm," Gray said, giving Garrett a smug smile. "A couple of days around me and she'll dump you like toxic waste."

Alicia couldn't help but laugh. "Remember, guys, I'm just a therapist. There is no one to dump."

"Uh-huh." Trevor tipped his bottle to his lips, his gaze shifting from Alicia to Garrett as he took a long swallow of his beer. "You say that, but I've got my eye on you two."

She lifted her gaze to Garrett. "Help."

He held up his hands. "What can I say? These morons are my friends."

But she caught the wink.

This should be a fun—and interesting—weekend.

GARRETT HADN'T WANTED TO COME THIS WEEKEND for a lot of reasons, the primary one being he felt less worthy because he wasn't a player right now. And many of his friends were hotshot players, all successful in their games.

He should have known better. He'd been tight with Gray, Drew, and Trevor in college. They'd bonded from freshman year, and nothing had changed in the four years before graduation. Sharing the suite had made them like brothers, and since he hadn't had brothers of his own, these guys had known all his secrets—both the good and the bad.

He missed spending time with them, but that's what adulthood and pro-sports careers did. Not all of the guys from his dorm had ended up in pro sports, but all his roommates had, something that had surprised the hell out of all of them. Garrett and the guys never failed to appreciate how lucky they had all been, but it had also caused them to scatter in different directions like leaves on the wind. With Gray in auto racing, Drew in hockey, and Trevor juggling both football and baseball, finding the time for all of them to get together was nearly impossible. Just getting this weekend together meant sacrifices for at least a few of the guys.

"So, how's the injury coming along?" Gray asked as they gorged themselves on juicy steaks in the lodge dining room.

"You should ask Alicia that question. She's the expert on my recovery."

Alicia looked up from her soup. "He's progressing nicely."

Trevor snorted. "That sounds like a pat answer. How's he really doing? Is he going to pitch this season?"

"I think he's an amazing pitcher, and he can be one again if he works as hard at his recovery as he did at pitching."

"Ohhh," Trevor said, shifting his attention to Garrett. "That sounds like she's laid down the gauntlet, buddy."

"Yeah. She pushes me. She's told me I've had my head up my ass about my recovery and I haven't worked hard enough." He lifted his fork and pointed it at her. "She even came to my house and banged on the door one morning when I tried to blow off therapy."

"No shit," Gray said, with something that looked an awful lot like admiration in his eyes.

"No shit," Garrett said. "She's tougher than she looks."

"I could use someone like you on my auto-racing team," Gray

said. "My crew needs a kick-ass motivator at times. And I pay well. Interested in defecting?"

"Hey," Garrett said.

Alicia laughed. "No. I'm happy where I am at the moment, but thanks, Gray. I'll keep you in mind."

"Seriously?" Garrett arched a brow at Alicia, who smiled sheepishly and shrugged.

"I have to keep my options open, you know."

"Ooh, she's cutthroat," Trevor said. "I might be in love with her."

"You don't know the meaning of the word," Gray said. "You're more a woman-of-the-week type."

"True. But if I was going to fall in love, it would be with someone like Alicia. Beautiful, smart, talented, and vicious. My kind of woman."

Alicia laughed. "I'm hardly vicious."

"I don't know about that," Garrett said. "I've been on the receiving end of one of your therapy sessions."

"Now you're going to give the guys the wrong idea about me, Garrett. I'm a marshmallow. Really." She batted her lashes.

"Somehow I think she's a mixture of both," Trevor said, studying her. "Which just makes me like her more."

"You should keep a tight hold on her, Garrett, before someone sneaks up and steals her right out from under you."

Garrett slid a piece of steak into his mouth and didn't answer Gray's comment. It was unlike his guys to be so taken with a woman. In fact, he would have sworn they'd be pissed off he'd brought Alicia with him. Instead, they'd been welcoming and seemed downright enamored by her.

He couldn't figure it out. Oh, sure, he knew she had a killer body. And a beautiful face, silky hair, long legs, and a perfect ass. She was smart and had a dry sense of humor that men would naturally fall for.

He took a long swallow of his beer and reminded himself that Alicia wasn't his girlfriend, a woman he was dating, or even having sex with. She was a professional, and she was here this weekend to torture his shoulder.

Nothing more.

He took a long swallow of his beer and reminded himself that
Alicia wasn't his girlfriend, a woman he was dating, or even having
sex with. She was a professional, and she was here this weekend to
rehab his shoulder.

Nothing more.

SEVEN

"WE SHOULD WORK OUT YOUR ARM," ALICIA SAID AS
they made their way back to the room.

It was past midnight, and they'd hung out in the bar after dinner, trading stories of college life. Garrett had a good time and
several beers, and after a long day, he was exhausted.

"I don't think so. I'm beat."

"Uh-huh. And the reason I came along was so you wouldn't
miss a day of therapy. I'll bet your arm is tight."

It was, but he'd be damned if he'd admit it.

"I realize it's late, and I'm not talking about a full-blown workout. But if we don't at least stretch it, you'll be even tighter in the
morning."

"Okay."

"Unlock the adjoining-room door after you change clothes, and
I'll get you loosened up."

After she shut her door, he went into his room and changed into a pair of sweats, leaving his shirt off. He unlocked his side of the adjoining-room door, then stretched and sat on the edge of the bed. Alicia came through a few minutes later. She'd changed into her yoga pants and had put on a T-shirt that fit snugly against her breasts.

Not that he would notice what his therapist was wearing.

But he definitely noticed everything Alicia did. Or wore. And as she leaned over him, he breathed in her scent, something musky that made him want to grab her hair and bury his face in her neck.

"I'm glad you left your shirt off. I can put some massage lotion on your arm and really work into it after I stretch it. Then I'll go down the hall and fill the ice bucket and ice you down."

He grimaced. "Sounds fun."

She smiled. "No, it won't be, but it'll loosen your shoulder."

"Let's get this over with."

"Lie down on your back on the side of the bed so I can get to your shoulder. We'll put some heat on it first, and then I'll stretch you."

He laid down, and Alicia kneeled at his side to put the heating pad on his shoulder. He turned to face her. "You're going to stretch me kneeling on the floor like that?"

"Yes."

"That can't be comfortable for you."

"It'll be fine. I've stretched people in more uncomfortable positions than this. And trust me, it'll be way more uncomfortable for you than it will be for me."

That made him smile. "So, what you're saying is that I shouldn't feel sorry for you."

"Not in the least."

"Okay. I hope you suffer."

She laughed. "That's the spirit."

"Did you have a good time tonight?"

She leaned back on her heels. "I did. Surprisingly."

"Why are you surprised?"

"I guess I wasn't prepared for—how nice and how much fun your friends were going to be."

"Yeah? What did you expect?"

"I don't know exactly. It's hard to come into new situations, be surrounded by a bunch of strangers. These are all your friends, and it's your reunion. I was the interloper. It could have gone badly. They might not have taken well to you dragging some strange woman in. They were very nice. So funny and so welcoming to me."

"I'm glad you like them."

"I do. You have great friends. You should see them more often."

"Okay, Mom."

"Hey." She shoved at him.

"It's not like any of us have the time for regular get-togethers. We all have busy careers. Or at least they do."

"You will, too, once I whip you into shape."

"I don't feel very in shape right now. Just whipped."

She let out a soft laugh. "Once we're finished working together, you're going to be a rock star on the mound again."

That's all he wanted.

She pulled the heating pad off and started lightly stretching his arm. She was right—he was stiff, and as she got deeper into the stretch, holy shit did it hurt. He ended up clenching his jaw as she pulled at his arm in those vicious, unnatural positions that ended up making him sweat.

But by the time she finished and went to grab some ice, he was looser. He was already seeing improvement in his range of motion, and for the first time in a long time, he felt hopeful.

"Here you go." She had brought wraps to put the ice in, so she laid it on his shoulder while he leaned up against the headboard of the bed.

"Thanks for doing this. My arm actually feels looser."

She dried her hands on one of the hotel-room towels. "It's no problem. And that's a good thing, right?"

"Yeah."

"Leave that on for ten minutes, then just dump the ice. I'll come back for the wrap in the morning."

"You're leaving?"

Her lips curved. "Yeah, I'm beat. And unless you have something early to do with the guys in the morning, I'd like to hit the fitness center with you for a full workout on your arm."

"No, nothing planned in the morning."

"Good. Say around eight?"

"That'll work."

"See you then. Goodnight, Garrett."

"Night, Alicia."

She closed the adjoining door. He waited for her to click the lock, effectively barricading herself in.

She never locked it.

For some reason, that made him smile.

Alicia was in the zone the next morning. After thirty minutes on the treadmill and another thirty on the bike, plus weight training and now stretching exercises, she had Garrett drenched in sweat and working the hell out of his arm when a guy walked in.

She actually had to do a double take because he looked a lot like Garrett. Tall, shaggy raven hair, but with the most piercing eyes she'd ever seen. He zeroed in on them with a cocky grin on his face.

"You look like shit," he said as he stopped beside Garrett.

Garrett raised his head. "Thanks."

"Is this your dominatrix, and does she always schedule early morning sessions to beat the crap out of you in the gym?"

"Yeah, it's my favorite new workout program. Drew Hogan, meet Alicia Riley, my physical therapist."

He stuck out his hand. "Hi, Alicia. Anyone who can make Garrett look like he's about to cry is a new friend of mine."

She shook her head. "Nice to meet you, Drew. Now get out of here so I can continue to torture him," she teased. "Unless you'd like to be next."

He shook his finger at Alicia but looked at Garrett. "I like her, Garrett. You should marry her. Or have at least a week's worth of mind-numbing sex with her. Why don't you two meet me for breakfast after your . . . uh . . . session?"

Garrett looked up at Alicia for confirmation.

"Sure," she said. "We'll be through here in another thirty, so about an hour?"

"Great. See you in the restaurant."

Alicia laughed as Drew left the gym. "He's kind of a force of nature, isn't he?"

Garrett grabbed the towel and swiped it over his face. "You have no idea."

They finished up their workout then went up to their rooms to shower.

Drew was waiting for them in the restaurant, along with Trevor and Gray.

"Where are the other guys?" Garrett asked as he held out a chair for Alicia. The waiter was right there to pour coffee for them.

"Lincoln, Hull, and Ted got up early to hit the golf course," Gray said.

Alicia looked outside. The sun was out, but it couldn't be more than forty degrees outside. "Die-hard golfers?" she asked.

"You'd have to be to play when it's this cold," Trevor said. "I won't drag my clubs out until it hits at least seventy."

"Wimp," Gray said.

"I don't see your ass out there making it a foursome," Trevor shot back.

"I had some business to do this morning. Couldn't make it."

"You lie. You just didn't want your balls to freeze in the cold." Drew gave Gray a smug look. "You might need to use them on—who was that pit bunny I saw when you were giving those interviews?"

Gray lifted his chin but smiled. "No idea what you're talking about."

"Whatever. Whoever you're currently having sex with, you don't want your equipment to malfunction."

Gray took a sip of coffee. "I have no pit bunny, despite what Drew thinks. I'm too busy working. Unlike Garrett here, who brings his work and play with him."

Garrett rolled his eyes. "I already explained who Alicia is. Believe me, she's all work. Not play."

"It's true," Drew said. "She had him bound up and crying like a girl in the gym this morning. She definitely had him by the balls, but not in the fun way."

Alicia slanted a smile at Drew, who winked at her.

"I wasn't crying. I was rehabbing. And if Alicia had me by the balls, trust me, I'd know it. And it *would* be for fun."

Alicia rolled her eyes. "Is it always like this with you guys?"

"Yes," Gray said. "Ever since college. It's like a sport."

"And I win," Garrett said. "Every time."

"In your dreams, Scott," Drew said. "How many times did you have to buy the beer?" Drew asked.

"Not very often. Because I won."

Trevor leaned over to whisper in her ear. "I never had to buy the beer. I just let these clowns argue it out until they declare someone the loser. Then I reaped the benefits."

"I heard that," Garrett said.

Alicia laughed, then sat back and listened while they bickered back and forth. It was like being in college again, partying at the frat houses. Lots of one-upmanship, who won what argument, who was the best at this or that. But it was clear that Garrett was relaxed and enjoying himself. She was glad. He needed that release of tension. This weekend would be very good for his state of mind, which was so integral to his recovery.

"I don't know what you morons have planned for the day, but I'm going to get Alicia out of here for a while. We're going into the city so she can have some fun that doesn't include soaking up all this testosterone."

Alicia turned to him. "What?"

"You'd take her away from all of this?" Drew asked, pointing to himself.

"Yes. Especially you."

"Have fun," Gray said. "But be back for poker tonight."

"Wouldn't miss it." He pushed back his chair and held hers out while she stood.

"What are you doing?" she asked.

"Treating you to a day of fun."

She stopped in the hall. "Why?"

"Because this is boring for you."

"No, it's not. And even if it is, I'm not your girlfriend, Garrett. I'm not here to be entertained by you. I'm here to work on your therapy. If I'm bored, I can always go up to the room and work on my treatment plan notes or read or watch TV."

"Oooh, sounds fun."

"Stop that."

"No, you stop. I feel bad enough for dragging you here this weekend. At least let me make it a little fun for you by taking you out and showing you around the city."

She inhaled then sighed. "Wouldn't you rather hang out with your friends? Isn't that the primary reason you're here?"

"I'll see plenty of them. And believe me, a little of those guys goes a long way. Besides, we won't be gone that long. I'll take you to Bricktown then to the outlet mall."

That got her attention. "There's an outlet mall?"

"There is. Unless you prefer the regular mall. There's a really nice one."

"Oh, no. I love outlet mall shopping."

He pressed the button for the elevator. "Outlet mall it is, then."

Alicia went upstairs, slipped into her boots and a sweater, then grabbed her bag and met Garrett in the hall. She was ridiculously excited to be going out exploring; she'd never been to Oklahoma City before. Okay, she'd never been in Oklahoma at all, so everything here was a new adventure.

"You're kind of . . . bubbly and wiggly," Garrett said as the valet brought his car.

"I know. It's ridiculous, really," she said as she slid into the seat.

"Tell me."

"I love travel. It's one of the highlights of being with the team. I'm so looking forward to hitting the road. When I was growing up, we didn't have a lot of money, so while I had friends who would come back after summer vacation and talk about all these fantastic trips they took, about the only thing we got to do was go camping. Locally."

He laughed.

"It's not funny."

"Oh, I know it's not. It's just the face you made was like tasting rotten food."

She pointed at him. "It was exactly like that. Imagine how I felt when my best friend came home, tanned and beautiful, from spending time with her grandparents in Florida. Me? I had mosquito bites from traveling a few hours up the road to a sucky campsite."

"Poor you."

"Fuck you."

He shook his head. "Such a mouth on you, Alicia. I should complain to your boss."

"Go ahead. Just remember who twists your shoulder. I can make it hurt even more."

He shot a glance her way. "Oh. Blackmail, too?"

She lifted her chin. "I'm not above it to save my own ass."

"The things I'm learning about you. And you look so innocent."

"Looks can be deceiving."

"Hmm, is that right?"

This time he gave her a long gaze that made her body heat up. Maybe that was just because the heater in the car had finally kicked in.

Or maybe it was because he was assessing her in a way that made her want to check her lip gloss and smooth her hair, which was decidedly girlfriendlike. Or datelike. And neither of those situations applied.

She didn't know what to expect, but as they drove along, she decided she liked Oklahoma City. It was more sprawling, less congested than most major cities. A lot like St. Louis, actually, and she loved where she lived.

He took her to the outlet malls first. When he parked, she turned to him and laid her hand on his arm.

"Are you sure you know what you're getting into?"

He laughed. "I've taken my mom shopping before. I can handle this."

"Okay. But I have to warn you—I'm like a storm trooper shopper. I'm relentless, and I'll go in every store."

"Have at it."

It was a great outlet mall with super bargains. And if there was one thing Alicia loved, it was a sale. By the time they'd been through the first half of the outlet mall, she had four shopping bags filled with clothes and shoes. And every time she came out of a store with a bag, Garrett took it from her hands and held it for her.

"Are you sure you don't mind holding those?" she asked.

"Nope. Go ahead and shop."

"Are you sure you're a human male? Your species mostly doesn't enjoy shopping."

He laughed. "You're having a good time, aren't you?"

"Well . . . yes."

"Then don't worry about me. I enjoy watching the people."

She shrugged. "Okay."

He even gave opinions when she tried something on. Surprisingly, he was very good at it, shaking his head or wrinkling his nose when he didn't like something, and nodding or smiling when he did. At least he wasn't one of those noncommittal or uninterested men who said everything she tried on looked "fine."

And the saleswomen nearly swooned after him. A gorgeous man who carried her bags and offered expert opinions on clothing? He was damn near perfect.

But she couldn't continue to take advantage. If left up to her, she could spend the entire day here winding in and out of every store. Surely, Garrett had to be bored out of his mind. And he needed to get back to his friends, which was the whole reason for the weekend.

"Are you getting hungry?" she asked after they left one of the corner stores near the parking lot.

"I'm fine. How about you?"

"Starving. We've been at this for hours, you know."

His lips curved. "I'm aware. You weren't kidding when you said you were serious about this shopping thing. You could teach a master class on the subject."

She hooked her arm in his. "Let's get out of here and go get some food."

He stopped and looked down at her. "You haven't even laid siege to the other half of the outlet mall."

She laughed. "I can live without laying claim to it. I'd rather have lunch."

"There's a great burger joint."

She gave him a look.

"Hey, they have soups and salads."

"Fine. Burger joint it is."

It had turned out to be a gorgeous day, with temps in the sixties, so Garrett took her to Bricktown, which was an outdoor area filled with shops and tons of restaurants. There was even a river and a water taxi to take you around the area. She loved it, and she could imagine how much fun this place was in the summer, with crowds jammed in, the nearby arena filled with people eager to watch events, then come out here after to drink some brews.

"This is awesome," she said as they settled in at a burger joint. They sat at a table with a beautiful view of the water, the sun beaming in on her face and body. She felt warm and good, so she turned to Garrett. "Thank you for this. It's been a great day, but I feel a little guilty."

He took a sip of the iced tea the waitress had brought. "Why?"

"Because this is your weekend to be with your friends."

"This is my weekend to do whatever the hell I want to do. I wanted to take you out so you could do something fun. Did you have fun shopping?"

She leaned back with her lemonade and grinned like a cat in a window filled with warm sun. "I did have fun."

"Okay, then. Let's eat lunch without you having some guilt meltdown."

"Fine."

He shook his head. "Women."

"Shut up."

He lowered his head, but she caught his smile. God, he was sexy when he smiled like that. Everything south of her belly button quivered when he gave her that half-lidded look and wicked smile.

The giant salad she ate ended up being delicious, as were the fries, and by the time they left, she was full and exhausted.

"I could use a nap."

"Stretch out in the car on the way back and sleep."

"No. It's okay."

"You can trust me. I won't grab you or anything while you're sleeping."

She turned to him and let out a soft laugh. "I didn't think you would."

"I might ogle your boobs if you fall asleep, though."

She burst out laughing. "You are so unpredictable, Garrett."

"Yeah? Good."

E I G H T

GARRETT DROPPED OFF ALICIA—AND HER MOUNTAIN
of packages—in her room when they got back to the lodge.

She said she was tired and she wanted to take a nap. When she
woke up, she promised to come find him.

He made a few business calls, relaxed in front of the television for a while, then went downstairs to the bar and found Gray,
Trevor, and Drew, who'd just come in from playing golf since the
weather had warmed up.

"You missed a great game today, Garrett," Trevor said, motion-
ing for the waiter to bring them all a round of beers.

"Yeah?" Garrett pulled up a chair at the table. "I suppose you
all kicked ass."

"We were killer out there," Drew said, tipping the bottle and
draining the last of the beer before answering. "Shot our best
games."

He knew they were lying. They always lied about their golf games. It was tradition. "Sorry I missed it."

"What did you do?" Gray asked.

"I took Alicia to the outlet mall. Then we went to lunch."

Gray arched a brow. "Shopping. How . . . exciting for you."

Drew gave him the once-over. "You sure she's not your girl-friend? Because it seems to me she's got you pretty well pussy whipped."

"Yeah? How so?"

"She calls, you come running."

"In what way?"

"When she wants you to work out, you go, right?"

He leaned back in the chair. "Mostly. She does control my pro-fessional destiny in that regard."

"And you brought her with you this weekend," Trevor chimed in. "Whose idea was that?"

"Mine, actually."

"Oh." Trevor took a long swallow from his bottle of beer. "Still, shopping? Dude."

"I wanted to get her away from all of you, show her the city and a good time. She was really nice to come along with me for the weekend."

"Isn't that her job?" Gray asked.

Garrett shrugged.

"Whipped," Drew said to the guys. "He's either already in her pants or wants in them bad enough to kiss her ass."

Garrett shook his head. There was no point in arguing with them when they had their minds set in one direction. If they wanted to believe he was sleeping with Alicia or wanted to sleep with her, there was nothing he could do about it.

"Why don't we talk about you instead?" he asked, turning his attention to Gray. "What was the name of that supermodel you were dating? Her name reminded me of a vitamin—Niacin or something?"

"Nisema," Gray corrected.

"That's a real name?" Trevor asked, turning to Gray. "It sounds like a face wash."

"We broke up a few months ago. Her career and mine didn't mesh."

Drew arched a brow. "Since when do athletes and supermodels not mesh?"

"She was always off on a shoot, and I was always working. And then we figured out neither of us missed each other when we were apart. We're both too career focused to be involved, so we just broke it off. It was pretty easy."

"She probably makes as much money as you do. That's why it was so easy." Drew leveled a smirk at Gray.

"I'm pretty sure she makes more money than me. I should be the one weeping over the breakup."

Garrett snorted. "Right. Like you'd ever be sorry over losing a woman."

"It could happen. Maybe." Gray looked over at the guys. "Okay, maybe it won't."

"I see you as the one who'll never get married, if for no other reason than to spite your father, who's looking for that "Preston heir," since it's obvious you're never going to walk in his senatorial footsteps," Garrett said.

Gray laughed. "You're right about that. Politics isn't my thing."

"No. You like loud engines and grease under your fingers," Drew said. "And to think you started off with a baseball scholarship. I still don't know how the hell you ended up in stock car racing."

"Oh this sounds like a great story. Can I sit in?"

Garrett looked up to see Alicia standing next to his chair.

"Have a good nap?" He scooted over and made room for her to sit in the booth, then signaled for the waiter.

"I did. I love shopping, but I don't do it very often. I guess I was worn out. It was great to lie down for a few minutes." She turned to Gray. "But now I want to hear about you and baseball and racing."

Gray shrugged. "Not much to tell. I came to school on a baseball scholarship. Now I race for a living."

"You didn't like playing baseball?"

"Loved it."

Alicia frowned. "I sense a 'but' in there somewhere."

The waiter came over, and they all ordered drinks.

"I played baseball all four years and was even sought after by several pro teams. But I'd always liked racing, did that on my free time. A friend of mine's dad raced competitively, so I worked with them on their cars and raced with them whenever I could. When my buddy got sick one weekend, I climbed into his car and raced for him. And I came in second. Nearly won the race.

"That was it for me. The only thing I wanted to do after that was get behind the wheel of a car and come in first. Baseball took second place, and I knew I couldn't play for the major leagues. I've been racing ever since."

"Much to your father's irritation," Garrett said.

Gray's lips lifted. "Yeah. But that's just a side benefit."

"He didn't like you playing baseball, either, if I remember right," Trevor said.

"No. He hated that I got the baseball scholarship to Oklahoma. He wanted me to go to Harvard and study law." Gray grimaced.

"His father was a little pissed off that he passed on the Harvard academic scholarship," Drew said to her. "Law and politics is the Preston family legacy."

Alicia stared at Gray. "Really. You got a scholarship to Harvard?"

Gray shrugged. "Like I said. Baseball was my thing back then."

"I take it you didn't want to be a lawyer," Alicia said.

"Oh, hell no. That baseball scholarship was my ticket out from under the Preston family shadow. I ran as far and as fast as I could."

"And then daddy cut you off." Drew lifted his beer and smirked before taking a long swallow.

"Yeah. Thankfully."

Alicia's eyes widened. "He did?"

"Yeah, he did. Best thing that could have ever happened. Without him threatening me with money, I could be free to do whatever the hell I wanted."

"Yeah, like the rest of us poor suckers," Trevor said with a laugh. "Poor being the appropriate word."

"You managed just fine without him, didn't you?" Garrett asked.

"You bet your ass I did. Got my own team now."

But Alicia noticed something distant and sad in Gray's eyes. She loved her family so much. She wondered what that break from his family had cost him.

"Are you gonna play poker with us tonight, Alicia?" Drew asked.

"Oh, I wouldn't want to intrude on your game."

"So that means you know how to play." Trevor rubbed his hands together.

"I know a little about poker."

"Then let's get this game going. I'm ready to take your money," Garrett said.

They moved into the card room, which was quieter and more private, with official dealers and everything.

Awesome.

Drinks were served, cards were dealt, and Alicia wasn't about to tell them just how good she was at poker. Poker was a weekly Riley family event. She'd learned to play when she was a kid, plus she'd played plenty in college. She might not be a Vegas pro, but she was shrewd, and she often won.

After about two hours of play, she had a sizeable amount of chips in front of her and four very irritated men glaring in her direction.

"Do you take weekend jaunts to Vegas on some casino's dime?" Trevor asked her, finishing a beer and signaling to the waiter for another round for the table.

Sitting comfortably, Alicia offered up her typical poker face as she scanned her cards. Two jacks and an ace. The dealer had a jack on the table. Sweet. "No, I just played in college. I'm probably a little rusty."

"Rusty, my ass," Garrett grumbled, throwing some chips in to bet.

When the dealer pulled up an ace, Alicia stayed perfectly still while she put in her chips and waited to see what everyone else was going to do. Gray folded; the rest of them bet.

"I'm all in," she said, pushing her chips into the middle of the table.

"Fuck," Drew said, tossing his cards on the pile.

"I'm folding, too," Trevor said.

"I'll see what you've got." Garrett went in with his bet. "Show me."

"Full house, aces and jacks."

"Sonofabitch. Three queens," Garrett said, flinging his cards toward the dealer.

The others laughed at him. "Did you purposely bring Alicia to play poker with us, knowing she was going to kick our asses?"

"If I'd known she was that good, I'd have never invited her," Garrett said. "Did you see the hand I had?"

Alicia grinned and dragged the winning chips over to her side. "Thanks, guys."

They broke to eat, and while the guys ate steak, she contented herself with an amazing tofu and nut salad. Then they went back to poker, where she tried hard not to kill them. Amazingly, they won some money back. Not much, but some. She still won a lot.

"You really are good at this," Drew said.

She shrugged. "I had a lot of play in college. And I have a very shrewd poker-playing family."

"Apparently," Garrett said, rolling his shoulders.

They'd been at this for seven hours. She finally stood and stepped behind Garrett, resting her hands on his shoulders. She felt the knots there when she pressed into his muscles. "As fun as it's been divesting you all of your money, I need to abuse your friend here for a bit before I fall asleep at the table."

A chorus of *ooob*s and catcalls went up. She rolled her eyes.

"Assholes," Garrett said, then pushed his chair back.

"We might come to the door and listen," Drew said.

"You can come watch if you'd like," she said.

"Garrett. Did you know she was such an exhibitionist?" Drew called after them as they walked away.

"You have to forgive my friends," Garrett said as they headed up to the room. "Actually, don't forgive them. They're pricks."

She laughed. "They're fun."

"Yeah, they are. And you've been great about it. I appreciate it."

"It was no problem. I've enjoyed it." She slid her key card in the slot to her room. "I'll just grab the heating pad and some lotion, and I'll be right in."

"Okay."

She changed into more comfortable clothes, piled up her stuff, then knocked on his adjoining door. He opened it, already in his sweats and naked from the waist up, which again caused that jolt of awareness she tried not to be so—aware of, but the female part of her was finding it harder and harder to disengage.

"You all get along so well. Was it always like that?" she asked as they waited for the heating pad to do its job.

Garrett laughed as he settled in against the headboard and pillows. "No. Not always. Young guys with hard heads and a lot of testosterone. You can imagine what rooming with those knuckleheads was like the first year. It took us awhile to find our footing."

"I can imagine. But you're such good friends now, so you obviously found a way."

"Yeah, eventually. It was pretty much sink or swim when you have to live together. So we had to learn to . . . live together."

"Oh, I don't know. You were all away from home with no one to depend on but each other. It probably didn't take long for the four of you to bond."

He looked at her. "You have a pretty keen insight for someone who wasn't there."

She shrugged. "I went to college, too, you know. I had the same experience. College life is like being dumped on an alien planet. You feel so alone, and the first thing you do is grab on to whatever lifelines you can. For me, it was my roommate. We stuck together through those first lonely months and became good friends. We're still friends today. I imagine it's the same for you and your guys. The fact you all played sports gave you even more of a common reference and glued you closer together."

He nodded. "I guess you're right about that. I never would have made it through that first year without the guys."

Alicia took the heating pad off and stretched Garrett. "I know. It's amazing how much those relationships change us."

She dug into his shoulder, watching his face for any expression of pain. She caught the wince, so she dug harder in that spot to loosen up the scar tissue.

"You do that on purpose," he said.

"What?"

"As soon as you know an area hurts, you hit it harder to cause me more pain."

"Would I do that?"

He gave her a look. "Hell, yes, you'd do that. I think you must get off on causing pain."

She laughed. "Then I'm in the right profession, aren't I?"

"Is sadism one of the job requirements?"

"Oh, definitely. I love knowing that I'm hurting you. It gets me off."

He gave her a look. "Really?"

She rolled her eyes. "No, not really. Unfortunately, pain sometimes means progress. When I find a spot that I know is tight and I focus on that area, it means I'm working on breaking up scar tissue to loosen up your arm."

"And here I thought you were getting some kind of sexual gratification out of all this torment."

"Now that would be a nice perk of the job, wouldn't it?" She gave him a wink and focused her attention on his workout.

When she finished the therapy, he was sweating and gritting his teeth. "You're enjoying this."

"I do love my job, but it's not causing you pain that I enjoy, Garrett. It's the end result that will be the most rewarding for me." She smoothed her hands over his shoulder and shook out the tension.

"The end result being me pitching again."

She nodded. "Of course. That's what I want most for you. You can sit up now."

He rolled over and rested on his elbows. "That must be the best part for you—the endgame. Being able to walk away from an athlete who's fully rehabbed."

"Yes. I look forward to the day I can finish your therapy and see you pitching again."

"Then you and I will be done with each other."

She grinned. "I'm sure you're eager to see that day. No more torture."

"I don't know. I'm kind of getting used to having you around."

She laughed. "Sure you are. You can't wait to get rid of me." She held her hand out to help him off the bed.

He grasped her hand, but instead of pulling up he surprised the hell out of her by jerking her down onto the bed, then rolled over next to her.

"Garrett. What are you doing?"

"I'm not sure."

He laid his hand on her stomach, and she was sure he could feel the out-of-control banging of her heart. She should shove his hand away and leap off the bed. She was his therapist, and they shouldn't be close like this, and she damn sure shouldn't be lying in the middle of his bed.

But oh, the press of his warm hand on her stomach and the feel of his hip connected to hers was unbearably hot, and she just didn't want to get up. Not when his face loomed over her and she wanted to reach up and swipe her hand over the slight stubble of beard at his jaw. There was so much of him she craved to touch, that she'd denied herself. And he'd thrown down the gauntlet.

He paused, no doubt waiting for her to protest, to push him away and jump off the bed.

But she didn't, because being next to him like this felt too good, catered to all the fantasies she'd had about him.

And when he leaned down and brushed his lips across hers, everything in her exploded with need and desire and want. She cupped the nape of his neck to hold him there as he explored her mouth, his tongue darting out to slide across her bottom lip, opening her to him.

Oh, God, it was so good. His lips were firm, coaxing, and she floated on a sea of erotic bliss. She could get so lost in Garrett.

She was shaking. This was wrong and was going to change everything. He'd lose focus, and she could lose her job.

She pressed on his chest, and he broke the kiss.

"Stop," she whispered, barely able to get the word out because the absolute last thing she wanted right now was for him to stop.

He hopped off the bed, and the first thing she saw was a very nice erection that she'd like nothing more than to spend the night exploring. But he grabbed her hand and pulled her off the bed, and just like that, it was over.

"Sorry," he said, dragging his fingers through his hair. "I don't know why I did that."

She straightened her T-shirt over her hips. "Don't be. You weren't the only one on that bed. But it's a mistake. And we both know why." She walked to the doorway leading her to her room, then stopped, unable to face him. "Thanks for being such a good guy about it."

She turned, and he was right there, palming the wall next to her head, his body inches from hers. Testosterone rolled off him in waves. If he stepped in just a little closer, they'd touch. If he leaned in a little, his mouth would be on hers again. She wasn't sure at this moment if she wanted that or not.

Oh, who was she kidding? She wanted it, wanted him. If he kissed her again, she wouldn't stop him this time.

His eyes were hard glints of steel as he hovered only an inch away from her. "Make no mistake, Alicia. I'm not a nice guy. I knew exactly what I wanted on that bed. I still want you."

She inhaled a deep breath, her desire for him warring with what she knew was best for both of them. She slid out from under his arm.

"I'll see you in the morning, Garrett."

He didn't move, just nodded as she closed the door on him. She laid her forehead against the closed door.

Yeah, she had to be the logical one. What a crock of shit that was.

For the first time ever, she really hated her job.

NINE

ALICIA SHOOK OFF THE CLOSE CALL WITH GARRETT and concentrated on the next step in his recovery, which would take place in—thank God—Florida. Since it was the dead of winter, Alicia had had to dig into the back of her closet for all her summer clothes. Normally, she'd be giddy about heading to Florida in late February, but this was work, not vacation.

She would be staying in his guesthouse, in close proximity to him every single day. Working together, sleeping nearby. After what had happened the other day, the living arrangements were going to make the situation between them even more difficult. She'd have to shore up her internal defenses and make sure Garrett understood that his recovery had to be his primary focus.

He'd gone down a couple of days earlier to get the house in order, giving her a break and promising her he'd head to the team facility and do daily therapy with Max. Which gave her a little breathing room, thankfully, and some time to shop and pack and see her family before she left. She'd had dinner two nights ago with her parents and said good-bye to them. Today she was going to see Liz, Tara, and Jenna for lunch before she hopped on the plane.

Tara insisted on hosting them at her place, though how she managed to organize it all with the new baby was beyond Alicia.

But Tara had a nice spread laid out with mini-sandwiches and three different kinds of salads.

"I don't know how you do this," Alicia said as she hugged Tara, then Liz and Jenna.

"Jenna and Liz helped."

"And don't you tell anyone I helped with the food prep or I'll cut your throat," Liz said with a mock glare.

Alicia laughed. "Your secret is safe with me."

They sat down and ate. Little Sam was asleep in the bassinet in the living room.

"How's he doing?" Alicia asked, dying to go over there, tickle his toes, and wake him up so she could hold him. But she knew better. Sleeping babies needed to be left alone, lest their tired mothers come after you with something sharp.

Tara sighed. "He's perfect. I'm so lucky. He sleeps well and eats well and is ridiculously healthy. I couldn't ask for more."

"Lucky her," Liz said. "She's had a Stepford baby. He hardly even cries."

"You're not here when he cries. Believe me, he has a very healthy set of lungs, and he uses them often."

"And then you hand him to Mick, right?" Jenna asked. "Tell me you do that."

"Of course I do." Tara gave them all a wicked grin. "What kind of woman would I be if I didn't let the big, strong, macho guy handle a screaming baby?"

"And does he fall apart?" Jenna asked.

"He's a total marshmallow."

"Ha. I knew it." Jenna gave them all a smug look. "Men are such babies when it comes to, well, babies."

"And how's your man?" Alicia asked.

"Delicious," Jenna said, popping a grape into her mouth.

"She's getting a lot of sex. You can tell by the content look on her face," Liz said.

"Please don't talk about sex. I haven't had any for a while, and I'm about to die."

Liz patted Tara's hand. "The downside of pushing an eight pound baby out of your vagina."

Tara glared at Liz. "Your day will come."

Liz shuddered. "I don't even want to think about it."

"Are you pregnant?" Alicia asked.

"Not yet. I told you, we're practicing. And enjoying the hell out of that right now, so don't rush me."

"Whatever," Tara said. "But as soon as you get pregnant, I have to be the first to know."

Liz rolled her eyes. "You'll be the first to know. As soon as Gavin's sperm does its magical explosion into my egg, I'll be sure to call you, day or night."

"Guys. I'm eating." Jenna grimaced.

"Wuss. So, tell us about Florida, Alicia," Tara said, taking a drink of tea. "I'm so excited you get to leave our dreary winter weather."

"I'm utterly jealous," Jenna said.

"I'm excited," Alicia said. "Nervous, of course, since this is for work. There's a lot riding on me getting Garrett in shape."

"He looks in pretty good shape to me," Jenna said. "At least from video and pictures I've seen. Is he hot?"

"Totally," Liz said. "Victoria Baldwin is his agent, and she's a good friend of mine, so I've had the opportunity to meet him. Believe me, he's hot."

"Lucky bitch," Jenna said.

"Please," Tara said to Jenna. "You have Ty."

Jenna popped a grape into her mouth. "I do. He keeps me very happy. Which doesn't mean I'm dead and I can't appreciate other sexy men. Like Garrett Scott."

"Amen to that," Liz said. "The day I can't ogle fine man flesh just because I have a hot man of my own is the day they bury me."

"Do you think the guys talk about women the way we talk about men?" Tara asked.

"Of course they do," Liz said. "Do you think they have blinders on when some cleavage-baring, minidress-sporting sexpot of a woman walks into the bar of the hotel when they're playing away games? Hell, no. Of course they look. They don't touch, but they sure as hell look their fill. They'd have to be mostly dead not to."

"You're right. And so will we, until we're too old to care." Jenna turned to Alicia. "How about you? Are you taking advantage of being able to put your hands on Garrett?"

Alicia paused, her fork filled with fruit salad as all eyes turned to her. "Um . . . of course not. He's my job."

Liz narrowed her gaze. "Which means what exactly? That you don't get to feel him up in the fun way?"

"I wouldn't even think of it."

Tara snorted. "I would totally be thinking about it. Every time I put my hands on his shoulder, I'd want to explore all parts of him, especially lower, like down in his pants."

"Girl, you so need to have sex," Liz said.

Tara hung her head. "I know. I'm so ashamed."

"You are not ashamed," Jenna said. "You're already thinking about when my brother is going to come home so you can jump him. And I can't even believe I just said that."

Tara laughed. "It's okay. And you're absolutely right. It's been too long for me, and I'm kind of madly in love with Mick."

Alicia was glad the topic of her and Garrett had been momentarily taken off the table. Because what was she going to say to them? That they were right, that she had been thinking about parts of him other than his shoulder, and she didn't know what to do about it?

Maybe she should talk to the girls about Garrett. Get some advice, ask what they thought. Though based on today's lunch conversation, she knew what the consensus would be.

Go for it.

If only it was that simple.

"So, I'll be heading down to Florida to see Gavin soon. I'll see you there?" Liz asked her.

"Definitely. You'll be staying at the beach house?"

Liz grinned. "Hell yeah. Private and secluded, just the two of us. Lots of time for sex."

Jenna sighed. "I should stop coming to these get-togethers."

"Shut up, Jenna," Liz said. "You know what we talk about. And you love us all anyway."

"You're right. I do love you. Maybe I'll start talking in graphic detail about my sex life with Ty."

"And that would bother us, how?" Tara asked.

Jenna sighed again. "It wouldn't. You guys suck."

"And swallow," Liz added.

Alicia snickered, and Jenna burst out laughing.

"I give up," Jenna said. "I wish Savannah was here. At least she isn't in love with my brother."

"No, she's in love with *my* brother," Alicia said. "And I don't want to hear about her sex life."

"Oh, come on, Alicia," Jenna said, leaning into her. "Misery loves company."

"That's okay, Jenna. I like your misery a lot better."

Jenna wrinkled her nose. "I hate you."

They finished lunch, and by then Sam had awakened from his nap, so they all got to ooh and ahh over the baby, who was filling out and becoming more adorable every time Alicia saw him. She got to hold him after Tara fed him. Content, he stared up at her, wide-awake, and she was certain he smiled at her.

She sighed and looked over at Tara. "He's gorgeous."

Tara's lips curved. "I think so. I don't know how I ended up with this happily ever after, but I thank God every day for Mick."

Alicia got teary eyed. "He's lucky, too, you know. We're all very lucky you're part of the family."

And then Tara's eyes welled up. "Thanks."

"Okay, everyone," Liz said. "If we're going to have a weep fest in here, I'm leaving."

"Actually, I have to be at the bar, so I am leaving. Though it isn't about all the emotion. I'm always happy to have a crying jag with you chicks," Jenna said.

"I have to go, too," Alicia said, carefully handing Sam over to Tara. "I have to finish packing."

She hugged everyone, thanked Tara for lunch, and said her good-byes, then walked out with Jenna.

"Hey," Jenna said as she stood at her car, which was parked behind Alicia's. "I caught you deflecting the whole conversation about Garrett."

Trying to play dumb, she frowned. "I'm not sure what you're talking about."

Jenna leaned her hip against her car door. "Look, I'm the absolute best at trying to deny what's right in front of me, and I wasted a lot of valuable time with Ty because of it. Do you have feelings for Garrett?"

Alicia could deny it, but what would be the point? She was closer to her family than anyone. They were better than girlfriends at keeping her secrets. "Honestly? There's physical chemistry between us. Crazy chemistry. But it scares me because my job is to rehab him, not jump him, you know?"

"Yeah, I get that. You're afraid for your job."

"And his. I need him to concentrate on his shoulder, not on getting into my pants."

Jenna laughed. "But if he's relaxed—and we all know sex can be relaxing—wouldn't that aid in his concentration?"

Alicia wagged a finger at Jenna. "You are no help."

Jenna winked at her then opened her car door. "Have fun in Florida, cousin."

ALICIA ARRIVED IN FLORIDA, GRABBED HER RENTAL car, and headed toward the beach house, though she was tempted to veer off course and just park at the beach for a few hours. It was gorgeous here and totally different from the cold weather at home. Preparing in advance for the abrupt weather change, she'd shed her coat and sweatshirt, shoes and socks, and rolled the window down to breathe in the fresh sea air as she made the drive along the coast highway.

When she arrived at Garrett's beach house, she parked and grabbed her bags. He came outside, already looking tanned in his shorts and sleeveless muscle shirt.

She ignored the flutter in her stomach as he greeted her with a wide smile.

"How was your flight?" He took her bags and hauled them toward the front door.

"It was good, thanks. You look tan."

"Do I? I've been doing beach runs twice a day."

"That's good."

He led her inside.

"Come on in. I'll take you on the tour."

Alicia was certain she'd stepped into paradise. A one-story, fully furnished house, it was open, expansive, airy, with wood and marble floors and more windows than she'd ever want to clean in her lifetime. There was so much light, and it was so warm here. She was so tired of cold weather she wanted to walk out onto the back deck, park her butt in one of the comfortable chaise lounges, and not get up for at least a month.

She turned to Garrett, trying once again not to notice his legs and his arms and his—oh, God, his everything. So much skin was exposed here.

Maybe she liked winter better. Though she knew what was underneath those clothes, at least the top half, and she'd spent more than enough of her personal time fantasizing about the bottom half, something she shouldn't be doing at all.

She'd also spent the past few days thinking about that kiss they'd shared, despite her vow to eradicate it from her mind forever.

Deciding that train of thought would get her nowhere but in trouble, she turned to face him. "It's . . . amazing. Do you stay here every year for spring training?"

He set her bags down. "Yeah. I know the people who own it. They're big baseball fans, so they're accommodating."

"How convenient."

"It's a good vacation spot. Unfortunately, sometimes they boot my ass out when they want to come down to watch a few games during spring training."

"Gee, that's tough."

He laughed. "Well, it is their vacation place."

Unfortunately, as she reminded herself, this was work, not her vacation, so as she wandered through the house, she found the workout room. It was huge and filled to her specifications with all the equipment she'd need.

"Really nice gym."

"Yeah. We brought in the extra stuff you asked for. The owners are going to do a remodel later this summer, turn this into some kind of yoga or meditation room or something, so they were fine with it."

"Excellent."

"There's a problem, though."

She turned around to look at him. "Yeah, what's that?"

"The guesthouse has been gutted."

Disappointment made her stomach tighten. Now she'd have to stay at a hotel. She'd really miss sitting out on that deck. "Oh."

He leaned against the wall leading to the backyard. "Yeah. I didn't know that when I made the reservations for this place, but Bill and Margaret—the owners—basically dismantled it since they weren't using it. They're going to use the space for some organic-gardening thing they're putting in."

Alicia folded her arms. "Okay. I can move to a hotel."

He frowned. "Look, Alicia, there are four bedrooms in this place. You can stay in one of those. One of the rooms has its own bathroom. It's the same thing as you would have had, only it's in the house instead of a few feet away from it. But if you're uncomfortable with that, I understand."

Relief washed over her. Commuting back and forth from a hotel to here would have been a logistics problem. She liked Garrett's solution better.

"No, it's fine. I'm not uncomfortable at all."

"Are you sure? I understand if you'd rather stay at the hotel."

"Now that would make me uncomfortable. Plus, it would be inconvenient for both of us, with you being here."

He nodded. "That's true. Look, Alicia. I'm sorry."

He was going out of his way to apologize, and she knew why.

But he was going to have to get over his discomfort, and she was, too, so they could get back to the job at hand, which was working on his shoulder. She'd have to smooth things over for both of them. "It's okay, Garrett. Why don't you show me around?"

Visibly relieved, Garrett turned and grabbed her bags.

"Bedrooms are this way." Beyond the workout room were three other rooms. Geez, this house was enormous. There were three good-size bedrooms and the master, which simply took her breath away. Decorated in warm shades, it appealed to her on every level. The king-size bed with its white frame and overhead ceiling fan was so inviting, especially with the killer view of the ocean. And the bathroom was truly something to behold. The shower had jets on both walls, and the oversize tub called to her.

But that was Garrett's room.

"You can stay in this room," he said.

She jerked her gaze to his. "No. This is your house. Your room. You've already been here a few days. You're settled in."

He laughed. "I can crash anywhere."

"That tub in there will be good for your therapy. So will the shower. I'm the employee, not a guest."

"And the guest should have the nice room."

She folded her arms. "No way in hell am I staying in this room. As your therapist, I insist you make use of that delicious shower and inviting tub."

He inhaled then let it out. "You're being difficult."

"No, you're the one being difficult. I'll tell you when you need a soak in that tub. And believe me, the further we get into this, the more grateful you'll be for that tub and shower."

"Do you always win arguments?"

She grinned. "Not always, but I'm going to win this one."

"Fine." He put her in the other large bedroom that had its own private bathroom. Plus, it had a stunning view of the ocean as well. It was lovely, decorated in pale mauves, and was roomy and spacious. Who were these people, anyway?

People with money, obviously.

She unpacked, changed into capris and a tank top, then set out to find Garrett. He was on the back deck.

Despite the shoulder injury, he was still in great form. He hadn't had to stop his normal workout program, which was good. Staying in shape was paramount to his recovery. Now if she could just get his mind to cooperate with his body, she'd have him back to the fierce competitor he was before he'd torn his rotator cuff.

She walked outside and stood next to him, breathing in the crisp salty air, orienting herself to the new location.

A fresh start. A fresh, professional start.

Garrett watched Alicia breathe and tried not to notice the way her breasts pressed against the skintight top she'd changed into.

He hadn't seen her for a few days, and despite being busy traveling and then meeting with Phil and Max, he'd be lying to himself if he didn't admit that he'd thought about her. That kiss they'd shared in the hotel in Oklahoma had stayed with him, and he'd thought about that a lot, about the way she'd kissed him back, the way her body had responded by surging toward his as if she'd wanted more of what he was offering. His dick twitched every time he thought about that night.

He should probably stop thinking about it.

He had a feeling Alicia wouldn't appreciate him getting hard right now. He could already sense the cool, professional walls she was trying to put up between them, so he understood what was happening.

Nothing. That's what was going to happen between them. Yeah, he got that they needed to be focused on his recovery, and getting it on with his therapist, who was also employed by the team? Likely a really bad move, plus it would put her job in danger. He wasn't an asshole; he knew she liked her job and didn't want to jeopardize it.

Besides, she wasn't the only game in town. If he wanted to get laid, there were a lot of ways to get there. He just needed to get his game on elsewhere and leave Alicia alone.

"Just to let you know, Max gave me a pretty thorough workout this morning."

She finally turned her gaze on him.

"You know, in case you had some of your now-famous torture in mind."

Her lips lifted. "The only thing I have in mind right now is to get near the ocean. Your therapy starts tomorrow. I'm too jet-lagged to even think about it today."

"Good. I was thinking more about getting something to eat. How about we do that first, and then we can walk on the beach after?"

She gazed longingly at the beach, but then she nodded. "I'm also starving, and hunger always wins. We'll eat first."

"Okay." He really had missed sparring with her, though. She challenged him, and he enjoyed that. And she was so damn pretty, and she had a smart mouth, and hell, she smelled so fucking good. And then there were her perky breasts . . .

"What are you doing?" she asked.

He blinked. "What?"

"You're ogling."

"I was?" He was.

"Yes. And you should stop it."

He should. But he probably wouldn't. An employee of the team or not, she had a hot body, just the kind he liked. He couldn't help noticing it. "So, do you like seafood and pasta?"

She gave him a dubious look. "I love pasta. The seafood I'll pass on since you know I'm a vegetarian."

He grinned. "I was just testing to see if you'd converted in the couple of days since I've seen you."

She rolled her eyes at him. "Should I change clothes?"

It gave him an opportunity to look her over again. "No, you're fine for where we're going."

They got into his rental car, and he drove down the beach toward town. There was a restaurant on the pier that served the best seafood he'd ever eaten.

"This place isn't fancy or anything," he said after he parked in the lot across the street.

"I don't need fancy. I just need food."

It was after five now, and he was so hungry they wouldn't be able to serve him fast enough. He hadn't eaten lunch, and then there was the workout. He couldn't go that long without food. He was a big guy.

They got a table near one of the windows, just in time to see the last of the day's rays disappear.

As soon as the waitress showed up, they grabbed menus and scanned them. Alicia must have been as hungry as he was, because she ordered her food at the same time as her drink. So did he.

"Maybe they'll bring the food faster," she said as the waitress wandered off with their order.

"I'd be happy if they brought the salads. Or bread."

She laughed. "I'm kind of embarrassed to be this hungry. My stomach is growling so loud you can probably hear it."

"I can't hear it over my own stomach. And I'm sorry. I should have thought about the food thing as soon as you arrived. We could have gone out to eat right away."

"It's okay. I'm a big girl, and I have a voice. I was too busy oohing and ahhing over the house and the beach to even think about food. That's what usually happens to me."

"What happens to you?"

"I get busy or distracted, then I forget to eat."

"That must be how you stay so thin."

She nodded. "That and my fast metabolism. And running around all the time. I also do yoga, which I love. Plus, my mom is still slender, so it must be a genetic thing. I'm very lucky."

The waitress brought their salads—and bread—so they both dug in, which meant conversation stopped for the moment. Once he had salad and bread in him, he felt more human.

He sat back and watched Alicia. She enjoyed the whole salad and three pieces of bread.

"You really do burn it off."

She swallowed then downed some water. "Wait till you see me handle the main course."

He laughed. He preferred women who liked themselves. There was something about self-confidence that was sexy. Obviously, Alicia didn't have any problems with her body, at least not that he'd seen.

And when her main course of pasta and vegetables arrived, she ate that with as much gusto as she'd devoured her salad, which meant he was free to dive into his lobster and crab.

Finally full, he sat back and wiped his mouth and hands, and took a drink of iced tea.

"Tell me about your family, Alicia."

She eyed him warily. "Isn't that venturing into the personal?"

"Come on. We're not robots here. We're spending every day together. Tell me about your family."

"I have two amazing parents who've been married forever and have been very supportive of my career. My brother, Cole, plays football for the Traders, and my cousin Mick plays for San Francisco. He's married, has a teenage son, and they just had a new baby boy. And you already know Gavin since he plays for your team."

"So you have an entire family of athletes."

"Yes."

"That's convenient. Did you practice your therapy moves on them?"

She quirked a smile. "As much as they'd let me, which wasn't often. They much preferred I'd give them massages, which is what they thought the whole sports medicine thing was about."

"That's what I used to think it was about, too."

"Yeah, well, until you're involved in it, either on the giving or the receiving end, you don't really know all that goes into it."

"I guess not." He took the bill from the waitress and tossed down some cash. They left the restaurant and drove back to the house.

"You ready for that walk now?" Garrett asked.

She looked over at him. "Definitely. I need it after all that food. Let me go grab my sweater."

She came back with a sweatshirt instead. "Couldn't find my sweater. I know I packed it."

"We can go shopping if you need some stuff. There's a mall a few miles away."

"You'd offer to shop with me again?"

"Not voluntarily, but if you need something, I don't mind taking you."

She shook her head. "How bizarre."

He opened the back door, and they walked down toward the beach. Alicia threw the sweatshirt over her head.

"How am I bizarre?"

"Men don't shop. It's unnatural."

"I was just offering to drive you there. Didn't say I'd go shopping or anything."

"Still, it's such a nice gesture."

He glanced over at her as they wandered down the beach. "I'm not even sure how to take that. No guy ever took you to the mall?"

"No." She slid her hands in the front pockets of her hoodie. "That's a girl thing."

He laughed. "You have some strange notions. You do see men at the mall when you're there, don't you?"

"I suppose."

"And men with women—together."

"Yes. I've just never gone shopping with a guy. Except with you, of course."

"You do realize I don't mean to pick out nail polish with you, right?"

She shot him a look. "Uh, yeah. I think I get that."

"Then I guess I'll have to take you again, just to prove guys aren't only interested in sitting in front of the television drinking beer and playing video games."

She stopped, tilted her head up. "We're here to work on your shoulder, Garrett. This isn't a vacation."

"I don't think you're going to spend twenty-four hours a day rehabbing me."

"You're right, of course. But you need to wrap your head around the fact that we're going to push it hard together while we're here."

The way she said it made his cock twitch. He should look on her as a professional, but in her oversize hoodie and those stretchy pants that clung to her great ass, it was hard to think about her as a physical therapist. They were going to be alone in a house together, and she was an attractive woman. And that kiss . . .

"You're doing it again," she said.

"Doing what?"

"Looking at me."

He shook his head. "So, now I'm not supposed to look at you?"

"Not that way." She turned and headed down the beach.

He watched her ass move as she walked.

He might be her patient, and she might be the therapist, but he was still a man.

And she still had a great ass that was going to be hard for him to ignore.

TEN

ALICIA FIGURED THE BEST WAY TO GET GARRETT TO stop giving her those looks—the ones that made her heat up from the inside out—was to get started on his therapy routine as quickly as possible.

He'd forgotten how awful it was—how awful she was. A quick reminder should take care of those hot looks he kept giving her.

The sooner he hated her, the quicker he'd regard her as if she were the devil. And she really needed him to hate her, because she sure liked the way he looked at her.

After their walk on the beach last night, she'd come back to the house and gone to her room to finish work on his treatment plan. She'd ended up falling asleep sideways on the bed, and had woken this morning disoriented and still in her clothes. It had taken her a minute to remember where she was.

That's what a comfortable bed and jet lag did to her.

She took a shower and dressed, then made her way to the kitchen and brewed a pot of coffee, tapping her fingers on the counter as she breathed in the scent. When she poured a cup and took her first sip, she groaned.

"That good?"

She looked up to find Garrett leaning against the wall.

He must have gone out for a run this morning; he was sweaty and his hair was still damp, curling against his neck. He wore sweats, a sleeveless shirt, and tennis shoes. Her stomach clenched as she drank in the sight of his muscular arms.

Seeing him at the team facility to work on his shoulder was one thing. Living with him and spending every minute of every day with him? Something else entirely.

She wanted to tell him to go away, but she had no valid reason to tell him that other than it bothered the hell out of her that he was so goddamn sexy.

"Yes, it's that good. Would you like a cup?"

"What I'd really like is orange juice."

"I'll get it for you."

Grateful to have an excuse to turn her back on him, she lifted a glass out of the cabinet and poured one for him.

"Thanks." And there he was, his body so close she felt some kind of vibration coming off him. She inhaled and breathed him in—the scent of the sea and musky, sweaty male, which unfortunately was not a turnoff to her. Definite sexual chemistry. She was afraid to even look up at him, and she was no coward.

But Garrett Scott represented her job, and if she did her job well, it would be a shot in the arm to her future with the Rivers. As one of the therapists in the lower echelon, she really needed to do well on this. Having the hots for her client was a terrible way to start.

She pushed off the counter.

"I was thinking omelets for breakfast. I know you're a vegetarian, but do you eat eggs?"

She stopped, turned, forcing herself to face him. "I do. Do you want me to fix your breakfast?"

He laughed. "No. I was going to fix breakfast. Unless you have some objection to that."

"Uh, no. No objection."

"Good." He laid his empty glass in the sink and grabbed a pan from under the counter. "I'm going to make bacon. I hope that doesn't offend you."

She couldn't help the smile that quirked her lips. "I won't run screaming as long as you don't make me eat it."

"Fine. You go work or something. I'll cook."

"How do you know what I want?"

"Eggs. I'm going to mix some vegetables in with it. Then I'll cut up some fruit, too. Would you like some yogurt?"

She sighed. He was just too good at this. She was going to have to keep her distance when she wasn't working with him. "That all sounds great, but I can help."

"It's okay. I've got this."

She went into the bedroom and grabbed her notebook, brought it out to the table, and tried to finish up her treatment plan, but it was hard to work when Garrett was cooking. Hot man in the kitchen? There was nothing sexier. He cracked eggs, sliced fruit, and she was certain he sizzled hotter than the bacon, which actually smelled delicious. Too bad she gave up meat five years ago.

She finally couldn't take doing nothing, so she got up, poured juice, and set the table. By then breakfast was ready, and Garrett filled their plates.

They sat at the table and ate. The omelets were delicious.

"You're very good at this cooking thing."

He waved a piece of bacon at her. "Amazing what a guy can do when he has to fend for himself."

"And you had to fend for yourself a lot?"

"Totally. You should feel sorry for me."

"This is where you're going to tell me you were homeless, you had to forage in the streets for food, you survived by using your street smarts, and you were some kind of baseball prodigy. That's how you got your scholarship, right?"

"You must have read the *Time Magazine* article about me. Dammit, and I wanted to impress you with my backstory. Now you've ruined it."

"Ha ha. Seriously, tell me about your family. I'm sure you were raised by loving parents and you're as boring as me."

He laughed and shoved a forkful of eggs in his mouth, followed by a couple of gulps of orange juice. "Yeah, just like your story. Very uneventful."

"I'm so disappointed."

He grinned. "I'm surprised you're not weeping into your napkin."

"So, what you're telling me is you had a very happy childhood, raised by two parents who adore each other, and there are no skeletons in your closet."

He popped a piece of cantaloupe in his mouth. "That's me. I'm pretty dull."

She finished her omelet and set it aside. "That's not what I've read. I read that you love to party, all women adore you and want to have your babies, but you steadfastly remain single. You haven't had a single serious relationship despite your immense popularity with the opposite sex, and you'll be turning thirty this year."

"Ancient, I know. I might as well hang it up now."

"Usually, all the sports studs carry on with some famous actress or model."

"And yet here I am, unattached."

"Maybe you're gay."

He arched a brow, searing her with his gaze. "Give me an hour in the bedroom and I'll prove that theory wrong."

Alicia's entire body went up in flames. She knew she shouldn't have baited Garrett that way, but they were having such an easy, fun conversation. He liked teasing her, and despite her attempts at wanting to establish boundaries with him, she couldn't help but respond to him. So she teased him back. All the distance she'd tried to create had evaporated with that one comment.

The look he'd given her, the way he'd said the words, and the challenge in them filled her mind with images of what he could do with her in the bedroom during that hour.

She realized it had been a very, very long dry spell for her in the sex department. Between finishing up her master's and getting her certification, then interning and working, sex had been more or less an afterthought for a long time. It was only natural for her body—and her mind—to want to jump all over the first really hot guy she was stuck in close quarters with. And she and Garrett had been together a lot—with her focus on his body. Of course she would feel connected to him in such a physical way.

Unfortunately, said hot guy attached to said hot body was most definitely off-limits.

"So . . . you game?"

She realized he was still watching her in a rather predatory fashion.

She blinked a few times to clear her head of all those dirty thoughts her mind had conjured up. "What? Game for what?"

"Me proving my utter heterosexuality to you."

"Uh, no. Definitely not."

He laughed. "I thought not. You'll just have to take my word for it, then."

She didn't need to take his word for it. He'd already proved it once when he'd kissed her. The memory of just how much of a man he was had been seared into every part of her body.

He got up and cleared the table. At a loss for a comeback, she helped him, nudging him out of the way so she could do the dishes.

"You cooked. I'll clean up."

"Sounds like a deal. I need a shower, anyway."

When he left the room, she exhaled. Maybe his disappearance would allow her pulse rate to return to normal. Though she didn't know what to do about her tingling nipples and throbbing pussy. That problem would likely have to be solved in the privacy of her bedroom tonight.

Or maybe Garrett would let her borrow his amazing shower with all those pulsing jets. She could have one hell of an orgasm in no time at all if she could direct one of those jets in the direction of her clit.

And once again, she thought of him in the shower, where he was right now. Only she was thinking of climbing in the shower with him, wrapping her hand around his cock, and massaging his ache at the same time she got herself off.

She'd wager that, like the rest of him, his cock was spectacular and that when he got hard, he knew exactly what to do with it. As she slipped her hands under the hot water, sliding a plate under to rinse it, she thought of what his cock would feel like as the shower water poured over both of them. Garrett's hands would smooth down her back to cup her butt, drawing her closer to his erection. She'd spread her legs so he could spear his cock inside her, shoving her against the wall as he did.

Sex with him would be hard. Passionate. All consuming. Oh so satisfying.

Her pussy clenched at the mental visual, and she drew closer to the kitchen counter, needing an orgasm so badly that just about any type of friction would get her there. But her hands were wet, and she had no idea how fast a shower Garrett took, so she wouldn't chance it. If she were alone, she wouldn't care. She'd dip her wet hands down the front of her shorts and take care of the matter right here. In her current state it wouldn't take long to get off.

If she hurried and finished the dishes, she could run into the bedroom and take care of this problem, and then maybe she could concentrate on her job instead of thinking about Garrett and his hot, thick—

"I feel a lot better now."

She whirled around, water flying everywhere. "What? I was just doing dishes."

His lips curved as he walked in. "I see that. Need some help?"

"No. Just finishing up with the last pan here." Her cheeks flushed hot, but she had no idea why she was blushing. Garrett had no idea that she'd been fantasizing about him, so she needed to calm down. She finished washing the pan and dried her hands.

"I'm going to . . . uh . . . . brush my teeth and floss. I'll be right back."

He looked up from the spot he'd taken on the sofa. "Sure."

She fled down the hall and shut the door to the bedroom, locking it behind her.

Two minutes. That's all she needed. An ease of tension, a release. Once she got that, she'd stop thinking about him, and she'd be normal again, instead of some crazy, libido-driven lunatic on the verge of a breakdown.

She lay down on the bed and took a deep breath, blew it out, then slid her hand inside her shorts.

She was still hot, bothered, and throbbing; the mere touch of her hand on her pussy sent her hips arching upward. She bit back the moan, though the bedroom was a long way from the living room. She could probably scream out loud, and Garrett wouldn't hear her. But she wasn't confident he'd stay in there, so she kept quiet as she skated her fingers over her swollen flesh. She closed her eyes, imagining Garrett pushing her up against the kitchen counter, dragging her shorts down, and putting his mouth on her aching sex.

"Yes," she whispered. "Yes, right there."

He had a sexy mouth, and she wanted it on her pussy. She bit down on her lip and rubbed her clit, already so close to coming she dug her heels into the mattress. But she wanted to delay, just a few more seconds, to enjoy the buildup as she envisioned him dipping two fingers inside her while he captured her clit between his lips. And when she tucked her fingers into her pussy, she couldn't hold back the moan that escaped, nor could she suppress the cry of delight as she released, tunneling her fingers deep and using the heel of her hand to rub against her clit.

She let her hips fall against the bed and breathed in and out, realizing that all she'd done was take the edge off.

The desire, the need—it was still there.

FUCK. GARRETT KNEW HE SHOULDN'T HAVE GONE TO-ward his room. If he'd stayed in the living room, he wouldn't have walked down the hall past Alicia's bedroom, wouldn't have heard the clear moan she'd made, wouldn't have figured out that she was in there masturbating.

His cock had gone fully hard in about three fucking seconds. And like some goddamn voyeur, instead of giving her privacy to get off, he'd lingered by the door and listened, hoping to hear more. He heard her breathing, whispering, and gasping when she came.

He'd never heard anything sweeter or anything that had turned him on more. As soon as he heard her moving around he'd hustled back out to the living room, then realized he should have gone to his room and jacked off. Now he had a hard-on he needed to get rid of in a hurry. But what if he tried to go to his room now, and she came out? It would be difficult to explain the erection sprouting in his pants. Alicia was smart—she'd figure out he'd overheard her.

So now he was stuck sitting on the sofa with a fucking pillow on his lap, feeling like a dumbass.

No good ever came from eavesdropping.

He just needed to breathe and think about unpleasant things.

Like therapy. And maybe never pitching again. Letting his team and his fans down.

Yeah, that took care of his erection.

Until Alicia came out of the bedroom, doing her best to look innocent, like nothing had happened. Except he'd been with plenty of women in his life, and he'd given a lot of them orgasms. And that rosy-cheeked look on her face was a dead giveaway.

"Sorry," she said, not meeting his gaze. "I finished unpacking while I was in there."

Since his balls were tied up in knots, he was a little resentful of her happy, I-just-came-and-you-didn't glow. "Hope it all went okay in there."

She cocked her head to the side. "Huh?"

"I mean, are there enough hangers? Do you have enough closet space?"

"Oh. Yes, it's an awesome bedroom."

Yeah, it had sounded pretty awesome.

She put her hands on her hips. "So, are you ready to get started?"

He clutched the pillow tighter. "I'm going to need a few minutes."

She frowned and came over to sit next to him. "Are you in pain?"

She had no idea. "No. I just want to digest breakfast. How about a walk first?"

"Great idea. It'll get the blood flowing. Let me go get my shoes on."

His blood was flowing just fine. To his dick. And if he didn't get his mind off sex and soon, he wasn't going to leave the sofa the rest of the day.

But by the time Alicia came back in, he'd managed to wrestle his cock—and his overactive imagination—under control.

"Ready to walk?"

There were about ten other things on his list right now, and all of them involved Alicia naked. Unfortunately, that wasn't what was going to happen, and he needed to get those visuals out of his head, because he didn't think he wanted to fight down another erection.

"Yeah, let's get outside."

ELEVEN

AFTER THE THERAPY SESSION, ALICIA HAD RETREATED
to the table to work on some notes and plans while Garrett had
plunked down on the sofa and watched a movie. He'd seemed rest-
less, though, and had gotten up several times to get a drink or something to snack on. They made sandwiches for lunch, but she stayed
at the table to work.

"Let's go out for dinner," he said.

She looked up from the book she'd been reading on her e-reader
and realized it was starting to get dark.

"Okay, sure."

"I need to get out of the house."

She laid her e-reader down. "Where would you like to go?"

"Do you like Italian food?"

She laughed. "I'm half Italian, so yes."

"Good. Put on a dress. I might want to go to a club after."

She arched a brow. "Uh . . ."

"What?"

"Should we be socializing together?"

He let out a snort. "Why shouldn't we be socializing together?"

"Because I'm an employee of the team." Surely he was as aware of the rules as she was.

"So? So am I."

"Exactly. And the team is in town, you know."

He frowned. "I'm not getting your point. Do you see us spending time together outside of therapy as some conflict of interest?"

"Yes, it could absolutely be seen that way."

He came over to her. "Are you . . . uncomfortable being around me? If you want to be alone, I can just go get my own dinner, and you can either eat here or go somewhere on your own." He leaned against the table. "You know, I've never even asked if you had a boyfriend or someone in your life who might not appreciate me hanging all over you. Is that why you pushed me away that day in Oklahoma City?"

"No." Her eyes widened. "No. That's not it at all. No boyfriend, no one. I just didn't want to cause any problems for my job, or for yours."

He seemed to relax. "Okay. Look, we'll be spending all our time together while we're here. It's just natural that we'll go out to eat together, and if I want to kick back and have some fun, I just assumed you'd want to get out of the house and come with me. You're under no obligation to do so. If you don't want to, I'll get you back here and go about my business. Fair enough?"

"Definitely."

She went into her bedroom to change clothes. That exchange had been awkward, but it had been her doing. Garrett didn't see anything strange about hanging out with her. As far as he was concerned, she could be just another one of the guys.

In a dress.

She changed into a short-sleeved cotton dress and slipped on a pair of wedge sandals, then glammed it up a little with makeup and pulled the sides of her hair up in a clip, some of the tendrils spilling over and curling toward her face. She added earrings and a bracelet, for some reason needing to feel feminine, though she had no idea why. Maybe so he *wouldn't* think of her as just one of the guys tonight.

Really bad idea, Alicia.

Ignoring that warning voice in her head, she left the bedroom and found Garrett on the back deck. He'd put on a pair of worn jeans and a long-sleeved button-down shirt. Even dressed casually, he took her breath away. So she inhaled another breath and let it out, determined to think of *him* as just one of the guys.

A really sexy guy she couldn't touch except in a therapeutic way.

"Ready when you are."

When he turned around, she caught the telltale appreciative look he gave her, and she couldn't help but tingle all over.

"You look . . . really nice," he said, giving her a head-to-toe once-over. More than once, actually.

"Thank you. So do you."

He laughed. "Just jeans and a shirt."

She looked down at herself. "Just a dress."

"Women are prettier."

"Oh, I don't know. I have a much finer appreciation for men than I do for other women."

"Good to know."

She grabbed a shawl, and they climbed into the car. Garrett drove them along the beach highway. Alicia squinted to get a look, but it was too dark now.

"It's too bad the sun's already gone down," Alicia said.

"Yeah? Why?"

"I would have liked to see the ocean."

"We'll be here for a while. I'll take you out for a drive one day along the beach."

She pulled her gaze away to look at him. "I'd like that. I love the ocean."

"Me, too. I love taking beach vacations."

"It's my favorite kind of vacation. I guess because I've always been landlocked."

"There's the river in St. Louis."

She snorted. "Not about to stick my toes in that, thanks. My idea of a vacation is warm weather, a beautiful blue ocean, and sand under my feet."

"Ever been to the Caribbean?"

"I've never left the US."

He glanced her way. "Seriously?"

"Yes."

"You should fix that. There are a lot of beautiful places outside the US."

"I always intended to go. I've just been busy with school and then getting a job after that."

"Ever been to Hawaii?"

"No, not there, either. But hey, I'm here, and this is great."

He frowned. "This isn't a vacation, as you told me today."

She let out a quiet sigh of contentment. "There's a beach and an ocean. It's close enough."

He made a turn, then pulled into the parking lot of the restaurant. The valet parked the car, and they went inside.

The restaurant was nice. Warm atmosphere, and oh, she could smell the bread already. Her stomach rumbled in delight.

The menu was extensive, and she had a hard time choosing.

"Would you like some wine?"

She looked up from the menu. Garrett was perusing the wine list.

"I'd love some wine."

He handed the list over to her. "I'll let you choose since I'm not a big wine drinker."

"Thank you." She went over the list, and when the waiter showed up, she selected a Chianti.

"Is that good?"

"I'm a traditionalist. I grew up having Chianti with my pasta."

He cocked a brow. "As a kid?"

She laughed. "Actually, some Italian families do serve wine to their children, in moderation and mixed with white soda. I had some at an early age. My mother is very old-style Italian."

"Interesting. I think I'd like your mother."

She smiled. "She'd definitely like you."

"Why's that?"

"You're an athlete, for one. She loves big, athletic guys. With appetites. Like my brother, Cole. And you like to eat. My mother loves people who love to eat."

"So, my secret is out, after such a short time together."

"I've been around you long enough to know that during your therapy, you're always complaining about wanting to stop so you can get something to eat. Or was that just an excuse to get out of doing your exercises?"

He reached for the bread as soon as the waiter put it down on the table. "No, I'm always hungry."

She laughed.

They ate dinner and she sipped her wine, which was delicious.

"Now that we've established you've been locked in the States your entire life, tell me your wish list for travel," Garrett asked as they ate their salads.

She lifted her gaze to his. "Italy is definitely on my list. My maternal grandparents were from Sicily. I'd love to go there someday."

"Italy's nice."

"You've been there?"

"Rome and Milan. Beautiful cities."

"I'm jealous. Where else have you been?"

He shook his head. "We're still on your wish list."

"Oh, okay." She dabbed her lips with the napkin and thought about it. "England, France, Scotland, Ireland, any and all of the Caribbean islands, Hawaii—though I know that's in the US, but I've never been to any of the islands. I suppose you've been to all of them."

"I've never been to the big island. I've heard it's great."

"Tell me all the places you've been."

"I've been to a few places."

Her fork balanced at the tip of her lips. "Go on."

He shrugged. "Some spots in Europe and Hawaii, of course."

As she chewed, she regarded him. "You're trying to downplay your travels so I won't feel bad."

He lifted the glass of wine to his lips and smiled. "Maybe."

"Don't. I'm perfectly content with the life I've lived."

"All right. I like to travel during the off-season, so I've been to England, Portugal, Italy, and France, quite a few of the countries in South America, and several of the Caribbean islands. Hawaii, of course . . ."

Alicia listened to Garrett recount his travels. He was a smooth conversationalist, which surprised her. Some athletes could only talk about themselves, their sports, and their stats, but he was well-rounded.

"You enjoy travel."

He smiled. "Yeah. I like meeting people. You can learn a lot from visiting other cultures."

"What about home?"

"I like that, too."

"Tell me about where you're from."

"Nevada. Lots of gambling."

She laughed. "So, you're from Las Vegas."

"Around that area."

"Is your family still there?"

"Half of them. My dad is."

He stopped with his glass partway to his lips. There was something he wasn't telling her.

"Wait," she said. "Where's your mom? I thought you said your parents were still together."

He laid his wineglass on the table and shrugged. "Oh. Did I?"

"Yes. You did."

"Huh."

"Garrett."

"I don't remember that conversation."

"Yes, you do. We just talked about it. You asked about my family, and I told you all about them. Then I asked about yours, and you led me to believe your family was exactly the same."

He didn't say anything, just grabbed another piece of bread and buttered it.

"Come to think of it, you never elaborated about your family at all."

He wasn't even looking at her, was tearing off small pieces of bread and leaving them on the plate. "My bad. My parents divorced when I was eighteen."

"I'm sorry."

He shrugged. "It's okay. It was a good deal for them. They fought a lot. The waters have been calmer since the divorce."

He seemed so matter-of-fact about it, when it had obviously hurt and probably still did. "It couldn't have been easy for you."

"No big deal."

She put her hand over his. "Tell me about it."

She ached for him, because she saw a man still hurting over the breakup of his parents' marriage.

"Nothing to tell, really. It was over and done with a long time ago."

And there he went again, his gaze riveted to his Chianti, as if it held all the answers. She squeezed his hand. "Garrett. Talk to me."

He lifted his gaze and met hers. "Trying to do the whole college and baseball thing while there was shit going down at home kind of sucked, but I got through it. They were both really supportive of me, didn't want me to think my world was coming to an end just because their marriage was."

She pushed her plate to the side and took a sip of wine. "I'm sure you thought it was."

"I was eighteen, not a kid."

"Eighteen *is* still a kid. It's hard for anyone to have their parents' marriage break up. I don't think it matters how old you are."

He gazed at her over his glass of wine. "I survived it."

"You're trying hard to downplay what had to be a really traumatic moment in your life. Why?"

He studied her, then grabbed the bottle and refilled her glass. "It's not something I like reliving. Frankly, it sucked. I was pissed at them for ending their marriage. I wanted them to stay together."

Now, she understood. "My best friend's parents divorced when we were sixteen. It devastated her. They argued a lot, and Casey worried over it, wishing they'd stop fighting. But it never occurred to her that they'd divorce. When they did, she was crushed. It tore her world apart. I hated seeing her so unhappy."

"Yeah. I was already away at college, but when I'd come home on breaks, seeing the life you knew dismantled and put in boxes, like it never happened . . ."

Alicia couldn't imagine the pain of having the relationship of the two people you counted on the most fall apart right in front of you. Hard enough to deal with as a child. It had to be harder when it happened as an adult. She reached out and laid her hand over his. "I'm sorry."

He looked down at her hand then lifted his gaze to hers. "It's okay. It was a long time ago."

"But you obviously don't like to talk about it, and I brought it up. I'm sorry for that."

He laughed. "Hey, it's not like my parents are dead. People ask about them. I have to talk about it."

"I'll drop the subject." She started to withdraw her hand, but he grasped her hand in his, squeezed it like a lifeline.

"Don't. It's okay."

Maybe he didn't think he wanted to talk about it, but she figured he really did.

"You said your dad still lives in Las Vegas. How about your mom?"

"She moved back to Southern California, near where my grandparents live."

"Oh, well, that was probably nice for her, to be near her family."

"Yeah. I visit her during the off-season and whenever we have games there."

"And your dad?"

He shrugged. "Not so often."

There was a story somewhere in there. She wasn't sure she should ask about it. But she'd come this far. He could always tell her to mind her own business or refuse to answer. "Why not so often?"

He paused, stared into the glass of Chianti. "He cheated on my mother."

She let her eyes drift closed for a fraction of a second, wishing she hadn't asked the question. When she opened them, he was staring at her.

"Oh, God. I'm so sorry, Garrett."

"Nothing to be sorry about. You didn't do it. My dad's the one who broke up my parents' marriage."

Maybe that's why he hadn't wanted to change the subject. She wondered if he'd ever had anyone to talk to about this.

She took a swallow of wine then leaned forward, glad they were in the type of restaurant where voices didn't carry. The place was lovely, but it was noisy, which meant they could have a conversation no one would overhear.

"Are you still angry with your father over the breakup of the marriage?"

He didn't meet her gaze. "It was a long time ago. Both my parents have moved on."

She leaned back. "How so?"

"My mom remarried about five years ago. Nice guy she met where she works."

"Oh, good for her."

He smiled. Finally. "Yeah. She really loves Henry. And he treats her like a precious diamond."

"So you obviously approve of him as a stepfather."

He laughed. "Yeah, he's great. And he loves baseball, which is a plus. Though he's a Los Angeles fan, so I have to deduct points."

She let out a soft laugh. "Well, yes, I could see how that would detract from his overall score. But I'm glad she's found happiness."

"Yeah. Me, too."

"What about your father?"

"He married the woman he cheated on my mom with. Like less than a year after he and my mom divorced."

"Oh." She let that settle a bit and worked on her meal. Garrett didn't offer up further details on his dad and stepmother. She wondered if he saw his father at all or if he'd cut all ties. She didn't want to ask, and obviously, he didn't want to talk about his dad, so she let it be.

Their plates were cleared, and they both declined dessert. Garrett paid the bill, and they left the restaurant and headed back to the house. He was quiet on the ride back. Alicia knew he must be thinking about his parents. Pain like that didn't just go away, especially if you never dealt with it.

When they got back to the house, he grabbed a beer from the fridge and went out onto the back deck. She opened a bottle of water and followed him.

It was a nice night. A little breezy, so she went back inside and put her sweater on, kicked her sandals off, and pulled her feet up onto the chaise, content to listen to the sounds of the ocean waves. Garrett leaned against the deck post, his back to her, giving her a chance to admire his great ass without him being aware of it.

She was worried about him. She could tell he wasn't relaxed as he took a swallow of beer and set it down on the deck rail. His shoulders were tight, his stance rigid.

Tension wasn't going to help his therapy. She pushed off the chair and came next to him.

"Are your muscles feeling tight?"

He looked up at her. "If I say no, will you leave me alone?"

She laughed. "That means yes. Come on. Let me give you a good stretch. It'll ease some of that tension."

"Ugh."

"Yeah, whatever, wuss. Suck it up."

She went into her bedroom, slipped out of her dress and into her yoga pants and a tank top so she'd be more comfortable. When she went into the workout room, Garrett was already there, shirtless and in low-slung sweatpants.

He still made her knees weak, but she swallowed and took a sip of water, mentally readying herself.

She put Garrett through the thirty-minute stretching session. He gritted his teeth and endured it, but he was tight, and his body was tense. When she finished, he sat up and grabbed a towel to wipe down his face and body.

"How about a massage?" she suggested.

He slanted a glance her way. "I thought that was against your rules."

"You're tense. You look like you could use it."

He grabbed a bottle of water and downed it in two swallows. "I'm fine."

He was not fine. "A massage will relax you. Therapist's orders."

He let out a resigned sigh. "Sure."

She set up the massage table with towels.

"Facedown," she said.

He smirked at her.

"What?"

He shook his head. "Nothing. Nothing appropriate, anyway."

"I have no idea what you're talking about."

"I know." He climbed onto the table, and she got out her massage lotion then turned on some music.

He lifted his head and looked up at her. "Really? You're going to play that new age shit?"

"Well, yes. It's very calming and relaxing."

"It'll put me to sleep."

"There's nothing wrong with you sleeping while I massage you."

"I don't really feel like sleeping right now. How about something a little edgier?"

She leaned her hip against the table. "Edgier doesn't seem very relaxing, Garrett."

He lifted up on his forearms and shot her a grin. "Maybe not to you."

"Okay. I'll find something . . . edgier."

She scrolled through her music until she hit something that rocked.

"That'll do," he said, and put his face down on the table.

Nope. Not relaxing at all, but if that worked for Garrett, so be it.

"I'm going to put some heat on your injured shoulder first. That way by the time I get to that part, it'll be warmed up and ready for me."

He lifted his head again. "God, you're not going to stretch the fuck out of it again, are you?"

Her lips curved. "No, I'm not going to stretch it. This will be a gentle massage. I promise."

"Good."

She put the heating pad on his shoulder then mentally centered herself by breathing in then out. After rubbing the lotion between her hands to warm it, she started in the center of his upper back and worked her way down, wanting to save his shoulder for last because she knew that's where the worst tension would be.

She was going to make him feel better and melt the knots in all his muscles. And maybe help him relax.

Though touching him like this wasn't going to be relaxing for her.

At. All.

TWELVE

GARRETT WASN'T MUCH FOR MASSAGE, THOUGH A LOT of his teammates swore by it. A lot of the guys got weekly massages to help with their sore muscles. Garrett just got in the whirlpool or a hot shower and otherwise sucked it up.

But Alicia was right. Talking about his parents tonight had knotted up the tension between his shoulder blades, and now his shoulder hurt. Of course some of that probably had to do with the way Alicia worked him in their therapy sessions.

Not that he'd tell her that. She was tougher on him than any of his previous therapists had been. He'd wanted to cry. And he never cried.

He hoped to hell whatever she was doing to him would result in some good. Because he'd take whatever pain she dished out if it put him back on the mound.

Right now, though? Whatever she was doing back there was

pure pleasure. He focused on the sweep of her soft hands over his back, the way she seemed to target every sore muscle, coaxing it into submission with her thumb or the heel of her hand.

He'd tried massage once or twice before and always seemed to get some tiny little woman who seemed nice but then proceeded to employ some Marquis de Sade technique of massage, determined to outdo her peers in how much they could hurt their clients.

Alicia didn't do it that way. Her hands glided over his back until he couldn't help but let out a groan of pure pleasure.

She rolled her fist down his spine, all the way to where his sweats rested low on his ass. He wanted her hands all over his body, rubbing him down front and back.

When she took the heating pad off and smoothed her hands over both his shoulders, he sank deeper into the cushioned table.

"You have magic hands."

She laughed. "Sure I do."

"No, really. This is a great massage."

"Your muscles are cooperating. Be quiet now. You shouldn't talk while I'm massaging you. Take deep breaths, in and out."

No, he shouldn't talk. He shouldn't think, especially not about Alicia. If he thought about her, about her hands moving over his body, and about what he'd really like her hands to be doing, he'd end up getting hard.

And if it wasn't bad enough feeling her, he had to listen to her, to the sounds she made as she touched him. Just hearing her breathe turned him on.

It sounded like sex, made him think about thrusting as she put force against his muscles. And when she exhaled . . .

Jesus. He really had to stop mixing Alicia and sex together. This was what happened when his mind went blank and he relaxed.

The music was pumping, but it wasn't helping to take his mind off Alicia, her hands, and the sounds she made. If he could sing a note himself, he would, but that would only send her screaming from the room, so that was out.

She leaned down to put a little pressure on his muscles. He caught a whiff of her perfume. No, not perfume. Soap or shampoo, maybe. Something citrusy. He sucked in a breath.

She stopped. "Is that a rough spot?"

He gritted his teeth. "No. I'm fine."

She laid her palms flat and moved down his back, then up.

"Talk to me, Alicia." Maybe if they carried on a conversation, he'd stop visualizing.

"You shouldn't be talking. You should be breathing. Deep, even breaths that'll carry oxygen to your muscles."

"I'm not talking. I want you to talk."

She paused. "Is it so difficult for you to relax?"

"Yeah. I like conversation."

She let out a soft laugh. "Okay. What do you want to talk about?"

"I don't know. I know about Gavin since we play together. Is that how you got interested in sports medicine?"

"Sort of. I watched a lot of sports when I was younger, obviously. The family is entrenched in sports with Cole and my cousin Mick playing football, and Gavin in baseball. Even the girls always played sports."

"The girls?"

"My cousin Jenna and I."

"What sports did you play?"

"I was on the dance team. And I played tennis and golf."

He lifted his head and looked at her. "You like golf?"

"I can play."

He sat up.

She frowned. "We're not finished."

"My muscles are relaxed. Let's talk golf. You didn't tell me you played that weekend we were in Oklahoma."

She shrugged. "You didn't ask me. Besides, no way would I have played in that weather. Too cold for me."

He laughed. "For me, too. So, you think you're good, huh?"

"No, I don't think I'm good. I *am* good."

"We should play."

She folded her arms. "You think you're ready to swing a club?"

"I don't know. You're the therapist. Am I?"

She studied him for a bit then said, "Actually, it would be good for your shoulder, help loosen you up for pitching. We should play."

If there was one thing Garrett loved, it was competition. "Good. I'll arrange a tee time."

"I don't have my clubs with me."

"Neither do I, so we're both at a disadvantage."

"Fine. We'll play. Now lie back down. I'm not finished with you yet."

He rolled his shoulders. "Honestly, I feel fine."

She pointed to the table. "Lie down. I haven't given you the full Alicia Riley massage yet."

He wanted to groan. Any more of her hands on him and he'd be hard the rest of the night. "No, really."

She gave him that glare he was getting used to seeing. The one that meant she was going to win, so he might as well not argue.

"Okay. Geez."

He flipped over, and she put more lotion on her hands then went back to work on him, this time spreading his arms out and rolling her hands over his biceps. Admittedly, that felt really good. She hit the rough spots and melted away the last of his soreness from the therapy today. But her touch and scent still set him off, so while he was relaxed, he was still keenly aware of her.

"That should do it," she finally said.

He stood and stretched. Alicia looked at him then quickly turned away. "All right, then. I'll just clean up in here, and you can head out. You should drink more water."

"Why?"

"Massage releases toxins and can make you sweat. The water will replenish you."

"Fine."

Maybe he wasn't the only one aware. He'd caught her checking out his abs—and lower. His cock tingled at the thought, but he brushed it aside. In these sweats hiding an erection wouldn't be possible. He left the room and went into the kitchen to grab a glass of water, downed it in a few gulps, then stepped outside for some air.

Alicia was right. He'd broken out into a sweat, and the cool night breeze helped.

"Feeling all right?"

He turned to her. "Yeah. Feeling great now. Thanks for the massage."

"You're welcome." She took a sip of water, then laid her glass on the table and took a seat.

He parked it on the top step, turning so he was half facing her, half facing the ocean.

"If I lived here, I don't think I'd ever leave the house," she said. "This place has a definite allure."

"It's great, but I think you'd get bored."

She laughed. "Remember where I grew up. This is heaven. The salt in the air, the amazing view of the ocean that never ends. Long walks on the beach. I doubt I could ever get bored with a place like this. Of course it's a wee bit out of my price range."

"You never know. You could end up becoming famous in sports medicine, and having a place like this would be chump change for you."

"Thank you for that."

"For what?"

"For thinking I could afford a place like this someday as opposed to thinking I'd marry someone rich who'd buy it for me."

He laughed. "I'm pretty sure you're a force to be reckoned with, Alicia. I don't think you'll ever need a man to take care of you, financially or otherwise."

"Thank you again. You're just full of compliments tonight."

"Well, I'm full of something."

Her lips lifted, and then she stared off into the darkness. But when she rolled her wrists and flexed her hands, he frowned.

"Did the massage make your hands hurt?"

She looked down at her hands and laid them in her lap. "No, I'm fine. Just releasing the tension in them. It's a normal practice."

He got up and went over to her chair, then kneeled in front of her and took her hands in his. "I don't want you to hurt yourself working on me."

She let out a soft laugh that made his balls quiver. "I don't hurt myself. It's my job."

"Your job has to be hard on your hands." He massaged them, rubbing his thumbs over her wrists.

"Oh, God, that feels good. Now who's the masseuse?"

He liked making her feel good. It surprised him how much he liked making her feel good. He didn't want her to hurt in order to fix him. "How hard is therapy on you?"

"What do you mean?"

"What you do to me—stretching my muscles or tendons—that takes some power, and you're not exactly a big person. How hard is that on your body?"

"I'm trained to do it, Garrett. I don't hurt myself."

He flexed her wrists. "Yeah, but who gives you a massage at the end of the day?"

"I don't need one."

"I'll bet you get sore working on athletes. I know what our bodies feel like. You're working on some hard muscles. And after this injury I've studied some anatomy—you're having to work with tendons and capsules and some of that other shit. You have to dig pretty deep—that's why what you do to me hurts so damn bad, right?"

She studied him. "It's good that you're so well-informed. It helps your recovery. But honestly, there's nothing wrong with my hands." She pulled them away from him and wriggled her fingers and flexed her wrists. "See? They're just fine."

He didn't believe her. "Are you sure?"

She made a move to stand, so he stood to get out of her way. "I'm positive. I haven't been at this as long as some of the veteran therapists. Now they might have some issues after years and years of practice. But me? I'm fine. I take good care of myself."

"Turn around."

She frowned. "What?"

"Turn around."

"Why?"

"I want to see if you're as tight as I was."

"Absolutely not. You don't get to be my therapist. I'm here to take care of you, remember?"

Ignoring her, he spun her around, and before she could object, he laid his hands on her. He was no expert, but he instantly zeroed in on the rock-hard muscles between her neck and shoulders.

"Just as I thought. Your muscles are tightened up."

She fought to turn around, but he pinned her between the chair and his body.

"Garrett. You are absolutely not going to rub my shoulders. Do you know how much money your arm is worth?"

"Yeah. My agent broke it down for me by the number of years of my contract. And then by month. She was very thorough."

"Exactly."

"And if I want to give a massage, I can." He was already pressing in on her skin, using his thumbs and fingers to try and release the tension. "Just think of it as more therapy for me."

"I'm thinking you're not listening to me."

"Yeah, whatever. I don't always take direction well."

Having her close like this was the worst form of self-torture. His nose was in her hair, and that citrusy smell drove him crazy. Her skin was soft, and with her butt nestled up against his crotch, he was going to have to do some calculations of earned run averages in order to avoid getting hard.

Alicia kept taking deeper breaths, which propelled her body closer to his. And she'd stopped talking—not a good sign. That meant she was concentrating on the movement of his hands. She either really liked the massage, or she had noticed what was going on in his pants. He took a step back, and she cleared her throat, lifted his hands off her shoulders, and turned around.

Big mistake. Because there it was, the erection that couldn't be avoided. And her focus went right to it, then her gaze shot to his, all wide-eyed and shocked.

"Um, we should go to bed."

He lifted a brow.

"Not together, of course. That would be . . . totally inappropriate. I mean, I'm going to bed. In my room. Alone. Thank you for the massage. It was great. I'll see you in the morning."

She moved past him, her body brushing the tip of his cock as she did. It was painful and exciting at the same time.

It was like being fourteen years old again, caught in the locker room with a hard-on because he'd been fantasizing about Miss

Smith, the hot twenty-three-year-old gym teacher who'd given them all wet dreams. How many times had he—hell, all the boys—tried to disguise erections when they'd been running track while Miss Smith had stood out in the center of the field working with the girls?

But he wasn't an awkward teenager anymore. He was old enough to control his libido around a desirable woman, especially a woman he had a working relationship with.

Fuck. He dragged his fingers through his hair and walked down the steps, deciding he needed a walk by the ocean to cool down his raging hormones.

He stood on the beach, his cock hard and throbbing and seemingly in no hurry to go flaccid.

Great. If he could just get thoughts of Alicia's body, her scent, out of his head, he'd go soft.

Instead, his head was filled with her, and his cock stayed hard. How was he going to explain that if he ran into her when he went back inside? She was already nervous and skittish around him, and waving his erection around would no doubt send her packing. He didn't want to scare her off.

Maybe he'd just jack off here at the edge of the ocean. There were no other homes within miles of this secluded beach property, no boats out on the water, which gave him plenty of privacy. He was hard and aching, and it wouldn't take much time to get off.

He drew his sweats partway down and pulled out his cock, taking it firmly in his grasp. It jerked in his hand, and he rolled his thumb over the head.

Garrett imagined Alicia walking out right now, seeing him like this. He knew how she'd likely react, but he imagined how he'd want her to react.

He'd want her to drop to her knees and put her mouth on him. His balls tightened at the mental image of her lips surrounding the swollen head, her tongue flicking out to lick up the pearly drops of fluid that spilled from the tip.

She had a beautiful mouth. He'd thought about kissing her again—a lot. Granted, he concentrated on her hands because she touched him, but her mouth—yeah, he wanted her mouth on him. On his mouth, on his skin, and definitely on his cock.

His balls tightened, and he gripped his cock, squeezing it as he jerked his hand over the soft skin. He tilted his head back and closed his eyes, so close to the edge he was ready to explode. But the fantasy of Alicia on her knees was too sweet to let go of.

Just a few more minutes.

ALICIA PRESSED A COLD WASHCLOTH TO HER NECK, splashed water on her face, paced back and forth in her room, and finally opened the window, hoping the night air would do something to bring her internal body temperature down.

But nothing worked.

Having Garrett's hands on her hadn't helped, and try as she might to convince him to stop, he hadn't. First her hands, then her neck and shoulders. He'd given her goose bumps.

In therapy training, they had all touched each other. She'd had plenty of great-looking men put their hands on her, and she'd never gotten turned on. Not once. After all, this was her job. She'd never been attracted to any of the men she'd gone to school with or worked with, either in a peer capacity or with a patient.

Until now.

Staying here at the house was only going to make things worse. This had been such a mistake. But she was stronger than her libido and her fantasies, and she could gain control over them.

Couldn't she?

She pressed her cool hands to her hot face. What was wrong

with her? She had to get a grip on herself, had to put some distance between them, put this sexual fire out, or she would never be able to do her job.

Because physical distance was an impossibility. She had to be able to touch Garrett and not go up in flames every time she did.

She opened the back door, letting the cool breeze fan the flames.

And then stopped, her jaw dropping as she caught sight of Garrett.

She blinked, certain she was imagining what she saw.

But as her eyes adjusted to the darkness outside, she made out Garrett's form at the edge of the water.

His sweats were drawn down low on his hips, and he had his cock in his hand, slowly drawing it through his fist. He had his head thrown back and his eyes closed, the tension in his body evident as he touched himself.

Her throat went desert dry. She couldn't swallow, didn't want to move, afraid the slightest movement would draw his attention. She had to get out of the light, so she took a step back, ashamed that she was watching him in this private moment but so enthralled by what he was doing she couldn't turn away.

He was beautiful, his chest bare, his back bowed as he thrust his cock into his fist, mimicking the act of sex as he powered his shaft forward.

Her pussy clenched; her clit fluttered, demanding her attention. She slipped her hand into her shorts and palmed her sex, needing release.

She whispered out a gasp as she watched his tempo increase, wishing she were bold enough to walk out there and face him, show him what she needed.

She wanted to give them both what they obviously wanted. But she couldn't. Staying hidden was thrilling, making her throb with want and need, but it was wholly unsatisfying when who she really wanted was standing out there on the beach, satisfying himself.

He'd wanted her tonight; the evidence had been so clearly outlined. And she'd walked away. Now he was taking care of his own needs when she could be out there, on her knees in the sand, her mouth on his beautiful cock, licking the crest, taking him between her lips, and sucking him until he exploded. Until they both exploded.

Her body taut with need, her legs shook as she swept her fingers over her aching pussy, her pulse pounding as she slipped her fingers inside, imagining what it would feel like if Garrett pushed her to the sand and plunged his cock inside her.

She let out a low moan, her fingers wet and her pussy gripping them tight as she watched him. His body was utter perfection as he rapidly jerked his cock. He looked like a god of the ocean out there, his body bathed in moonlight, his head tilted back as he moved with the fluid grace of someone who knew his own needs so well.

He was close to coming. So was she as she rubbed the heel of her hand against her clit.

She wanted him to fuck her, wanted to feel his muscled body hot and slick against hers, driving relentlessly into her, rolling against her until she splintered.

And when he thrust his hips forward and come jettisoned from his cock, she bit down on her lip and forced back her cry as she released, burying her fingers inside her pussy as waves of orgasm poured from her. They were coming together, and all she wanted was Garrett inside her, gripping her hips as he pounded his release into her.

Damp and shaken, she turned away, resting against the wall. She pulled her hand from her shorts as she caught her breath and closed her eyes, reliving the moment over and over again as her body pulsed with the aftereffects of that amazing orgasm.

When a few minutes had passed and she dared to take a peek out the window, Garrett was gone.

She went into the bathroom and stared at herself in the mirror. Her cheeks were pink, her skin was damp, and her whole body trembled.

So much for fleeing in here to cool her body down. She was a wreck. Her nipples tingled and her pussy quivered. She was still turned on, the images in her head nowhere near going away.

Facing Garrett tomorrow was going to be very difficult.

Running away from him tonight hadn't helped at all. It had only made it worse.

THIRTEEN

GARRETT GOT UP AND WENT FOR A RUN EARLY, THEN grabbed some juice and went right to the gym for a lifting workout. That's where he met Alicia, who came in dressed in tight-fitting spandex yoga pants and a tank top.

"Mind if I work out with you?" she asked, setting her towel and bottled water on the elliptical.

Jacking off last night hadn't put him in any better mood. He figured the run might generate some endorphins, but he was still in a mood. "You can do whatever you want. There's plenty of equipment here."

She didn't seem bothered. "Okay, thanks."

She plugged earbuds in, turned on what he assumed was music, and started her workout. Instead of concentrating on her fine ass moving up and down on the elliptical, he was determined to focus on his workout. The one thing he could always count on to distract him was training his body. He worked with the weights, at least the ones he was allowed to do on his own, which meant legs and abs. Upper-body training was off-limits except under the direction of his trainers or his therapist, so he'd have to wait for Alicia.

He'd lost track of time, but he hadn't lost track of Alicia, who after working up a sweat on the elliptical had moved to weights.

She was strong. She hadn't once asked him to spot her, and despite being slight, she could heft a decent amount of weight on her own. He was impressed, and he liked watching her body.

Which he shouldn't be doing at all since that's what had put him in a bad mood to start with. He should do less ogling of her form and more paying attention to his own.

"You ready for me to work with you on your upper body?" she asked, swiping the towel over her neck and chest, which only made him focus on her breasts, which weren't large but still made him want to run his tongue across her cleavage. She was damp with sweat, which only made him think of getting her sweaty in other ways.

Naked.

Dammit.

"Sure." The sooner he finished this workout, the sooner he could avoid her, which was his new plan. Avoidance.

"Let's start with a light bench press to warm you up," she said, and off they went on the upper-body work.

He went through the motions, did the workout, then grabbed his towel.

"We're not finished, Garrett," she said.

He frowned. "That's the normal routine."

"I thought we'd change it up today, add a little more weight."

"Really."

"I think your shoulder needs to have some stress added to it. We need to get you warmed up to start throwing pitches."

The idea of throwing a pitch made him ache in the pit of his stomach. Since the injury, it was all he could think about. This was everything he was working for.

And everything he feared.

But he refused to back down, refused to let the fear control him.

He was either going to get back in the game again or have to accept that his days as a pitcher were over. And there was only one way to find out.

He tossed his towel down, excited to be challenged. The day was already looking up. "All right. Let's do it."

Two hours later, his enthusiasm had waned. Between the weights and the therapeutic exercises and more of that god-awful stretching that was beginning to remind him of some form of sadism on Alicia's part, he was as limp as an overcooked noodle. He sat slumped on the living-room sofa while his evil therapist updated her notebook.

"I think you're trying to kill me."

She momentarily lifted her gaze to his and smiled. "Wimp."

"Admit it. The other teams in our division have paid you to destroy me."

Another quick look. "Oh, suck it up. Yours isn't even the worst injury I've ever seen."

He stayed quiet for a few minutes, watching as she concentrated, typed, chewed her bottom lip, then made a few more notes. He noticed when she was focused, she could shut out everything, including his constant complaints, which were obviously falling on deaf ears.

Tired of himself, he got up and fixed them sandwiches for lunch.

"Hey," he finally said, hollering to her from the kitchen.

"Yes?"

"Lunch."

She stood and came into the kitchen. "Really? You made lunch? I could have done that."

"You were working. And I can throw a turkey sandwich together. Though yours is without the turkey. Hope you don't mind avocado and all that vegetable and grass stuff."

She laughed. "I love avocado." She sat at the table and took a bite, then made a moaning sound that made his balls quiver. "Oh, you have mad sandwich-making skills. Thank you. I was getting hungry."

"You were working away in there."

She swallowed and nodded. "I have big plans for you."

His shoulder winced in response. "Great."

"You're going to like it. I promise."

He doubted it. "The only thing I'm going to like is when the Rivers put me back in the starting rotation."

She took a bite of her sandwich and studied him like a science experiment. She was no doubt pondering new ways she could tear his shoulder apart. He finished off his sandwich, trying not to watch her watching him. He had to admit it unnerved him.

"Why don't you tell me how you got hurt?" she asked.

"I'm sure all that crap's in my chart. You read it, didn't you?"

"Yes, but it's not the same as hearing it from you. I want to know what you were doing, what you remember about your body mechanics. We want to make sure you don't reinjure yourself when you hit the mound again."

He shrugged. "I was pitching."

"What pitch?"

"A slider. I reared back, threw the pitch, and felt a pinch. After that, I was sore."

"But you didn't come out of the game right away."

"No. I finished the inning."

"And pitched another after that."

He grimaced, remembering the leadoff walk, the base hit, and the three-run home run before the coach pulled him from the game. It had been a nightmare. He knew his shoulder was hurt, knew he'd been throwing nothing but shit and there'd been nothing on his fastball. But when the pitching coach came out after the base hit, he'd promised the coach he still had it, that he could get the next batter out.

Nothing like pitchers and their egos. They never wanted to admit defeat. But this had been different. He was hurt and he knew it, and he still continued to pitch. And it had cost his team.

"Coach should have pulled you. And even worse, you should have told them you were injured. You cost the team three runs because of that."

It was like she was reading his mind. "Wow, you don't pull any punches, do you?"

"I don't see any reason to blow smoke up your ass when you know it's the truth. One of the things I try to work on with athletes is reading the signals of your own body. When you're injured, your recovery time can be a lot quicker if you step down as soon as you feel pain."

He rolled his eyes. "Oh, come on, Alicia. If I stopped pitching every time I felt an ache or a pain, I'd be out of the game."

"Don't feed me that line of bullshit. You know the difference between discomfort, fatigue from overuse, and 'Oh, no, I've really hurt myself.' You knew it that day, didn't you?"

He didn't answer.

She leaned back, obviously confident that she was right. "That's what I thought. You didn't want to come out of the game, which is normal. I understand that. My brother and cousins are hardheaded like you. They play injured. You all do. It's part of your psychological makeup as athletes to think you're impermeable. But look where are you now. You missed the second half of the season with this injury. You're lucky the tear didn't cost you your career."

Irritation bristled through his nerve endings. "Not the first time I've heard this lecture, you know."

"I'm sure it isn't. But it might be the last time if it doesn't sink in. How many more times do you think that shoulder's going to take this kind of abuse? You've got a rocket arm and a wicked fastball. Tears like that develop scar tissue, and a repeat of an injury like this will end your career."

Well, she'd painted that picture in big fucking letters on a clear blue sky, hadn't she? The doctors had at least sugarcoated it for him with smiles and positive thinking, told him he'd be back in the rotation in no time at all.

Only he hadn't been back in the rotation, and all these months later he didn't feel like he'd ever be ready to pitch again.

And the opening of the season was bearing down on him like goddamn Armageddon.

"Any more soft words of encouragement you'd like to give me?"

She pushed her plate to the side. "Come on, Garrett. You didn't choose me because I'd pat you on the head and tell you how awesome this was all going to be. You chose me because you knew I'd be blunt with you, just like I was that first day. And the one thing you can always count on from me is honesty. I'm also going to force you to be honest with yourself, and that means recognizing how important it is to learn to read your body's signals."

"I hate being pulled from a game."

"Of course you do. You're an athlete and a damn good pitcher."

"But I fucked up that day, and it cost me my arm."

She gave him a smile. "Not permanently. We're going to fix it, and you will pitch again. I believe it. Now you have to believe it, too."

After lunch, Alicia disappeared, claiming she needed to make some calls. Garrett went outside and took a walk on the beach to clear his head.

Reliving the day of his injury hadn't been a picnic. He never wanted to think about it, because when he did, it made him realize what an arrogant asshole he'd been that day.

He should have walked off the mound as soon as he knew he was hurt. Instead, he thought he was invincible, that he could save the inning, save the game, and that nothing could stop him, not even the pain.

What a fucking dumbass he'd been. He'd let down his team and screwed himself over in the process.

He'd always had to learn lessons the hard way.

Alicia was right. He had to do better about listening to his body, because he never wanted to go through this again.

When he came back in after his walk, she was waiting for him. She'd pulled her hair into a ponytail and slipped on tennis shoes. She had a gym bag slung over her shoulder.

"Going somewhere?"

"*We're* going somewhere. Go change."

He cocked a brow. "Into?"

"Comfortable workout clothes."

What now? Burying him in the sand and making him sweat? Maybe stringing him up somewhere or stretching him out on one of those medieval torture racks? She could get pretty inventive. And scary. "Where are we going?"

"You'll find out when we get there."

He changed, and they got in the car. He turned to her. "Where to?"

"The baseball stadium."

Now that he hadn't expected. Dread and excitement churned in his stomach. He started up the car and headed down the highway toward the stadium. Spring training was underway, and he wasn't part of it. God, he really wanted to be.

"The team's not here today, you know," she said as he pulled into the empty parking lot. "They have an away game."

He turned off the ignition. "I know the schedule." He knew every game, where the team was, who they were playing, and the fact he wasn't playing with them. With every passing day he felt the season slipping through his fingers. Spring training had been underway for a while now. And he was missing it. He counted down the days until the start of the season. That had always been his target date to get back on the mound. Now that date was breathing down his neck like an ugly beast—shadowing him every damn day and making him lose sleep at night.

She grabbed the bag and they went to the door. They showed their credentials to the guard, who let them into the stadium.

When they stepped onto the field, his stomach twisted and he broke out into a sweat.

Alicia took a baseball glove and ball out of her bag. Garrett's heart leaped in his chest.

"What is that?"

"My glove. A ball. Kind of obvious, don't you think?"

She pulled his glove out of her bag and tossed it to him. He frowned. "Where did you get that?"

"From your coach."

He hadn't brought it along, figured they wouldn't get far enough for him to need it.

"I thought we'd play a little catch today."

He arched a brow. "You play catch."

"Of course."

"Like the kind of catch a pitcher can throw at you?"

She laughed. "You're not ready to throw a fastball yet, stud. We'll take it slow to begin with, then start working on your mechanics."

She moved behind the batter's box and waited. Garrett stared down at his glove, then over at the mound.

"Well?"

He shifted his gaze to Alicia, who was throwing the ball up in the air and catching it in her glove.

"Let's warm up that arm," she said, then tossed him the ball.

Instinct took hold and he caught it, then walked to the mound. He stood on the mound, the palm of his hand curled around the ball, his target a short ninety feet away. Everything was so familiar yet felt so fucking alien to him. Where he'd once felt so comfortable—the pitcher's mound was like a second home to him, after all—he now felt like he'd never stood here before. Like this was his first time.

In a way, it was a first time. It would be the first time he'd throw a ball since he got hurt, since he'd felt that twinge of pain that had blossomed into something bigger and threatened to sideline his career.

Sweat rolled down his brow. He swiped at it with the back of his sleeve and focused on Alicia waiting patiently for him to toss her a simple, slow, underhanded pitch. She didn't know, had no idea how goddamned monumental this moment was.

Or maybe it really wasn't a big deal at all. He was making more out of this than it was.

Just throw the fucking ball, dumbass.

"Everything okay out there?" she asked, her voice light and easy, but he knew she was concerned.

"Fine. Just getting . . . my head organized. I'm a little rusty."

"Take your time. I'm in no hurry."

It had been a hot day like today—only the heat of summer and in Cleveland—when he'd reared back and thrown the slider that had started it all. He flipped the ball around in his hand, remembering that day like it had been yesterday instead of months ago.

"It's just catch, Garrett. No pressure."

It was more than catch. This was his future, his career. If he couldn't do this, something simple like this . . . it was over for him. He squeezed the ball in his hand, frozen, unable to move.

"You want to try it again another day?" She started toward him.

He straightened, held out his hand. "No. Just gimme a sec."

She stopped, then nodded. "Sure."

He'd never pitch again if he didn't throw—if he didn't at least try. She was right. It was just catch.

He swallowed, or tried to—his throat had gone sand dry.

He was sweating, and his goddamn legs were shaking, but he held his head up and nodded. "Okay."

"No pitches yet. Don't put any finesse on the ball. Just toss it to me. Start underhanded."

"What? This isn't softball."

"I know that. But we need to warm up your arm, including all those muscles and tendons that haven't gotten use in a while. We'll throw a few underhanded, then we'll move on from there."

Not exactly the pitching clinic he was looking for, but it was a start.

He took a shaky breath and tossed the ball—underhanded—to her.

"How did that feel?" she asked.

"Girlie."

She rolled her eyes and threw the ball back to him. "Good. Throw me a few more girlie pitches."

He did, his arm not as stiff or sore as he expected. And it didn't hurt.

"Can I throw one overhanded now?"

"No. I'll let you know when."

Frustrated, he threw more pitches. Underhanded. Weakly. Twenty-six more times until his teeth were clenched so hard his jaw hurt.

Alicia finally nodded. "That's good. Now throw one over-handed. Gently. I can't stress the word *gently* enough, Garrett."

"So you want me to rocket a fastball so hard into your glove that I'll knock you on your ass?"

She leveled him with a glare. "Not if you want to pitch this year."

He finally relaxed his shoulders and smiled, some of the tension lifting. "You have no sense of humor."

"Not when I'm working, I don't. Gently."

She'd even lowered her voice when she said the word, as if he was so dull witted he didn't understand the concept. He hadn't gone through months of grueling rehabilitation to fuck it up with one throw. He rolled his shoulder, which felt good, then threw the ball overhanded. *Gently*.

It didn't hurt. Goddamn, it didn't hurt to throw a ball, even if he had thrown it like a pussy.

"How did that feel?"

"It felt fine."

"No twinges or sudden sharp pains?"

"None at all."

"Good. Do it again. Easy, still."

Excited, he threw again, doing his best to follow her instructions and keep his throw as soft as he could. No pain.

They lobbed the ball back and forth for about fifteen minutes, until Alicia told him they were taking a break.

Frustrated, he walked off the mound toward her. "I was just getting warmed up."

She reached into her bag for two jugs of water. "It'll be a short break."

They sat in the dugout and Garrett took several swallows of water, staring at the mound, anxious to get back out there.

He turned to her. "I want to throw a pitch. A real pitch, Alicia."

Alicia shook her head. "You're not ready yet."

"We're already in spring training. And I'm missing it. I threw the ball and felt fine."

She lifted her gaze to his, and he saw the understanding in her eyes. "Tossing a few balls ninety feet isn't the same as the mechanics of pitching, and you know it. Those weren't even warm-up pitches. There was no velocity to them. We're just stretching your muscles right now, getting your arm used to throwing again."

Disappointment ate away at him. He stared at the mound, a place that suddenly felt a million miles away.

"How soon can I pitch?"

"We'll go back out there in a few minutes, and you can throw again."

"I mean pitch. A curve, a slider, a changeup."

"And a fastball?"

"Yeah, that, too." He was itching to really throw some heat, see how it felt. He missed pitching.

"Sooner than you think."

"That would mean today. My arm feels fine."

She stood and tucked the water into the bag. "Your arm isn't ready today. Let's go throw some more."

He wanted to argue, and when he got to the mound, he wanted to take a windup and blast a heater into her waiting glove.

Logically, he understood what she said made sense. Rushing his recovery could hurt his progress. But damn if it didn't take every ounce of restraint he had to pull back and lob those weenie balls.

But as he continued to throw, he began to see the wisdom in her approach. After thirty minutes his arm felt fatigued. He didn't want to quit, because, sonofabitch, he wasn't even throwing pitches. They were playing catch and nothing more.

But Alicia had some kind of freaky sixth sense. She approached the mound, the ball in her hand.

"I think that's enough for today. Let's go back to the house and ice you down."

He didn't want to admit defeat. "I can go a little longer."

"No, you can't. That's enough for today."

Without waiting for his next argument, she pivoted, left the mound, and packed up the bag.

Game over.

He'd gotten back onto the mound. He'd thrown a ball.

But it sure as hell felt like a loss today.

FOURTEEN

ALICIA HAD READ THE DEFEAT ON GARRETT'S FACE after they left the field.

She'd thought he'd be excited to get out there and throw again, but she didn't factor in that he wanted to pitch—real pitches—or how much not being able to do so would devastate him.

When he'd first taken the mound, she'd read the fear on his face, and for a while there she'd been afraid he wasn't going to be able to muster up the courage to even lob balls underhanded. But he had. And then she'd seen him fired up and excited, and she'd been excited for him. Until he found out he wasn't going to be able to throw his standard pitches. Then he'd been pissed off. She understood his frustration, but she also knew what was best for his recovery, even if he didn't.

Men and their egos. It was bad enough that so much of what a man considered his self-worth was tied to his penis. There was also the not-so-small matter of career. Sex and career were the deal breakers. Lose the ability to perform either one of those, and it spelled doom for a man—at least in his mind.

She was fairly certain, though it was a guess and likely a fantasy on her part, that Garrett was a master in the sex department. His career, on the other hand? That part was still up in the air.

She would have loved to let him pitch today. She'd seen the game films. Hell, she'd been to the games and watched him. Garrett was magnificent. He had a sneaky slider and a wicked fastball. She wanted to see him throw that heat again.

But he wasn't ready yet. Deep down, she knew he was aware of that, but she hated seeing the disappointment on his face.

He was going to be ready soon. His arm had moved easily today, and he hadn't exhibited any signs of pain. It wouldn't be long before they could start easing into throwing actual pitches.

But he wasn't going to be patient, which meant she was going to have to encourage him and give him a realistic plan so he'd get on board and not try to rush things. She knew he was impatient, and the last thing she wanted was for Garrett to suffer a setback. That could destroy him.

After stowing her gear, she went into the workout room to take off the ice pack she'd put on Garrett's shoulder. She stopped at the doorway, struck by the sight of him reclining on the cushioned futon, his back against the wall. His legs were stretched out, his eyes closed, just the right amount of stubble peppering his jaw, which of course drew her focus to his mouth.

That stubborn set to his jaw was also part of what made him so sexy.

She'd like to straddle him and put her lips to his, taste that mouth, just to see what he'd do. Then she'd rock against him and find out how long it would take him to get hard.

Realizing she'd taken her visual fantasy down to his crotch, she snapped herself out of her dirty daydream, shocked to discover his eyes had opened. He was watching her with a full-on look of hunger that sent a stab of desire to her core.

She'd spent a very sleepless night reminding herself that he was a patient, she was his therapist, and she was going to stop fantasizing about him or thinking about him in any personal way.

That resolution hadn't lasted long, had it?

Some rock you are, Alicia.

She cleared her throat and walked in, keeping her focus about a foot above his head. "I think you've cooled down enough." She reached for the ice pack, but his hand snaked up and wrapped around her wrist, forcing her to look down at him.

"I'm not cooled down."

She sat next to him and laid her hand on his shoulder. It was cold from the ice pack. "Are you feeling pain?"

His lips curved. "Yeah, you could say that."

"Tell me where it's hurting."

"Right where you were looking when I caught you staring at me."

Her eyes widened, and she started to pull away, but his hand on her wrist stopped her. Mortified, she tried to jerk away again, but he held her still.

"Why are you fighting this? It's what we both want."

She finally looked at him. "I don't want it. Let me go."

He released her wrist, and she walked out of the room, feeling like a coward.

Because he was right. She did want him. So damn much her body throbbed all over. She went into her room and shut the door, climbed onto her bed, and laid her face in her hands, feeling ridiculous for running away.

She wasn't some scared teenager who didn't know how to have a conversation with someone of the opposite sex. And she certainly wasn't a virgin. She should have stayed and had a rational talk with Garrett, explaining the obvious conflict of interest. That her career was more important to her than satisfying her sexual urges and that he needed to spend his time focusing on his recovery, which had to remain his number one priority. And that whatever she might want—or he might want—it wasn't going to happen.

It was so easy to play the conversation out in her head after the fact. It was so simple. After all, as soon as she'd said no, he had let her go. It wasn't like he was being difficult. Garrett of all people understood the importance of one's career. He'd get onboard with this. He might want her, but he'd deal with the fact that nothing was ever going to happen between them. It was simple and logical. He was a man. Men weren't emotional. He'd get it.

Armed with new resolve, she slid off the bed and went in search of him, finding him in the kitchen, foraging in the refrigerator.

"Garrett."

He didn't look up. "Yeah."

"We need to talk."

"I'd rather eat. I'm starving." He closed the refrigerator, then looked over at her. "I want a steak. I can fix one of those tofu things for you. Maybe with a baked potato and salad?"

She vaguely registered his list of menu items. "Uh, yeah. Sure. But we need to talk."

"We can talk over dinner, when my stomach isn't growling. I'll fire up the grill. How about you make the salad?"

He walked out of the room and left her standing there, her fiery prepared speech wilting as fast as her confidence.

Maybe he'd gotten past it quicker than she thought.

Or maybe he felt rejected, his feelings were hurt, and he was hiding it from her by pretending the conversation in the workout room hadn't happened. That's probably how she'd deal with it.

But he was a guy, and she was a woman, and women were emotional, so she had no idea what he was really thinking.

Shit.

DINNER WAS . . . UNREMARKABLE. OH, THE FOOD WAS
fine, but Alicia barely remembered eating it.

Refusing to let the conversation she intended to have with Garrett be pushed to the side, she'd made a list in her head of all the
points she wanted to discuss with him.

After dinner, though, just in case it resulted in upsetting him.
No sense in ruining the meal.

And okay, she was stalling because it was going to be uncomfortable. But at some point tonight the two of them were going to
talk.

When they finished, they did the dishes. She'd no more than
hung up the dish towel when she turned around to find Garrett had
disappeared. She flipped off the light and found him flopped on
the couch channel surfing. Alicia hovered nearby, ready to crawl
out of her skin. She made some notes about today's pitching
session until Garrett finally found a movie and stopped flipping
channels.

She grabbed a glass of wine and fished a few pieces of chocolate
from the bowl on the coffee table, all the while watching. And waiting. And waiting some more.

She didn't want to interrupt his movie, but it was an old one,
and she was certain he'd probably seen it before.

Now was the time.

"Garrett."

He ignored her. She tried again. "Garrett."

He frowned. "Yeah? What?"

"We need to talk."

His gaze jerked from her to the television and back again. "Can it wait? I'm watching this movie."

She sighed. "Sure."

An hour and a half later, she'd polished off two glasses of wine and more chocolate than she'd intended. She'd also read half a book and the movie was over. Garrett grabbed a drink and resumed channel surfing.

Oh, no. This wasn't happening. He couldn't avoid her forever. She moved over and grabbed the remote from him.

"Hey. I was—"

"Avoiding having a conversation with me."

He rolled his eyes. "Fine. What do you want to talk about?"

"What happened earlier. In the workout room."

"Nothing happened. You made it clear you didn't want anything to happen. I'm no rocket scientist, Alicia, but I hear the word *no* when it's stated."

"Okay. That's good, and I appreciate it."

"But you know as well as I do that the *no* from your lips isn't what your body is telling you."

She shuddered in a breath. "What I want and what I'm going to have don't have to be mutually inclusive. I'm your therapist. This is my job. You're my patient. Your recovery is paramount. Getting involved with each other would alter our client/patient relationship and might end up hurting both of us—professionally and personally."

He stretched out on the sofa, looking lazily sexy. "We don't have to get 'involved,'" he said, using air quotes around the word. "But we can ease some tension and have fun at the same time."

"I take sex very seriously, Garrett."

He pushed off the sofa, coming over to her side. His breath was warm on her cheek as he tucked one of her curls behind her ear. "Oh, believe me, Alicia. So do I."

Oh, God. She shouldn't have said that. "That's not what I meant."

His gaze roamed over her face, his eyes meltingly sexy, his lips just a fraction of an inch from hers. "Then tell me what you meant."

She swallowed, her throat so dry she could barely speak. Her heart pounded so hard she could barely hear, her carefully formed list obliterated by Garrett's close proximity. She laid her hand on his chest to push him away, but the solid feel of him tempted her in ways she could no longer deny. She clutched his shirt in her hand instead, her nails digging into that solid wall, testing and teasing. She wanted to scrape her nails across his bare skin as he pounded relentlessly into her.

"Alicia."

His voice, his breath, whispered across her cheek.

She lifted her head to look at him, moistened her lips, and like an animal tracking prey, his gaze followed.

"I love my job, Garrett. I won't do anything to jeopardize it. You know what the risks are for both of us if we get involved."

"I would never do anything to jeopardize your job. If this isn't what you want, I'll back away."

"You have to think about your career, about your recovery."

His gaze narrowed. "I'm so fucking tired of thinking about it. It's all I've thought about for months. I want to shut it down for a while and think about something else, like holding a beautiful woman in my arms."

Alicia shuddered. Torn between knowing she shouldn't and wanting him so badly she vibrated with the need for him, she didn't know what to do.

She swallowed, her whole body consumed with hunger for him.

She was tired of this battle she had no hope of winning. The only option was surrender.

"Dammit, Garrett."

He cocked a brow. "Is that a yes or a no?"

She fisted a handful of his shirt and hauled him closer. "Kiss me."

FIFTEEN

"I'LL TAKE THAT AS A YES."

Tight with tension, Garrett breathed a sigh of relief, then took
her mouth in a kiss he felt like he'd been waiting months for.

Her lips were sweet and moist and he sank into the kiss, sliding
his tongue between her lips to taste her.

She tasted like wine and chocolate—sweet and sexy, just like he
knew she'd be. His cock sprang to life, hardening as he pulled Alicia across him, folding her into his arms to deepen the kiss.

Her body was perfect against his. He'd been dying to touch her,
to run his hands over her hips and legs. She'd changed from her jeans
into a pair of cotton shorts, and her thighs were buttery smooth as
he caressed her. Garrett wondered if her chest was as tight as his, if
she found it as hard to breathe as he did.

He never went crazy over a woman. He liked them, and he
loved having sex with them. Fortunately, there were always plenty
of women around, and he was lucky enough not to have to work

hard to get one into his bed. That was mostly due to the allure of his career and his success, and he knew it. But Alicia was something different, and she had been since the first day he'd noticed her in the pack of therapists all claiming to know what was best for him. Despite the ugly uniforms, he'd picked her out, liked her smart mouth, and being with her the past few weeks had only increased his desire for her.

And now that he had her in his arms and she was winding her hands in his hair, moaning as he rubbed his lips against hers? Yeah, that was the jackpot.

That she was torn about doing this with him only ratcheted up his desire for her. It was wrong that her internal battle fed his hunger, and he knew it, but there wasn't a goddamn thing he could do about it. He wanted her, and she'd said yes. Unless she changed her mind, he was going to touch and kiss and lick every inch of her tonight, because short of his goal to return to the pitcher's mound, she'd been all he'd been thinking about.

She shifted, and her scent wound around him. Whatever it was she showered or shampooed with drove him crazy, and whenever they worked together he found some way to breathe deeper. She sifted her fingers through his hair, letting her nails massage his scalp as she leaned into the kiss, her breasts rubbing against his chest.

Her touch was a magic balm to his sore shoulder, and every ache seemed to melt away when she laid her hands on him. He knew the difference between a medicinal touch and one meant for sex, and when Alicia touched him now, there was a tenderness that had nothing to do with therapy.

Or maybe she'd always had that magic touch, and he'd been so wrapped up in his own head he'd never noticed. All he knew was he shared some kind of connection with her. Maybe that was basic chemistry. He didn't want to define it. He just went with it, and what he knew was he liked her hands on him, in whatever way she touched him.

He pulled away, loving the way her eyes had changed. She was always so . . . in control. Now, her eyes were half lidded, drowsy from passion, and her lips were plump from kissing. Her hair was messy, and desire was written all over her face. She had no control now, and he liked her that way.

If someone could bottle that look and sell it on the open market, they would make billions, because nothing could rev a guy up faster than a woman who looked at a guy the way Alicia looked at him now. She made his balls tighten, and he wanted to throw her down on the sofa and bury his cock deep inside her until she screamed his name.

"Change your mind yet?" he asked, rimming her bottom lip with the pad of his thumb.

She shook her head. "No."

"Good. Because we're all in now, so if you want to stop, now would be the time to tell me."

She let out a soft sigh. "Don't stop."

He drew the strap of her tank top off her shoulder, then the other, leaving them at her elbows. There was something about a half-dressed woman he found so sexy. He leaned in and pressed a kiss to the side of her neck. She shuddered.

"Cold?" he murmured against the soft column of her throat.

"No. Just keep doing that."

"This?" he asked, flicking her earlobe with his tongue.

"I'm pretty sure I'm going to like anything you do with your mouth."

He growled out a laugh. "I hope so, because my mouth is going to be all over your body tonight."

She held tight to his shirt, clinging to him like she was afraid she was going to fall. He liked that he could drive her crazy.

And they hadn't even started yet. But they were about to. He kissed his way across her shoulder, taking a little nip out of her skin, feeling the goose bumps pop up there. He was unable to resist a smile. Her body was so responsive; he couldn't wait to get to all the good parts.

He drew her tank top down. Her breasts were contained in a very hot black and pink satin bra that made his cock tighten. A matching checkered bow sat in the center of the bra.

He lifted his gaze to hers. "My guess is the panties match."

She looked down at him and graced him with a wicked half smile and a nod.

"Let's take a look." He dropped to his knees and grabbed her shorts, then pulled them off, sitting on his heels to admire the view. "Wow."

"Stop it," she said.

"Alicia. You're beautiful."

Especially when she got those two bright spots of color on her cheeks, adding to the overall effect of her slender body, small breasts, and beautiful long legs. Her dark hair, a little mussed, spilled over her shoulders, one curl teasing her right breast. He spread her legs and nudged between them, easing closer so he could play with that curl, teasing the swells of her breasts with it, watching them rise and fall with her heaving breaths. And when he bent to kiss the mounds, she let out a short gasp.

He lifted his head, studied her. She was breathing rapidly. "How long has it been for you?"

She took her bottom lip between her teeth, obviously deciding whether or not she wanted to tell him.

"About a year."

He arched a brow. "That's a long time."

"I've been busy."

He laid the heel of his hand against her pussy. Her mouth

opened, and she moaned. "You should never be too busy to have sex."

"I didn't say I haven't had an orgasm."

He rubbed his thumb over her clit, soaking in her soft moan. "Giving them to yourself isn't the same as having someone do it for you."

"Don't I know it."

"I'll take care of you tonight, Alicia. I'll give you as many as you can stand."

OH, GOD. GARRETT WAS GOING TO KILL HER, AND SHE was going to be dead before she could ever come. The way he talked to her in that low, sexy voice, making promises about giving her orgasms . . . She could die on the spot. Or just climax from his voice alone.

She pushed aside all reservations, that annoying voice in her head that told her they should be concentrating on Garrett's recovery, that she was being unprofessional. She'd likely suffer a major guilt crisis—tomorrow.

Tonight, she was going to have him, though right now he was having her, drawing circles over her sex with his fingers. And he hadn't even taken her panties off yet. Her body pulsed and she lifted her hips, arching toward the center of that pleasure.

All he had to do was keep rubbing her, and she'd come. It would be so easy. She was pent up and ready. After all, she'd been thinking about him, fantasizing about him, aching for him. It wouldn't take much to send her right over the edge. Her body was an inferno, a tight knot of pent-up nerve endings just waiting to burst. A few caresses from his magic fingers and she'd get there.

Instead, he moved his hands over her hips, her belly, the intensity only getting worse as he rested his fingers on her rib cage, his gaze roaming over her body as if he'd never been with a woman before, when she knew damn well that wasn't the case. But she had to admit, she liked the way he looked at her. It caused her breasts to swell and her sex to coil with need.

And when he rolled his hands over her breasts, she bowed back, offering them to his questing hands.

With one deft move, he released the clasp at the front of her bra and pulled the cups aside, baring her.

"So pretty," he said, leaning forward to take one bud between his lips.

Watching her nipple disappear in his mouth was torture, the sensation arcing like hot lightning between her legs. She tingled all over, and she never did that.

Then again, she never did a lot of things, like fantasize about a man, invade his privacy by watching him get off, or jeopardize a patient's recovery by getting personally involved. And she'd done— was doing—all of those things. It was like she was in some other woman's body, a body she'd lost all control over.

And she'd given over control to Garrett, who masterfully pulled on her nipple, eliciting gasps she had no hope to hold back.

He let her nipple slide out of his mouth and lifted his gaze to hers, giving her the kind of wicked bad-boy smile that made her quiver in anticipation. And when he buried his head between her breasts and began a slow trek down her body with his tongue, she knew whatever he was offering, she wouldn't want to miss a moment of it, no matter the consequences.

"You smell so good, Alicia," he said, murmuring against her stomach as he snaked his tongue out to tease her navel.

She sighed, watching as he eased toward the top of her panties and pressed a kiss to her hip bone.

"I like your mouth there."

He lifted his head. "You're going to like my mouth a little lower in a minute."

"How about now?"

His lips curved. "Impatient?"

"Yes."

"Good. I want to make you scream."

She was about to . . . from frustration. Anticipation built, making her stomach knot. His breath wafted warm over her belly, and when he pressed a kiss to the top of her sex, she nearly bolted off the couch. She was wet, throbbing, and embarrassingly close to an orgasm, and he hadn't even put his mouth on her yet. This slow seduction was making her lose her mind.

But he had all the control here. She didn't want to be rude and demand he lick her pussy, but damn, it had been a really long time. And now that she had decided to do this with him, she wanted it right now. She didn't need finesse and slow seduction, she needed a goddamn orgasm.

So when he peeled her panties down her legs, she released a sigh. And when he cupped her butt and swept his hand over her thighs, she bit her bottom lip, hoping he wouldn't laugh when she came so quickly. Because she knew she would. She was already tingling, could already sense that he was going to be so—

"Oh, Garrett. Yes." He put his mouth on her, his tongue hot and delicious as he found her clit. She fought the trembling, but the sensations were overwhelming. And damn if he didn't have the most expert lips and tongue she'd ever felt, all warm and wet, knowing exactly where her hot buttons were. He didn't poke or jab, just lazily sailed along, swirling around her sex like he had all day, just the way she liked it.

She lifted, feeding her pussy to him, and when he slid two fingers inside her, she could already imagine what it was going to be like when he fucked her. Her imagination had gone there before, and when he began to move his fingers and sucked on her clit, she flew, her orgasm slamming into her with all the force she'd expected—and then some.

"Oh, I'm coming," she cried, bucking against his face with unabashed pleasure.

Garrett replied with a hum against her pussy and buried his fingers inside her as she rode out the wild pulses, licking her through the most intense orgasm she'd had in a very long time. He held her, his mouth firmly clamped to her sex, while she rocked against the pulsing waves that seemed never ending. When it was over, she felt light-headed, spent, yet still wanted more.

He took her down easy, kissing her hip bone and belly as he moved up her body, bringing her back by lingering at her breasts, using his thumbs to tweak her nipples, which fired her body to life all over again.

This had just been an appetizer. She was ready for the main course.

She was ready for Garrett.

SIXTEEN

FEELING ALICIA'S HEART POUND NEXT TO HIS CHEEK
was sweet satisfaction for Garrett.

She'd been so responsive, her body like a live wire as she'd bucked against his mouth when she came. He'd loved listening to her, tasting her, feeling her body shudder against him. But they were just getting started, and he intended to rev up her heart rate all night long.

He stood, then grabbed her hand and pulled her off the sofa.

"Let's finish this in the bedroom."

Before she could say anything, he scooped her up into his arms.

"I can walk, you know."

He grinned at her as he carried her down the hall. "And ruin my chance of playing your knight in shining armor?"

"I'm more worried about your shoulder."

He gave her a look. "If I can't carry someone as lightweight as you, I might as well retire."

"Okay, fine. I'm not hurting your shoulder. But this is a little . . . provincial."

He kicked the partially ajar door open and deposited her on the bed. "You're ruining my moment, Alicia. You're not big on romantic gestures, are you?"

She sat up on the bed, and he had to admit he liked seeing her naked. She had a beautiful body. And those long legs that he couldn't wait to feel wrapped around him.

Just the thought of being buried inside her had his cock straining against his sweats.

She graced him with a soft curving of her lips. "Sorry. It was very romantic. You should get naked now."

He let out a laugh. He had to give her credit for being practical and to the point. She didn't need to be swept off her feet or wined and dined. She wanted sex. So did he. That made this whole thing a lot easier.

And damn, was she ever a sexual creature. Going down on her gave him a lot of pleasure. She was responsive and hot, and she tasted so good that as soon as she came he wanted to take out his cock and plunge inside her.

But there were some things a guy really did need to finesse, and the first time with a woman was one of those things. So whether she liked it or not, she was going to get the best he had to offer.

Starting with him getting naked. He yanked off his shirt, then shoved his pants to the floor. Her eyes gleamed and she smiled appreciatively.

He climbed onto the bed.

"I have a confession to make," she said.

He swept her hair behind her ear. "Yeah? What's that?"

"I saw you last night. On the beach. When you were jacking off."

His lips curved. He liked the idea of her watching him. "You did?"

"Yes."

"What did you think?"

Her breath came out in a soft pant. "What did I think? It turned me on."

He pushed her back on the bed and laid his hand on her stomach. Her skin was so soft; he wanted to touch her all over. He snaked his fingers upward, teasing the tight points of her nipples. "Yeah? Did you do anything about it when you watched me?"

"Yes. I slid my hands in my panties and touched myself."

His cock twitched at the visual of her watching him, being so excited by what she saw that she had to dip her hands inside her panties to touch herself. "Did you get off?"

Her breathing deepened. "Yes."

"Show me."

She gave him an off-kilter smile. "Well, I'm not wearing panties right now."

He gave one of her nipples a teasing pinch. "Smart-ass. Show me how you touch yourself. You got to watch, but I didn't. Though I have a confession of my own to make."

Her lips parted, her breaths coming faster as she slid her hand between her legs. His balls tightened as he watched her spread her pussy lips to tease her sex. "What kind of confession?"

"The afternoon you locked yourself in your room and got yourself off? I was at the door listening."

She gasped but not in outrage. She lifted her hips and swept her fingers over her clit. "You listened? I tried to be quiet."

"Not quiet enough. I walked by and could hear you breathing. Not just regular breathing or I'm-having-an-asthma-attack breathing, but I'm-sexing-myself-up breathing." He covered her hand with his. "Trust me, babe, I have radar that tells me when a woman is on the verge of orgasm."

She sighed. "Good to know. And did you enjoy yourself?"

She was wet, and he coated his fingers with her, sliding them over her plump lips. "I got hard thinking about what you were doing in there. Listening but not being able to see you drove me crazy. I had to use my imagination."

When he slid his fingers inside her, she let out a whimper. He pressed his cock against her hip and rocked against her, the need to be inside her nearly breaking him.

"And what did you do after?"

"Later that night, I went into my room and jacked off."

She lifted her hand and wrapped it around his aching dick. "Another missed opportunity."

He pushed her hand away, using his thumb to circle her clit. Alicia raised her hips and he knew he could make her come. But this time, he wanted to be inside her when she did.

"I think it's time we do each other instead of ourselves," she said. "I want your cock inside me."

He couldn't agree more.

"I like the way you think, Alicia." He rolled over and kissed her, diving into her mouth like he was starving for a taste of her. She met his kiss with a fervor that drove him between her legs, the tip of his cock hovering near the entrance to her pussy.

It would be so easy to plunge inside her right now. But he jerked away and reached into his nightstand for a condom.

Alicia licked her lips, her body quaking with anticipation as she watched Garrett roll the condom on. He laid one hand on top of hers, wound their fingers together, and inched inside her.

"I like the way you talk to me," he said, his voice low and dark, coiling around her belly and making her tighten with need. "I like that you're honest with me, that you tell me what you want, what you think about, what you need."

"What I need? This."

He buried himself deep then stopped, his cock pulsing.

"You're what I need, too, Alicia. Everything I've needed ever since I met you." He swept her hair away from her face. "You feel good surrounding me."

She clenched around his cock, his words causing her belly to tumble.

She expected him to give it to her hard and quick. She'd come in a hurry, she knew it. Instead, he eased out then inched back in again, a slow, deliberate torment that made her feel all of him, every sensation, as if they were making love in slow motion.

Taking it leisurely like this destroyed her. A fast, furious fuck would have been emotionless. Like this, his gaze riveted to hers, was so intimate, took so much from her. More than she was willing to give. She closed her eyes and just felt, letting each stroke carry her to a place where nothing mattered but the incredible sensations threatening to drive her to the brink and over.

"Alicia. Look at me."

She couldn't. It was just too damn good, and she was already in over her head. She hadn't expected this. Not with Garrett, and not so soon.

But when his lips brushed hers and he took her mouth in a kiss that was so deep her toes curled, she wrapped her legs around him and squeezed his hand.

"Open your eyes," he whispered against her lips. "Do this with me."

She sighed, then lifted her lids.

His eyes compelled her. So clear, so filled with desire and a hunger that matched hers. She shouldn't be a coward, but he asked for so much. And when he pulled back and thrust again, ever so slowly, she let out a shaken gasp, sure he was going to own her in ways she'd never let anyone possess her before.

This slow, intimate lovemaking tore her apart. She wanted fun and sexy and raunchy, not this tenderness, this ease with which he slipped through her defenses and made her want to scream his name and burst into tears.

He leaned down to lick her nipples, taking long, slow sips while moving with deliberate intent inside her, shredding her with every thrust, taking her closer and closer to the climax she knew was going to be monumental.

"Garrett."

His name fell as a whisper from her lips. He kissed along the column of her throat, eliciting goose bumps along the way to her mouth. He kissed her again, still holding her hand, and when he rolled against her, levering his hips so she'd get the right amount of friction, she tightened.

"That's it," he said, the desperation in his voice inflaming her need. "Let go, Alicia."

She panted, raised her hips, and matched his movements, daring him to fuck her harder, to make this less personal. But still, he ground against her, giving her bone melting sensations that were meant to make her explode.

She held back, until he brushed his lips across hers and she met his gaze again.

"Trust me," he said. "You aren't in this alone."

He knew. He felt it, too.

She let go.

He watched her come, and she let him. She knew she gave him so much in this orgasm, revealed so much, but she wasn't able to stop herself from letting Garrett have this level of intimacy. And when he began to thrust hard, plunging in and out of her in rapid succession, he gave her everything in return, meeting her gaze with fierce abandon as he rolled through his own climax. She gripped his hand and held tight to him as he shuddered. She had never felt so connected to anyone before.

He finally collapsed and buried his face in her neck, but even then he continued to kiss her throat, and never once let go of her hand.

As she came down, one thought continued to spin through her head.

What just happened?

She was wasted, thoroughly spent, and surprised as hell that it had been so emotionally intimate.

Sex was always physical and fun, but she had an emotional connection to Garrett that shocked her. And when he rolled over, he pulled her against him. She felt the strong beat of his heart.

He hadn't yet said anything, and she wasn't about to. Not about this.

She was also lying on his injured shoulder.

She lifted her head then pushed away to sit up. "Am I hurting you?"

"My shoulder's fine, Alicia." He grabbed her and drew her close. "Lay your head on me and stop fussing over me."

She was being overly concerned, she knew. She knew his capabilities and his limitations. Lying on his shoulder wouldn't hurt him. Maybe she was searching for distance, especially after that— she had no idea what the hell had just happened between them. Certainly whatever it was had been something she'd imagined. It had been awesome sex, that much was certain. But it hadn't been epic or anything.

Except that it had been epic. And monumental.

And that's all it had been. Just really great sex. He hadn't rocked her world or anything.

Other than like an earthquake.

This was ridiculous. She needed to get her mind off sex with Garrett and back to reality, which meant the first thing she had to do was get out of bed. Cuddling up naked next to him let her mind wander into dangerous places, like imagining him as some kind of sex god. Which he certainly wasn't. He was just an average—okay, make that above average—lover.

She sat up and slid to the edge of the bed.

"Where are you going?"

She could barely meet his gaze, but she was no coward. Might as well face the situation, so she looked over at him, trying to keep her expression light and easy. "Back to my room."

He arched a brow. "Why?"

"To sleep."

Now he grinned. "Do I smell?"

She laughed. "No."

"Was the sex bad?"

"Oh, God, no. It was really . . . wow, it was amazing sex, Garrett."

Now he smiled, stood, and came over to her side of the bed. He pushed her back on the bed then climbed in after her. "I thought it was pretty fucking good, too."

He pulled the covers over both of them, then tucked her in against his side.

Alicia stared out at the moonlight and took a deep breath.

"But I really should sleep in my own bed, Garrett."

"Why?"

She opened her mouth then closed it.

Hell if she could come up with a good enough answer for him.

"I give up. I don't have any idea."

"Good." He tugged her against him. "Because if you sleep with me, I can do this." He rocked against her, his cock hardening again. A rush of desire flooded her body, her nipples tightened and her pussy quaked. When he cupped her breast and slid his cock between her legs, she arched back to rub her butt against him.

"Now that's going to give me ideas."

She laughed. "You already had ideas."

"True." He rubbed his thumb over her nipple, making her gasp as pleasure bloomed.

He licked her earlobe, then her neck. "I want to fuck you this way. Open for me, Alicia."

Already eager to feel his cock inside her again, she lifted her leg while he put another condom on. He was back in a hurry, this time sliding inside her with one thrust.

Their coupling was passionate and furious as she ground against him while he pistoned his cock deep, fucking her with fast, hard strokes that made her crave an orgasm. When she reached between her legs to rub her clit, Garrett slowed down his thrusts.

"Make yourself come. Let me feel your pussy squeeze the come right out of me."

She loved the low, dark tone of his voice. It spurred on her movements and brought her ever closer to the climax she was seeking. And when Garrett pulled her onto her knees, she went willingly. She dropped her chest and head to the mattress, and raised her butt in the air, letting him drive his cock deep into her, needing him inside her as far as he could go.

She swept her hand over her clit while he pounded her with his cock. He gripped her hips with his fingers, the pain and pleasure combined sending her spiraling over the edge.

"Garrett, I'm coming," she cried, her pussy squeezing his cock like a vise as she felt the rush of her orgasm.

"I'm going to come in you, Alicia," he said, his fingers digging into her as he slammed his cock deep, then shuddered against her. He wrapped his arm around her, and they both fell to the mattress as they rode out their orgasms.

Alicia caught her breath as Garrett rolled them over, then got them a washcloth and towel to clean up.

"Thanks," she said with a smile.

"You made me sweat," he said. "You're always making me sweat."

"Uh, you're welcome. Or I'm sorry."

He brushed his lips across hers. "No apologies for that sweat session." He kissed her deeply, so deeply her toes curled.

She felt light-headed and ridiculously content.

GARRETT LISTENED TO THE SOUND OF ALICIA'S breathing and felt her body as she nestled against him in bed.

She was tense. A couple of orgasms should have taken care of that tension, but apparently being in bed with him made her anxious.

It took her about a half hour to fall asleep. Her body finally relaxed and her breathing became deep and even.

But she'd struggled with falling asleep. It hadn't come easy for her.

Maybe he should have given her another orgasm. She needed to loosen up a little more. After all, she hadn't even wanted to sleep with him.

Maybe he wasn't as good as he'd like to think he was.

But he knew that wasn't the case. He liked to watch her come, and damn, had he liked feeling her come when he was inside her. That slow burn had been agony for him, but worth every second. A fast fuck was always fun, and he'd really needed to get off, but he'd loved feeling every inch of her, her pussy clenching around his dick, tightening around him every time he slid deep inside her.

His cock hardened as he thought about what it felt like to be connected to Alicia that way.

He'd fucked a lot of women in his lifetime, but he hadn't made love to very many. Hell, hardly any. He wasn't much for deep emotional connections. They only got in the way of having a good time. But there was something about Alicia that begged for more than just a fast fuck, and like it or not, he was into her.

He knew it couldn't last. She was his therapist. There was already a conflict of interest, and eventually, they'd have to part ways. But tonight they'd had a hell of a good time, and he wanted more of it. So while they were working together, they could also play together.

Because they'd just gotten started, and he wasn't nearly finished yet.

And hey, sex was good for recovery. Something about orgasms and increased blood flow to healing tissues or something, right?

He'd discuss that with his therapist in the morning.

He smiled and closed his eyes.

SEVENTEEN

ALICIA HAD SLIPPED OUT OF BED BEFORE DAWN,
wanting to get up before she and Garrett woke up together. Avoiding the inevitable awkwardness was always best, and despite sleeping with him last night, this was the light of day, and she was much more clearheaded now about where things stood.

She didn't regret what had happened between them. She was an adult and had made an adult decision. She hadn't been coerced, she'd walked into sex with Garrett more than willingly. Which didn't mean it was going to be repeated. Falling into a relationship with him—sexual or otherwise—would be a huge mistake. Her job was to focus on his recovery, and that meant getting him on the pitcher's mound. That was her number one objective, and she couldn't allow herself to get sidetracked. She had a schedule to stick to, and spending days—or nights—playing with him could be disastrous to that timeline. Which wouldn't be good for his career or hers.

She was hoping he'd see it the same way this morning. He was probably like a lot of guys when it came to sex. One time was great, more than that meant a relationship. Surely he was more interested in getting back to work than having repeat sex performances, right?

She went into her room to take a shower. When she dressed and came out, he was nowhere to be found. That gave her a reprieve, so she made some coffee and grabbed her notebook. She was in the dining room charting some notes when Garrett came inside from his run.

She chanced a quick glance at him as he headed into the kitchen. His back was turned to her as he reached into the cabinet for a glass to pour his orange juice into. His arms were glistening with sweat, his hair wet from the run. He wore shorts and a tank top and as he leaned against the counter, she could still remember what it felt like when he was moving inside her last night.

Her body responded with a tight coiling. She pushed the feeling aside and focused on her treatment plan.

"I woke up alone this morning."

She squinted her eyes shut. She was kind of hoping he'd want to avoid the topic. Obviously not.

"Yes. I woke early and didn't want to disturb you."

He came over to the dining room table and sat across from her. "It was warm in the bed. We could have taken up where we left off last night."

Her nipples tightened, her body all over that idea. It was still early. The bed was probably still warm.

No. She wasn't going there. *They* weren't going there, and it was best she suck it up and have this discussion with him now. She lifted her gaze to his. "You know that's not a good idea."

He grinned. "Since when is sex not a good idea?"

"Are you really going to make me be the bad guy here?"

He finished off his juice and set it on the table. "I guess I am.

Because I don't see anything wrong with what we did last night. Or with continuing it today. We both had fun. Nobody got hurt." He moved his arm around. "Even my shoulder survived."

She resisted the urge to smile. "It's not a good idea. Your primary goal is pitching. Not having a sexual relationship with your therapist."

But he did smile. "Oooh, you make it sound dirty when you say it that way."

She rolled her eyes and stood, then headed into the kitchen to make breakfast. Garrett disappeared, which allowed her to exhale and get her riotous libido under control. She might have mentally resolved that she wasn't going to have sex with him again, but her body hadn't yet come to grips with that decision. So it was going to take a little time and probably more than a little mental fortitude.

She never had one-night stands. She'd always had relationships. This time, it would be a one-night stand. They'd had great sex, she'd gotten the release she'd needed, and now she could move on. She was totally over it. She was strong, and she could take working close to him. Touching him and not having him would be hard.

Just like he was hard—his body was hard—and she'd like to glide her hands over him and . . .

"Here, Alicia, let me—"

She almost dropped an egg on the floor as Garrett scooted in next to her to help her cook.

"I can do this."

"No reason for you to be my cook when I'm perfectly capable." He cracked the eggs over the pan then started scrambling.

"I'll do the bacon, then."

"Sure."

She laid the bacon in the other pan, and they worked side by side. She tossed bread in the toaster while he grabbed orange juice. It was companionable. She was conscious of him, of his body brushing against hers in the confined space. Every time he touched her she wanted him to grab her, push her up against the counter, and kiss her like he had last night.

Yeah. She was over it all right. He had taken a shower and he smelled like soap—clean and delicious—and she wanted to lick him all over, then wrap her hand around his cock and slide him inside her. She was practically vibrating just thinking about it.

She couldn't handle it. His scent, his body close to hers, was driving her crazy. She still wanted him. Last night had just been a sampling, and she wanted more.

She moved away.

"I don't bite, you know," he finally said. "Well, I do bite. You might like it."

She leaned against the counter. "I can't do this."

He frowned. "Do what?"

"This. You and me. Last night was a mistake and we both know it."

"I don't agree." He moved in closer, and she backed away.

"I'm serious, Garrett. I'm serious about getting you ready to pitch and I can't do that and . . ."

"And what?"

"And have sex with you."

"Why not?"

"Because I have to focus. I have to think about you as my patient, not my lover. I have to be detached and clinical, not emotionally involved. I just can't."

"Okay."

"Have you got this?" she asked him while not looking at him. "I'll be right back."

"Sure."

She pushed away from the stove and left the room, needing a

few minutes in her room to compose herself. She shut the door and paced, her arms wrapped around her middle.

That hadn't gone well.

This was ridiculous. She was a hands-on therapist and it was going to be impractical to dash out of the room every time she got within a few inches of Garrett.

Time to suck it up and deal, Alicia. You made this bed.

More like she'd unmade the bed.

She inhaled deeply then went back to the kitchen.

"Breakfast is ready," he said.

"Great. Thanks."

They filled their plates and ate in the dining room. Alicia was happy for the space between her and Garrett, though she knew that was only going to last as long as breakfast, because after that they had therapy. At least he seemed content to stop talking about what happened between them last night.

After they ate, she did the dishes. Garrett said he was going into the workout room to warm up, while she lingered a little too long over scrubbing the skillet.

She finally gave up. It was time to do some therapy, so she grabbed her notebook and headed into the workout room.

Garrett was on the bench press. She laid her notebook down and went over to him.

"You shouldn't do these without me being here."

He paid no attention to her, so she laid her fingers under the bar while he lifted the weight.

"This is a heavier weight than you normally lift."

Again, he didn't answer her, but he didn't seem to be straining, so she let him go, but she still stood above him to spot him. He did twelve reps, and she helped rack the bar when he finished. He sat up and leaned over to take some deep breaths.

"How did that feel on your shoulder?"

"It felt fine." He tilted his head back to look at her. "I'm not having any pain."

"That's good. But don't add weight without consulting me."

He arched a brow. "You think I don't know what I can handle?"

"I think you have a therapist for a reason. How about you let me be the therapist, and you be the patient?"

"I think you laid out the ground rules about who was who in this relationship pretty clearly earlier," he said. "I don't need you to draw me a picture, Alicia. I got it."

He stood and went to the pulleys, then waited for her. The room temperature seemed to have dropped about ten degrees, the chill between them evident.

Okay, she could deal with this.

When she came over and selected a weight, he said, "Your weights are too light. Add more."

Now he was acting like a patient. A surly, frustrated athlete. That she could wrap her head around. That she could deal with. As long as she focused on Garrett as just another athlete, she could keep it impersonal.

She looked down at her notes and shifted the weight by five pounds. He tilted his head and gave her a look. "Come on, Alicia."

"Start there. Do twelve."

He blew out a breath and did twelve. Easily.

"See? No problem. Now add more."

She added another five, and he did twelve more. Also without effort. She had him do two more sets, then came up behind him and felt his shoulder, digging in deeply to see if he tensed with pain.

He didn't. That was a good sign, so she put him through a more rigorous workout, adjusting her notes as he went about the circuit. He was making drastic improvement, but she'd see how he felt at the end of the day. Pushing the muscles and tendons was one thing while he was doing the workout. It was the aftereffects that concerned her the most.

She really wanted him to pitch, however, he needed to rotate that arm. That was going to be the true test of whether he was going to get through this injury or not.

But she liked what she saw. And she wanted to see more.

After weights, she'd run him through his therapeutic exercises, pushing him harder than she had previously. He'd taken it without complaint. Then they'd each had a sandwich, sharing the kitchen space—not in an unfriendly way, but not in a particularly friendly way, either.

So after lunch, she said, "Let's go pitch."

The only reply she got to that was a shrug, followed by him walking away to get ready.

Distance was good, right? This was what she'd asked for.

On the drive over to the ballpark, he was silent. Okay, so some guys didn't appreciate being dumped. Not that she was exactly dumping him since they were still going to see each other every day.

That was the problem with working together and sleeping together. It never worked out. Not that she'd ever slept with a colleague or, God forbid, a patient before. She'd always kept her work life separate from her personal life, vowing to never mix the two. She'd always figured that was one complication she didn't need.

She should have stood by that vow. Garrett had to trust her. They had to be partners in his recovery. How was that going to happen with this added tension between them?

She pushed that quandary aside and got him up on the pitcher's mound, repeating what he thought were the same warm-up underhanded pitches from yesterday, following up with some soft overhand pitches.

She could tell he was bored and frustrated, and she needed to challenge him. His recovery was going well, and she wanted to know

now before they got any further what his pitching mechanics were going to be like.

She held the ball in her hands. "Now, get into your windup, but don't throw hard. Just loft one over, but throw a little harder than what we've been doing. And I don't mean serious heat. Just a little faster."

He stared at her. "I think I got it, Alicia. I don't need you to draw me a road map."

Oh, yeah. He was irritated. She got into the normal catcher's stance, squatting down and prepping to receive a pitch.

"Would you like me to give you a signal?"

"Funny." He paused, wound up, then threw her a hard ball that smacked into her glove. It stung, but she'd taken pitches from the pros in rehab before. She knew it was going to hurt.

She stood. "How did that feel?"

"Fine." He waved at her with his glove. "Get back down there and let me throw some of my other pitches."

"Okay. Again, no serious velocity on these."

"Yeah, yeah."

He burned the next five pitches into her mitt, and didn't once pull up or wince like he was having any pain.

She caught the last ball and stood, pulling the ball out of her glove. "Your form looks good. How did those feel?"

He stepped off the mound. "Like I could pitch at least six good innings."

She smiled and met him halfway. "Good. Let's throw a few more, but still not too hard."

He nodded, took the ball from her, and stepped back on the mound. They went at it for about forty-five minutes, and he did what she asked, using correct pitching form but not throwing too hard. Alicia kept watch to be sure he wasn't favoring his right arm or giving off any signals that he was having pain. When he threw what she thought was enough pitches, she stopped him.

"That's enough for now."

Again, he didn't complain, just tossed her the ball and left the mound, content to grab a bottle of water and cool down.

"How's the arm?" she asked as they climbed into the car.

"It's good. A little sore, but I'd expect that after not pitching for so long."

"We'll ice it down when we get back to the house. Then I'll massage you."

"Okay."

He was being uncharacteristically cooperative. And businesslike. Which was exactly how she liked her patients to be. But not how her relationship with Garrett had been since they'd met. Now there was no banter, no easy conversation. She'd effectively shut that all down with her dismissal of them and the relationship they'd begun.

Admittedly, she missed it, but this was how it was supposed to be, how it must be. He was obviously coming to grips with the fact that they weren't going to have a personal relationship. If that made her feel sad and empty—tough. It was exactly what she wanted, so she might as well get used to it.

She laid her gym bag on the floor when they got back to the house, then turned to him. "Ready for some ice?"

He shrugged. "Sure."

"Come on. Let's go into the workout room."

He followed her into the room. She was conscious of him behind her, watching her as they headed down the hall. She wanted to turn to him or wait for him so they'd walk side by side, but she didn't. Instead, she kept walking until they were inside the room. He walked right past her and to the cushioned bed where he stretched out and waited for her.

Ignoring the pang in her stomach, she retrieved the ice pack from the freezer, wrapped it in a towel, and brought it to him.

"Ten minutes," she said.

He grabbed his music player and slipped in his earphones. "Got it."

He'd tuned her out, deepening that ache in her stomach. She walked out of the room and hunted down her notebook. She set a timer and began to chart today's notes in Garrett's file.

The ten minutes passed much too quickly. But when she went into the workout room, she found only the ice pack lying there. Garrett was nowhere to be found. She loaded the ice pack back into the freezer and left the room.

Thinking Garrett had gone into his room, she walked out into the hall, but his door was open. She peeked her head in. He wasn't there.

"Garrett?"

He didn't answer, and she didn't hear the shower running, so she went out back and found him standing at the edge of the sand staring out over the ocean. She walked outside and stood at the edge of the deck, watching him.

What a picture he presented in his bare feet, shirtless, the sun beating down on him while the wind blew his hair. She wondered what he was thinking as he stood there examining the waves. It had been a rough day, both physically and emotionally. Was he thinking about that, irritated with her, or just pondering the future of his career? Was he thinking about her?

She'd definitely thought a lot about him today, about more than just his shoulder.

She'd had his body last night, had felt every rock-hard ridge and plane. He'd been inside her. He'd tasted her and had made her come—more than once. They'd just begun mapping each other's bodies, and no matter how much she talked the talk about professionalism and how they should stay away from each other, the bottom line was, she felt cheated. There was so much more she wanted to know, to find out about Garrett, his wants and needs, what turned him on and what got him off.

She gripped the edge of the railing, desire igniting inside her like a flash fire. She blazed hot for Garrett. No man stirred her as quickly as he did. Just one look, one thought, and she was consumed. All rational thought fled, and every wall she'd so carefully constructed throughout the day crumbled around her.

He was right. What difference did it make if they had sex? She knew her job, knew what it would take to get him ready to pitch. She could do her work efficiently and the two of them could still have a smoking-hot sexual relationship.

She'd be insane to walk away from something like this. She knew he wasn't looking for a girlfriend. He had his career to resume once his rehab was over with. That would consume all his time. And she sure as hell wasn't looking for a committed relationship. She was building a career that had been her primary focus for years.

So they both worked for the same team. It wasn't like she was going to be engaged with him on a one-on-one basis after he finished his rehab and the season started. Unless he was injured, they wouldn't have much contact at all. She could protect her job, and no one would ever know about the two of them.

She was an adult. So was he. They could manage their sexual relationship. She could manage it.

She kicked off her shoes and stepped off the porch.

EIGHTEEN

A STORM WAS COMING. GARRETT HAD BEEN WATCHING the clouds gather, darkening the sky and shifting the atmosphere from bright and sunny to ominous and gray.

He knew the feeling. His own mood had darkened throughout the course of the day. But that was on him. Not on Alicia. He knew she was out on the deck watching him. He didn't turn around, didn't go to her, figured if she had something to say she'd come talk to him.

He'd kept things professional between them today. That's what she asked for, and he knew her job was important to her, so he did his best.

It was hard. Hell, she made him hard. He'd be lying to himself if he didn't admit he wanted more of her, and a lot more of what they'd had last night. But if she didn't want that he'd have to respect it.

The problem was, he knew she was torn, and it would be easy

to get her to change her mind. He could be persuasive if he put his mind—and his charm—into it. But that would make him an asshole, and he'd like to think he wasn't one. So he backed off and kept things between them business only. If he had to go through this therapy thing with a throbbing hard-on, that was his problem. Eventually, he'd get over it.

Besides, he had bigger problems to deal with than whether or not he'd ever get Alicia in the sack again. Like getting himself on the pitcher's mound. It was time he started concentrating on that.

So when he caught sight of Alicia stepping off the porch and coming toward him, he figured she was going to drag him inside and perform some kind of stretching torture on his arm. He turned to face her, waited for her to say something.

She didn't. A strong gust blew in from the ocean, slapping strands of her hair across her face. She didn't bother to push them away. Her gaze was fixed on his, and he read the intent in her eyes. He recognized that heat, because it had been boiling inside him all day long. Her desire crashed into him with a force stronger than the wind.

He didn't understand the sudden turnaround. He could question her, especially since she'd been the one to put up the wall between them. Now she was tearing it down?

But he realized he really didn't give a shit why she'd changed her mind. He only needed to know one thing.

"You sure about this?"

"Yes."

She didn't hesitate, and he wasn't going to ask again. He swept his hands over her cheeks and pushed her hair away, then slanted his lips over hers, needing his mouth on hers. There was no figuring this out—whatever it was between them that drove him crazy, and probably her, too.

He only knew he wanted her with a primal force as strong as the wind slamming them into each other. He drew his arm around her waist to hold them both steady. And when the first raindrop smacked him on the cheek, he broke the kiss, grabbed her hand, and they ran like hell toward the house as the skies opened, drenching them in the short distance to the deck.

Alicia lifted her gaze to his. Her hair was plastered to her head, her tank top was molded to her chest, and droplets of water slid down her body. He'd never had desire gut punch him like it did right now.

Lightning arced across the sky as thunder clapped around them, shaking the foundation of the house. The skies had grown so dark it was like night. The rain came down so hard he couldn't even see the water anymore. The force of the storm mixed with his hunger for her, and he pushed her against the wall of the house and fixed his lips to hers.

She met his kiss with equal force. Maybe it was the weather, the storm bringing out primal desires. And maybe he just wanted her that much. He lifted her shirt and swept his hand across her stomach, felt the ripples in her muscles as he wound his arm around her so he could draw her closer to his body. She moaned against his mouth, tugged at his bottom lip with her teeth.

He growled in response, his need for her fierce as he pulled her wet shirt off and undid the clasp of her bra. There was no one outside, no neighbors within viewing distance. Even if there were, no one could see anything in this driving rain anyway. Alicia didn't seem to care as she helped him peel the rest of her clothes off, then his.

Fed by the storm, the two of them stood outside, leaning against the porch, their wet bodies steaming as the rainstorm cooled the air around them. He didn't care, but she had goose bumps. He wrapped his arm around her and used his body to shield her from the wind, his lips and hands to give her heat. He grasped her breast in his hand, using his thumb to graze a nipple already hardened from the wet and cold.

She shuddered and wrapped her tongue around his, sucked it into her mouth, and nearly brought him to his knees. He groaned and pulled his lips from hers, gazing down at her face. Her lips were trembling.

"I need to be inside you," he said.

She lifted her gaze to his. "Yes. Now."

If it wasn't for the lack of a condom, he'd have driven inside her right there—on the deck in the pouring rain. But he took her hand and pulled her inside the house, both of them dripping wet as they dashed toward the bedroom. He turned on the shower, waited until the water was steamy hot, and pulled Alicia inside, shoving her under the spray.

"Get warm," he said. "I'll be right back."

He grabbed a condom and set it on the shelf, then met her in the shower. Her eyes were closed, the water pouring over her head. She opened her eyes and smoothed her hair back, then reached for him.

He stepped into her arms, his body chilled to the bone. But her breasts against his chest and her mouth on his heated him up fast. She met his lips in an eager kiss that made him shudder, and it wasn't from the cold. He smoothed his hand down her back, remembering what it felt like to hold her body against his last night.

It hadn't been enough then, and now, he mapped her curves as he moved his mouth over hers, wondering what it would take to get his fill of her. Steam enveloped them, and she wrapped her hand around his cock, stroking him with gentle, fluid motions, making him ache to be inside her.

He backed her against the wall and slid his hand between her legs. She was so soft, like the petals of a flower. He wanted to be gentle, but she dug her nails into his arms in response, her body quivering as he began to ease his hand back and forth across her sex.

"Oh, God," she said. "Yes, just like that, Garrett. Put your fingers inside me and make me come."

He loved that she talked to him, told him how to give her pleasure. And despite how fragile she felt under his hand, she demanded more than just a gentle stroke. He increased the pressure, resulting in her low moan, which tied his balls into knots and made his cock twitch. He leaned into her, rubbing against her as he moved his fingers and rolled the heel of his hand across her sex, giving her what she asked for.

"Ohhh," she said, tilting her head back as she shattered against his fingers, her pussy clamping tight around him. Her lips fell open, her nails scoring down his arm as she tilted her pelvis toward his thrusting fingers while she rocked through her climax.

He reached for the condom wrapper, tore it open, sheathed himself, then spread her legs. "Do you know what it does to me to watch you come?"

She swallowed, then licked her bottom lip. "Tell me."

"My balls tighten up like a fist, and my cock gets even harder. It makes me think about nothing but what it's going to feel like to be inside you, fucking you with long, slow strokes."

Even with the water beating down on them, he heard the short, panting breaths she gave him in response. "Yes. I want that. I thought about you all day, Garrett. I missed your body against mine."

He raised her arms above her head and slid inside her pussy. She moaned against his lips and wrapped one leg around his hip, drawing him deeper.

Damn, it was good to be this close to her, to feel her nipples rub against his chest as he pumped inside her. He twined his fingers with hers and wrapped his tongue around hers, grinding against her until she tightened around his cock, squeezing him.

He tilted his head back, watching the way her eyes widened whenever he pushed deep. He reached between them and found her clit, wanting her to go off and take them both into orgasm.

"Yes, touch me there," she said, twining her hand around the nape of his neck to bring his mouth back to hers. "Make me come again."

He kissed her deeply as she tightened around him, her whimper of satisfaction spurring him to thrust deep and join her in her orgasm. He swept his arm around her waist and held her while he shuddered and spent himself inside her.

He caught his breath, still feeling her pussy grip him with pulses from her climax.

"You kill me," he said, resting his forehead against hers.

"I'm hardly a bundle of energy here."

He laughed. They washed, got out of the shower and dried off. When Alicia started to head out of the room, he grasped her hand and tugged her into his bed.

"Do you have some problem sleeping with me?" he asked. "Do I need to tie you to my bedpost?"

She arched a brow but settled in next to him. "Intriguing idea. I didn't know you had that kind of kink in your repertoire."

"There's a lot you don't know about me, Miss Riley."

She swept her hand over his arm as he cuddled in close to her. "Is that right? Do tell."

"Stay in my bed and you might find out."

She didn't move. Instead, she wriggled her butt against him and made a contented hum.

He'd call that a win. For tonight, it was good enough.

THROWN BY A CURVE

with hers and wrapped his tongue around hers, grinding against
her until she tightened around his cock, squeezing him.

He tilted his head back, watching the way her eyes widened
whenever he pushed deep. He reached between them and found her
clit, wanting her to go off and take them both into orgasm.

"Yes, touch me there," she said, twining her hand around the
of satisfaction spurring him to thrust deep and join her in her orgasm. He swept his arm around her waist and held her while he
shuddered and spent himself inside her.

He caught his breath, still feeling her pussy grip him with

NINETEEN

AFTER THE PREVIOUS NIGHT'S STORM, THE DAY
dawned sunny and dry, with just a hint of a cool breeze.

Alicia figured today was a great day to play golf since she'd challenged Garrett earlier and told him she was a better-than-average
golfer. Plus, it added variety to his therapy and would be a good way
to work his shoulder.

Waking up in his bed this morning had been strange. And exciting, especially the way he roused her before dawn with his hand
caressing her breast and his hard cock nestled between her legs.
They'd made love slow and easy, until it had become more heated,
and Garrett had pulled her on top of him to finish them both off.
Then they'd showered together, laughing as they washed each
other, then dodged flying suds during a soap battle.

All in all, not a bad way to start the day.

Now, on the eighteenth hole of the golf course, she was in therapist mode, watching Garrett's every move. His swing was easy and he hadn't once seemed to tighten up or wince. A very good sign.

"How are you feeling over there, champ?" she asked as he teed up.

He shifted his gaze from the ball to her. "You trying to throw off my concentration?"

She leaned against the shaft of her club. "You're ten strokes ahead of me, asshole. I don't have a chance in hell of beating you, so I don't think distracting you is a viable strategy for me."

He gave her a sexy grin, then turned and took his shot, a nice, straight arc that landed in the middle of the fairway.

Prick.

She took her tee shot, a decent one, but it had nowhere near the distance his had. They grabbed their clubs and went to find their balls.

By the time they arrived at the putting green, she had a good opportunity to make par. Garrett was about six feet from the hole with a fair chance of hitting a birdie shot.

Which he missed by barely an inch.

"Fuck," he said, then tapped his ball in for par.

She missed hers and bogeyed the hole. "Ditto," she said.

They ordered lunch in the clubhouse.

"You were right," he said after taking a long swallow of iced tea. "You're good."

"It wasn't even close to being my best game," she said, taking a sip of soup, "but I haven't played in a while. You're good, too. How does your shoulder feel?"

He rolled his shoulders. "Surprisingly good, considering I haven't played golf in a couple of years."

"That's a great sign. Golf is good therapy for you, now that you're healing so well. You should play more."

He speared his salad and took a bite. "You should play with me."

"You're not good for my ego. I need to play with someone I can beat."

"Wuss. Suck it up."

She laughed. "Next we have to do your therapy. Then we'll see who the real wuss is."

"You'd persecute me like that after I just put my shoulder through eighteen holes of golf?"

"It is my job, you know."

"And you enjoy it so much."

"I do."

He gave her a mock glare over the rim of his glass. "I think there must be a little sadist in therapists."

"You think?"

She expected there to be some tension between them, uncomfortable silences. And maybe that was on her—her own fears about what she thought might happen after she slept with him.

There was none. They'd had a fun morning and were at ease with each other.

So much for her worries.

When they got back to the house, she washed up and changed into her workout clothes. Garrett was in the gym when she got there, sitting on one of the benches, ice pack already on his shoulder.

She leaned against one of the machines. "Doing my job for me now?"

He looked down at the ice pack then back up at her, giving her a knowing smirk. "I think I'm familiar enough with the routine now."

"Is that right? Maybe you don't need me anymore."

"Oh, I need you, all right. I have an ache."

From the look he gave her, she knew exactly what kind of ache he was referring to, and it had nothing to do with his shoulder.

Heat speared her, need coiling low in her belly. She came toward him. "Is that right? Tell me where you hurt."

He put his hand between his legs. "Right here. Do you think you can do anything to make me feel better?"

She straddled him, the hard ridge of his erection pressing up against her quivering pussy. "Oh, I can definitely make you feel better."

He grasped her hips and rocked her against him, drawing her quivering pussy against his shaft. She licked her lips and laid her hands on his chest. "I could come like this," she said, her voice lowering as desire flushed through her nerve endings.

Garrett figured there was nothing better than a beautiful woman getting herself off on his cock. Having Alicia writhing fully clothed on his lap had gotten him from semi-hard to fully erect in a matter of seconds. He'd been thinking about her while he'd put on the ice pack. She'd looked hot today on the golf course. He'd never found golf sexy at all until he'd played with Alicia. She was competent in her swing, and it didn't hurt that she'd worn those capri pants that showed off her toned calves. Plus, he let her walk ahead of him so he'd gotten an awesome view of her great ass as she moved with confidence through the course.

Who knew that golf would get him hot? But having her sit on him like this was definitely melting the ice pack on his shoulder.

He shrugged off the pack and drew Alicia against him for a kiss that rocked him all the way to his balls. She was fully into it, slipping her fingers into his scalp to tug on his hair. It gave him chills and made his cock as hard as the metal bars he lifted here in the gym.

But then she moved away from him and dropped to her knees.

"Slide your legs over," she said, looking up at him.

He sat forward and swept his legs over the side of the bench, laying his feet flat on the floor. Alicia shouldered herself between them, then tugged on his sweats, drawing them and his boxers down and off.

His balls tightened as she grabbed hold of his cock and began to stroke it from base to tip, never once drawing her gaze away from his face. He leaned down and kissed her again, brushing his lips against hers, coaxing her to open for him. Her lips trembled, her excitement clear.

God, that turned him on. He dipped his tongue inside, licking and tasting her until she pulled back.

"Let me taste you," she said, rolling her thumb over his cock-head.

He shuddered, then leaned back and laid his palms flat on the bench, giving her access to him. He was riveted, watching her as her tongue slid between her lips. He found himself swallowing, his throat dry as he anticipated her next move.

She licked the underside of his shaft, starting at the base until she got to the tip. Then she covered his cockhead with her lips and flicked her tongue over it.

He couldn't hold back the groan of sheer pleasure. He'd never felt so hard or so ready to shoot a load of come. He ached with the need for it, and when she shifted, then took him deep into her mouth, he let out a curse.

She had him. She owned him, and he'd give her anything as long as she kept sucking him like that, bathing him with her tongue and covering his dick with her sweet, hot mouth.

He swept her hair to one side so he could watch her cheeks hollow as she clamped her lips together and increased the pressure, bobbing up and down on his shaft until he dug his feet into the carpet and held on. Sweat beaded and rolled down his back as he thrust against her mouth.

"I'm going to come, babe," he said, unable to control the thrust of his hips as she sucked him fully into her mouth. "God, you're going to make me come."

He gave her the option of pulling back, but she grasped his shaft and took him deep. Unable to hold back, he held her head and let go, bursting into her mouth as what felt like gallons of come erupted from him, making him shudder and yell out as he came.

He was shaking as he released, and Alicia took everything from him until he collapsed forward, fisting her hair and holding on to her for what seemed like his goddamn life.

She laid her head on his thigh and let him recover. When he could form words, all he could say was, "Christ, that was good."

She tilted her head upward and licked her lips. It made his dick twitch. Damn, she made him insatiable.

"You're killing me, Alicia."

"So, you're saying you don't want to lift weights now?"

He laughed. "Uh, no. But I'd love a glass of ice water."

She got up. "Me, too. I'll go get us one. You should get dressed."

Before she could get away, he grasped her wrist and pulled her into his lap for a deep kiss. "Thank you."

"It was my pleasure."

"Oh, your pleasure is coming."

She grinned. "I'm counting on it."

While he pulled his clothes back together, Alicia came back with two glasses of water and handed him one. He drank it down in about three greedy gulps while she sipped hers.

"You really do need to do a workout, you know," she said.

"I know. I just need a minute to catch my breath. And I don't know, maybe a snack. You depleted all my stores with that blow job."

She snorted. "Toughen up. We're working on your stamina, stud."

"I think you're trying to kill me."

But she did relent, and they had a snack, then went to work on his therapy. He had to admit, therapy was a lot more fun after sex, though his cock kept twitching while he fantasized about all the different ways he'd like to have Alicia in the workout room. She noticed, too, shooting a glance at his crotch and lifting her gaze back to his.

"Exercising with a hard-on doesn't get your blood flowing to the right muscles. I need it in your shoulder—not your cock."

He shrugged as he worked the pulleys. "I can't help it. I keep thinking about bending you over the bench. Or throwing you down on the futon and fucking you."

She gave him a glare, but it was only a halfhearted one. "Well, stop it. We're in work mode now. We can have sex later."

"Is this a work-reward kind of thing?"

"Will it make you stop thinking of sex if I say yes?"

"Maybe. It would help if I could have a little tease right now." He walked away from the pulleys and toward her. Alicia backed away.

"No, Garrett. Work now."

He advanced on her. "Just a little play. Then back to work."

She laughed as he pressed her up against the wall. "I'm serious."

"Oh, so am I. Dead serious about getting my hands down your pants and—"

"So, is this a new form of therapy?"

Garrett turned in a hurry, his throbbing erection dying as he faced the one person he really didn't want to see right now.

His agent—Victoria Baldwin.

TWENTY

ALICIA WANTED TO DIE RIGHT ON THE SPOT. THE WOMAN that had come in and interrupted them was gorgeous and smartly dressed in a business suit, her brown, chin-length hair perfectly coiffed. Alicia felt at a distinct disadvantage, especially being caught by surprise.

"Victoria," Garrett said, obviously not shocked at all that someone had come into the house unannounced. But he did take several steps away from Alicia. "Ever think of ringing the doorbell?"

Victoria gave them a wry smile. "I did ring the doorbell. No one answered. I saw the car and figured you might be at the beach, so I came around back. Your slider was open, so I came on in. I didn't know you were—uh—occupied in other ways." She slanted that smile Alicia's way.

Alicia's face flamed with mortification. She had no idea who this Victoria was, but obviously, it was someone Garrett knew well.

"Well, since you're here—" He turned. "Alicia Riley, this is my agent, Victoria Baldwin. Alicia is my physical therapist. She works for the Rivers."

Victoria walked over, her hand extended. "Very nice to meet you, Alicia."

Oh. His agent. Great. Just freaking great. The last person she wanted to catch Garrett and her nearly having sex in the workout room. She was doomed. "Nice to meet you, too, Victoria. Would you like something to drink?"

Victoria waved her hand. "Don't go to any trouble. I just popped in to check on Garrett's progress. I had no idea I was interrupting something else."

Alicia heated all the way down to her toes. She wanted to disappear into the floor. "It's no trouble. And you weren't interrupting anything. I'll go fix us some iced tea."

They left the workout room and headed into the kitchen. It was obvious Alicia wasn't going to vanish in a puff of smoke and avoid this rather embarrassing moment, so she was just going to have to deal with it.

"So, how's the workout going?" Victoria asked Garrett. "And even more importantly—how's the arm?"

"My arm feels great. Alicia's doing a fantastic job."

"Yes," Victoria said with a wry smile. "It certainly looked that way."

Alicia cringed as she filled a tray with drinks. This was what she was afraid would happen if she got involved with Garrett. She had no idea if they could trust Victoria, but the last thing she needed was Phil or Max finding out she was sleeping with one of her clients.

Doomed. She was doomed. Doomed and fired and disgraced, and she'd never get another job again.

Pasting on a pleasant smile, she turned around. "The tea is unsweetened, so I've put regular and artificial sugars, and some lemon on the tray. You can fix it however you like. Why don't we go into the living room?"

Alicia set the tray down then swiped her sweaty palms on her pants, nervous as hell about Garrett's agent being here. And she'd found them fondling and kissing each other in the workout room. Talk about bad timing.

Alicia wanted to throw up.

Victoria fixed a glass of tea and sipped it, her gaze alternating between Garrett and Alicia, all the time not saying a word. But she was smiling, in an I-know-exactly-what-you-two-are-doing kind of way.

Kill me. Kill me now.

Alicia needed to regroup, put on her professional demeanor, and panic later.

"Garrett's shoulder is showing definite signs of improvement," Alicia said, unable to bear the awkward silence. "He's even thrown some pitches. With no pain. I'm really excited about how well he's performing."

"Is he now?" Victoria arched a brow. "I assume the performance you're referring to relates to his shoulder?"

"Tori." Garrett's tone came out as a warning.

Victoria laughed. "Come on, Garrett. I'm just teasing."

"Alicia doesn't know you like I do."

"It's okay." Alicia hated people talking about her like she wasn't there, and she couldn't handle the suspense. "I'm sure if Victoria has something to say, she can just say it."

"Oh, honey. Whatever you're doing with Garrett outside of working on his shoulder is absolutely none of my business. Garrett and I go way back. I signed him when he was an annoying kid with more attitude than talent."

"Hey," Garrett said.

Victoria ignored him, her focus remaining on Alicia. "And

we've been close ever since. Whatever you have going on is between the two of you. My only interest in Garrett is in how his injury is progressing. I need him back on that pitcher's mound."

Alicia relaxed a little. "My main goal is to get him there."

Victoria nodded. "Good to know." She turned to Garrett. "And you're sure the arm is good?"

Garrett wound his arm around. "It feels great."

He told her about the different types of therapy Alicia had employed since they'd started. "Some of it's been pretty unusual, too, including rock climbing."

Victoria arched a brow. "You got him to rock climb with an injured shoulder?"

Alicia nodded. "It's good for stretching the tendons and muscles. Often someone with an injury will favor that area. My goal is to make him use the arm, and not just with the average therapeutic exercises and weight lifting. I like to do activities like golf, swimming, and even rock climbing. It'll make Garrett use the arm without realizing it."

Victoria actually nodded and looked impressed. "I'm in awe of your talents, Alicia. He's needed someone to kick his ass a bit."

"Just doing my job."

"I hope you do it well. We need to get our guy pitching."

"That's my intention."

"That's all I care about, then."

So why did Alicia still feel so tense? And defensive? And scared to death that everything was about to change? She needed to get a handle on this situation and get her head screwed on straight again.

"You're here to see other clients, too, Victoria?" she asked.

She gave Alicia a smile. "Yes. I have several playing down here. Then I'm off to Arizona to check out a couple of more."

"You must have quite the client base. How many play for the Rivers?"

"Just two. Garrett and new outfielder Raul Hermosa."

"I've heard great things about him. He's got amazing speed and a hell of a throwing arm."

Victoria grinned. "And he's all mine. Well, technically, he belongs to the Rivers now, too, but I nabbed him first."

"He's a good kid," Garrett said. "Gavin said he has a rocket arm and a killer bat. I can't wait to see him in action."

"Then get your ass back on the mound," Victoria said with a wry smile.

Garrett leaned back against the sofa. "I'll be there. No doubt about it."

"You're singing a much different tune than the last time I saw you."

"Am I?"

"Yes. You were mopey and unsure about pitching a couple of months ago."

"I've healed since then. And done a lot more therapy," Garrett said, throwing a glance at Alicia.

"And he's thrown a pitch or two. Now, he's anxious to get out there with his team," Alicia said, feeling a little more comfortable now that the topic of conversation had moved away from her and Garrett, and onto baseball and Garrett's recovery.

"Do you think he's ready for that?" Victoria asked.

Alicia shifted her gaze to Garrett, who looked as hopeful and expectant as Victoria.

"I think he's ready to start working out with the team."

Victoria stood. "That's the best news I've heard today."

"You're worried about my contract," Garrett said. "Or the continuation of my contract."

"That's what you pay me for, isn't it?"

Garrett shrugged. "Yup."

"Well, don't you worry. First, your contract isn't up for a while.

And second, I have every faith in you—and Alicia, here—that you'll be pitching this season, so your contract isn't going to be an issue."

Alicia liked Victoria. She put Garrett at ease about his contract and gave him confidence. The one thing he didn't need was something else to muck up his head.

"Thanks, Tori. You're right. I don't want to be worrying about that shit."

"That's why you have me. And why you pay me so much of your hard-earned money."

Garrett laughed. "You're right there."

"And now I have to get going so I can check on my other guys."

"Already?" Alicia frowned. "You sure you don't want to stay and have dinner with us?"

"That's so sweet of you, but I can't."

"You sure we can't convince you to stay?" Garrett asked. "I can throw some steaks on the grill. It's not gourmet cuisine, but it won't suck."

"You're so sweet. You've cooked for me before," Victoria said. "It was burgers on the grill as I recall, and I don't remember you poisoning me. Sadly, I can't stay. We'll catch up when you're back in town for the home opener." She laid her hand on his arm. "And I'll be expecting you to pitch."

Garrett gave her a grin. "I'll do my best."

"I'm sure you will."

They walked her to the door. Victoria turned to Alicia. "It was nice to meet you."

"You, too, Victoria."

"Work his ass off, okay?"

"I'm doing my best at that every day."

Victoria gave her the once-over. "You know, somehow I believe you really are. And I think he needs someone like you—in more ways than just the rehab."

Alicia had no idea what Victoria meant by that, but she didn't elaborate, just waved and headed out the door.

"Well. She's interesting," Alicia said after Victoria left.

"She's a kick-ass agent. She wasn't kidding when she said she plucked me out of obscurity. She got me my chance with the Rivers when I was just a kid. I owe her a lot. She's a good friend."

Alicia shut the door and leaned against it. "Your good friend almost caught us having sex in the workout room."

Garrett grinned. "Yeah, she did. And she'll be discreet about it, so you don't have to worry about her saying anything to Manny or Max or Phil."

He was like a mind reader. She pushed off the door and followed him back to the workout room. "I'm thinking she was probably concerned I was paying more attention to your cock than I was to your shoulder."

"Believe me, if Victoria had a concern about that, she'd have voiced it. She knows I'm in a much better place now than the last time she saw me. And if she wasn't relieved about how well I was doing, she would have stayed instead of making this a short visit. Then she would have grilled me—and you—for hours about every aspect of my therapy, which would have included conference calls with Max and Phil."

Alicia stopped what she was doing to look up at him. "Is that true?"

"It is. She's thorough as hell where her players are concerned, and she has no problem butting in if she thinks shit isn't getting done. So trust me when I tell you, she has confidence in your abilities, and she doesn't care what's going on personally between us."

She relaxed. "Okay, then."

"Okay, then," he reiterated. "Now, let me ask you a question."

She paused at the pulleys. "All right."

"Am I really ready to start working out with the team?"

She was expecting that question. "I don't say things I don't mean, Garrett. I would have never said something like that otherwise. When the team's back in town tomorrow, we'll start integrating your workouts with them."

She saw the light flash in his eyes, the excitement on his face. She laid her hand on his arm. "I don't want you to get your hopes up too fast, though. You're not ready to pitch a game just yet. This will be just warm-ups and workouts."

"I get that. But I'll be with the team, and that's a move in the right direction. I know I'll be pitching soon enough."

She hoped so, and she hoped her treatment plan was spot-on, because if she disappointed him, or if his arm wasn't ready yet, he'd be devastated. And she wasn't sure he'd recover from that.

TWENTY-ONE

GARRETT LOVED THE SMELL OF A BALLPARK. THE ONE here in Florida wasn't even a major-league park, but it was still a baseball field. The smell of the dirt and the feel of the grass under his cleats as he walked out onto the field reminded him of opening day, of what he'd spent the last eight years preparing himself for at the start of every season.

He'd been so afraid that he was going to miss out on this, that for the first time since he'd graduated college, he'd be left behind and be forced to spend the season sitting in the dugout.

It could still happen, but for the first time, he had hope, and that was the one thing that had been lacking all these months since his injury. At first he'd been scared, and then when his arm hadn't healed right away, he'd been down and depressed, certain his career was over. All the therapy in the world hadn't gotten into his head or kicked him in the ass, forcing him to work for the goal.

Alicia had, though. She'd known what it was going to take for him to get there, to reach for what he wanted, and to really work at it. All the tools had been right there in his grasp; all he'd had to do was put in the effort.

They were far from finished. He knew that. But for Garrett, it was more than just the chance to get back to work. It was being at the ballpark again, surrounded by his peers. And the crowd. God, he loved the fans, the sounds they made, even the boos when he had a bad game.

He'd been isolated for so long that he'd even take a rousing chorus of boos, as long as he could just be here.

Even better, Alicia was here with him, working with him on the sidelines. He might not be throwing warm-up pitches with his teammates, but he was at least throwing pitches today. They still weren't the kind of pitches he wanted to throw, but he had to focus on his recovery and his arm, and not on Walter Segundo, the fiery right-hander who was his fiercest competitor and no doubt a lock to start on opening day.

Walter was currently throwing off the mound and firing bullets into the catcher's mitt. His accuracy was off the charts, and his ERA was nearly as good as Garrett's had been before his injury. Garrett knew he'd been the best pitcher the Rivers had—before he'd screwed up his shoulder.

Would he be that good again? That was the multimillion-dollar question, wasn't it?

"Hey."

He shifted his gaze to Alicia, who was kneeling with a catcher's mitt in her hand. "Yeah?"

"Pull your head out of your ass and focus on me, not on Walter or the other players. You want to be here at the ballpark? Then eyes on me."

He wanted to make a smart remark about how he'd rather have his eyes on her great ass or maybe it would be better if she was naked or several other completely inappropriate remarks, but there were other guys hovering nearby. So instead, he nodded and said, "Yeah. Got it. Focus."

"Good. Throw a slow one at me."

"I've been throwing slow ones at you for the past hour."

"Good. Fling me a few more, and quit whining about it."

He heard the snickers of his teammates, which didn't bother him in the least. It wouldn't be the first time they'd ribbed one another about a workout with a trainer. Hell, if Manny wasn't chewing your ass out on a daily basis, you felt like he didn't like you anymore. Alicia was a kitten by comparison.

Speaking of the Rivers coach, he made his way over to them when the rest of the team took a break.

Alicia looked wide-eyed and terrified at Manny's approach, which amused the hell out of Garrett. He gave her credit for continuing with what she was doing, which was taking pitches from him.

Manny stood and watched for a while, then sauntered over to Garrett.

"I see she's finally got you throwing some pitches."

"Some weak ones, but yeah, I'm finally throwing."

"They look like shit," Manny said.

Alicia looked horrified. Garrett grinned. "Yeah, they do. But it's more than I've thrown since the injury. And my arm feels great."

Manny scrutinized Garrett, then Alicia. Garrett always thought Manny looked like an old grizzled pirate when he gave that squint. Manny finally nodded and slapped Garrett on the back. "Good enough. Keep it up."

When he walked away, Alicia slumped and dropped her glove. Garrett walked down the field toward her then leaned over.

"Are you breathing?"

She lifted her head. "I can't help it. He scares the crap out of me."

"You? The one who stood in the therapy room that day and told me I had my head up my ass, then stood up in front of Manny, your boss, the team doctor, and the entire therapy team and told them all that their method of dealing with me sucked? And you're afraid of Manny?"

She stood, kicked at the dirt. "I had a moment of madness. I didn't know what the hell I was talking about."

"So you're saying you have no idea how to treat me."

She lifted her chin and glared at him. "I know exactly what I'm doing."

When her hackles were raised and she got defiant like that, he wanted to jerk her into his arms and kiss her. It was such a turn-on when she went all fiery and independent. "Good. Then quit letting Manny intimidate you."

She blinked. "You know what? You're right."

"Of course I am."

Alicia rolled her eyes and pointed. "Back to work for you. How's your arm feeling?"

"Pretty good, actually."

"Okay, throw me some harder stuff. And by harder stuff, Garrett, I don't mean a blinding fastball or—"

"God, Alicia. I know what you mean. Put a little more effort into it but not game-situation strength. Just a little harder than what I've been throwing."

She nodded. "Now you're getting the picture."

He turned and walked away. "You don't have to draw me a fucking road map. I'm not a goddamn moron."

"I heard that."

He turned to face her. "I know. That's why I said it loud enough for you to hear."

She crouched down into position. "Are we going to talk all day, or are you going to throw me a pitch?"

More snickers from his teammates. He shook his head, wound up, and threw a pitch just hard enough that Alicia winced when it hit her glove.

That might shut her up for a while. She scowled at him but tossed the ball back without saying a word.

"Not quite *that* hard yet, asshole."

More laughs from the other pitchers, but the laughs were still directed at him.

Good. Just where he wanted them.

GARRETT WAS OFF TALKING TO THE OTHER PITCHERS, so Alicia took a moment to update her notes.

"You look all official and therapylike."

She turned around and smiled at her cousin Gavin, then gave him a quick hug. "And you look all baseball-like. How's it going?"

"Good. How's rehabbing Garrett going?"

"Great. He's coming along."

"So I've heard. Among other things."

Alicia cocked a brow. "Other things."

"Oh, you know. Word gets around pretty fast in a ball club."

Crap. "Tell me what you've heard."

"Some of the guys talking about how easy it is between the two of you, a lot of laughing and . . . things."

"Things? What things?"

"Look. I don't pay much attention to gossip and rumor, you know that. But I did watch you two together today. It's pretty obvious there's some body language between the two of you."

"Body language?" She knew all she was doing was repeating what he said, but she was sinking fast. She had nothing to say in her own defense, so the longer she could delay the inevitable, the better.

"I know it's none of my business, but is there something going on between the two of you?"

There would be no use denying it to Gavin. He'd find out eventually from Liz, who told him everything. "Uh . . . sort of."

Now it was Gavin's turn to raise an eyebrow. "What does 'sort of' mean? This isn't high school, Alicia. There either is or isn't. You know I'm not going to tell any of the guys on the team. You can trust me."

She knew her cousin wouldn't talk. "Yes, there's something going on between us. I just don't know that we've really defined it yet, and I'd really appreciate it if you could do whatever you could to not promote any talk among the other players. I'm rather fond of my job."

"Hey, you know I didn't come over here to get gossip from you."

She nodded. "I know. Which is why I told you."

Gavin looked over at Garrett. "He's a good guy, you know."

"Yes, he is. But my primary focus is on his recovery, not on dating him. I mean, we're not even dating. We're just—"

She gave Gavin a blank look. "I cannot have this discussion with you."

Gavin looked as horrified as she did. "Thank God. Because I do not want to discuss sex with you."

She laughed.

"Good thing Liz is in town," Gavin said. "It might be better if you talk to her about this shit." He pulled off his ball cap and dragged his fingers through his hair. "Why don't we get together for dinner? You can come to our beach house."

"I'd love to see Liz." Then she thought about it. "You're not going to grill Garrett about our relationship, are you?"

"Uh, no. Because then the whole sex topic would come up again, and believe me, that's the last thing I want to talk about with your guy."

Her guy. He wasn't really her guy. Was he? "Okay, I'll talk to Garrett about it and call you."

He kissed her cheek. "Later."

When warm-ups were finished, they stayed and watched the game. She kept her eye on Garrett to see how he reacted to being relegated to watching rather than playing. Fortunately, as a pitcher, he wasn't always in the rotation. He seemed to handle it fine, cheering on the players as the Rivers beat Atlanta, three to two.

He did great, even making his way down to the bullpen to rally the relief pitchers in the later innings while she stayed in the dugout.

While the crowds filed out and the team headed to the locker room, Alicia spent some time with the other sports-medicine folks, catching up on what had been going on. Annamarie was there, the only other female sports-medicine therapist. Alicia and Annamarie had been hired around the same time and had bonded as females in a sea of testosterone. Annamarie was tough and capable and also fairly gorgeous, Alicia had always thought. She had a saucy attitude to go with her Italian/Mexican/German heritage. While Alicia's hair was sort of the same color, the two of them could never be confused. Annamarie's hair was thick as hell, and she often braided it to keep it out of her way. Plus, she had gorgeous olive skin and beautiful eyes and the kind of lush body that couldn't be hidden under the team's hideous medical uniforms. She and Annamarie had become fast friends and would always commiserate about their bottom-of-the-totem-pole status.

"I've missed you," Annamarie said, sitting next to Alicia in the dugout. "We haven't had a chance to get caught up since you got assigned to Garrett. Lucky you. He's a hot one."

Alicia laughed. "Yeah. It's been an interesting case."

"How's he coming along?"

"He's doing well."

"And you get all this one-on-one time with him as his specialist. What a great career move for you. It puts you front and center in the eyes of the team. I'm kind of jealous."

"Yes. It also puts me front and center in the eyes of the team, if you know what I mean."

Annamarie cocked her head and frowned, then said, "Oh. Right. You're like a giant target."

"Exactly. If I don't get him up on the mound and pitching, it's not going to look good for me."

Annamarie half turned on the bench to face her. "Quit worrying. I've seen you work with the guys, Alicia. You're very good. You have this almost sixth sense about therapy and rehab, and your outcomes are in the highest percentiles. Do you have any doubts that you'll have Garrett pitching this season?"

That day in St. Louis when Garrett had asked her what her opinion was, she knew with certainty that she could fix him. She still felt that way. "No. None at all."

"See, that's where you and a lot of therapists differ, where you and I differ. I know there's still so much I have to learn, but you've always had this ballsy confidence. You plunge headlong into whatever you're doing with this uncanny conviction that the outcome is going to be a one hundred percent rehabilitated player."

Alicia looked at Annamarie. "I'd never thought about it like that. I must be out of my freakin' mind. There are no certainties like that, especially in this field, because there are so many variables, including the players themselves. You know as well as I do that their level of cooperation is paramount in their recovery."

Annamarie laughed. "Of course I do, which is why I'm not as confident as you are. But I think your confidence stems from your ability to sweet-talk them into cooperating. Look how well it's working with Garrett. You've made amazing strides with him so far, haven't you?"

"I suppose I have." She had. A lot of that had to do with Garrett's willingness to cooperate and the way he approached his therapy. She'd been tough on him, but he'd been equally hard on himself.

"Then don't change anything you're doing. It's working."

She squeezed Annamarie's hand. "Thank you. I needed this. It's been a real confidence booster."

Annamarie laughed. "That's what friends and colleagues are for. Call me anytime. And when this crunch is over, we need to have lunch together. I've missed you."

"I've missed you, too."

After Annamarie left, Alicia thought about what her friend had said. It made a lot of sense, but it also freaked her out. Was she really that fearless in her treatment plans and the way she handled players?

She had been with Garrett. And so far it was working, so maybe she shouldn't overthink it.

She looked around. Where was Garrett anyway? She realized she'd been talking to Annamarie so long that the stadium had cleared out.

"We're about to shut out the lights, miss. You coming?"

She looked up to see one of the stadium crew members.

"Actually, I'm waiting for one of the players. I think he's still out in the bullpen. Garrett Scott. He might be out there with one of the coaches."

The crewman grabbed his phone and sighed. Obviously, there was somewhere he needed to be.

"We'll lock up if you need to go. I'm sure Garrett or the coach he stayed behind to work with can get the keys to you tomorrow since we'll be back here early. I want to work with him on his throwing before the team shows up for warm-ups."

"You sure?"

"Positive. Go on."

He nodded. "Okay. Thanks. I'll take care of the stadium lights. You can turn off the ones in here before you go." He handed her the keys, and she went and locked up the gates behind him.

After the lights had shut down, it was dark and a little bit scary in the dugout. She waited, figuring as soon as the stadium lights went out, Garrett would appear.

He didn't.

They had come in the same car. Surely, he wouldn't have left her here alone, would he?

She went into the locker room, but it was empty, so she high-tailed it outside to scan the parking lot, just to be certain. The car was still there, but Garrett was nowhere to be found.

She went back inside, through the locker room, and back out to the dugout.

A single light was still on across the field toward the bullpen. She crossed the dugout and picked up the phone the coach used to call for relief pitchers.

The phone rang several times before Garrett picked it up.

"Yeah?"

"I was hoping you were out there considering you drove us here."

"Sorry. I'm still here."

"What are you doing out there?"

"Thinking."

"You're alone?"

"Yeah."

Huh. "What are you thinking about?"

"Some stuff."

She wondered where his mental state was. "Are you okay?"

"Yeah, I'm fine. I stayed behind to talk to a few of the guys. When they left, I found myself not wanting to go."

She took a seat on the bench. "Okay. You want to talk?"

She heard his soft laugh. "About?"

"I don't know. I'll let you decide. We could talk about your therapy. It is going well, Garrett."

"I don't want to talk about therapy. Or my shoulder. Or anything having to do with my recovery or rehab. I'm taking the night off from thinking about it."

"All right. How about we talk about the game instead."

"It was a good game. Sorry I bailed on you. I wanted to hang out here with the other guys."

"You don't have to stick to me like glue, you know. You were right where you were supposed to be—with the other pitchers."

"Thanks. It felt good to be back here. Did you enjoy the game?"

"I did. I'm glad the team won. They look good this season."

"Yeah. They do."

This conversation was superficial. There was something he wasn't telling her, something bothering him.

"Garrett—we'll get you out there. This is still preseason."

He paused. "I know."

She had to get his mind off baseball and what he wasn't able to do right now. "So . . . what are you wearing right now?"

He laughed. "Are you trying to phone sex me from the dugout, Miss Riley?"

"Maybe."

"Are we alone?"

"Yes. Crew is gone."

"In that case, I'm naked out here."

If only that were the case. "Really. Since you're naked, you should take your cock in your hand and stroke it for me."

She heard him take in a deep breath. "You know I'll do that. Out here. If you slide your hands in your pants and touch yourself."

Now, her breathing quickened. She knew they were alone. It

was dark in the dugout. No one would see her. She slid her hand down the front of her pants. Garrett was so close, but he couldn't see her, either.

"Touch yourself for me, Garrett."

"I'm hard already. You know I'm going to fuck you here."

She palmed her sex, already wet and quivering in anticipation of him doing just that. "Then get over here and do it."

"Hanging up now."

She hung up, too, and sat on the bench. The light in the bullpen went out, bathing the entire ballpark in darkness. She heard the squeak of the bullpen door, and a short time later she caught sight of Garrett's tall, lean form making a determined trek across the field toward the dugout.

She didn't get up, not until he walked down the few steps toward her. Then she stood. He tugged her against him and kissed her.

The passion in his kiss never failed to ignite her, to take her right into the maelstrom of desire and need, where she wanted to be naked and feel him inside her right away. She toed out of her shoes and frantically clawed at her zipper while Garrett turned her around so her back was to him.

He cupped her chin with one hand, tilting her head back while she dropped her pants to the ground.

"I really hate this uniform of yours, Alicia," he said, licking the side of her neck.

She trembled. "Me, too."

"You should be in a skirt tonight. Or a dress I could lift up so I could shove my cock in you and fuck you hard."

Her sex quivered at the mental image while she shimmied out of her panties. "You're not making this any easier."

He sat on the dugout bench and unzipped his pants. "Yeah, well, I'm getting harder. Come sit on me."

Thank God she had condoms in her bag. She might have cried if they didn't have any. She straddled him, bending her knees to slide them across the bench on either side of his hips.

"Ever make love in a ballpark?"

She laughed. "This is definitely a first for me."

He swept his hands across her thighs, holding her in place while she eased down on his cock.

"I like being a first," he said, sliding his hand under her shirt.

He was definitely a first. For a lot of things.

He lifted her bra over her breasts, filling his hands with them while she sank down on his shaft.

"Christ," he said, stilling as she buried him inside her. He squeezed her breasts, brushing his thumbs over her nipples, then brought her forward to lick them. When he blew on them, his warm breath caused a fire to burn deep within her. She grasped his arms and brought a nipple to his mouth.

"Do that again."

His lips curved, and he caught one of the buds between his lips, sucked it between his teeth, and flicked his tongue over it.

So achingly sensual, the painful pleasure seared her.

The night was hot and steamy, not the slightest bit of air blowing to cool off her heated skin as Garrett began to thrust upward. She held onto his shoulders and lifted, then sank onto him again, the sensations heating her to boiling.

"Your skin is silver in the moonlight," he said, wrapping his hand around the nape of her neck to draw her down for a kiss.

When he kissed her and made love to her, her toes curled, her hair stood on end, and everything in between ignited. She dug her nails into his shoulders and rode him, bombarded with sensations that brought her to the breaking point.

And when he pulled away, she arched her back, giving him access to the most intimate parts of her. He rubbed her clit and she shattered, gripping his cock as waves of orgasm convulsed within her.

"Christ, Alicia." He swept his arm around her back to pull her against him. He thrust deeply into her and his harsh groans were the sweetest sounds in the quiet night as she rode out her climax, then took him along for the ride.

Clasped tightly to him, she stroked his sweat-soaked back. He pressed a kiss to her neck, then eased her off his lap and set her on her feet.

She held on to him. "My legs are shaking. And I'm not sure I know where my panties are."

He laughed. "We should probably find them or we'll have some explaining to do to the crew tomorrow morning."

"Yes, and speaking of the crew, they left me the keys to the gates, which means an early workout for you in the morning."

He put his arm around her and tugged her against him, his eyes still heavily lidded with passion. "Worth it, don't you think?"

She shuddered and pressed her hands to his chest. "Definitely. I've never had dugout sex before."

"Me, either." He kissed her thoroughly, his fingers diving into her hair to hold her firmly against his mouth while his tongue plundered. By the time he pulled away, she was more than ready for round two. But they should probably get out of there before they pressed their luck and someone showed up. Not that she expected anyone to haunt the ballpark after hours, but one never knew.

They searched and found her panties under the dugout bench. She dressed and fished the keys out of her pocket so they could get out and lock up.

On the way back to the house, she remembered her conversation with her cousin earlier. "Oh, by the way, Gavin suggested we all have dinner together."

Garrett arched a brow. "He knows about us?"

"Yes. Apparently, rumors are floating around the team about how close we've become."

"Yeah? Huh."

He didn't seem bothered by it. Maybe she shouldn't be, either. Gavin said he'd be discreet. In the meantime, she'd try to be less . . . close to Garrett in the future. At least publicly.

"Anyway, Liz is in town, and he wants to get together at his place."

Garrett didn't say anything for a few minutes. She wondered if he was worried about the whole rumors thing.

"Gavin's going to grill me about our relationship, isn't he?"

She laughed. "No. He's aware we're . . . having sex, and he said that's the last thing he wants to talk about. I think you're in the clear."

"Good. Then dinner sounds fine."

"Why? Because you're afraid to face my cousin, or afraid to answer questions about our relationship?"

He spared her a quick glance as he drove. "Neither. And both."

Confusing answer. She wasn't sure what to make of it, or whether she liked it. A part of her understood his reasoning for being uncomfortable. After all, Gavin was her cousin. Family was always tricky. Even she couldn't define their relationship, if they even had a relationship.

They were having sex. Plus, they had a working relationship. That's all it was between them.

Wasn't it?

TWENTY-TWO

GARRETT STEPPED UP TO THE FRONT DOOR OF GAVIN
Riley's beach house with more than a little anxiety.

Gavin was, after all, Alicia's cousin. Family. Protective of Alicia,
no doubt. Plus, he was Garrett's teammate. They'd been playing
together for years, had gone out for beers after games, had gotten
along well. Garrett had to be able to count on Gavin at first base,
needed to know Gavin had his back. Relationships in baseball were
everything. So was trust.

All things Garrett hadn't thought about when he'd dragged
Gavin's cousin to bed. Of course, Gavin hadn't been front and center on his mind when he'd gotten Alicia naked.

"Are you okay?" Alicia asked as they waited at the front door.

He stopped staring at the door long enough to slant his gaze
toward her. She looked beautiful tonight with the sides of her hair
pulled up, the remainder of it cascading down her back in loose,

soft waves. He wanted to bury his face in her hair, then tangle his fingers in it. But he kept his distance.

"I'm fine. Why?"

"You look nervous. I told you not to be nervous. This is going to be fun."

Yeah. Like a beheading was fun.

The door opened and Elizabeth Riley stood there. He'd met her several times before, both with Gavin and accompanying his agent, Victoria, since the two of them were not only peers, but friends.

"Hey, it's about time you two showed up," Elizabeth said.

"We're not late," Alicia said, hugging Elizabeth as she walked in. "You know Garrett."

"I do. That bitch Victoria has you as a client. You're not currently pissed at her or anything, are you?"

"No."

"Dammit," she said, then winked at Garrett. "Who wants a drink? I have beer, wine, and tea."

"Beer's good for me," Garrett said as Elizabeth led them toward the kitchen. Wearing capris, a sleeveless silk top, and ridiculously high heels, Elizabeth was a stunner with knockout red hair and curves any man would be happy to get his hands on. Gavin was a lucky man.

She handed him a beer. "Thanks, Elizabeth."

"Call me Liz. The other is way too formal."

Gavin came in from out back. "Oh, you guys are here. What's up?" He shook Garrett's hand and caught Alicia around the waist, pulling her in for a hug.

"You're tan," she said to Gavin.

"Went out on the boat for a while today since we had an off day."

"I, of course, am not tan, being one of those fair-skinned redheads who burn. So I lathered on the sunscreen and tried not to fry out there. Lord, it was hot."

"Bitch, bitch, bitch," Gavin said, but gave Liz a wink.

"Yeah, but who caught the fish today, stud?" she asked.

"You did, my beautiful but not tan wife. And you'll never let me forget it, will you?"

"You bet your ass I won't."

Alicia laughed as she gave Liz an incredulous look. "You caught fish?"

Liz pulled out a chair at the bar. "Sit. Make yourselves comfortable. And yes, I caught fish. I'm getting pretty damned good at this fishing thing."

"She's even learned to bait her own hook without cussing or complaining," Gavin said, taking a long swallow of beer.

"Or wanting to throw up," Liz added.

"Yeah, that, too."

"I'm so proud, Liz," Alicia said. "We'll have to go to the lake in the summer. I love fishing."

Garrett looked at her. "You like to fish?"

She lifted her gaze to his. "I love it. My family always used to camp. My dad taught Cole and me to fish when we were kids. Do you fish?"

"I've done it here and there."

"You'll have to come, too."

She made it sound like he'd still be in her life in the summer. Would he? He hadn't thought much beyond the here and now, because that's the way his life had always been. Relationships had never been long-term for him, which suited him just fine and had fit with his career goals. It was hard to have a relationship and do what he did for a living, always being on the road. Plus, he'd never known if someone was in it for him or for who he was and what he did.

Alicia was different, though. Their relationship had been anything but traditional. They'd never even had what he would consider a date. He didn't know how he felt about what was going on between the two of them. The sex sure as hell was smoking hot, and he definitely felt something, but what was it?

Maybe it was time to start figuring it out, because at some point this whole therapy thing was going to be finished, and they'd be left with . . .

What?

"I've got steaks out on the grill—except for you, Alicia, of course," Gavin said. "You're having this amazing pasta salad that Liz fixed for you."

Alicia grinned at Liz. "Awww, you cooked."

"I boiled, mixed, chopped, and tossed. Gavin will be cooking," Liz corrected.

"Don't let her fool you," Gavin said. "She's a hell of a cook. Garrett, want to grab your beer and come outside with me while I turn these steaks?"

Oh, shit. It was time for the inquisition. "Sure."

The night was clear and warm, every star visible in the moonless sky. Garrett followed Gavin down the steps and over to the side of the patio where the grill was located. He took a long swallow of beer and contemplated his life as it stood right now.

What if he never pitched again? What would he do? He'd never much thought about life after baseball, but he wasn't going to do this forever. And if he didn't get his arm working, he'd have to figure out something to do. Maybe he should start planning that sooner rather than later and get a strategy in order.

"Been missing you on the team, man," Gavin said.

"Been missing being there. How's it going?"

Gavin shrugged. "Typical preseason. Ups and downs. Sure could use you."

Garrett took a long swallow of beer. "Working my ass off to get back."

"How's your shoulder?"

"It feels a hell of a lot better, but I haven't had the chance to pitch in a game situation yet, so there's a lot up in the air."

Gavin leaned against the deck. "Scary shit, man. I think all of us who play know what you're going through, how you're feeling. We're all one injury away from that big 'what if.'"

"Yeah. It's definitely got me thinking about what I'm going to do if I can't pitch anymore. I've pushed it to the far corner of my mind for a long time now, but I have to face reality and come up with a backup plan."

"None of us ever want to think about life after baseball." Gavin looked at him. "Do you even have a backup plan?"

Garrett laughed. "Not yet. I guess it's time to figure that out."

"You'll pitch again. My cousin is damn good at her job. She's dedicated and fierce. She'll have you on that mound, good as new."

He loved that Gavin believed in Alicia. "She is good at her job. She's pushed me harder than anyone—hell, harder than I ever thought about pushing myself."

Gavin smiled as he tipped the beer to his lips. "That sounds like Alicia. The words *no* and *I can't* aren't in her vocabulary. When she got hired on to the team, I knew if I ever got hurt, I'd want her in charge of my recovery."

"Seriously?"

"Hell yeah. For as long as I've known her, she's wanted to help people. In high school she knew she wanted to go into sports medicine, even bullied the high school football coach into letting her apprentice with the team athletic director, just so she could get some on-the-job practice before she went off to college. This is her life's dream. She's so goddamn dedicated to making sure athletes stay healthy, recover, and play at the top of their game. It's more than just a paycheck to her, you know."

"I can see that. I've seen it in action. She puts a lot of heart into what she does. And I'm really grateful for what she's done for me. I think very highly of her."

Gavin paused while he flipped the steaks then turned to Garrett. "I know this is really tricky territory, because you and I are friends, and she's my cousin. I don't want to butt in because it's none of my business. The only thing I'll say about it is, I just don't want her to get hurt."

He knew Gavin would say something. The responsibility of looking after family and all. Not that he had much experience in that department since he rarely saw his own. But from what he'd heard about Alicia and her family dynamics, he knew they were close, so he'd expected this. "I don't want her to get hurt, either. I'll do everything not to let that happen."

Gavin stared at him for a minute then nodded. "I believe you. You're not one of those assholes."

Garrett laughed. "Uh, no. I'm not. I won't hurt her, Gavin. That's not what this is about."

"Okay. Good talk. Let's move on to how we're going to kick Baltimore's ass tomorrow."

ALICIA TRIED TO PEER OUT INTO THE DARKNESS, SO she could get a read on what was going on between Gavin and Garrett. She couldn't see them, though. And she also couldn't hear them, which was a good sign there was no arguing going on.

"What are you looking at?" Liz asked her as they sat at the bar drinking wine.

She pulled her gaze toward Liz. "Trying to figure out if they've come to blows yet."

Liz snorted. "Gavin isn't going to punch Garrett just because the two of you are having wild monkey sex."

Alicia's eyes widened. She thought about denying it, but this was Liz, who would poke and pry until she got the truth out of Alicia. "How did you know?"

"Please. I know that nervous look. Besides, Gavin told me. You're afraid Gavin is going to go all protective cousin on Garrett."

"Maybe."

Liz waved her hand. "Not going to happen. Believe me, the last thing Gavin wants to talk about is your sex life."

She relaxed her shoulders. "You're probably right about that."

"How's it going with the two of you?"

Alicia took a sip of wine and smiled at Liz. "Garrett's shoulder is doing good. He's starting to throw pitches."

Liz slanted her a look. "Nice evasion, but you know that wasn't what I was asking."

She hadn't thought it would work, but it was worth a try. "I don't know how it happened."

"I do. You're hot, and so is he. It's Chemistry 101, honey."

"It shouldn't have happened at all. He needs to be concentrating on his recovery, not on sex."

Liz snorted. "Sex is great for recovery. All that blood churning through his veins. You're the expert. A player in a good mood is not a bad thing, is it? I mean, a lot of his recovery is mental, isn't it?"

"That's true, but his cock has nothing to do with his shoulder."

"Oh, come on, Alicia. If you're keeping him content in the sack, he's relaxed and more apt to work harder on his rehab. He's less tense since you've been having sex with him, isn't he?"

Alicia narrowed her gaze at Liz. She was right on in that department. "Well, who made you such a fucking expert on all things sports medicine?"

Liz laughed. "Honey, I don't know a goddamn thing about sports medicine. But I know a lot about sex and how to keep my man relaxed and happy. And when he's relaxed and happy, he plays great fucking baseball. So quit second-guessing your every move with Garrett, and enjoy what's happening between the two of you."

Alicia lifted the wine bottle and refilled her glass and Liz's. "Has anyone ever told you how smart you are?"

"Not nearly often enough." Liz lifted her glass and clinked it against Alicia's.

Maybe Liz was right and their relationship was good for Garrett's recovery. She'd told him at the very beginning to get out of his head. When he wasn't so focused on his shoulder and every step in the process, she could make inroads with his rehab.

What better way to do that than with sex?

A definite benefit—to both of them. Because there was no downside to having sex with Garrett.

THEY HAD DINNER AND GREAT CONVERSATION, AND Alicia spent the evening not worrying about anything for a change. Apparently, Garrett chilled, too, because when he came inside after being with Gavin, he put his arm around her. He even kissed her in front of her cousin, which she thought was more than a little monumental.

She supposed she could even call this evening a date. They laughed, had drinks, talked baseball, and she couldn't remember seeing Garrett this relaxed. He'd stuck close to her all night, touching her in small ways that made her stomach ripple with desire.

He'd trail his fingers down the side of her neck or rub his thumb over the back of her hand, all seemingly innocent gestures that fired up her nerve endings and made her wish they were alone so she could touch him in intimate ways and make him feel half the things she was feeling.

"What are you doing?" she asked him at one point in the evening when he laid his hand against the small of her back, his fingers creeping dangerously low to her butt. She kept her voice at a low whisper, so Gavin and Liz couldn't hear

He gave her a sexy, innocent smile and an "I don't have any idea what you're talking about" as a response.

She had a feeling he knew exactly what he was doing to her. In return, she draped her hand over the top of his thigh, letting her fingers dangle ever so close to his cock. Then she drummed her fingers while she carried on a conversation with Liz. When she looked up at Garrett, he glared at her.

Ha. Payback.

By the time they left Gavin and Liz's, she was a bundle of taut tension. Garrett might appear to be unruffled as he leaned back in the seat as he drove, but she was strung up with the need to get him naked and climb all over him.

He knew it, too. She could tell from the lazy sweep of his fingers down her leg to his relaxed posture in his seat. He was smug and confident, and he knew exactly what he'd been doing to her all night—driving her right to the brink.

She wasn't about to let him know she was ready to explode. She'd just look out the window and pretend everything was fine.

Until his fingers started a slow trek up her thigh, raising her dress.

She snapped her gaze to his and pulled the hem of her dress down. "What do you think you're doing?"

Giving her an innocent look, he said, "Me? I'm just touching you. I like touching you. Do you want me to stop?"

"Yes. No. Yes. I don't know."

He cocked a brow. "Care to clarify?"

"You were driving me crazy all night."

"Was I?"

"Yes."

"Yeah, well, you were doing the same to me."

It was good to know she'd had some effect on him. "I like you touching me."

"Then let me, Alicia. Lean your seat back. Spread your legs."

She looked outside. "We're in the car, Garrett. You're driving."

"On a two-lane road. It's late, and there are hardly any cars. Trust me to protect you."

She did trust him. Arousal beat a hot pulse between her legs.

"Alicia. Let me touch you."

"You should focus on the road."

His lips curved. "I can do both."

She sucked in a breath. She'd just bet he could. "How about I watch the road for you?"

"You won't be watching the road. You'll be concentrating on what I'm doing."

"Is that a challenge?"

He gave a quick, wicked smile, but to his credit, he kept his eyes on the road.

"Lean your seat back, Alicia."

She tilted the seat back and spread her legs, chewing her lip the entire time.

"Lift your dress so I can see what you're wearing underneath."

She drew her dress up, revealing the hot pink underwear she'd worn to match the pale pink and white sundress she had on.

"Sexy." And that was the only look he gave her. Eyes on the road, his fingers crept over her thigh and between her legs, causing a shock of pleasure when he cupped her sex. She melted against him, arching toward his searching fingers.

"This makes me hard, Alicia, makes me think about all the things I want to do to you when we get back to the house."

The outline of his erection was visible against his jeans. "I want to touch you."

He shook his head. "No. I want to make you come. Just relax."

She let out a shaky breath and half turned toward him, giving him better access. He took advantage, sliding his hand down into the silk, touching her bare skin.

She moaned and gripped his wrist as he found her clit, then slid his fingers lower, teasing her pussy. She didn't know if it was being in the car, the idea of this being so public, but she was throbbing, her clit tingling with pulses of need.

"You're wet, babe," he said, taking a quick glance at her. The hunger in his eyes undid her as he swirled her moisture over her clit. "I'm going to make you come."

"Yes," she said, sliding her hand over his, helping him get her there. She pressed down on his hand and shoved his fingers deeper inside her. "Harder."

She swallowed, her throat dry as he increased the pressure. She couldn't control the desire now, and didn't care who might be watching. She undulated against the most exquisite sensations as she shattered against his hand with a loud cry.

"Oh, yeah," she heard him say, but she was lost, bucking against his fingers as she came in wild, seemingly endless bursts that left her hot and shaking. It was only after the trembling stopped that Garrett removed his hand.

And when he licked his fingers one by one, she shuddered, hoping they'd be back at the house in a hurry.

"Glad you kept your eyes on the road the whole time," he teased.

She realized Godzilla could have stepped out of the ocean and onto the road in front of them and she'd have been totally oblivious to it. She smoothed her dress down over her legs. "Okay, I might have been a little distracted."

He cocked a grin. "Just the way I like you."

Now it was her turn. She leaned over and laid her hand on his thigh, wanting to make sure his erection didn't go anywhere. His jaw clenched as he drove the rest of the way back to the house.

By the time he pulled into the driveway, his clamped jaw had worked itself into a decided twitch. She was rather proud of that, because he'd driven her absolutely out of her mind with pleasure, so she felt obliged to return the favor. Her fingers danced over his fully hard cock, and if he hadn't been driving, she'd have unzipped him and would've stroked or sucked him. But she did prefer he pay some attention to the road, so this tease was enough torture for him.

She gave him points for being a very good driver.

He opened her car door and pulled her out, pressing her against the side of the car to fit his lips to hers and grab a handful of her ass.

She was more than ready for him, and when he scooted her across the car to lay her flat on the warm hood, pressing his hot, hard body against her, she was sure he was ready to take her right there, his body surging against hers.

Not that she'd object—much. She flattened her palms against his chest and gave him a little push. "Shouldn't we take this inside?"

He pressed a kiss against her jaw. "Not sure I can wait that long."

She loved that he wanted her that much. The feeling was mutual, and if they hadn't left the porch light on and it wasn't so brightly lit out here, she might just consider it, because he was rubbing his hard cock against her sex. A few more minutes of that and she'd be ready to explode.

Fortunately, he pulled her up and nearly dragged her to the front door.

They didn't make it far inside, though, because as soon as he shut the front door, he drew her to the floor, pulling her down on top of him. She landed with her skirt over her hips. Garrett took advantage, slipping his hand into her panties to roam over her bare butt.

"I've been wanting to get my hands on your naked ass all night."

She lifted up, resting her hands on his chest. "We should get into bed so I can touch you."

He shook his head. "It's too far into the bedroom. Touch me here."

"Get undressed."

He half rose, and within a couple of seconds, his shirt was off, exposing his well-sculpted abs. She splayed her hands across them then leaned over him to press a kiss to his nipples.

He gave her a look. "That's not where I want your mouth, Alicia."

"Really." She kissed his neck. "Here?"

"A little lower."

She slid her tongue down to his rib cage and moved along his stomach. "How about here?"

"You're getting a little closer. Keep going."

When she laid her hand on his cock, he tensed. "Yeah. There. With your mouth."

She loved that he had no problem telling her what he wanted. And how he wanted it. She popped the button on his pants and slowly drew the zipper down. He kicked off his shoes, and she lifted off him momentarily so he could shove his pants off, freeing his cock for her to grasp in her hands.

He was naked now, and she gloried in just looking at him. She always loved seeing him naked, being able to run her hands over his magnificent body, which she did now, snaking her hands up his abs and over his chest.

"Now you."

She pulled her sundress over her head, leaving her in her underwear, which she took care of by standing and straddling him. She popped the clasp on her bra, removed it, and cast it aside, then shimmied her panties down her thighs.

Garrett grasped her ankles while she stepped out of her panties and threw them in the pile.

She stood, straddling him and looking down at him. He smiled up at her and took a deep breath. She knew what he was looking at. She'd never been shy about her body, but oh, the way he was looking at her made her blush from her toes to the tips of her hair.

"Now, there's a beautiful sight. Come sit on me."

She squatted down and sat on his thighs, grasping his cock with both hands. "Actually, this is a beautiful sight. I love touching you, Garrett. All over."

He laughed. "I like your hands on me." He thrust his shaft upward. "When you touch me, it makes my cock throb."

She twisted her hands around, watching his face go dark. When she leaned forward, her hair spilled around him. He fisted it in his hand, forcing her gaze to his.

"Suck me, Alicia."

Her pussy clenched at his command, exciting her, dampening her as she moved her lips to his cockhead. She licked her lips, then put her mouth on him, her tongue swirling around the wide head.

"Christ," he said, surging forward to propel his shaft into her waiting mouth.

She took control then, closing her fist around the base of his shaft and sucking him deeply into her throat. His loud groans told her he enjoyed what she did. She wanted him to come hard, like he'd made her come in the car, so she pressed the roof of her mouth tight against her tongue, sucking as she brought his shaft deeper, cupping his balls, and giving them a squeeze.

"That's going to make me shoot my come in your mouth, babe," he said, pumping into her mouth with hard, rapid thrusts.

She held tight to him, squeezing him until he let out a harsh groan and came, spilling onto her tongue. She swallowed and held him while he shuddered and called her name. He held tight to her until he dropped to the floor and relaxed his body. She pressed a soft kiss to his shaft then climbed up his body to lay next to him while he recovered.

"Jesus Christ, I can't even breathe." His voice was hoarse.

She smiled and swept her hand over his chest, smoothing away the fine sheen of sweat that had gathered there. "I'll go get us some water."

"I'll meet you in the bedroom."

She got them each a glass of ice water. He had the covers turned down and the fan on, the door to the deck partially open to let the night breeze in. Garrett was on the bed waiting for her, so she handed him the glass, which he downed in about four quick swallows. She climbed onto the bed next to him and cuddled beside him.

"I'm not sure I have the strength to make love to you," he said.

She grinned. "It's not necessary. Besides, I think you already did."

He laid the empty glass on the table and turned to her. "Bullshit. That was foreplay."

Before she could even blink, he had shifted her under him, his body hot and hard and covering hers. He framed her face in his hands. "I want as much of you as I can get, Alicia."

There was something he wasn't saying. Like he wanted her while it was just the two of them, before they headed back to St. Louis, before the season started, before real life intruded and they were torn apart?

She knew what they had was only temporary, and she was living in a fantasy world with him right now. Logically she knew it, anyway. They weren't going to stay together for so many different reasons, the least of which was both of their careers.

She swept her hand across his jaw, always a turn-on to caress the rough beard there. She shuddered and pushed aside the temporariness of their relationship. For now, he was hers, and she'd have him for as long as she could. And when it came time to walk away, she would. Because her career came first, just like his did. They were both adults, and they could handle this.

She could handle this.

Right now, she only wanted Garrett, only wanted to concentrate on his body moving over hers, inside her, and on the way he made her feel. She sparked so fast with him, and like it or not, she was different when she was with him. He brought out so much passion in her, made her feel so free.

And as he clasped his hand with hers and they went over the edge together, she knew what she'd always known.

He was something amazing. Undeniably special. And he made her feel special.

And she was in love with him.

Which was going to make that whole walking-away-at-the-end-of-all-this thing really damned difficult.

TWENTY-THREE

GARRETT APPROACHED THE TRIP BACK HOME TO ST. Louis with both excitement and bone-shaking terror.

Spring training had ended, and while he'd gotten in some work with the team and he knew he'd made significant progress, he'd pitched no games. In the back of his mind, he'd thought maybe he'd be strong enough to pitch before the end of spring training.

Alicia had made no promises to him and in fact told him it likely wouldn't happen, but she'd do her best to get him ready so he could pitch in the regular season.

He'd made a mental note that she hadn't said she'd have him ready by the start of the season. He refused to remind her that when they very first started working together, she'd told him she'd have him on the mound by the start of the season. He'd considered it a promise at the time.

He'd believed her, and she'd gotten him further along than he'd thought. That was good enough. He considered it a miracle he was this close to pitching again.

But the regular season was about to begin, and that meant it was make-it-or-break-it time for him.

He wanted on the mound in the first series. If he couldn't be the first game starter, then he wanted in the rotation.

There was no doubt his shoulder was in great shape. His therapy with Alicia had been going well. They'd moved from those small pitching sessions and had begun working him out with the coaches again. He'd started throwing again—regular pitches this time.

Everything felt good. His shoulder was strong, he was getting velocity on his pitches, and every day he felt better and better, like his old self again. Alicia still put him through his grueling therapy sessions, and every day they hurt less and less. Alicia told him it was a day-by-day thing and all a matter of time.

He hoped like hell that wasn't some standard bullshit spiel she said to all the players in recovery, because he was so goddamn ready to pitch he could taste it.

Today they were on the field working position practice. He was over with the pitchers taking warm-ups, though Alicia was there with him, along with the pitching coach, who was watching his mechanics. As he wound up and threw his curveball into the catcher's mitt, Bobby Sloane, the pitching coach, frowned.

"Do it again."

He did. And Bobby frowned. Again.

"One more time," Bobby said.

After Garrett threw the pitch, Bobby still didn't look happy. Not that Bobby ever smiled, but if you threw the pitches right, Bobby walked off and terrorized a different pitcher. This time he stayed. "Something's off with your curve. You're not hitting the strike zone. Is it your shoulder?"

Garrett rolled his shoulder. "It feels fine."

"Throw a few sliders."

He did then some changeups and fastballs, all according to the coach's directions.

Bobby watched them all, then shook his head. Instead of talking to Garrett, he turned to Alicia. "He's off, Alicia. I don't like those pitches just yet. They don't have the trademark Garrett Scott finesse."

Alicia stepped beside Bobby and nodded. "I'll work on him in the treatment room. It's likely he's still just a little bit stiff since he hasn't thrown in so long. Therapy and just working through the pitches will get him back on the mark."

Bobby walked away and Alicia came over to him. "Are you in any pain?"

"No."

"You threw a lot of pitches at practice today. How does the arm feel?"

He walked off the mound with her. "Do you have any idea how fucking tired I am of hearing that question? I never want to hear that goddamn question again."

Her lips lifted. "Well, guess what? It's not the last time you're going to hear it. From me or the coaching staff. So deal."

"Yeah, yeah."

He was grouchy and he knew it. He'd expected to get on the mound and start throwing pitches the same way he had before he got hurt. It wasn't looking like that was going to happen, and it pissed him off, which was no reason to take it out on Alicia.

"Hey," he said, pausing just inside the tunnel leading toward the locker room. "I'm sorry."

She cocked her head to the side. "For what?"

"For snapping at you."

She laughed and touched his arm. "This is a big deal for you, Garrett. You're entitled to be tense about it."

She understood. Of course she did. Right now she knew him and what he was going through better than anyone. He leaned in and brushed his lips across hers. "Thanks."

Except a few of the players took that moment to come in from the dugout.

"Whoa, Garrett." Tommy Maloney, a fellow pitcher, gave Garrett a shove. "Shouldn't you two get a room or something?"

"I don't know, Tommy." Dedrick Coleman crossed his arms, his glove dangling from his fingers. "I'd say we've got a pretty good show going on right here. I might want to stay and watch."

"Fuck off, Deed," Garrett said, seemingly unconcerned that they'd just been caught making out in the tunnel.

Dedrick laughed, and he and Tommy headed toward the locker room.

"Sorry about that," Garrett said, turning back to Alicia.

Her eyes were wide with shock. "Oh, God. That's the worst thing that could have happened."

Garrett frowned. "What? Oh, the guys? Don't worry about it."

"Are you serious? The last thing I need to have happen is for my boss to find out about the . . . about what's been going on between the two of us." She took two giant steps back. "That can't happen again. I'll meet you inside the therapy room."

She hurried away, and he wondered what she meant by "that." Kissing her in public or being with her at all.

Their time together in Florida had been nearly perfect. They'd had a lot of alone time, especially in the house together. He'd been free to touch her, to taste her, to make love to her without anyone around. Yeah, once they'd gotten to the ballpark, it had been professional and hands-off.

Except in the dugout that night . . .

He smiled remembering the way her body had arched when he'd been inside her, the sounds she'd made when she'd come.

He'd like to do it again. Here in this dugout. Or maybe in the bullpen.

His cock tightened, but he pushed aside his own needs. Alicia was pissed. And scared. And all he was thinking about was having sex with her again, getting close to her, touching her.

He needed to respect her boundaries.

He went into the training room and found her, head down in that damn notebook where she charted—whatever the hell she charted about him. He knew her notes were all about him since right now he was the only one she worked with.

She looked up. "Let me loosen up your shoulder. You had a hard workout today."

"Sure." He changed, and she put heat on him then loosened him up with a series of stretches that not that long ago caused agony. Now it felt good to have his muscles and tendons stretched. Plus, having Alicia's hands on him had a whole different meaning than it did back then. He craved her touch, the way her hands slid over his shoulder and down his arm.

And all the while, she didn't even make eye contact with him, not even when she bent down to push deep into his muscle, when her face was so close to his, if he lifted up even a little bit, their lips would touch.

"Alicia."

"Yes."

"You can look at me, you know."

She gave him a brief glance, but she backed away first. "Am I hurting you?"

"No." But they weren't alone in the treatment room, and he knew she was freaked out by what had happened earlier with Dedrick and Tommy. He wasn't going to be able to talk to her about it now, because there were other athletes and other therapists in here.

Later. They'd talk later.

Except later, after they had both left—and he'd noticed that she'd hightailed it out of there as soon as she'd finished with his therapy—he'd called her and asked if she wanted to come over to his place. She'd told him she was busy with some family stuff and couldn't see him tonight. And she'd gotten off the phone with him in a hurry.

A cold knot formed in his stomach. Maybe she was being honest, and she really did have family obligations.

Or maybe she was creating distance in more places than just the ballpark.

And to Garrett, that just wasn't acceptable.

The next day, he tried again. After workouts and therapy, making sure they were alone in the treatment room, he asked her.

"What are your plans for tonight? I thought maybe we could go out for dinner."

She paused, mid stretch of his arm. "Um . . . what?"

He tilted his head back to look at her. "Dinner. That thing where you get food. I get food. We eat. Talk. You remember that, don't you?"

"Of course I know dinner. But I can't. Actually, I was going to talk to you about tonight."

"You were?"

"Yes. My cousin Jenna's new music club is opening tonight. The whole family is going to be there. I was wondering if you'd like to come."

Now it was his turn to pause. He sat up and she stepped back while he swung his legs over the table. "What?"

"I'm inviting you to come with me to my cousin's club opening."

He wanted time with her. Alone. Not with her entire family. He didn't do family. The whole family thing was awkward and uncomfortable, like with his family. "Oh. No thanks."

She cocked a brow. "Why not?"

"It's your family. I'd be intruding."

"It's not a private thing, Garrett. The club is opening to the public tonight. My family is going to be there to help celebrate. Jenna and Ty—hell, my entire family has worked hard on making this happen. I'd love for you to be there."

"Yeah, I don't do the family thing. But thanks for asking."

She shuttered her feelings behind a blank stare. "Okay. Lie back down so I can finish stretching you."

He'd hurt her. She'd backed off, he'd pursued, and then when she'd relented and invited him back in, he'd turned her down. What kind of a dick was he, anyway?

Dammit. How could he explain to her how uncomfortable family gatherings were for him? Every time he saw his mother, despite how happy she was with her husband, it reminded him of the pain of his parents' breakup and how it had shattered him. And his dad? Yeah, that rarely if ever even happened. His dad was off in his own world, his own life with the woman he'd left them all for. His father couldn't be bothered with his son.

He liked Alicia's cousin, Gavin, mainly because they'd been teammates before Alicia and he had ever gotten together. And maybe he never thought what was going on with him and Alicia was ever going to be anything more than just a right-now kind of thing. Nothing long-term, and sure as hell nothing that involved interacting with each other's families.

"Okay, we're done here. I'll get the ice pack."

"Alicia."

She stopped. "Yes?"

"About this event tonight. Let me explain."

She offered up a smile that didn't transform her face like her typical smiles did. "No explanation necessary, Garrett. I'll be right back with that ice pack."

Shit. He raked his fingers through his hair. Somehow he'd have to work around this. He didn't want to hurt her feelings, but damn if he wanted to thrust himself into the middle of her family tonight.

But after expressing her fear about the two of them being seen together, she'd offered up an olive branch.

And he'd just snapped the branch in two.

Maybe he was an asshole after all.

TWENTY-FOUR

ALICIA WASN'T ONE FOR DRESSING UP OR GOING TO clubs. Not that Jenna's club was fancy. She'd created it to be casual and welcoming, just like the original Riley's bar.

But it was opening night, and this was a big damn deal, so she'd bought a new dress and some strappy high-heeled shoes that were expensive and sexy as hell, just like the thigh-skimming dress that showed off way more leg than Alicia typically did.

Riley's Club was officially open, and there was already a line outside to get in. Jenna must be out of her mind with nerves and excitement. Alicia hadn't even had a chance to talk to Jenna tonight, other than a quick hug when she'd come in an hour ago. Jenna had looked gorgeous in a skintight short black dress and knee-high black high-heeled boots, her hair in its customary spiked-up short cut with purple tips, her left ear adorned with a multitude of piercings, her body a tattooed map of her life experiences.

Jenna was a former wild child tamed by the love of her life, hockey-stud Ty Anderson, the smiling, calming influence standing by her side right now, his hand around her waist while she welcomed everyone into the club.

"They look stunning together, don't they?"

Alicia nodded at Savannah Brooks, her brother Cole's girlfriend—no, make that fiancée. When they'd returned from their extended vacation, Savannah had been sporting one hell of a sparkler on her ring finger and a glow on her face that told Alicia they'd had a very special, very romantic vacation.

"They look about as much in love as you and my brother."

Savannah grinned. "That man melts my butter. Sorry, I know he's your brother, but he's more than I could have ever dreamed of."

Alicia linked her fingers with Savannah's. "I think he's pretty lucky, too, Savannah. You saved his career."

Savannah waved her hand. "He turned his own career around."

"Oh, I think you were right behind him with those awesome high-heeled shoes of yours, giving him the kick in the ass he needed."

Savannah's lips curved into a knowing smile. "Maybe now and then. He didn't need as much of a butt kicking as everyone thought. Even as much as he thought. He's a very special man."

And that's what love was all about. People who saw through the flaws and loved you anyway, who helped you when you needed it most, who would always be there for you, and who always had your back. Alicia wondered if she'd ever experience love like that.

She'd never been in love before. School and her career had kept her relationships mainly superficial.

Until Garrett. She'd let him in, let him wrap around her heart, and now she was afraid she'd made a huge mistake, because there was so much she still didn't know about him.

Like why he was so reluctant to be around her family. He'd had no qualms about spending time with Gavin and Liz. Then again, that had been a more intimate gathering. Granted, her family en masse was nothing short of epically overwhelming. She understood that, but everyone was focused on Jenna as the center of attention tonight. She thought inviting Garrett would pull a little of the focus away from him.

She realized after that episode in the tunnels the other day that she likely had overreacted. No one from upper management had come running to tell her she was fired. None of the players had even looked at her funny. Garrett had either said something to them, or the only person freaked out about the whole thing was her.

She thought inviting Garrett to Jenna's club opening would be a fun way for the two of them to hang out. It would be packed in here tonight, they could get lost in the crowd, and he would get a chance to meet her family at the same time.

So why had he balked at the invitation? Was it just the whole meeting-the-family thing? Had it been too much for him? Maybe that was too close to a relationship for him, and he just didn't see the two of them that way.

She sighed and went to the beautifully distressed antique bar to order a glass of wine. Eric, one of the bartenders, had shaggy blond hair that fell over his forehead and searing blue eyes that seemed to look into your very soul. Eric poured her wine with a sexy smile. At the other end of the bar was Penny, built like a centerfold, with a slender waist, legs that went all the way to Ohio, and one hell of an impressive rack.

Jenna so knew how to choose bartenders. They were going to make a lot of tips, and they were going to sell a lot of booze.

"What do you think, Alicia?" her aunt Kathleen asked as Alicia wandered around to visit with family members.

"I think this is going to be another Riley success. This place is packed with both the curious and people wanting to sing tonight. Such a brilliant idea."

Her uncle Jimmy beamed a wide smile. "I'm so proud of Jenna. She's worked so hard to get this place in shape in time for the opening. There was even a write-up in the newspaper about it."

"I saw that. You should be proud. And I'm excited. I can't wait to hear Jenna sing. I've heard she's incredible."

"She's amazing," her aunt said, fighting back tears. She fished in her purse for a tissue. "I'm going to blubber all night."

Alicia patted her aunt on the arm. "I think you deserve to."

The music had already started up. The club featured a wide range of acts—anyone who wanted a chance to sing or play music could. Right now a guy had the mic and bellowed out a country-rock song that had people clamoring to get on the dance floor.

After visiting with her aunt and uncle for a few minutes, Alicia wandered off again, running into family members and friends of the family wherever she went. But it wasn't only family members crowding into the club. There were people she didn't know. Obviously, word had gotten out about the great new club, which was excellent news for the new business.

She decided she'd better elbow her way toward the front door so she could say a few words of congratulations to Jenna before her cousin got so busy she wouldn't be able to talk to anyone the rest of the night.

The only problem with that was the solid wall of people standing in her path. Short of pushing and shoving, she was stuck where she was. Instead, she leaned against one of the wood beams and decided to sip her wine for a while. She'd catch up with Jenna later.

"Need a bodyguard to help you make your way through?"

She laughed and turned her head, shocked to see Garrett standing there.

And oh, did he look good in dark jeans and a white button-up shirt that hugged his lean, muscular body.

"What are you doing here?"

He cocked a brow. "I was invited, remember?"

"I do remember. You declined my invitation."

"I was a prick. I'm sorry."

She wanted to ask him why he had turned her down in the first place, but it was so noisy in there that their voices would have to be raised, and this wasn't the venue for that particular conversation. "I'd like to know why, but how about we table that topic for another time?"

"Sounds good."

He held a bottle of beer in his hands, and he looked so delicious she wanted to lean against him and not let go. "Thank you for coming tonight."

"I'm glad to be here. Take me around and introduce me to your family."

"Are you sure? There's a lot going on around here. Chances are we could hide out in the back of the room and not be noticed."

He slid his hand in hers. "Alicia. Introduce me to your family."

Something melted inside her. "Okay."

The whole introduction thing took awhile since the family was spread out and people were packed in the club like sardines. But she found her parents and her aunt and uncle together, so they were first.

Her mother grinned from ear to ear when Alicia introduced Garrett.

"So you're the one Alicia's been working on. How is your shoulder?"

Garrett graced her with his trademark smile. "It's doing great. Your daughter is very good at her job. I'm hoping to be able to pitch soon."

That made Alicia's dad grin. "I'm glad to hear that. Scared the hell out of me when you got hurt last season."

"Believe me, Mr. Riley, it scared the hell out of me, too."

"I'm glad Alicia invited you," her mother said. "And you and Gavin are friends, too?"

"We are."

"I hope you have a good time," her mother said. "Thank you for coming to support Jenna. And look—she's about to take the stage."

They all turned as Jenna grabbed a mic.

"I want to welcome you all to the club tonight. Thank you for making Riley's Club's opening night such a rousing success. I won't stand here and give a long speech since that isn't my thing. How about some music?"

Everyone cheered. The band started up, and Jenna began to sing. Alicia knew Jenna wrote a lot of her own music. This song was upbeat and fun, the kind of song everyone would want to dance to. She had people crowding the dance floor, clapping their hands, and shaking their hips as she gave it her all. By the end of the song, they were whistling and cheering for her.

"Your cousin has an amazing voice," Garrett said.

Alicia grinned. "Yes, she does. I'm so proud of her. So thrilled for her. Not just for the club, but because she's living her dream. Finally."

Garrett cocked a brow.

"It's a long story," Alicia said. "I'll tell you sometime."

"Okay." He turned to Alicia's parents, and her aunt and uncle. "Congratulations. This place is going to do very well."

Her aunt couldn't possibly smile any wider. "We think so, too. Wasn't Jenna wonderful?"

"I don't know why she's singing here when she's better than half the people selling records right now."

"That's what I keep telling her," Alicia's uncle said. "But she insists this is the only place she wants to be."

When they wandered off, Gavin turned to Alicia. "No grilling?"

"Oh, if I invited you over for Sunday dinner, there would be grilling. They're cutting you some slack tonight because it's crowded and noisy in here. They're just being polite."

"Lucky me, then," he said, sweeping his knuckles across her cheek.

"At least where my parents are concerned," she said as she saw her brother bearing down on her with a decided scowl on his face.

Garrett straightened as Cole approached. Garrett didn't look at all threatened as he casually slipped his arm around Alicia's waist.

"Been looking for you," Cole said, his fingers linked with Savannah's.

"I've been here for a while. I guess we kept missing each other in the crowd. Cole, this is Garrett Scott. Garrett, this is my brother, Cole, and his fiancée, Savannah Brooks."

Savannah shook his hand. "Garrett, so nice to meet you. I've heard great things about you."

Cole shook Garrett's hand, too. "You're the one she's been working with. Shoulder injury."

"Yeah."

"Rehab finished yet?"

"Not yet."

"Think you'll pitch this year?"

"Hell yeah, I'll pitch. And when I do, a lot of the credit for that will go to Alicia."

She felt a tug in the vicinity of her heart at his statement and lifted her gaze to his. "Thank you, Garrett."

Cole gave Garrett the kinds of looks a brother would give any guy she was . . . whatever it was she and Garrett were doing. She knew Cole was being protective, but really. Cole didn't know what was going on, so he could stop being all Neanderthal about this.

"I've read your career history, Garrett," Savannah said, obviously trying to defuse the tension. "I do image consulting, especially for athletes. So it's kind of a specialty of mine to dissect you all. You've had an amazing career."

"Thanks. I just hope I get to continue it."

"Season will be starting soon," Cole said.

Master of the obvious, wasn't he?

"Yeah," Garrett said. "Between Alicia and the coaches, they're prepping me nonstop to get ready to pitch."

"Yeah? And how's that going?"

"The past few months have been living in hell. I've been under the goddamn microscope so long all I want to do is disappear."

Something in Cole seemed to switch off at that point, and he relaxed. "Dude. Been there. Not that I got hurt—" Cole looked at Savannah. "But yeah. Been under that same microscope. I've never had an injury before. It must be a downer having to deal with all the uncertainty."

"It sucks."

Cole laughed. "Want to grab these ladies a seat? And I need a beer."

"Me, too." Garrett switched his gaze to Alicia. "Ready to sit down?"

Alicia was so relieved to feel the ice thaw between Garrett and her brother. She nodded at Garrett. "Like you wouldn't believe. My feet are killing me in these shoes."

He grabbed her hand. "Let's go muscle up a table, then."

"Good luck in this crowd."

"Come on," Cole said. "We're VIP's. We'll get Jenna to find us one."

Jenna did find them one, in a spot she'd reserved near the stage for family members. Which gave Alicia a chance to introduce Garrett to both Jenna and Ty, at least for the minute and a half Jenna spent with them before she dashed off to see to her customers and introduce new musicians to the crowd. But at least they had a table. And seats with the rest of the family. Tara was thrilled to have a night out without Sam, though she kept texting Nathan, her teenage son who was on babysitting duty. And despite Mick's assurances that Nathan could capably handle the baby, who had been fed and was sound asleep, Tara kept staring at her phone.

Garrett seemed to be handling being surrounded by her family members well. He'd even bonded with Cole, the two of them talking golf of all things.

"He's very hot," Savannah said, keeping her voice low as the two of them huddled close.

Not that it would have mattered, since Garrett and Cole had their own huddle going on.

"Who? My brother? Too much information, Savannah."

Savannah gave her a look. "Ha, ha. And you know I was talking about your smoldering new boyfriend."

"He's not my boyfriend. He's . . ."

She had no idea how to describe him.

Savannah arched a brow. "Do go on. He's what? Just the current athlete you're working on that you decided to invite to a family event?"

The knowing look Savannah gave Alicia told her that her hesitation was ridiculous. "Okay, so we're involved. I just don't know how to describe it."

"Why is it so difficult to describe it?"

"I don't know. We've never defined it. It just kind of happened between us. There's really nothing going on." She realized even as she said it that her explanation sounded stupid.

"You seem afraid." Savannah offered up a serene smile and rimmed her wineglass with the tip of her finger. "Do you have reservations about this relationship?"

"Well, we do work for the same team. And I'm currently his therapist. There's a major conflict of interest going on here."

"I understand. Believe me. I had much the same problem with my relationship with Cole. Not in the same way as yours, of course. But you can't let that mess up what the two of you have. If, in fact, you have something you think is worth the risk." Savannah paused and shot Alicia a direct look. "Is it?"

Alicia glanced across the table to where Garrett was bent over in conversation with Cole. Just looking at him caused butterflies to take flight in her stomach. In the short period of time she'd known him, he'd completely wrecked her well-managed, orderly routine. Now, she couldn't imagine that life without him in it.

She returned her gaze to Savannah. "I'm crazy in love with him."

Savannah's lips curved. "Does he know that?"

"Oh, God no. We're not there yet."

"Well. Learn from my experience. Cole and I did everything wrong, and it cost us both a lot of pain. Talk to him. Tell him how you feel."

Somehow, Alicia didn't think Garrett was ready to hear those words from her yet. Inviting him here to meet her family was a big step. That he was gracious enough to show up was a move forward.

That was enough for now.

OKAY, SO MAYBE ALICIA'S FAMILY WASN'T AS UNCOM-fortable to be around as Garrett had imagined. Once they'd gotten past the initial discomfort, he and Cole had bonded fast over their mutual love of golf and poker, and then they'd launched into a discussion of some of their favorite video games. He probably could have spent all night talking to him, except Cole's fiancée, Savannah, had dragged him away, claiming the current band up on the stage was playing a slow song she wanted to dance to.

Garrett realized he'd pretty much abandoned Alicia, though she and Savannah had seemed engaged in an animated conversation of their own. He shifted to face her.

"Sorry to leave you hanging. I like your brother."

She grinned. "So I noticed. I think he likes you, too."

"Would you like to dance?"

Both her brows went up. "You dance?"

"Not really. But I like having my hands on you, and that's about the only way I'll be able to do that with your whole family watching."

She laughed. "Then by all means, let's dance."

He pulled her onto the jam-packed floor and drew her into his arms. There was a band with a lot of horns playing something slow and jazzy. He stroked up her back, liking the dress she had on. It was short and sexy and clung to her body, showing off all her curves and her great legs. He hadn't yet told her how good she looked tonight.

"I like this," she said.

"The band, or my hands on you?"

"Definitely your hands on me. But the band is good, too, now that you mention it."

There wasn't much room for maneuvering, which suited him just fine since he had no finesse on the dance floor, so they mainly swayed back and forth in time to the music. What he really liked was having Alicia's body pressed up against his, her breasts pillowed against his chest. With her high heels on, she was much taller. He didn't have to bend down so far to see her beautiful eyes.

"You're quiet."

He smiled. "Doing inventory."

"What?"

"Feeling you. Watching you. Thinking about how beautiful you look tonight, which I failed to mention earlier."

"Wow. Thank you. You feel good, too. And you look amazing. Though I have seen you in ads all dressed up before. There was that one in the tux. You were hawking men's cologne, I think."

He grimaced. "Damned uncomfortable photo shoot."

"Yeah. All those half-naked models draped over you. I'm sure it was a hardship."

"Seriously. Those things take hours, and the models were unfriendly as hell. In between takes they would sip water, text on their phones, and otherwise look bored. They had no idea who I was and thought I was some newbie model dude at my first shoot. They couldn't be bothered with me."

She laughed. "Really?"

"Really. It was kind of embarrassing. But not as embarrassing as the one commercial I did for a razor where I had to spend an entire day with my face coated in shaving cream while wearing nothing but a towel around my waist."

"Oh, I saw that commercial. Lord, you looked hot with that towel slung low on your hips. I had fantasies about you while watching that commercial."

He grinned. "Yeah? Would it burst your bubble to know I had my boxer briefs on under that towel?"

"Totally."

"No way was I going commando with twenty crew members there. Doing those commercials and print ads are never as fun or as sexy as the finished product. It's all work."

"Oh, poor you."

He squeezed her hand, then twirled her around as the music picked up. "I can tell I'm not going to get any sympathy from you."

She laughed. "No. Poor famous guy."

"If I don't start pitching again, I'm going to be has-been guy."

"You are pitching, in case you haven't noticed."

"I'm practicing. That's different. I'm reserving judgment until I pitch a minimum of six innings in a real game."

"Oh, is that a challenge?"

"Would it help if I said yes?"

"It's not going to make me work any harder on you, so no. We're doing the best we can to get you ready, Garrett."

"I know you are. But this is my career. Hell, it's my life."

She pulled away from his embrace. "Do you think I don't know that? Do you think I approach any of my clients any differently than I do you? That I don't take this seriously?"

She walked off the dance floor. He followed. "Alicia, that's not what I meant."

She turned to face him. "Then what did you mean? See, this is the problem with you and me."

How the hell had they gotten from a dance to talking about his rehab to some kind of issue in their relationship? "What problem between you and me?"

"This. What we've been doing. You think after we—" She paused to glance around, then moved in closer. "You somehow must think that us sleeping together has caused me to approach your therapy differently. Like I'm on some goddamned vacation. Like I've slacked off with you instead of giving it my all."

"That's not what I said. When did I say that?"

She pointed her finger at his chest. "Well, let me tell you, stud. At no time have I ever given you less than everything I've got to give. In fact, I've given you more. A hell of a lot more."

She went to the table, grabbed her purse, and headed for the exit, leaving him standing there with several sets of Riley eyes zeroed in on him.

Shit.

The only one to come up to him was Cole, though.

"What was that about?"

He dragged his fingers through his hair. "Hell if I know. We were talking about some of the PR work I used to do, and then we started talking about my rehab, and the next thing you know she's pissed as hell at me and making a fast dash for the exit."

Cole followed Garrett's gaze toward the front door where Alicia had walked out. "Huh. Women. Who can figure them out sometimes? And my sister? I wish I could offer some advice, man, but she's always been a big mystery to me."

Garrett had thought for sure Cole would take a punch at him for upsetting his sister. "I don't know what I did. I swear I wasn't trying to upset her."

Cole offered up a wry smile. "Don't worry about it. I can get her from zero to rage demon in about four seconds just by saying hello."

Somehow he figured Cole was exaggerating. "I'm sure I did something or said something that irritated her. I need to say I'm sorry. Well, first I need to figure out what I did wrong. Then I need to apologize."

Cole laughed and patted him on the back. "Yeah, good luck with that."

TWENTY-FIVE

MAYBE SHE WAS PMSING. THAT WAS ALICIA'S ONLY EX-
cuse for her lunaticlike behavior at the club.

She'd built up a good head of steam heading out of the club,
carried a body full of smoke to the car, but by the time she'd gotten
home and into the driveway, the fog had cleared, and she was, unfortunately, much more clearheaded.

And mortified that she'd let her emotions get the best of her,
that she'd stormed out of the club, out of Jenna's opening night,
without saying good-bye to her family and without thanking Jenna
and telling her what a great success the club was going to be.

Alicia owed Jenna a big, fat apology. If she ever left her house
again, which at this point was debatable considering what a spec-
tacle she'd made of herself.

This was the reason she'd spent the last several years focusing
on her education and her career and most definitely not on men and
relationships. Men made women crazy. Or at least they made her

crazy. Okay, one man in particular was making her lose her ever-loving mind.

As she sat at her kitchen table sipping the cup of hot tea she'd made to try and mellow herself out, she replayed their conversation over in her mind. What had the trigger point been?

Having Garrett show up at the club had been wonderful, and she'd been grateful and thrilled that he'd gotten along so well with her family, especially with Cole. And when he'd asked her to dance, she'd been happy to be able to touch him and feel his body close to hers. They'd talked, and he'd made her laugh with his stories of advertising and commercials, until they'd gotten on the topic of therapy . . .

That's when everything had gone awry, and she'd gone up like an erupting volcano because he'd challenged her abilities. Or at least that's what she'd thought she'd heard. In a packed club with the music blaring and people talking all around her, for all she knew he could have been talking about the hottest new brand of goat cheese.

She decided she'd blame it all on the wine. Alcohol made people do dumb things all the time. Too bad she'd only had two glasses spread out over four hours with multiple waters in between, so she wasn't even drunk. Not even slightly buzzed, as a matter of fact.

The bottom line was, she'd overreacted.

"Ugh, Alicia. You're an idiot." She laid her head down on the kitchen table, deciding at that instant to become a hermit. She'd give up her career and become a hoarder. She enjoyed shopping online anyway.

A knock at the door interrupted her self-pity party. She picked up her phone to look at the time. It was pretty late. Who could be here at this hour? Alarmed, phone in hand just in case it was someone she didn't know, she crept to the door and looked out the peephole.

Garrett. She laid her head against the door.

She couldn't face him. She was a moron. What would she say? *Oh, I'm dramatic like that all the time. Wouldn't you love to continue having a relationship with me?*

"Alicia. I know you're there. I heard your shoes on the floor."

Even worse, she sucked at stealth, too. Good thing he wasn't a burglar. Unsure what to say to him but knowing she wasn't going to leave him standing out there, she opened the door.

He stood there, his hands stuffed into the pockets of his pants and his head cocked to the side. He wasn't smiling.

"Hey," was all he said.

So she gave him a "Hey" in return.

"Can I come in for a minute?"

Despite having no idea why he'd want to be within miles of her at the moment, she stepped away from the entrance. "Sure."

She closed the door and locked it after he walked in, but she stayed near the door, just in case she'd have to let him out right away.

He turned to face her, looking about as miserable as she felt.

"I'm sorry," he said right away. "I was a jerk. I shouldn't have made you doubt that what you're doing for me—what you've done for me—has been anything less than a goddamn miracle."

Great. Now she felt even worse. She moved toward him. "No, I'm the one who's sorry. I behaved terribly, acted like the type of woman I absolutely loathe, the kind who throws tantrums and acts like a diva because things don't go her way. I can't apologize enough for overreacting to what you said."

"You didn't overreact. I was an asshole."

"You weren't an asshole. I'm just doing my job, and you have a right to feel about it however you feel about it. It's natural for you to have concerns about your career. I made it about me. Even worse, I made it about you and me. I should know better."

He swept one of the escaped tendrils of hair behind her ear. "I think it's okay to talk about you and me like there really is a you and me."

Something fluttered in her belly. "Is there?"

"I think so. Don't you?"

"I don't know what to think sometimes. It scares me."

"Hell, everything scares me, Alicia. The fact I might not pitch again scares me. Being in a room full of your family tonight? That was terrifying, given how I feel about my own family. You and me? That definitely scares me. That argument we had tonight was minor in comparison."

She loved that he was being honest with her. Knowing what frightened him—that the two of them and their relationship ranked at the top of that list—helped her understand him better. It scared her, too. Her feelings for him absolutely petrified her, because they gave him the power to hurt her. "You're right, and I handled it badly. It won't happen again."

His lips lifted. "Don't make promises you might not be able to keep."

She laughed. "Okay, I won't. I have some hot tea made. Would you like some?"

"No. I want to kiss and make up." He pulled her close and cupped the back of her neck, drawing her lips to his. There was power in this kiss, a desperate passion she grabbed on to like a lifeline.

Maybe it was an apology, but every time they came together, it always seemed more powerful than the time before. It could be that it was all in her mind, that her love for Garrett was growing and that's why touching him, kissing him, and being with him felt so all consuming to her each time they were together. But there was something incredibly magical about the way he stroked her neck. Surely those goose bumps she felt weren't her imagination.

He slid his fingers along her scalp to release the clip that held her hair up then trailed his fingers down to find the zipper of her dress.

With her zipper drawn halfway, he led her into the bedroom where he turned on the beside lamp, then stood her at the side of the bed and pulled her against him again to take her mouth in a searing kiss that left her breathless.

"I've been waiting all night to get you out of this dress, to see what kind of underwear you had on," he whispered against her ear, finishing what he'd started in the living room by pulling the zipper of her dress the rest of the way down.

When she stepped out of the dress, his gaze roamed appreciatively over her black push-up bra and matching thong panties. She hadn't expected to see him tonight, but she'd selected the underwear anyway, secretly hoping he'd be there.

"Uh . . . fucking wow," he said. "And with those sexy high heels? Double fucking wow."

She blushed under his heated gaze. "Thank you. You next."

He unbuttoned his shirt and shrugged it off, then slipped off his shoes and pants, modeling his black boxer briefs for her.

She laughed. "Sexy."

"Yeah, not even close. He dropped his briefs, his erection bobbing up and making her quiver in anticipation.

He teased his fingertips over the swell of her breasts. "This underwear is very hot, Alicia. Did you wear it for me, hoping you'd see me tonight?"

"Yes."

"I like that. Thank you. Why don't you lie on the bed and let me show you how much I appreciate you?"

She sat and started to take off her shoes, but Garrett put his hand over hers and grasped her ankles. "Oh, no, babe. These shoes have to stay on. I want you to dig them into my back and my ass when I fuck you tonight."

Her pussy quivered. She laid her palms flat on the bed. "God, Garrett. You make me wet when you say things like that."

"I like making you wet." He gave her shoulder a gentle push, and she lay back on the bed, her legs dangling over the edge.

When Garrett lifted her legs and pressed a kiss to her calves, she shivered.

"I really like these shoes, Alicia. You should wear them more often." He swept a hand over her ankles, calves, the backs of her knees, and under her thighs, worshipping one leg, then the other, ignoring the throbbing spot between her legs that begged for his touch.

When he drew her panties over her hips and down her legs, she was ready for him to touch her, pet her, lick her until she screamed. But he only caressed her legs again, kissing his way up her calves and knees, making his way to the promised land but bypassing it again to move his lips over her hips and ribs.

"Garrett." His name sailed from her lips on a shaky sigh.

"Mmm," was his reply as he reached the swell of her breasts. He snaked his tongue over the edge of the cups of her bra, teasing her. Her nipples tightened, and she was so hot she felt like she might spontaneously combust. He undid the clasp at the front of her bra to draw the cups aside, releasing her breasts.

"You have the most beautiful breasts, and pretty nipples I like to suck on."

His words sent her up in flames. She watched him as he took one nipple between his lips and sucked it into his mouth, the sensation shooting straight to her core. She reached down to touch herself, but Garrett grasped her wrist and laid her hand down on the bed next to her.

"Uh-uh," he said, before flicking his tongue over the other nipple then grabbing it with his teeth to gently nibble on it.

"You're killing me."

He looked up at her and shattered her with a wicked grin. He moved up and took her lips in a kiss that destroyed what few brain cells she had left. She was limp, lifeless except for every tingling nerve ending begging for him to satisfy her, and when he made the slow trek south again, she wanted to sing with joy.

She trembled as he teased her inner thighs and dropped to his knees, draping her legs over his shoulders as he scooted her to the edge of the bed.

When he finally put his mouth on her sex, her entire world spun. She lifted up on her elbows, desperate to see what he was doing to cause those delicious, sinful sensations. Seeing her legs flung over his shoulders, his tongue gliding over her sex, and the way he devoured her pussy made her entire body convulse with pleasure.

"I'm not going to last, Garrett. I'm going to come, and I'm going to come fast."

He murmured against her sex, laying his tongue against her and, oh, God, was he vibrating it against her clit?

She exploded in a mind-numbing orgasm, grabbing on to his hair and screaming his name as she rocked her climax against his face, unashamed to let him know just how damn good it was. And when she flattened against the bed, out of breath and out of energy, she was certain she had died.

But then he was there, framing her face with his hands and kissing her, renewing her, his erection brushing her hip as he turned her around in the bed.

Maybe she wasn't dead after all, because his mouth and his tongue brought her back to life. His hands roamed her body, brushing her nipples and touching her everywhere. Then he rolled her to her side so she could touch him, too.

She loved the feel of his body, every muscle and ridge that she had come to know so well. She caressed his shoulder, kissed it, even took a little bite.

He growled in response, and her nipples tightened.

And then he pushed her onto her back and grabbed a condom.

"I need to be inside you."

She reached for him, guiding him into her, loving the moment when he buried himself inside her. The sensation of him filling her, becoming one with her, was an emotional as well as a physical sensation that always brought her an amazing sense of wonder. She wanted to tell him that, to tell him how he made her feel, but now wasn't the time, not with passion rising so fast it engulfed her.

He lifted and bent her knee toward her chest, smoothing his hand along her leg. When he caressed her ankle, he turned back toward her, and his lips curved.

"Oh, yeah. I fucking love these shoes."

He thrust into her, slow and easy, taking his time driving her crazy, taking her right to the very brink, burying himself so deep she thought she might die from the ecstasy of it.

She reached for him and tangled her fingers in his hair, tugged on it. He groaned and powered even deeper.

He was going to make her come again, but this time she was taking him with her. And when he increased his tempo, when his brow furrowed and his lids dropped to half-mast, she knew he was on the brink.

"Come inside me, Garrett," she whispered, and he dropped down on top of her, grabbed her butt, and lifted her hips, bringing them even closer together. That's when she dug into him and made him fuck her harder, made him give her everything he had.

Sweat poured from him. He was relentless, muscles bulging in his arms as he rolled his hips over her, shattering her. He kissed her when she cried out, groaning against her lips as he emptied inside her. They shuddered together as they climaxed, her body tightening around his cock as they rode it out, both of them sawing out breaths as if they'd just run a marathon.

Spent, she lay with her head on his chest, listening to the sound of his heart beating. She wanted to tell him how she felt. There were so many things they needed to talk about, but right now she was content and satiated and utterly exhausted.

That big talk about important things could wait for another time.

For now, she just wanted to sleep.

TWENTY-SIX

AFTER A GRUELING DAY OF WORKOUTS AND PRACTICE, Garrett had been called into Manny Magee's office.

They'd be heading to Chicago tomorrow for the season opener. He was hoping he'd get to pitch in this series. He already knew he wasn't the first-game starter. The ball had been given to someone else. But he wanted to pitch—he was ready to pitch.

Alicia had been brought in with him. He wasn't sure what to make of that. The look she gave him told him she had no idea, either.

Manny came in, along with Bobby, the pitching coach, and Phil and Max.

Manny, never one to take a seat behind his desk, leaned against the edge of it in front of where they were all sitting.

"Let's get right to this, Garrett. We're going to work you back into the rotation."

Garret's stomach tightened. Excitement drilled through him. This was what he'd been waiting for.

"Right now we want you to pitch middle-inning relief. We don't think you're ready to start just yet. We want you to get some pitches in, and a couple of innings a game is a good way to warm you up."

His stomach dropped. Fuck. Not what he wanted to hear. "I can start, Coach. My arm's good. I'm ready."

"Bobby and I feel that middle-inning relief is good for you right now."

"The MRI and scans we did on you show you've healed," Phil said. "A very good sign. Now it's just a matter of time until you get your mechanics straightened out."

"I am straightened out." Garrett focused his attention on Manny. "You know I can pitch a good game for you."

"I know you can. After you do a few games in middle-inning relief, we'll move you back into the starting rotation. Work with Bobby on tweaking the finesse of your pitches and continue your therapy with Alicia." Manny stood. "You'll get back there, kid."

The one thing you didn't do was argue with Manny Magee. Once he slotted you into a position, that was your position. If you didn't like that position, your next alternative was AAA ball. Or maybe a new job outside of baseball.

The meeting was over, and Garrett knew it. "Sure. I'll give it my all."

Manny slapped him on the back. "Knew you would, kid."

Garrett walked out of Manny's office, unable to process what had just happened.

Middle-inning relief? Fuck. He'd rather be a closer than spend time as a middle-inning reliever. Hell, he'd rather not pitch at all.

"You're pissed," Alicia said as they walked down the hall after everyone else had dispersed.

He shot her a look. "You think?"

"Garrett."

He was eating up the hallway with quick, angry strides, Alicia hurrying along to catch up. Not now. He wasn't in the mood to talk. He'd rather head down to the workout room and take out his irritation on one of the punching bags or the weight bench. Maybe he'd run a few miles out on the track. There was a goddamn fire in his belly, and right now it wasn't motivation. It was pure, white-hot fury.

But Alicia grabbed his arm, forcing him to stop. "Listen to me. You're going to pitch. At least you're going to pitch. This is good practice for you."

"Practice? You think I care about that?"

She kept her hand on his forearm. "I know this isn't what you wanted."

"No. It isn't at all what I wanted. What I wanted was to be a starting pitcher again."

"And you will be if you stop being such a baby about not getting what you wanted."

That got his attention. He glared at her.

"So you aren't starting a game. Do you think you're the first pitcher to come out of rehab and not start right away? You're lucky you get to pitch at all. Many of them sit on the bench for months, unable to throw a pitch. Your arm is strong, but your mechanics are off a little. This is a way to get your finesse back without losing control of the game. So quit feeling sorry for yourself, pay attention to your pitching coach, let me continue to work with your arm, and let's get you back on the mound as a starter."

He turned and walked away.

"Garrett."

He didn't look at her. "I'm going to the therapy room. Come work on my shoulder. It feels tight after today's practice."

There was nothing worse than being called on the carpet by your therapist of all people.

She was right. He hadn't taken the news well. He'd wanted to start in the rotation, not do middle-inning relief.

But he was going to pitch. And she was right about that. He could have ended up benched.

So he'd deal. He'd be the best goddamn middle-inning reliever they had, and when they realized that, they'd put him back in the starting rotation.

He'd give it a week. A week and he'd be a starter again.

A WEEK LATER, HE WAS STILL PITCHING MIDDLE IN-nings. He'd done fine in relief, had walked a few, struck out some, and put a couple on base. He'd given up two runs, which sucked. Still, he would liked to have left those players on base.

But he was getting his form back, his arm felt good, and he was pitching some innings.

Middle innings.

Fuck, this was driving him crazy.

To make matters worse, he had the media crawling up his ass about his shoulder and his new position as a middle-inning reliever. He'd explained, and the coach had explained, that this was only temporary, that this was part of his rehab, and that he'd be starting games again in no time. Which had gotten the media into a frenzy, speculating that there was still something wrong with his shoulder and he'd never be a starting pitcher again.

He'd rolled his eyes over that one. As if he didn't have a moun-tain's worth of his own self-doubts weighing him down, the media had to add to it?

"You ready for me to stretch you?"

He looked up to see Alicia standing over him. He hadn't even realized there was anyone else in the workout room. But now, there were other players filing in to do their pregame warm-ups.

It was the home opener today. Normally, he'd be excited as hell about the home crowd, the home stadium. Normally, he'd pitch the home opener. He always had. At least since he'd been a starting pitcher.

Today, Walter Segundo would start the game. Maybe, if he was lucky, he'd get to throw some middle-inning pitches, but Segundo was a strong pitcher and could often carry the game until the closer came in, in the eighth or ninth. Garrett might not get to pitch in the opener at all.

"Garrett," Alicia said again. "Let's stretch that shoulder."

He looked up at Alicia, wondering if he'd made the right choice a few months ago when he'd told the doctors and coaches that he wanted to work with Alicia. Maybe he should have stayed with Max, the head of the sports-medicine department.

He felt disloyal to Alicia just thinking it. He was pitching now, where before he'd done nothing but feel sorry for himself, convinced he'd never pitch again.

He was pitching again, just not the way he'd envisioned. Surely that wasn't Alicia's fault. Or maybe it was. She was responsible for his recovery, wasn't she? She'd told him she'd get him on the mound again. She'd done that, but not in the way he wanted.

Shit. He didn't know what to think anymore.

"Garrett?"

He got up and followed her. "Yeah. Sure."

At the table he kept his eyes closed, concentrating on his arm, on what it was supposed to be doing that it wasn't, while Alicia stretched him.

"You're very quiet today."

"Just thinking."

"About the game?"

"Yeah."

"I hope you'll get some work in today. Be sure to keep your arm loose."

"I don't think you need to tell me what to do in the bullpen."

She didn't say anything after that, which was fine with him. They hadn't seen much of each other over the past week. They'd been on the road, and the two of them hadn't spent much time together other than her doing his therapy. They'd met on the field and in the workout room, but there'd been so much going on with media interviews and the games that they'd had no alone time. Alicia was rooming with the other female therapist, and Garrett had one of his teammates as a roommate.

They'd hardly spoken, other than as player and therapist. Not since he'd snapped at her when he'd found out he was going to be assigned as a middle-inning relief pitcher.

Which had probably been for the best. Garrett hadn't exactly been the best company lately.

He hadn't called her when they'd gotten back into town, either. Too much was going on in his head, and none of it was pleasant. She probably knew it, too, because she hadn't said anything about it, just showed up at the facility with her usual smiling face, patiently working on his shoulder as if nothing had changed, when in fact everything had. At least for him.

He didn't deserve to have someone like her in his life.

Her hands on him felt good, though, and when she rolled him over to massage his back and shoulders, she released some of the tension he'd been holding in. At least physically.

There was nothing she could do to take away the doubts in his mind.

"Okay, sit up," she said.

He grabbed his shirt and pulled it over his head.

She looked at him, and he was reminded that, despite those ugly physical therapy uniforms they wore, she was still beautiful. He didn't know how he hadn't noticed it all those months ago.

She gave him a smile. "You're going to do great today."

"Yeah, if I get on the mound at all."

She looked around the room, then brushed her fingertips across his knee. "Give it time, Garrett. Recovery is never fast. You'll get there."

"Yeah. Sure I will." He slid off the table, then left the treatment room.

During the game, Garrett watched from the bullpen. Segundo pitched a shutout through eight innings, and Maloney closed the last inning for him. Garrett never got to pitch.

He'd never ached to be on the mound more in his life. He'd have given anything to even pitch the middle innings.

But what he really wanted was his own game. He wanted to start so badly it hurt.

In the locker room after the game, Garrett showered, dressed, then sat in front of his locker, hoping like hell the media would be more focused on Gavin and Dedrick and Stan, the playmakers who'd driven in the winning runs, and Segundo for his stellar turn on the mound today, and less on the fact that Garrett had been nonexistent. He couldn't face them, had nothing to say.

Max came in and sat next to him. "You doing okay?"

He lifted his head and nodded. "Fine."

"Your shoulder is fine, too, you know. But maybe it's time for a change."

Garrett frowned. "What kind of change?"

"You've been working with Alicia for a while now, and while she's gotten you this far, maybe it's time you let me take over and get you the rest of the way."

"The rest of the way?"

"Your mechanics are good, but you're not there yet. I have a few ideas for tweaking the small amount of scar tissue that's still left in your shoulder, and I think we can get you back in the starting rotation."

That would mean dumping Alicia. "Alicia's been a lifesaver, you know. She really worked me back into shape. I wouldn't be where I am now without her skills."

"Oh, I know she did. Better than I thought she would, frankly. Now, let me take you the rest of the way."

Garrett swallowed. This was his career, and he had to put it first. Even above Alicia's feelings. It wasn't like she'd be fired or anything. She'd done her part, and God, he was grateful. But he had to be a starting pitcher again, and if Max could make that happen . . .

"Fine. Whatever you think needs to be done, let's do it."

TWENTY-SEVEN

SOMETHING WAS GOING ON WITH GARRETT. ALICIA HAD no idea what it was, but she'd bet it had something to do with his unhappiness at being stuck in middle-inning relief.

She knew his shoulder therapy was still going well. He had full range of motion and exhibited no signs of pain when throwing the ball. The problem was, he'd pretty much climbed up into his own head and refused to talk to her. And when a player got into his own head, it was never a good sign. That's where Garrett had been when she'd started working with him, and it had taken some effort to get him out of there.

Unfortunately, they hadn't had any alone time together, first because of the road trip, then because of the string of home games, plus the media circus in St. Louis. She couldn't even fathom the pressure Garrett must be under right now, but the last thing she was going to do was add to it with any kind of emotional stuff related to the two of them.

He had enough going on. There would be time later for the two of them to kick back and talk about their relationship. Right now she was more concerned about his career and where his head was. She needed to convince him that his pitching days weren't over just because he wasn't currently a starting pitcher.

She believed in him and in the work they'd done together. She knew he'd start again. The key was in convincing him.

She walked out onto the field where the pitchers were taking practice throws, ready to work with him and with the pitching coach. She and Bobby had gotten into a rhythm of diagnosing Garrett's mechanics and working on adjustments that would affect his positioning. Bobby would ask her if that would hurt his arm in any way, and she would have Garrett throw and gauge his pain level.

These days, nothing seemed to cause him any pain, which was a very good sign, but she could tell afterward, when she did therapy, if any of the throwing mechanics had an adverse effect on his shoulder. The last thing they needed was to take any step backward in Garrett's recovery.

This morning, Max was out there, and Garrett was already throwing. She grabbed her notebook and opened it, checking Garrett's warm-up time. No, she wasn't late.

"Morning, Max," she said as she headed out onto the field.

"Alicia. Garrett, why don't you come over here for a second? Give us a minute, Bobby," Max said.

"Sure," Bobby said, moving over to work with one of the other pitchers.

"Garrett and I spoke yesterday," Max said. "You've done an excellent job, Alicia. But in order to effect more progress in his recovery, it's time for a change."

Alicia looked from Max to Garrett, who positioned his gaze somewhere over her shoulder, not at her.

"I don't understand."

"Just to shake things up a bit. I've got a few ideas that I think will eliminate the remainder of the scar tissue in Garrett's shoulder and will get him back on the mound as a starter."

"Yes, Max, so do I." She flipped open her notebook. "If you look here . . ."

But Max waved his hand. "It's okay, Alicia. I've got this now. Transfer your notes on Garrett to my desk. Why don't you go tape up Cleron's ankle? He's complaining of some soreness."

"But—"

"That's the final word, Alicia. You're off Garrett's case."

She looked at Garrett, who gave her a short nod. "I'm sure Max will do a good job of getting me the rest of the way. Thanks for all you've done, Alicia."

Thanks for all you've done? That was it? It was like they were strangers. And just like that a chasm opened between the two of them, a distance she'd felt for a while now but had ignored.

She pasted on a professional smile and nodded to Max.

"Okay, Max, sure. I'll have those notes transferred to your files right away."

She turned and headed toward the locker room so she could grab her kit that held the tape for Cleron's ankle. With every step, the emptiness in the pit of her stomach grew.

It wasn't personal, despite the devastation she felt. This was part of her job, so the ache in her stomach could just take a hike.

It was time for distance between her and Garrett, anyway. He needed to focus on his pitching, and she needed to get back to what she did, which was work for the sports-medicine team in whatever capacity they needed her.

Their time together was coming to an end. Or maybe it had ended a couple of weeks ago, and Garrett had been the only one to notice it while she'd been working so hard on his arm, trying so desperately to put her feelings on the back burner. Because it had been his career that had been so important to her, and his feelings that she'd been tiptoeing around.

While he'd just crushed hers without a second thought.

Tears pricked her eyes. She swiped them away, refusing to be such a girl about the situation. She was at work and she was going to be a goddamned professional. This wasn't about her and Garrett as a couple; this was about Garrett, her client.

Getting personally involved with a client had been the problem all along. She'd known this would happen as soon as the two of them had climbed into bed together.

Ending their personal relationship was for the best. She knew it, and obviously Garrett knew it, too. She'd known from the beginning they wouldn't be able to work together once his shoulder healed. And being together while they worked for the same team was a conflict of interest. There was no way she was giving up her job. She loved her work with the Rivers, had fought hard to get this job. It was iffy as it was with her cousin playing for the team. Having a relationship with another player? If that was discovered by her bosses, it would be death to her career.

It was time she categorized her relationship with Garrett where it belonged—a wonderful interlude, something she'd remember fondly, but not something that could be continued.

It was over. Door closed. Done. Already forgotten.

She pulled up Garrett's treatment file on her notebook and sent it to Max. When she came out of the locker room, she headed straight for the bench, focusing only on Cleron. She didn't once look up, didn't once search out Garrett. She had to make a clean break from him, not let her emotions cloud her logic.

She kneeled in front of Cleron. "Okay, Jeff. Let's take a look at that ankle."

GARRETT WATCHED ALICIA WORK ON CLERON'S ANKLE. She never looked over at him, not even a glance over her shoulder.

What did he expect after the way he treated her? The shock in her eyes when Max had told her he was taking over, followed by the look of pain that crossed her face when Garrett had basically given her a kiss-off still stuck in his gut like a hard punch.

"Garrett. You're not focusing," Bobby said. "You haven't hit the strike zone in six pitches."

Garrett walked off the mound, his concentration broken. He shouldn't be focusing on Alicia. This was his chance to change his pitching style, to have Max finish off his rehab, and to finally—finally—get back his starting pitching job. He couldn't take this personally, and neither should Alicia. It wasn't personal, it was his career.

And, unfortunately, hers. She had probably taken it personally, and she likely thought he was dumping her personally on top of dumping her professionally.

Shit. He took off his ball cap and threaded his fingers through his hair.

You didn't treat someone you loved that way.

Wait.

Loved?

He shot his gaze across the ballpark toward the dugout.

Alicia was gone. Cleron was back in the outfield, but Alicia was nowhere to be found.

He already felt the emptiness.

"You gonna count daisies out here all day, Scott, or do you maybe feel like throwing some pitches?" Bobby asked.

Garrett scanned the ballpark one last time, but didn't see Alicia. He didn't know what he'd do if he did see her.

He'd fucked up and didn't know what to do about it. Instead, he turned and stepped back up on the practice mound. "Yeah, coach. Let's throw some pitches."

TWENTY-EIGHT

IF THERE WAS ONE THING ALICIA DIDN'T DO, IT WAS avoidance. She was a direct, in your face, let's-put-it-all-out-there-and-resolve-the-problem kind of person. Things that festered tended to get ugly, and she was a big believer in communication.

Which was why she was sitting at her aunt's house on a Sunday afternoon watching the Rivers play baseball instead of being at the ballpark.

"Shouldn't you be working?" her dad asked, munching on a pretzel as the family gathered around her uncle and aunt's television to watch the game.

"We do occasionally get days off, you know."

"Yeah, when the team is off," her father said.

She rolled her eyes. "There are plenty of sports-medicine specialists to handle injuries. We don't all work every game day. I'm not on today."

"But you get free game tickets, and you can go to the ballpark any time you want, right?" Jenna asked.

Alicia shot Jenna a look that plainly said, "Shut. Up."

"Yes. Just didn't feel like going today."

"Hmmm," Jenna said.

"Hmmm, indeed," Savannah added.

"Besides, it's Dad's birthday. I specifically asked for today off so I could be here for the big family party."

Her dad grabbed for another pretzel. "I dunno, sweet pea. I'd rather be at the game."

Cole snorted. "Me, too, Dad. Alicia should have given us her tickets."

"I could have gotten you seats if you'd asked. Gavin can get you tickets, too."

"That's true," her uncle said. "Though these are pretty good seats, too."

"Better instant replay," Jenna said.

Alicia would rather be watching some old black-and-white romance on television at home while crying into a gallon of chocolate chip ice cream, but it was her father's birthday, and her aunt and uncle had decided to host a barbecue at their house today, so she had no choice but to attend. It was either that or go to the game, and being at the game meant being near Garrett, and right now that was not a place she wanted to be.

"Aunt Kathleen, can I do anything in the kitchen?" Anything to avoid the game on television.

"No, thank you, honey. I made the potato salad and slaw last night. The ribs are soaking in barbecue sauce, so everything's ready."

"I could grill the ribs."

Her uncle scowled at her. "That's my job, missy. Don't even think about it."

Jenna snickered. "Well, I could use a little girl gossip upstairs."

Bless Jenna. "Sure."

Savannah stood. "I'm coming with you."

"Me, too," Tara said, handing Sam off to Mick, who grinned and snuggled the baby in the crook of his arm.

"Liz will be unhappy she's at the game today and missing out on this," Tara said after they moved upstairs and got comfortable in Alicia's aunt's room.

"Alicia looked like she needed a break from all things baseball," Jenna said, looking to Alicia to start the conversation.

The last thing she wanted to do was talk about it, but when faced with her family, it all came pouring out. She told them everything that had happened with Garrett, including being taken off his case.

"What a dick," Jenna said. "I can't believe after all you did for him that he dumped you like that."

"Men can be so obtuse at times," Savannah said. "Have you spoken to him since that happened?"

"No. He did call, but I didn't answer. I don't see the point."

Tara, who'd pulled up a spot on the bed next to Alicia, patted her hand. "You can't hide from him forever, you know. Eventually, the two of you are going to have to have a conversation."

Alicia sighed. "I know. I'm just not ready yet. We've been through so much, and he really needs to concentrate on his pitching."

"Oh, bullshit," Jenna said. "He really needs to come over to your house, beg your forgiveness, and kiss your ass for what he did to you."

Alicia let out a laugh. "I wouldn't go that far. He has to do what he thinks is best for his career."

"You're what's best for his career." Jenna lifted her chin, clearly on Alicia's side no matter what.

And that's why Alicia loved her. "Max is the head of sports medicine. It's not like he sucks at what he does."

"And you're the one who got Garrett pitching again, aren't you?" Savannah asked. "Is it possible he took his frustration at not becoming a starter right away out on you and let this Max person sway him into switching therapists? As I recall, Max wasn't very happy about getting the boot in the first place, was he?"

Savannah had a point that Alicia hadn't considered. "No, he wasn't."

"So there could have been some behind-the-scenes maneuvering on Max's part to shift you out and put himself back in charge of your guy's therapy. Then, when Garrett moves back into the starting rotation, who gets all the credit?" Tara asked.

"Max likely will," Alicia admitted.

Tara nodded. "That's what I thought. Jenna and Savannah are right. You need to talk to Garrett."

Alicia stared at all of them. "And tell him what? That I'm pissed he pushed me out? It's his prerogative. He can choose which therapist he uses. Max is the best."

Tara cocked a brow. "Is he the best for Garrett? Or are you the best for him?"

"I think I'm the best for him. I got him to stop moaning about never pitching again. And goddamn it, he *is* pitching, just not the way he thought he'd be. And he will be a starter again."

"Then tell him that," Jenna said. "And when you're doing that, also tell him he acted like an asshole."

"One would think he'd come to that realization on his own," Savannah suggested.

Alicia sighed. She didn't know what to do. But she definitely wasn't going to go begging to Garrett. He would either figure out he needed her or he wouldn't. In the meantime, she had other players she was assigned to and her own job to protect.

Her own heart to protect.

"But it's more than just your job and your working relationship with Garrett, isn't it?" Tara asked, keying in on what was really bothering Alicia.

"Maybe."

"No maybe about it. You're in love with him, aren't you?"

She turned to look at Jenna. "Yes. I'm in love with him. Or I thought I was."

"Is he in love with you?" Savannah asked.

"I don't know. We never talked about it."

Savannah slanted her a look. "Did you ever tell him how you felt?"

"It was never the right time."

A collective chorus of groans filled the room.

Alicia drew her knees up to her chest and wrapped her arms around her legs. "So now what do I do? After what happened, I'm sure as hell not going to tell him I love him. It would seem like begging for my job back."

"No, you can't tell him now," Savannah said. "The ball is definitely in his court. He has to come to you. He owes you that much."

"So, now I wait?"

Jenna nodded. "Since you're in love with him, I guess waiting is the best thing to do. I agree with everyone else—you can't go to him. Not with all those feelings you have. Then if the two of you end up together, you'll always be left wondering. It's definitely his move. If he's worth it at all, you shouldn't have to wait long."

"And if he doesn't come to me?"

Tara shot her a look of sympathy. "Then he's not worth waiting for, honey."

TWENTY-NINE

IT HAD BEEN A REALLY GOOD DAY. GARRETT HAD pitched two solid innings. Things were going well. He'd been working with Max, who seemed to think therapy was progressing nicely.

Manny had told him his pitches were getting stronger, hitting the mark, and if all went well, he might be rotating into the starting lineup within the next month or so.

Things were looking up.

But he still felt an emptiness inside that couldn't be filled, because Alicia wasn't in his life, wasn't the center of his universe, and that just plain sucked.

He'd called and texted her a few times after Max had removed her from his case, but she hadn't answered. And like a coward, he'd stopped trying, focused instead on his pitching, figuring that maybe it had been for the best, that maybe they'd had a great fling and he should just look forward, not back.

Problem was, she filled his head at night when he lay in bed, and on the road all he could think about was talking to her. When he was at home, he wanted to see her, be close to her. He wanted her at his place. He wanted to have dinner with her, sit on the couch with her watching movies. He wanted her in his bed.

He ached for her. Like it or not, she'd become an integral part of his life that had nothing to do with rehabbing his shoulder. His shoulder was fine. He was nearly 100 percent recovered now, and eventually, he wouldn't have needed her for that anymore anyway.

But he'd always need her to fill the space in his heart that had opened up and let her in.

And that's what he needed to tell her. He couldn't allow fear to keep him from having something—someone—that meant so much to him.

She'd been busy working on rehab for some of the other guys, so he rarely got the chance to talk to her during treatment and workouts anymore.

On an off day, he waited until she finished and showed up at her house that night, hoping like hell she hadn't moved on, that she didn't have a date over when he rang the doorbell.

When she answered, she was wearing skintight yoga pants and a long-sleeved shirt. God, she looked good. He wanted to pull her into his arms and kiss her. But he couldn't. He'd lost that right because he was stupid.

Her eyes widened when she saw it was him at the door.

"Oh. Hi," she said.

"Hi yourself. I know I should have phoned, but you didn't answer the last few times I called you, so I thought I'd drop by."

"Yeah. Sorry. My feelings were a little hurt about being dumped as your therapist."

He loved that she was so forward and honest. "Can I come in?"

She hesitated. He didn't know what he'd do if she said no.

"Sure."

He stepped into the living room and turned. "I feel like I'm always apologizing to you."

She didn't say anything.

"Maybe it's because I'm always fucking up. I'm not very good at this relationship thing. I've never had one before. I've dated here and there, but nothing long lasting. You and me—I think we've got something special, and I feel like I let it go."

"You didn't let it go. You're mixing the work aspect with the personal."

He took a deep inhale. "But they are mixed together. Or they were. In my head, anyway." He dragged his fingers through his hair. "I got used to seeing you every day. I got used to you taking care of me. And when you weren't there . . ."

She frowned. "So you're upset I'm not your therapist anymore?"

He was screwing this up. He shook his head. "No. I mean, yes. What you did for me—you turned my life and my career around. I can't thank you enough for that. Manny thinks I'll be a starting pitcher again soon."

"That's good news. I told you that you would be."

"I know you did. I guess when I started pitching again, I wanted it to happen right away. And when it didn't, everything got confused for me. I looked for someone to blame for that."

She crossed her arms. "And I was convenient?"

She wasn't going to make this easy for him. "Yeah, I guess so. You were responsible for my recovery, for helping me pull my head out of my ass and make me see that I could pitch again. And when things didn't go the way I wanted them to, I blamed you. When Max came to me and told me that he could get me the rest of the way, I jumped at the chance."

"I could have gotten you there, Garrett."

"I know. Which is what I told Max. He's very good at what he does. But he's not you."

She stepped closer. "You told Max what?"

"I told Max that while I appreciated his working with me, I've grown used to you as my therapist, and I'd rather work with you."

She gaped at him. "You did not say that to him."

"I did. He's fine with it."

Her lips lifted. "I'm pretty sure Max isn't fine with it."

"I don't care if he is or not. What I do care is how you feel." He crossed the distance between them and picked up her hand to hold it; he'd missed her touch so much. "I hurt you that day. And I let you walk away from me. I'm sorry for that. I've missed you."

"I've . . . missed you, too, Garrett."

"I love you, Alicia."

Her eyes widened. "You do?"

"I do. I can't tell you how much that scares me. The breakup of my parents' marriage kind of soured me on the whole idea of love and permanence. You know how I am about family. Hell, I don't even see my own much anymore because it makes me so damned uncomfortable to be around them. It reminds me of pain and loss and things I don't want to remember. But then I see you with your whole family—and the love that surrounds you—and it makes me believe that maybe we could have something like that, that maybe that kind of love actually does exist."

Alicia was swamped with so many emotions at once she couldn't process them all. Relief that he'd shown up—that he'd come to her and laid his feelings on the line—and utter shock that he'd told her he loved her.

He'd even apologized and taken responsibility for hurting her. It took a strong man to stand up to his failings. A lot of men couldn't do that.

She laid her hand on Garrett's chest and tilted her head back to look into the face she loved so much. "You did hurt me. I've put everything I have into making you a pitcher again. And you threw it all away because you got scared."

This time he didn't look away. "Yes. I'm sorry."

"You can't run every time the world doesn't turn in the direction you want it to. You might not become a starting pitcher again at the time you think is right for you, but you will start again, Garrett. I know you will. I believe in you. I've always believed in you."

She felt his shudder. He clasped his hands over hers, brought her hand to his mouth and pressed a kiss there. "You've always believed in me, even when I didn't believe in myself."

"Yes, I did."

"Thank you for that. And now I have to ask if you'll forgive me for hurting you, even though I don't deserve it. Because I love you, and I want to be with you."

"How will that work, Garrett? I can't be your therapist and your girlfriend."

He cocked a brow. "Why not? There's no rule that says you can't work for the team and have a relationship with a team member, is there?"

"Of course there is. It's in my contract with the team."

He took a step back. "Seriously?"

"Seriously. How can you not know that? I just assumed you did, or that it's in your contract, too. I can't fraternize on a personal basis with any team member without losing my job. Why do you think I was so freaked out when the other players caught us kissing?"

"You have got to be kidding me. Why didn't you tell me this sooner?"

She shrugged. "Well, first, and again, because I thought you already knew. And second, because I thought what you and I had was a fling, a temporary thing. I figured as long as we hid it well, no one would ever know. Now . . ."

She was elated by his declaration of love, and miserable at the same time.

He sat on the sofa. "This sucks."

"Yes."

"And it's unacceptable." He pulled his phone out of his pocket and punched a number, looking at her as it rang. "Victoria, it's Garrett. We have a problem."

THIRTY

ALICIA CHEWED HER BOTTOM LIP AS SHE WAITED IN
the team conference room with Garrett, his agent, Victoria Baldwin, and Lucas Birdwell, an attorney Liz had hired to represent
Alicia in this matter.

Her boss, Max, Manny Magee, and the team's attorneys were
all present as well.

Alicia's throat had gone utterly dry. That night when Gavin had
told his agent he wanted to be traded, she'd nearly collapsed on her
living-room floor.

"Now that we've outlined the issue, I'm sure you can see why
Garrett has asked for this trade," Victoria said, looking so well put
together in her stylish navy blue suit and gold stacked heels that
Alicia felt frumpy in comparison in her simple black dress and
black high-heeled pumps. But the last thing she wanted to do was
call attention to herself. She'd pulled her hair back in a low ponytail
and hadn't worn any jewelry. It was much better for Victoria to

have all the attention, and that she did with her hair smartly cut in a short bob, her perfect manicure, and her expertly applied makeup. The woman was utterly stunning and completely confident as she addressed everyone present.

"Wouldn't it be simpler for Miss Riley to secure another position?" asked one of the Rivers' attorneys whose name Alicia couldn't remember since there were five of them present.

"Simpler, yes. But Garrett has requested the trade, so Miss Riley doesn't lose her job. As we've discussed, the two of them are in a relationship and determined that Miss Riley doesn't lose a job she's so well qualified to perform. She enjoys her position with the Rivers and doesn't want to compromise it."

"Wait," Manny said, with a frown on his face. "So Garrett and Alicia have fallen in love, have I got that part right?"

"You have, Manny," Victoria said.

"And this is a problem, how?"

"Miss Riley's employment contract specifies she can't personally fraternize with any of the players," Alicia's attorney explained.

"What a crock," Manny said. "Why don't you just rewrite her contract then. She stays, Garrett stays, and everyone's happy."

Victoria looked over at the attorneys. The one whose name Alicia couldn't remember said, "If we did that, Mr. Magee, we'd have to do that for all the employees of the team."

"What? You think there's gonna be a bunch of fraternizin' then? There's only one other female member of the sports-medicine team, and she's already married, isn't she?"

"Yes," Max said. "She is."

Manny leaned back in his chair. "Then it seems to me the problem is solved. I'd rather not lose one of my best pitchers just because he happened to fall in love with a woman who works for the team. Dumb rule if you ask me. Who writes these contracts anyway?"

No one on the Rivers legal team answered that question.

"Is it possible to revise Miss Riley's contract?" Lucas asked.

The suits conferred, then Mr. Teers—Alicia finally remembered his name—answered. "I think we can do that as long as Miss Riley and Mr. Scott agree that she'll no longer be directly responsible for Mr. Scott's therapy."

"I don't think so," Garrett said. "What difference does it make if she does my therapy or not? She's the one who got me back on the pitcher's mound."

"Garrett," Alicia said, placing her hand over his. "You can't win everything. It's okay."

"She's right, Garrett," Victoria said. "Take this as a victory. Alicia keeps her job, and you get to stay with the Rivers. Surely there are many fine sports-medicine specialists working for the Rivers who can handle your physical therapy."

"There are," Alicia said, looking over at Max, who so far hadn't betrayed his feelings on the matter with any sort of expression. "Work with Max."

Garrett inhaled, then sighed. "Fine."

"Then it's agreed," Lucas said.

After some legal language maneuvering, the meeting was over. Alicia found the whole process exhausting, and was still shocked Garrett had even contemplated the trade in the first place.

After thanking Lucas for his time, Alicia stood outside with Garrett and Victoria.

"Thanks, Tori. I knew I could count on you," Garrett said.

"You make me want to drink, Garrett, you know that?"

He grinned. "I doubted they'd let me go. Even though I'm not a starting pitcher yet, I'm too valuable to the team."

Victoria patted his cheek. "That's what I love about you. All that ego." She looked over at Alicia. "Keep him healthy, even if it's on the down low."

Alicia laughed. "I'll do my best. And thank you."

"You're welcome, honey."

She linked her arm with Garrett's, but ran into Max and Manny in the hall. She started to pull her arm away, but Garrett held her hand, keeping them firmly linked together.

Max's lips stayed compressed tightly together. Manny grinned.

"That ended up good for everyone, but it would have been easier if you'd have just come and talked to me about all of it," Manny said.

Garrett shrugged. "It was Alicia's deal I was more worried about. I needed to protect her." Garrett looked over at Max, who shrugged.

"We don't arbitrarily dump our best therapists, Garrett," Max said. "We'd have found a way to work it out. We'll see you tomorrow, Alicia."

Shocked, Alicia could only stare dumbfounded as Manny and Max walked away.

"So, he likes you."

"Apparently. Or he was just blowing smoke up my ass."

Garrett laughed. "I don't think Max hands out compliments all that easily."

"I have no idea. This has been a nightmare. Let's go home."

"Your place or mine?" he asked.

"I don't care."

"I have an idea. How about we take this relationship public?"

He took her to Charlie Gitto's on the Hill. She had a ridiculous amount of penne primavera, and he had steak and pasta. They both had the most wonderful glasses of Chianti, and by the time they left, Alicia was full.

"I need to walk," she said.

The night was cool, but she didn't care. Garrett wrapped his arm around her, and they strolled around the block a few times.

"It does feel good not to worry about someone seeing us together."

He stopped and pulled the edges of her jacket closed, then pressed a kiss to her lips. "I love you. And you don't have to worry about being seen with me anymore. Unless I get demoted or can't pitch."

He said it with a laugh, but before they could resume walking, she laid her hand on his chest and stopped him. "You do realize I don't love you because you're a famous ballplayer, right?"

"Yeah. You love me in spite of it."

Now it was her turn to laugh. "You've got that right."

When she felt like she had sufficiently walked off the enormous meal she'd eaten, they climbed back into the car. She expected they'd head to either her place or his, but she was surprised when he stayed downtown and pulled into valet parking at the Lumiere, a hotel and casino.

He took her inside, and though it wasn't quite like Vegas, bells were ringing, cards were being dealt, and she was ready to play.

They hit the poker room, and Garrett fronted her some money. Four hours passed before she realized it. She and Garrett both did well. She was several hundred dollars up and ready to stretch her legs, so they wandered around, played a few slots, and, unfortunately, lost money.

"I think I'll stick with poker," she said.

"I agree. You're a hell of a lot better at poker than you are at slots."

She laughed and tucked herself against Garrett's side. "Thank you for taking me out tonight. I've had a great time."

"Oh, the night isn't over." He led her to the front desk, showed his ID, and was given a room key.

When they walked off, she looked up at him. "We have a room here?"

"We do. And bags are being brought up. I asked Savannah to pack an overnight bag for you. I hope you don't mind. I figured however this thing turned out today, we'd need an overnight get-away, just the two of us."

"I don't mind at all. Thank you."

The room was a suite, overlooking the St. Louis Arch and the riverfront. It was beautiful and spacious, and she loved it. What she loved the most, though, was being alone with Garrett and no longer having to worry about anything other than being in love with him, spending time with him, and then going to work and doing her job.

She liked the simplicity of it all.

"I like this chair," he said, referring to an overstuffed chair sitting near the window.

"Do you? And why's that?"

"I think because I'd like to see you holding on to the arms of that chair while you're bent over."

Her body warmed at the visual. "Would you like me to keep my dress on, or take it off?"

He came over to her and pulled her against him, kissing her thoroughly until that warmth she felt turned into a full-blown heat explosion. He raised her dress over her butt, smoothing his hand over the red silk panties she'd chosen to wear today.

He peered around her. "Oh, dress definitely off. Turn around."

She turned and he unzipped her dress, drawing it off her shoulders. He kissed each shoulder, then pulled her ponytail holder out, moving her hair to the side so he could kiss her neck. She shivered, goose bumps breaking out on her skin.

"Cold?" he asked.

"Definitely not cold. You make me hot."

He drew her dress down her arms and over her hips until it pooled on the floor, leaving her in her heels and underwear.

"Oh, yeah," Garrett said, cupping her breasts, teasing her nipples through the flimsy silken fabric.

Alicia leaned back against him, watching his hands as he played with her. They were so large they dwarfed her breasts. She put her hands over his and pressed in, loving the pressure. He drew the cups down and brushed his thumbs over her sensitive nipples.

"I like you touching me."

He rolled her nipples with his thumbs and forefingers. "Like this?"

She gasped. "Yes. More. Harder."

He gave her nipples a light pinch, and she rubbed her butt against his quickly growing erection.

"And I like that," he said. "I love when you rub that sweet ass of yours against me. Bend over, Alicia. Grab on to the chair."

He took her breath away. She held on to the arms of the chair while he swept his hands over her rear, worshipping it with the lightest of caresses. When he gave it a light tap, she gasped and half turned to look at him.

"Hurt?"

"No."

"More?"

"Oh, yes."

Her pussy tightened when he gave her another swat, and when he drew her panties down to her thighs and spanked her again, still gently, she felt naughty.

"I love seeing you like this. It makes me hard."

She looked at him, her pussy quivering with delight at this unexpected turn in their sex play. "It makes me wet."

"I like you wet and quivering for me."

She did. He swatted her again, this time a little harder. She cried out, but it was in pleasure, because he smoothed his hand over the spot, then bent and kissed her where he'd spanked her.

"You're so hot with your smoking red panties pulled down and your butt red where I've spanked you. I had no idea you'd like that."

"I didn't, either."

"Is your pussy wet?"

"Yes."

He slipped his hand between her legs to cup her sex. She nearly died from the ecstasy of his touch.

"Yeah, you're wet." He tucked two fingers inside her and used his thumb to swirl over her clit.

"Oh, God," she said, throwing her head back as he began to fuck her with his fingers. And when he tapped her butt with his other hand again, her pussy clamped around his fingers like a vise.

"You do like that, don't you, Alicia?"

She couldn't answer, because he was going to give her an orgasm if he kept doing that. "Spank me. Rub my clit and spank me. I'm going to come."

He did, and oh, dear God, it was too much. She climaxed on a wild cry, bucking against his fingers, hoping he'd hold her right there because it was so damn good she didn't want it to stop.

The waves kept rolling while Garrett tore open a condom wrapper. Then he was behind her, inside her, holding on to her hips as he rammed into her with one glorious, hard thrust.

She heard him groan as he seated himself fully inside her, and she was still throbbing from the aftereffects of that amazing orgasm. He stilled, and she knew he felt her.

"God, Alicia, you feel so good." And then he began to move inside her, taking her there again so quickly she wasn't sure she'd be able to remain standing. Her legs trembled as he withdrew, then thrust, smoothing his hand over her back, then leaning over her to nip at the nape of her neck.

She loved this animalistic, out-of-control, passionate side to him. She loved everything about him. And when she thrust back against him to draw him deeper inside her, he groaned, dug his fingers into her hips, and slammed into her, his balls slapping against her as he gave her what she asked for.

She reached between her legs to rub her clit, needing another climax, needing to feel her pussy grip him in that tight fist again.

"Alicia," he said, his voice going taut with tension as he neared the edge.

"Come inside me, Garrett. Make me yours."

She climbed onto her knees on the chair and lifted her butt up. He used his fingers to swipe her juices onto her anus and teased her there.

"Oh, yes," she whispered. "More."

He lubed her butt and inserted a finger into her ass while he fucked her. She rubbed her clit, and the sensation of his finger inside her anus and his cock in her pussy sent her over the top.

"Make me come," she said. "I need to come again."

Mindless with pleasure, she was a bundle of nerve endings, each tuned into the riotous pleasure he gave her.

Out of control now, Garrett fucked her deep, and when she felt him nearing the end, she let go, screaming at the orgasm he gave her. He yelled out when he came, too, and they rode the crest together.

He pulled out and turned her around, pressing his lips and body to hers, wrapping her in a cocoon of hazy afterglow.

"Will it always be like this?" she asked, brushing her lips against his.

"Like what?"

"So . . . intense. Lovemaking with you burns out a few of my brain cells every time."

"Yeah, I know. And yes, it'll always be like this."

She loved his confidence.

They showered, dressed in their sweats, and climbed in bed. Garrett ordered room service dessert and coffee, then they settled in among the many pillows to watch a movie—some romantic comedy that Alicia had seen probably twenty times, but Garrett claimed to have never watched before.

He took some foam from her cappuccino and made a moustache on her face. She giggled and grabbed her napkin to swipe it away, but not before she made him a goatee from the last of her foam.

"Oh, I like that goatee on you. You should grow one."

"Will I get more sex with the goatee?"

"Maybe."

"Then consider it done."

She laughed.

He stared at the TV. "You like this mushy stuff, huh?" he asked as he fed Alicia a chocolate-covered strawberry.

She savored the chocolate and strawberry mixed together. "Totally." She took a sip of her cappuccino. "You don't?"

He polished off the last of the cheesecake, then set the plate aside. "Not saying. But I'll bet he ends up meeting her at the train station, even though he told her he was going to take that job in Europe."

She sat up. "You *have* seen this movie before."

"No, I haven't. I'm just guessing. Isn't that the way all these kinds of movies end? Boy meets girl, they have a hot romance, both determined they're not going to fall in love, but by the end they realize they can't live without each other, so they find a way to make it work?"

She lay back against the pillows and rubbed her feet against his. "Sounds a lot like our story."

He looked over at her and entwined their fingers. "If the person you fall in love with is worth it, you'll move mountains to make it work."

God, she was in love with this man. He might not ever make it easy on her, but he was worth fighting for every step of the way.

Alicia snuggled against him with a smile on her face and settled in to watch the happily ever after.

EPILOGUE

ALICIA WASN'T ON DUTY FOR THE DAY'S RIVERS GAME. Instead, she sat just above the player's dugout, thanks to great tickets provided by her awesome hot boyfriend, Garrett.

Liz was with her today, along with her parents and Gavin's parents, who sat in the same row.

Liz squeezed her hand. "Nervous?"

"No, not nervous at all. Terrified is more like it."

"Relax, honey. Garrett is going to do great."

God, she hoped so. He was still working with Max, but she couldn't keep her hands off of him, both from a therapeutic and a personal perspective.

"He looks good, Alicia," her dad said.

"Yes, he does."

"Even more, he looks ready. Fired up," her uncle said.

She smiled. They'd been working on his form and his pitching motion for a month now, ever since Garrett had put his career on the line and offered to be traded just so the two of them could be together.

Now he was in the starting rotation again, and today he'd start his first game since his injury last year.

He'd given her the news two days ago, and since then she wasn't sure who was more nervous—her or him. He'd told her about it after the game with Atlanta, shrugging it off like it had been no big deal.

She'd hooped and hollered and launched herself into his arms. That night, they'd celebrated by having dinner out, then hot sex after.

It had been pretty memorable hot sex, too.

"There he is," Liz said.

The crowd roared. Alicia leapt to her feet, so thrilled to hear the thunderous applause as Garrett took the mound.

He looked so good in his uniform, tall and lean and in great shape. He looked ready to take on anything.

She hoped he soaked in the adoration, and that it helped fuel the fire she knew had been burning inside him ever since his injury last year. He'd worked so hard on his recovery, and he deserved this moment.

She loved him so much and wanted nothing more than for him to succeed.

And he would, because she believed in him.

GARRETT WOULD BE LYING IF HE SAID THE HOME crowd applause when he took the mound hadn't caused chills to skate down his spine. He'd waited seemingly a lifetime for this, and now that it was here, now that he had the mound and the ball in his hand, he was going to make damn sure to shut down Houston.

But when the first batter came to the plate, his knees shook a little.

He closed his eyes and rolled the ball around in his hand.

Focus on the familiar. You've been doing this practically your whole goddamn life, Garrett. This is as familiar to you as brushing your teeth. You can do this.

He opened his eyes. His catcher, Sanchez, called for the signal. Garrett nodded, took a deep breath, got into his windup, then tossed a hard fastball that whizzed right by the batter and into Sanchez's waiting glove.

Hell, yeah.

Sanchez called for a curve. Same thing, and the batter hit a grounder right to Gavin, who stepped on first base.

Out number one.

The next batter came up and Garrett smoked a fastball. The batter bit right away, a pop fly to right field.

Out number two.

Feeling a little more relaxed, he faced the next batter and tried out his sinker. First one was a ball, so he adjusted and threw a fastball.

Strike one.

Sanchez called for the sinker again. Garrett threw it again, and the batter fouled it off.

Strike two.

This time Garrett wanted to blow this guy out of the water. Sanchez called for a curve, but Garrett said no. When Sanchez suggested the fastball, Garrett nodded and wound up, threw the heat, and the batter swung.

At nothing but air.

Strike three and he was out.

The crowd roared and Garrett walked off the mound.

Easy first inning.

He stayed in his own head through eight innings, allowing only two hits and no runs. His arm was tiring and it showed. He'd walked two batters in the eighth and Manny told him he didn't want him to stress out his arm. Though he wanted to pitch the whole game, he also didn't want to hurt himself. Manny brought in Maloney to close it.

"You pitched one hell of a game, Scott," Manny said as he took the ball from him. "Welcome back."

Garrett couldn't help the slight smile on his face. "Thanks, Coach." He walked off the mound to a standing ovation from the crowd. That felt damn good.

They won the game four to nothing. His teammates celebrated the victory in the clubhouse after. The media asked him how it felt to be in the starting rotation again.

"It feels pretty damn good," was all he could say, while giving a lot of credit to his teammates for their batting and fielding, and Maloney's stellar job as a closing pitcher.

After the game, he met up with Alicia in the parking lot. She threw her arms around him and kissed him. "I knew you could do it."

He kissed her back, long and hard, holding tight to her for an extra few seconds. "Because you believed in me, even when I didn't."

She squeezed his arms when she pulled back. "How does your shoulder feel?"

"A lot like overcooked spaghetti."

She laughed. "That's normal, given that's the first time you've pitched so many innings. I'll give you a massage tonight."

"Naked massage?"

"See, that's your problem. Always thinking with your cock."

"That's a problem?" he asked, arching a brow. "Usually it results in an orgasm or two for you."

"Hmm, you make a valid point. But we're supposed to meet my parents and aunt and uncle for a celebratory dinner."

He sighed. "Okay, dinner first. Naked massage later."

He wound his arm around her and walked her to her car, unable to remove the smile from his face.

He'd had a great game tonight. He was a starting pitcher again, and he had an amazing woman by his side. His life couldn't be any more perfect right now. He didn't know what he'd done to get so lucky, but as he pulled Alicia close to him and kissed her again, he thanked whatever fates had brought her to him. She'd saved his career and filled the hole in his heart.

She'd made him believe in love again, and that was more important than anything.

"I love you," he said, brushing his lips across hers.

She smiled up at him. "I love you, too, Garrett. Now let's go get this dinner thing over with so I can get you naked."

He grinned. Like he'd said . . . just damned perfect.

TURN THE PAGE FOR A SNEAK PEEK AT
JACI BURTON'S NEXT PLAY-BY-PLAY NOVEL

ONE SWEET RIDE

THERE WAS NOTHING THAT GOT GRAY PRESTON'S motor running more than a well-running engine, a fast car crossing the finish line in first place, and a hot, willing woman waiting for him at the end of a great day.

Too bad a blown engine had sent his car into the wall three laps shy of the finish line in Michigan. He'd been in second place and coming up alongside his competitor in a hurry, certain he'd be able to wrestle first place from Cal McClusky before the checkered flag.

That dream had gone up in smoke. So had the hot woman, one Sheila Tinsdale, a frequent visitor to his trailer and his bed over the past month. Smoking hot, platinum blonde, and stacked, Sheila put no strings on him and liked sex as much as he did. She was damn near the perfect woman.

Unfortunately, Sheila also had her eye on McClusky, and she bedded winners. So when McClusky crossed the finish line and

Gray hit the wall, Sheila hit McClusky's trailer faster than Gray's Chevy had spun out on turn three.

Not that he was surprised, and it hadn't hurt his feelings. Much. He wasn't emotionally invested in Sheila, and there were plenty more like her on the racing circuit.

So he had a big fat zero for today's events. No win, a smashed-up car, and no consolation sex. Plus, he'd dropped two spots in the points race and had a disappointed crew to deal with. As the owner of two cars in Preston Racing, and the driver of car number fifty-three, responsibility weighed heavily on him.

It was his goal to make something of himself, especially since he'd broken away from his former owner and gone out on his own two years ago. He had a lot to prove—to himself, his team, his fans, and . . .

It probably didn't do him any good to think about just how much he had to prove. And how much it would cost him, financially and otherwise, if he failed.

At least it was still early in the season. There was time to make up the ground he'd lost in today's race.

He made his way to the team garage where his crew was busy, their heads under the hood of his car.

His crew chief lifted his head. "That sucked today."

Gray nodded at Ian Smart. He and Ian had been together since Gray had first climbed into a race car, before he'd ever gone pro. "Understatement. Oil temp was screaming high toward the end. I pushed it too hard. But damn—I was so close."

As Gray leaned over and inspected the engine, Ian nudged him with his shoulder. "That's what you gotta do to win the race, buddy. Nothing you can do about it. We'll get 'em next time."

Yeah. Next time. He knew all about loss. His father was a senator, so he'd grown up around campaigns, around strategies for winning, and what you did to regroup when you didn't win.

Though his father rarely lost a race. He'd be disappointed in Gray's performance today. That was if he ever bothered to watch him race, which Gray knew damn well he didn't. Mitchell Preston wouldn't be caught dead lowering himself to watch auto racing. He considered it a redneck sport and beneath him. His father was involved in a big election this year and was more interested in his own race—which Gray had no doubt his father would win.

Gray lost a hell of a lot more races than his father ever had. Something his dad absolutely hated. Then again, his father disliked everything Gray did, and he had ever since Gray had turned down the Harvard scholarship and chose the sports scholarship to Oklahoma. Royally pissed off his dad, too.

At least that memory put Gray in a decidedly better frame of mind.

"Donny did pretty good, though. He rolled in twelfth."

Gray dragged his attention back to Ian. "Not bad, but I know he can do better. He needs to work on his focus more. I'll talk to him and his crew chief."

At least he could salvage something out of this shit day. Donny Duncan drove the new car Gray had brought into Preston Racing this season. At twenty-four, Donny was still coming on, having just made the switch to this level two years ago. But the kid had raw talent and great instincts. Gray was confident if he continued to push Donny he'd see winning results.

Gray made the turn to head toward his trailer and saw someone waiting at his door.

Not just someone. A very attractive, way-overdressed-for-the-track female wearing a business suit and very high heels. He gave her an assessing look as he made his way toward her.

Media, maybe? Though he'd finished his interviews earlier.

She pulled down her sunglasses and gave him the once-over, too.

"Grayson Preston?"

Wow. She was a stunner, with her strawberry blond hair expertly pulled up, her blue eyes assessing him, and her lips perfectly glossed. She sure as hell didn't belong here. Besides, nobody on the racing circuit called him Grayson. Hell, only his mom called him by that name. And his father.

"Yeah. And you are?"

She walked toward him, her steps sure and confident, then held out her hand. "Evelyn Hill. Do you have a moment?"

For her, he had a lot of moments. He shook her hand, noticing her manicured nails. Not those long, fake, clawlike nails some of the women around here wore. Evelyn's were short and unpainted. "Sure. Come on in."

He opened up the door to his trailer and waited while she climbed the stairs, which gave him an opportunity to ogle her very shapely legs and mighty fine ass. Too bad her skirt covered her knees. Normally the women around here wore their skirts a lot shorter. Then again, normally the women hitting on the racers didn't dress like they were going to have high tea somewhere.

She moved into the living area and he shut the door.

"What can I do for you, Evelyn?"

She turned to face him and gave him a smile. A practiced, professional, very businesslike smile. "I'm here representing your father, Senator Preston."

Just as he was focusing his radar on her, she had to go and ruin it by working for his father. Though at least he was sending better emissaries now. Gray went to his fridge and grabbed a beer. "Want one?"

"Oh. No thank you."

He popped the top off the can and took a long swallow, his throat parched from all those laps and the interviews he'd had to do after the disastrous finish. "Did you see the race today?"

"As a matter of fact, I did. I'm sorry about your wreck, but I'm relieved you weren't hurt."

He shrugged. "It wasn't that hard a hit." He pointed to the small table. "Take a seat, Evelyn. You sure you don't want something to drink? I also have water and pop."

"No. I'm fine. But it was nice of you to offer."

Wasn't she polite? She slid into the booth and crossed one long leg over the other. He cleared his throat. "Okay, then, what did my father send you all the way to Michigan to talk to me about that one of you couldn't have called to say over the phone?"

She swept a curl behind her ear and folded her hands together on the table before focusing those gorgeous clear blue eyes directly at him. "As you are aware, or at least I hope you're aware, now that Senator Preston has dropped out of the presidential race he has a good chance at being considered a viable candidate for vice president in the election this year."

He leaned back in the booth. "I knew he dropped out of the race, but didn't know he has a shot at the VP spot. Good for him. What does that have to do with me?"

"He'd be very grateful if you could assist him in his efforts."

Now this was a first. His father hadn't wanted anything to do with him for a long time now. "Is that right? And how am I supposed to help him?"

"You've done very well for yourself in this sport, Mr. Preston—"

"If you're going to keep talking to me, Evelyn, you'd better call me Gray."

She opened her mouth, paused, then nodded. "All right, Gray. As I was saying, you've become very successful in auto racing, which means you have a very dedicated fan base. A very dedicated nationwide fan base."

Evelyn sure was pretty, and there was a light sprinkle of freckles across the bridge of her nose that spread to her cheeks, which did nothing to diminish how damn sexy she was, or how commanding her eyes were. Her beauty also didn't distract him from the very clear message she had just delivered on behalf of his father.

"I get it. A very dedicated nationwide fan base of registered voters who you think I could persuade to cast a few for my dad and the presidential candidate. And if I agree, that makes Mitchell Preston an even more attractive potential vice presidential candidate, what with all those critical southern votes I could help him garner."

She didn't avert her gaze. "Yes."

"Why didn't he come to me when he was running for president?"

"He would have, had his presidential bid continued."

"Huh. You do realize my father and I don't exactly see eye to eye on a lot of things, political issues included."

"I know a lot about you, including your likes and dislikes—politically, that is."

He wanted to laugh, but he could tell Evelyn was doing her best to do the job she'd been assigned. It wasn't her fault she'd been assigned to Mitchell Preston's uncooperative sonofabitch of a son. "I'm surprised, given that I've never spoken publicly about my likes or dislikes—politically, that is."

She lifted her chin. "Your father has briefed me."

Now he did laugh, then took a long swallow of beer before answering. "Has he? My father doesn't know shit about me. We don't speak much at all. And since I inherited my trust fund from my grandfather when I turned twenty-five, he can't blackmail me into giving him what he wants by refusing to give me money, so we have no reason to communicate at all and I have no reason to give him my assistance."

He watched Evelyn squeeze her hands so tightly together that her knuckles turned white. "I see."

He started to get up. "So we're done?"

She didn't move. "Your mother wanted me to tell to you that she would greatly appreciate your cooperation in this. She's sorry she didn't get a chance to talk to you herself, but she's been very busy on the campaign trail with your father, and of course, you're very difficult to get hold of now that you're racing every week."

Damn. "Cheap shot, Evelyn." He could tell his father to stick it. But he loved his mother and would do anything for her. Well, almost anything. His mother was well aware of his relationship with his dad and she skated that ice carefully, usually not interfering. But for some reason she adored the bastard and supported his political career.

Evelyn gave him a sympathetic look. "I'm sorry. I realize this is . . . difficult for you. But your support would help your father's campaign."

"My father is a misogynistic prick who treats women like servants. Why in hell are you working for him?"

Her lips curved. He liked her smile. "Obviously you haven't spent much time around your father lately, have you?"

"Obviously the old man has you snowed, or you're utterly gullible."

She arched a brow. "I can assure you, Gray, I am never gullible."

He was sure Evelyn thought she knew all there was to know about Mitchell Preston. But Gray had grown up with the man and knew him better than anyone. And the one thing he'd witnessed time and again was how his father treated women. It was a wonder there were any women at all on the campaign given his father's irresponsible, dickhead behavior toward them, especially if they were young and vapid. And this was a man they were considering for the VP nomination? His father was an overbearing, unemotional douchebag. Gray didn't know how his mother had stood by his dad for thirty-three years without smothering him in his sleep or poisoning his coffee, but he'd never understood their marriage anyway.

"So, can we count on you for your cooperation?" Evelyn asked.

He couldn't help but laugh at her audacity to think he'd still be agreeable. "Not a chance. Let me walk you out."

She looked stunned. Obviously, she was used to people falling at the senator's feet. He wasn't one of them.

She stood. "Seriously?"

"Seriously. Sorry, Evelyn, but I don't kiss the senator's ass. You're going to have to find some other way to get votes for him."

"You do realize this could be beneficial for you. Think of the exposure you'd get, the new fans you could bring on board."

"I have plenty of fans already, but thanks." He handed her bag to her, rested his hand on her back, and directed her toward the door.

She stopped and turned to him. "This could be a way for you and your father to repair your relationship."

He could tell she was grasping at straws now. "My father knows my phone number. And my schedule. If he wanted to repair our relationship, he could have done that years ago."

That's when he saw the fight leave her eyes. "Then I'm sorry to have wasted your time."

"You didn't waste my time, Evelyn. You wasted yours." He held the door for her and walked her down the stairs.

She didn't even look back as she headed toward the parking lot.

Too bad she was here representing his father. Evelyn Hill was one hell of a beautiful woman, and he wouldn't have minded spending some time with her. But now that he knew she was associated with his father, he wanted nothing to do with her.

* * *

EVELYN THREW HER BAG DOWN ON THE BED IN THE hotel room, kicked off her shoes, and flung herself onto the chair, wincing as she curled her toes.

Stupid shoes. She grabbed the remote and turned on the television, which was set to the sports channel. Too tired to channel surf, she ordered room service, rolling her eyes as the replay of today's race events came on TV. Despite the childishness of the act, she stuck her tongue out at the screen when Gray Preston's handsome face appeared before her.

"Dickhead," she muttered, then grabbed her phone to check her email, grimacing when she saw one from the senator asking for a status update.

The most important task he'd ever given her, and she'd failed on the first try.

She lifted her gaze to see Gray's smiling face as he was interviewed by the media.

She'd been thwarted more than once in Washington, and she'd never given up. Where was her fight, her determination to win? That was how she'd gotten as far as she had. And she was so close to getting what she wanted, to being able to live her dream.

She knew exactly what she needed to do.

She scrolled through her phone and punched the number, grinning as it rang. If Gray thought he could say no and it was over, he'd soon realize she was more formidable than he thought. She'd never go down without a hard fight.

"Mrs. Preston? Hi, it's Evelyn . . . I'm fine, thank you, but we have a problem. It's your son, Gray."